SONGBIRD IN THE GALLOWS

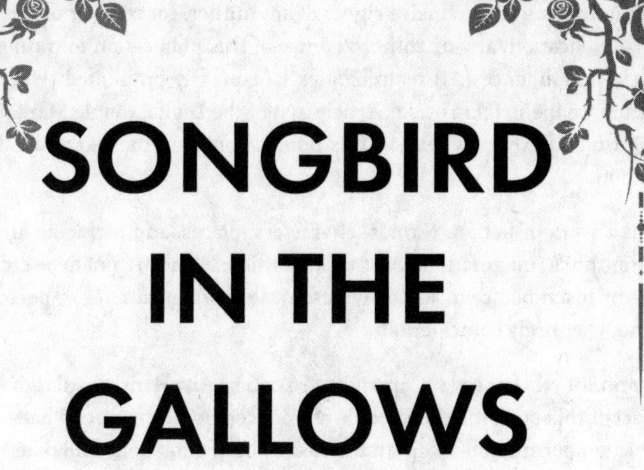

SONGBIRD IN THE GALLOWS

A Novel

ALTA HENSLEY

An Imprint of HarperCollinsPublishers

*To those who embrace dark humor, twisted imaginations,
and the ability to give any villain their happily ever after.*

<u>PLAYLIST:</u>

"I Can't Decide" ~ Scissor Sisters

"Providence" ~ Poor Man's Poison

"St. James Infirmary" ~ The Bridge City Sinners

"Wednesday" ~ Ethan Gander

"Gossip" ~ Måneskin

"The Plank" ~ The Devil Makes Three

"Birthday Suit" ~ Cosmo Sheldrake

"the fruits" ~ Paris Paloma

"Hey Mister" ~ Poor Man's Poison

"Pick Your Poison" ~ The Bridge City Sinners

"Burn Your Village" ~ Kiki Rockwell

"Hammer and Nails" ~ The Bones of J.R. Jones

"Gladiator" ~ Jann

"The Killing Moon" ~ Echo & the Bunnymen

"Bloodletting" ~ Concrete Blonde

"Black Car" ~ Leon Else

"engravings" ~ Ethan Bortnick

"Silverlines" ~ Damiano David

"Bloodsucker" ~ Cil

"Something Blue" ~ VOILÀ

"In Hell I'll Be in Good Company" ~ The Dead South

"Femme Fatale" ~ Twin Temple

"Seven Nation Army" ~ Scott Bradlee's Postmodern Jukebox

TRIGGER WARNINGS

- Murder presented as a love language
- Facial hair . . . it's not for everyone
- Serial killer you can't help but love
- Kidnapping via antique luggage (surprisingly roomy)
- Fire, blood, and gore
- Corpses repurposed as floral arrangements
- Explicit sexual content and not the vanilla kind
- Axes used for purposes other than chopping wood
- Romance conducted in rooms with decomposing audiences
- Death of loved ones and grief trauma
- Detailed descriptions of decomposition
- Romance that redefines "till death do us part"
- Small-town gossip involving body counts
- Stabbing and blood . . . maybe some vomit
- Basement wine cellars with non-wine contents
- Third floors that are absolutely, definitely off-limits
- Fairy-tale endings that require significant cleanup
- Greenhouse activities that have nothing to do with botany
- Handcuffs used for non–law enforcement purposes
- Belt accessories repurposed for bedroom activities
- Public displays of affection in very public places
- Consensual breath play that may alarm sensitive readers

SONGBIRD
IN THE
GALLOWS

CHAPTER ONE
SAYLOR

Once upon a time, I believed in right and wrong.

Before I learned the truth. Learned it in the spray of my father's blood, felt it hot across my face while I choked on the urge to scream. The sound of him dying is still inside me, a metronome to every choice I make.

There's a bone-deep truth. A blood-written truth . . .

It's not what you do, but why you do it.

The driving force that lives beneath your skin, pulsing with every heartbeat, whispering justifications in the dark hours when sleep won't come. When you understand someone's why—when you relate to it, fall in love with it, cradle it against your chest like a secret—that's what can turn the villain in any story into the hero.

But maybe this is the real question: Who is the villain?

Can you be the villain in your own story? Can you watch yourself make choices that would horrify the person you used to be, and still believe you're doing the right thing?

Can you go from rabbit to wolf and convince yourself it was always your true nature, that the innocence was just a costume you wore until the world forced you to shed it?

I think about this now, when my hands are steady and my conscience is quiet. When the weight of what I've done settles into my core, and I can look in the mirror without flinching at what stares back. When love means something different than it did before. It's deeper, more honest, written in a language that most people are too afraid to learn.

* * *

They say you can disappear in New York. Become someone new between one subway stop and the next. I should know—I've been Saylor Mitchell for so long now that sometimes I forget I was ever *Sara* Mitchell.

But here's the thing about running: You can change your name, dye your hair raven black, build a whole new life, but some things follow you. The phantom weight of your father's blood on your hands. The sound a throat makes when it's being cut. The way your real name sits like a stone in your chest, even when no one's called you that in years.

These nights performing at the White Note are the only time I feel like both versions of myself can coexist. Where scattered applause and clinking glasses create their own kind of percussion, and cigarette smoke curls through the air like visible notes. Where Saylor Mitchell sings jazz for tips, but Sara Mitchell's rage hums underneath every note.

I'd considered changing my last name too—new identity, clean slate. But Mitchell was my father's name, and as much as I needed to disappear, I couldn't bring myself to lose that last piece of him. So Sara became Saylor, but Mitchell stayed. A small rebellion against my own survival instincts.

The cabaret is dimly lit, smoky, a place where secrets thrive in dark corners. I scan the crowd as I slink across the stage, my scarlet-red sequined dress catching the light. My fingers find the compass necklace at my throat—Dad's compass. Antique brass on a simple chain, the face no bigger than a quarter. It clashes with everything I wear, too practical for sequins and satin, but I haven't taken it off since that awful night. North still points north, even when everything else in my life points nowhere. I give it a quick touch for luck. Same ritual every night since I started singing here.

As the sultry melody from the band fills the room, I adjust the rose in my slicked-back black hair and take hold of the microphone. It's time for me to seduce the crowd and lose myself in the music.

I close my eyes and let my body move to the rhythm, swaying my hips and running my hands down my curves. The audience is captivated, their eyes following every movement of my body.

My voice comes out low and smooth as I sing the first line of "Fever," a classic jazz song that never fails to get hearts racing. It's not my favorite song—too mainstream for my tastes—but Joey, the club owner, insists I start each set with it. Says it draws in the regulars.

Sometimes I wonder if the regulars would recognize Sara in Saylor. But Sara was an eighteen-year-old girl from Seattle who watched her father die, who ran to New York with nothing but the clothes on her back and a fake ID she bought at Port Authority. Saylor is twenty-three, trying to be confident, and attempting to never look over her shoulder. Sara hid in closets. Saylor owns every stage she steps on. Not that anyone here knows there's a difference.

The music shifts into something slower, sultrier. My hips follow the rhythm as I work through the standards. Songs that pay rent and keep me invisible. Each performance is a balancing act between being memorable enough for tips but forgettable enough that no one asks too many questions about where I came from.

I open my eyes and scan the crowd again, checking faces out of habit. Making sure no one looks too interested, too familiar, too dangerous. Every time I check faces, I expect to see one of them—the Crow who leaned close to wipe his blade on my father's shirt, his grin etched so deep I still see it when I close my eyes. I see my father's back as he shoved me into the closet, hear his whispered command to stay quiet, stay hidden.

Obedience saved me. Cowardice haunts me.

But that's when I see him.

He's not a Crow from that night, but there's something about him . . .

Sitting alone at a corner table, he stares through the audience, pinning me in place. I almost miss my next line—something that never happens. But this man is throwing me off balance for some unknown reason.

Dark hair falls across his forehead, and there's something dangerous in the curve of his smile that's hidden by a thick beard that makes me want to run my fingers through it. It's long and dominates his face, but I can still make out the distinct line of his jaw beneath it. His mustache is subtly curled at the ends, giving the villain vibe I didn't know I wanted—maybe even needed—until now. This is a man who clearly is comfortable in his own skin, who exudes confidence and danger in equal measure.

His suit is impeccable, but there's a wildness in his presence that tells me he's anything but tame.

The suit is obviously expensive, perfectly tailored. It's an understated luxury that whispers money instead of shouting it. Most men his age in jazz clubs wear leather jackets, trying to look younger, cooler. But this man doesn't need to try.

Dad would have said that confidence belonged to men from his generation, not mine. Maybe he's right . . .

This guy's got to be in his forties at least. Old enough to know better than to look at me like that. Old enough that I should know better than to like it.

I can practically taste the mystery rolling off him in waves.

I've had my share of admirers, sure. Being a singer in a jazz club, you get used to the attention. But I've never been one to mix business with pleasure. Music has always been enough—that and staying inconspicuous, staying safe, staying one step ahead of whoever might still be looking for Sara Mitchell.

But this man . . . he's different. His gaze holds mine as I continue to sing, and I feel exposed, as if he can see past the stage persona I've carefully crafted. As if he can see through Saylor Mitchell straight to the frightened girl who chose her new name in a Greyhound bathroom stall with shaking hands.

I hold his stare as I continue to sing, my voice growing huskier with each verse. My fingers trail along the microphone stand suggestively. I'm performing for the whole room, but in this moment, it's just for him.

As the song reaches its climax, I descend from the stage, weaving between tables like I do every night. The patrons reach out, trying to touch me, but I dodge their grasping hands with practiced ease. I'm heading straight for my mysterious observer.

I reach his table just as the final notes fade away. Up close, I can see the glint in his dark eyes, the slight curl of his lips that hints at cruelty. The lines edging his thick lashes that confirm what the suit suggested—he's got at least twenty years on me.

I should care. I don't.

I smile, a simple gesture that feels more genuine than any I've given in this club before. Then I turn and make my way back to the stage, my heart racing as I feel the intensity of his stare following my every move.

I return to the stage and finish my set, but my mind is elsewhere. As I belt out the final notes of my last song, I steal a glance in his direction. He hasn't moved, hasn't taken his focus off my face for a second.

The applause washes over me as I take my bow, but it's all background noise. There's a hum in my ear. The same hum I felt that night, minutes before they slit my father's throat. The one that says danger is coming.

But this time, I don't run.

After my final song, I head to the bar, deliberately passing close to his table. My throat is dry from singing, but that's not the only reason I need a drink.

His gaze burns into me. I'm a match and he ignites the flame.

"Whiskey, neat," I tell the bartender, my body buzzing from my performance and—

"Make that two," a deep voice says from behind me. The sound is low and rough, like gravel wrapped in velvet. The voice of someone who's lived long enough to know exactly what he wants.

I turn, coming face to face with the stranger. Up close, his eyes are even more mesmerizing—dark and cavernous. There's a scar running underneath his right eye that makes me wonder what stories his body could tell. Yes, he's older than me, but in the sexy mmmm . . . daddy way.

My father would have chased him off with a shotgun if he knew his little Sara was having the kind of dirty thoughts I'm having now.

I raise an eyebrow, a smirk playing at the corners of my lips. It's a façade, I know it, I just hope he doesn't. "Buying a lady a drink? How quaint."

He chuckles, but it doesn't lighten the darkness and shadows that engulf him. "I assure you, there's nothing quaint about my intentions."

The bartender slides our drinks across the counter. I pick mine up, swirling the amber liquid before taking a sip. The whiskey burns pleasantly as it slides down my throat.

"And what exactly are your intentions?" I ask, my voice a purr. I don't even sound like me, but my body and mind seem to be taking over, and I've lost all sense of control. Saylor is in charge now. Sara would have already run.

He leans in close, his breath hot against my ear. "To unravel you. To see what's beneath the perfectly polished exterior." His hand slides to the small of my back, pulling me closer. The heat of his touch sears through the thin fabric of my dress.

Who in the hell says things like this?

I should walk away. I should end the night now. I should . . .

I pull back slightly, meeting his gaze. My body constricts, but I try to remain cool and collected. I've played this game before, but something about this man tells me the stakes are higher. I can already tell he's three steps ahead of me, and I find it slightly in-furiating.

"Bold of you to assume there's anything beneath the surface. I *am* perfect. Always polished," I counter, taking another sip of whiskey to aid in the courage I need to continue this banter. The scald in my throat matches the fire igniting in my veins.

His laugh is dark, almost menacing.

"Oh, I think we both know that's not true. I saw you up there, singing. I know there are flaws—delicious imperfections."

"And what makes you think you're the one who gets to unravel them?" I ask.

I focus on his beard and, with the light cast from the neon signs peppering the bar area, I see now that it's meticulously groomed, the edges sharp and precise. It's not just a beard, it's a statement. A mask, perhaps, hiding secrets I'm suddenly desperate to uncover. And then I see something more.

There's a hue to the blackness of the hair. A midnight blue that catches the light. His beard is so black that it somehow breaks the color spectrum and now shimmers with an otherworldly blue tint.

"Blue," I say.

"I never told you my name."

"Your name is *Blue*?"

He lifts my hand and kisses it, an oddly old-fashioned gesture that somehow fits him perfectly. "Nice to meet you."

I laugh at the absurdity of the name, and yet it also somehow seems so right. "Blue what? Blue . . . Beard? What's your last name?"

His eyes flash with amusement at my question. "Just call me Blue. And what should I call you? Little songbird? Girl in the red dress who could very well send me to the gallows by the end of the night?"

I surprise myself by leaning closer, my lips brushing against his ear. "Tonight, you can call me whatever you want."

Who. Am. I. Right. Now?!

He growls low in his throat, his grip on me tightening. "Dangerous words, love. I might just take you up on that offer."

I pull back, meeting his intense stare. "I'm counting on it. I'm curious now. Is all your hair blue?" My gaze lowers as I lick my lips suggestively.

Oh dear god, did I just say that? I've lost my mind. I've completely lost my mind.

"I don't usually do this," I say, surprising myself with my honesty. "Mix business with pleasure, I mean."

He leans in closer, his presence overwhelming in the best possible way. "And what makes tonight different?"

"I don't know," I admit. "Maybe it's the music. Maybe it's the whiskey." I meet his gaze. "Maybe it's you."

Blue smirks, finishing his whiskey in one smooth gulp. He sets the glass down with a decisive clink. "Shall we take this somewhere more . . . private?"

This man could be a psychopath. *I'm actually on the run from killers.* So while some people would go home with their one-night stands, there is no way in hell I'm going to, no matter how strong this man's pull is on me. I need to be smart. I need to—

However . . .

I could always . . .

I down the rest of my drink. Fuck it. I'm going to act impulsively for once in my life. Before I chicken out, I take his hand and lead him to my dressing room.

The space is small, cluttered with costumes and makeup, but it's private. As soon as the door clicks shut behind us, Blue pushes me against it, his body pressing into mine. His lips crash against my neck, beard tickling my skin as he trails kisses down to my collarbone.

"Tell me," he groans against my skin, "what's a beautiful girl like you doing with a man like me?"

I laugh breathlessly. "Looking for trouble, it seems."

He pulls back, his gaze connecting with mine. "That's the answer I was hoping for."

In one swift motion, he lifts me up, my legs wrapping around his waist. He carries me to the small couch in the corner, laying me down with surprising gentleness. But there's nothing gentle about the way he looks at me, like a predator eyeing its prey.

I reach up, running my fingers through his beard. "So, Mr. Blue, are you going to show me if the carpet matches the drapes?"

He smirks, slowly unbuttoning his shirt. "Patience, my songbird. Good things come to those who wait."

As he reveals more skin, I see tattoos peeking out from beneath his clothes. Intricate designs that seem to shift and move in the dim light of the dressing room.

He's marking every single box on my must-need sexy checklist.

- ✔ Yes.
- ✔ Yes.
- ✔ Yes.
- ✔ Yes, please!

In one fluid motion, he sheds his shirt completely. The tattoos cover his entire torso, a tapestry of chaotic colors.

He leans down, capturing my lips in a searing kiss. His tongue explores my mouth, tasting of whiskey and something darker, more primal. I moan against him, my fingers tracing the living artwork on his chest.

As we kiss, I feel a strange tingling sensation where my skin meets his tattoos. It's as if they're reaching out to me, trying to pull me in. The room starts to spin, and suddenly I'm not sure if it's from desire or something more sinister.

"Wait," I gasp, breaking the kiss. "I need to know . . . are you going to kill me?"

He pulls away, visibly stunned but only for a split second. "Do you ask all the men you're with this question?"

I freeze for a moment, not wanting to reveal that I've never done anything like this before in my life. One-night stands have never been my jam, but I'm enjoying this ruse of being daring, bold, and spontaneous.

"Only the interesting ones," I reply with an impish raise of my lip, my fingers still tracing the tattoos on his chest. The tingling sensation intensifies, and I can't tell if it's excitement or fear surging through my body.

He leans in close, his breath hot against my ear. "Oh, I do want to devour you. But killing you? That would be such a waste."

His hand slides up my thigh, pushing my dress higher. "I have much more . . . entertaining plans for you."

I reach out and place my hand on his lower abdomen. "Maybe *I* have plans for *you*."

"Are *you* going to kill *me*?" he asks.

I laugh, a husky sound that echoes in the small dressing room. "Maybe. But first . . ." I reach for the button of his pants.

With deft fingers, I undo his fly, sliding my hand inside. My breath catches as I feel him, hot and hard against my palm. And there, in the dim light of the dressing room, I see it—a faint blue shimmer amidst the dark curls.

"Well, well," I murmur, stroking him slowly. "Looks like Mr. Blue is full of surprises."

He groans, his hips bucking against my hand. "You have no idea, little songbird."

Suddenly, he grabs my wrists, pinning them above my head with one large hand. His other hand slides up my thigh, pushing my dress higher until it's bunched around my waist.

His fingers then hook into the lace of my panties and pull it aside. When his mouth finds my pussy, I gasp and my hips jerk off the couch.

"Look at me," he says against my skin.

I force my eyes open. He's watching me while his tongue works, and something about that eye contact makes everything more intense. His beard scrapes against my thighs—rough, then soft, then rough again.

"Blue," I manage to say.

He makes a sound low in his throat that I feel more than hear. He releases my hands and grips my thighs hard enough to leave marks, spreading me wider. Whatever restraint he had before is gone now. This is hungry and desperate and nothing like I expected.

When he pushes two fingers inside and curls them, I come hard. My back arches and I actually cry out—loud enough that someone in the club definitely heard.

He keeps going until I'm shaking and trying to push him away because it's too much. He finally lifts his head, his beard wet, smiling like he just won something.

"Tonight is just about you," he growls. "I like to spread out my fun over multiple nights. Tonight . . . I just want a taste."

CHAPTER TWO
BLUE

I never visit the same establishment more than once if I can help it, and most definitely not two nights in a row. My profession—scratch that—my old profession of hired killer makes me wary of patterns and predictability.

But I'm retired now. I'm a new man. Or so I keep telling myself.

The truth is, I wouldn't be here at all if it weren't for the phone call. Tommy Vance, low-level information broker with a talent for finding people who don't want to be found. Five years of searching, five years of dead ends and false leads, and suddenly he claims he's got a lead on Sara Mitchell.

"White Note cabaret," he'd said. "Meet me there tomorrow night. I think I found your girl."

Your girl. As if she belongs to me. As if I have any right to her after what happened to Peter.

The smoke in this place is thicker tonight, clinging to everything like guilt. Every shadow in the corner could be hiding threats, every patron could be a Crow who followed me here. Old habits. They die harder than the people I used to kill.

I scan the dimly lit bar, my old instincts kicking in despite my best efforts to quell them. The bartender is the same as last night. He catches my eye and gives a slight nod of recognition. Damn. So much for anonymity, but it was important for me to come to the bar last night to scope it out before this meeting. I like knowing what I'm walking into. In my line of work, surprises equal death.

I sidle up to the bar, trying to appear nonchalant. "Whiskey, neat," I mutter, avoiding eye contact with the bartender. He slides the drink over without a word, but I can feel his gaze lingering. Taking a sip, enjoying the fire liquid as it sizzles down my throat, I check my watch for the tenth time in as many minutes. Where the hell is Tommy?

Peter's dying message plays in my head on repeat: *"Blue, they found me. If something happens, promise me you'll find Sara. Keep her safe. She's all I have left, and she's perfect. She deserves better than this world I pulled her into."*

I'd been three whiskeys deep in some dive bar, drowning in my own demons after a job gone sideways, when his call came through. Let it ring. Figured Peter could wait an hour while I finished feeling sorry for myself.

By the time I called back, Peter Mitchell was dead.

The man who was trying to save my soul, and I couldn't even answer his fucking call.

We were opposites in every way that mattered. He believed in second chances, I believed in permanent solutions. He saw the good in people, I saw the targets they painted on themselves. But somehow we'd ended up walking the same dark circles, two men from different worlds trying to survive in a business that didn't have room for conscience.

Peter was the light trying to pull me out of the darkness. I was the shadow that followed him, cleaning up the messes his decency couldn't handle.

Peter and I met fifteen years before on a job in Prague. I was supposed to eliminate a witness. Some college kid who'd seen too much. Peter took one look at the boy, barely eighteen and shaking like a leaf, and stepped between us.

"There's another way," he'd said, calm as death. *"There's always another way if you want it badly enough."*

He was right. We made the kid disappear instead. New identity, new life, clean slate. Peter paid for it out of his own pocket. Never asked for anything in return except a promise that I'd think twice before my next kill.

That one conversation changed everything. Peter saw something in me that I'd never seen in myself—the possibility of redemption. He was the one who convinced me to walk away, to try building something instead of just destroying.

"You've got enough blood on your hands for ten lifetimes, Blue," he'd said the last time we spoke in person, about a week before he died. *"Maybe it's time to find out what those hands can create instead."*

Peter believed in second chances the way other people believe in gravity. With absolute, unshakeable faith. He was probably the only decent man I've ever known.

And I failed him when it mattered most.

The singer finishes her set, and the sparse applause dies down. As she slinks off stage, I catch her eye. She winks, a coy smile playing on her crimson lips. I raise my glass in a silent toast. Oh yeah, there's going to be a repeat of last night. No doubt about it.

Her Amy Winehouse meets Wednesday Adams vibe is everything I ever craved. She's darkness wrapped in delicate silk, with just enough edge to keep me on my toes. And in my line of work, *former* line of work, I remind myself, staying on your toes is a matter of life and death.

Everything about the way she looks is familiar, yet dangerously new. Her dark hair cascades in waves, framing a face that could launch a thousand ships—or sink them, depending on her mood.

Cliché? Fuck yes, it is. But everything about her pulls that kind of sap from me.

I remember how she tasted last night. It was like licking the lining of a whiskey bottle filled with honey—a bizarre mix of sweet and sin that shouldn't work but somehow does.

A hand claps down on my shoulder and I nearly reach for the blade I no longer carry before recognizing Tommy Vance's nasally voice.

"Blue. You look like shit."

I turn to face him. Rat-faced, twitchy, with the kind of nervous energy that comes from a lifetime of selling secrets to killers. "You said you had something on Sara Mitchell."

Tommy orders a beer, takes his sweet time settling onto the barstool. The little shit's enjoying this. "Maybe I do. Depends how much you're willing to pay for maybes."

"Cut the games, Tommy. What do you have?"

"Girl matching her description. Dyed her hair black, used to be lighter according to my sources. Early twenties, showed up in the city about five years ago with nothing but a badly forged ID and a story about being from Seattle." He takes a swig of his beer, watching me over the rim. "Been singing in clubs around the city, keeping her head down, blending in with the crowds."

My pulse quickens despite my efforts to stay calm. "Where is she?"

Tommy's grin widens. "That's the beautiful part. She's been right under your nose this whole time."

He nods toward the stage, where the singer is adjusting her microphone for the next set. "Currently going by Saylor Mitchell. Stage name or something. Been here almost every night for the past two years, singing her little heart out."

The whiskey glass slips from my numb fingers, exploding against the bar in a shower of crystal and amber liquid. The crash cuts through the ambient noise like a gunshot, and half the bar turns to stare.

No.

No, this isn't possible.

But even as my mind rejects it, the pieces slam together with brutal clarity. The familiar way she tilts her head when she's thinking, exactly like Peter used to do when he was working out a problem. The stubborn set of her jaw, the way she sings like she's pouring her soul out through her voice, the same way Peter hummed old jazz standards while he worked.

Oh fuuuuuuck . . . I didn't just go down on a stranger last night.

Holy shit.

I had my mouth on Peter's daughter. His unsuspecting, perfect, angelic daughter! Made her come with my tongue while she moaned my name in that dressing room.

Peter always said he'd put a bullet in any man who touched his little girl inappropriately. If he wasn't six feet under, I'd be a dead man.

What the fuck did I just do?

As if I didn't already carry enough guilt about Peter, now I've violated his daughter. The girl I swore to protect. The innocent he died trying to save.

My stomach lurches, and for a moment I think I might vomit right here at the bar. The weight of what I've done crashes over me—not just what happened between us, but the complete and utter failure of everything I promised Peter. She's been here for two years. Two years I could have been watching over her, keeping her safe, honoring my debt to the only man who ever believed I could be better.

Instead, I've been drowning in my own self-pity while Peter's daughter sang in dive bars, alone and unprotected.

"Jesus," Tommy breathes, apparently reading my expression. "You know her."

I can't answer. Can't do anything but stare at her as she starts her next song. Her voice carries across the smoky room, raw and beautiful and heartbreaking, and I hear Peter in every note. He used to sing to her when she was little; I remember him telling me that once, years ago. How she'd fall asleep to his old blues records.

This girl learned music from him. Learned to find beauty in dark places the way he did.

The way I never could.

"I need to go," I manage, my voice coming out rougher than sandpaper.

"Hey, what about my payment?"

I pull out my wallet and drop a thick roll of bills on the bar without counting. "This conversation never happened. And Tommy?" I lean closer, close enough that he can probably smell the whiskey and regret on my breath. "If anyone else comes asking about Sara Mitchell, anyone, you've never heard the name. Are we clear?"

He nods so fast his head might fall off.

But even as I threaten him, the cold reality settles in my chest like a stone. If Tommy fucking Vance can find her, so can the Crow. It's only a matter of time before they put the pieces together, before they realize the girl they've been hunting is singing every night in a Greenwich Village jazz club.

She's not safe here. Hell, she's not safe anywhere, but especially not out in the open like this.

I leave him at the bar and push through the crowd toward the exit, but I can't stop myself from looking back. She's still singing, still lost in the music, and she has no idea that the man she let put his mouth on her last night is the same man who failed to save her father.

In the smoky light of the club, she's achingly beautiful. Tonight she's wearing a deep emerald dress that hugs her curves, different from the scarlet sequined number from last night but equally stunning. Her dark hair falls in waves past her shoulders, framing a face that's all sharp cheekbones and soft lips. She's smaller than I remembered, probably no more than five-foot-four in those heels, but she owns that stage like she's ten feet tall. There's something ethereal about the way she moves, graceful but with an edge that speaks to the darkness she's been carrying.

Peter's eyes, I realize with a jolt. She has Peter's dark, intelligent eyes, but where his held warmth and humor, hers burn with barely contained fury. The same stubborn chin, the same way of tilting her head when she's lost in thought. But everything else about her is uniquely Sara—the defiant set of her shoulders, the way she transforms pain into art with her voice.

She's twenty-three years old and more beautiful than any woman has a right to be, especially one who's been missing since she was barely eighteen.

Peter's little girl, all grown up and hiding in plain sight. The guilt threatens to choke me.

She has no idea who I really am. The same man who's been hunting her for five years.

The same man who now has to figure out how to keep her alive while fighting the urge to finish what we started in that dressing room.

If I can't protect her this time, she'll be my failure all over again.

CHAPTER THREE
SAYLOR

The applause dies down as I step off the stage, the spotlights dimming behind me. Eddie, our piano player, is already loosening his tie when I walk over.

"Not bad for a Thursday night," he says, flexing his fingers. "Though you kept scanning the crowd during that last song."

"Was it that obvious?" I lean against the piano, catching my breath.

"Only to someone who's been watching you perform for two years." Eddie starts gathering his sheet music. "Your mysterious friend from last night show up again?"

I glance around the cabaret. The crowd is thinning but there are still plenty of people nursing drinks at their tables. "He was here. Then he wasn't."

"Ah. The old disappearing act." Eddie pauses in his packing. "That why you look like someone stole your favorite toy?"

"I don't look like anything."

"Right. And I don't have arthritis in my left hand." He grins. "So what happened? Guy seemed pretty into you last night."

"Nothing happened. That's the problem." I run a hand through my hair. "He just . . . vanished. Right after my set."

"Maybe he had somewhere to be."

"Or maybe I'm reading too much into things." I lower my voice as a couple walks past our corner. "Eddie, you ever get the feeling someone's watching you? Like, really watching you?"

His expression shifts, becoming more serious. "All the time in this business. Why?"

"For the past week, I've felt like I'm being studied. Not the usual drunk patron bullshit—something different."

"Then keep your eyes open. And maybe consider that hooking up with dark strangers in tailored suits isn't the smartest move when you're already feeling paranoid."

"Oh, so now you're my life coach?" I cross my arms. "What's next, Eddie? Going to tell me to eat my vegetables and get eight hours of sleep?"

He chuckles, shaking his head. "Just saying, kid. Timing seems a little convenient, doesn't it?"

"What, so I should swear off men because I'm feeling jumpy? That's a fast track to becoming a crazy cat lady."

Eddie laughs as he finishes packing up. "Fair point. Just . . . be careful, all right?"

"Always am." I push off from the piano. "See you tomorrow night."

But as I watch Eddie head for the exit, that crawling sensation between my shoulder blades gets stronger. Time to get out of here.

The ride to my apartment is silent except for the low hum of the engine and the city noise filtering through the windows. I lean forward in the backseat of the cab, watching the driver's mirrors. There's a black sedan three cars back that's been behind us since we left the club. Could be nothing. Could be everything.

The driver doesn't seem to notice my paranoia, or maybe he's just used to neurotic passengers having breakdowns in his backseat.

When we pull up to my building, I notice another car parked across the street. A man sits behind the wheel, and when our looks collide in his side mirror, he looks away too quickly.

Something tightens in my chest. This isn't paranoia anymore. This is confirmation.

I fumble with my keys at the front door, my hands shaking. Was this always going to happen? Had I been living on borrowed time, thinking I could stay under the radar forever? Maybe I should have run the first time I felt those eyes on me. Maybe I got too comfortable, too careless. Maybe this was always how it would end.

The lock that's been broken for months suddenly seems less like a minor inconvenience and more like a death sentence. What kind of idiot lets something like that slide when she's running from the people who killed her father? I should have been on the apartment manager's ass about it from day one. Should have fixed it myself. Should have moved to a building with better security. Fuck, I got sloppy. Complacent. Started thinking like Saylor Mitchell instead of

Sara Mitchell—the girl who knew that broken locks could get you killed.

Maybe I should call the police. But what would I say? That I'm scared? That someone might be following me? Nothing's actually happened. I sound like some paranoid woman afraid of the dark. There's nothing to report. I'm just in my head, spiraling. Calm down. Get a grip. This isn't the first time I've been scared shitless and nothing happened.

I climb the three flights to my apartment, listening for footsteps behind me. The hallway seems longer than usual, darker. Every shadow could hide a threat, every creak of the old building could mask the sound of someone following me. When I reach my door, I freeze.

It's slightly ajar.

I always lock my door. Always. Even when I'm just running downstairs to check the mail.

My heart tries to break free from my ribs as I push the door open and step inside.

The apartment is empty.

Not just empty of people—empty of everything. My furniture, my clothes, my books, even the coffee mug I left in the sink this morning. All of it, gone.

All except for a large steamer chest sitting in the middle of the room like some Victorian relic. Dark wood, brass fittings, and big enough to hide a body.

"What the fuck?" The words tear out of my throat, raw and disbelieving.

I spin in a circle, taking in the bare walls where my photographs used to hang, the empty spots where my bookshelf and couch should be. Even the curtains are gone. It's like someone erased my entire existence in the span of a few hours.

"This is insane," I say to the empty room, my words echoing off the bare walls. "This is completely fucking insane."

But even as I say it, a cold certainty settles in my stomach. This isn't random. This is them. The Crows. The ones who killed my father. The ones I've been running from for five years.

They found me.

And they're going to make me completely disappear. Poof. Gone.

I walk over to the steamer chest, my footsteps echoing in the empty space. It's old-fashioned and ominous, like something you'd find in a haunted attic. The lid is unlocked, and when I flip it open, it's completely empty except for a faint smell of cedar and mothballs.

What the hell is this thing even for?

"We've been looking for you for a very long time."

The voice comes from behind me, low and smooth with just a hint of an accent I can't quite place. I spin around to find three men standing in my doorway like Death's own welcoming committee. The one in the middle is tall and lean with graying hair and cold eyes that remind me of winter mornings. The other two flank him like bookends—one built like a truck, the other wiry and sharp-faced like a snake.

"Sara Mitchell," the middle one says, and hearing my real name spoken aloud after all these years makes my blood freeze. "Or do you prefer *Saylor* Mitchell these days?"

These are them. I know it with the same bone-deep certainty that told me something was wrong tonight. The Crows. The bastards who destroyed my life.

"I don't know what you're talking about," I say, but my voice comes out smaller than I intended.

The middle one smiles, and it's the kind of smile that would give children nightmares. "Of course you don't. You've done such a good job disappearing. Five years is a long time to stay hidden. But you can't sing in public and expect to remain invisible forever."

"The White Note," the truck-sized one rumbles. "Beautiful voice. Just like Peter said."

My father's name on this monster's lips makes something snap inside me. The fear is still there, cold and sharp, but now it's wrapped in fury. "Don't you dare talk about him."

"Peter Mitchell was a good man," the middle one continues, stepping farther into my apartment like he owns it. "Shame he got mixed up in business that wasn't his concern. But then, you know all about that, don't you? After all, you were there."

The memory slams into me—Dad's blood, warm and sticky on my face. The wet sound of his throat opening. His eyes finding mine through the crack in the closet door, love and terror warring in his gaze.

"You killed him," I whisper.

"We did our job," the snake-faced one says with a shrug. "Nothing personal."

Nothing personal. They cut my father's throat and it was nothing personal.

The rage burns brighter now, hot enough to push back the fear. I take a step toward them, my hands clenching into fists. "You want to finish what you started? Come on then. I'm not hiding in a closet anymore."

The middle one laughs, actually laughs. "Oh, you have more fire than your father ever had. Good. That'll make this more interesting." He nods to his companions. "The trunk."

"Fuck you," I spit. "And fuck your trunk."

It happens fast. The big one lunges for me while the snake-faced one circles around. I dodge left, my heels skittering on the hardwood, but there's nothing to grab, nothing to defend myself with in the empty space. I aim a kick at Truck's knee, but he catches my leg.

"Let go of me, you knuckle-dragging mouth-breather!" I twist in his grip and manage to rake my nails across his face, leaving four bloody furrows down his cheek.

He roars and backhands me hard enough to make my ears ring. "Crazy bitch!"

"That's the best you got?" I laugh, tasting blood. "No wonder it took you five years to find me."

The snake-faced one circles closer, grinning. "She's got a mouth on her. Just like daddy did before we shut him up."

Pure fury floods through me, white-hot and blinding. If I ever get the chance—when I get the chance—I'm going to kill these fuckers slowly. I'm going to make them beg. I'm going to make them understand exactly what they took from me.

"You want to know what Peter's last words really were?" the middle one asks, pulling out a syringe. "He said 'please don't hurt my little girl.' Pathetic, really."

I launch myself at him, all claws and fury. "You lying sack of—"

The big one grabs me from behind, trying to wrestle me toward the trunk. I sink my teeth into his forearm, biting down hard enough to taste blood.

"Fuck!" He jerks back. "She bit me! Like a rabid badger!"

"Get her in the damn trunk!" the middle one snaps.

I thrash wildly in Truck's grip. "I'm going to shove that syringe so far up your ass you'll be sneezing chemicals for a week!"

But even as I fight, the needle slides into my neck. The middle one's cold smile is the last thing I see clearly.

"Nothing personal," he says, echoing his partner's words.

The world starts to blur at the edges. My legs feel like they're made of rubber, and I stumble, trying to keep my balance.

"No," I slur, trying to fight the drug coursing through my system. "No, you assholes, I'm not . . . I won't . . ."

But I'm already falling, my vision tunneling down to a pinprick of light. The last thing I see before the darkness takes me is the steamer chest, its mouth open like a hungry beast.

The last thing I think is that I should have run the moment I felt him watching.

I should have listened to the fear.

CHAPTER FOUR
BLUE

The axe knows when death is coming.

I can feel it humming against my palm where it rests on the passenger seat, the Damascus steel blade singing a song only I can hear. Fifteen years of spilled blood have taught me to trust that song, and right now it's screaming that something's about to go very, very wrong.

The street outside Sara's building looks normal enough—a few pedestrians shuffling home from work, parked cars lined up like sleeping metal beasts, the usual symphony of urban decay. But something feels wrong. The air tastes metallic, charged with the kind of tension that comes before violence erupts.

I adjust my grip on the axe handle, worn smooth as silk from years of use. Most killers prefer guns—clean, distant, professional. But there's something honest about an axe. When you split someone's skull with forty inches of hickory and steel, you have to mean it. There's no taking it back, no claiming it was just business. It's personal, intimate, final.

The axe hasn't tasted blood in three years. Not since I went cold turkey after Peter's death—well, not immediately after. First came the bender. Two months of hunting down every piece of shit who'd ever crossed my path, every lowlife who preyed on the innocent. I told myself it was grief, that I was honoring Peter's memory by cleaning up the streets he'd died trying to protect. But the truth was uglier: I was drowning in rage and the axe was the only thing that made the pain stop.

The only targets I avoided were the Crow. Oh, I wanted to. Every fiber of my being screamed for Brutus's blood, for the satisfaction of watching my former brothers bleed out in the dirt. But I held back. Told myself when I was thinking clearly their time would come, when I could plan properly instead of acting on pure fury. The Crow deserved more than sloppy vengeance.

They deserved methodical destruction.

But the truth was darker than strategic patience. Peter wouldn't have wanted the bloodbath I was painting across the region, regardless of how much every bastard I killed deserved it. Not in his name. Not in his memory. Peter believed in justice, not vengeance. He believed in protecting the innocent, not becoming the very evil we were supposed to fight against.

Something had to stop. I had to stop.

So what does any self-respecting serial killer do when he wants to stop killing? He finds a therapist, obviously.

It took my therapist Dr. Jay Finch six months to convince me that revenge wasn't therapy, and another year to admit that maybe—just maybe—I'd become the kind of monster Peter would have been ashamed to call his friend. Jay specializes in what he calls "murder sobriety"—though I'm pretty sure most therapists don't keep a stress ball on their desk specifically for when their patients describe dismemberment techniques.

Everything in me is telling me to turn around and drive back to Grimlock, the town I call home on the Pacific coast. A sanctuary where the residents understand certain unspoken codes, where people like me can find refuge among their own kind. She'd be safe there in ways she could never be safe here. This is insane. I shouldn't be here, parked outside her building like some lovesick stalker, wrestling with the decision that's been eating at me since I left the club. But she's not safe in New York. It's only a matter of time before the Crow find her, and when they do—

I could walk up to her door like a normal person. Knock. Explain the situation. Ask her to come with me to my estate where I can protect her behind twelve-foot walls and enough security to make the Secret Service jealous. But we both know what her answer would be. She'd tell me to go to hell, probably in more colorful terms than that. And I don't have time to court her into saying yes. I don't have time to be charming or persuasive or anything resembling a decent human being.

The truth is simpler and uglier than that: Sara Mitchell is coming home with me tonight whether she wants to or not. Because the alternative is watching Peter's daughter die the same way he did, and I'll be damned if I let that happen.

My thoughts scatter as the apartment building's front door bangs open and my driver comes stumbling out like he's been wrestling with a tornado. Hans is built like a brick shithouse with the brain of a gentle giant, which makes him perfect for the simple tasks I usually give him. The fact that he looks rattled sends alarm bells clanging in my skull.

He approaches the car with his massive hands held up in surrender, his usually pristine black suit rumpled but oddly clean—no bite marks, no signs of struggle.

I roll down the window. "Problem, Hans?"

"Boss . . ." Hans runs his massive hands through his hair, looking like a man who's just discovered his lottery ticket was a fake. "The apartment, it is . . . how do you say . . . completely fucking empty."

My blood turns to ice. "What do you mean empty?"

"I mean empty like a church collection plate after the pastor runs off with the choir director." Hans gestures helplessly toward the building. "No furniture. No belongings. No Sara. Nothing. It's like someone took a giant eraser and rubbed out her entire existence."

The axe hums louder in my grip, steel singing with anticipation of violence. They got to her first. The Crow got to her before I could.

"You checked every room?"

"Ja, every room. Kitchen, bedroom, bathroom, even looked in the closets in case she was hiding. Nothing but dust bunnies." Hans shakes his head. "Professional job, boss. Clean sweep."

"The Crow," I say, and it's not a question. Hans nods grimly.

"Had to be. This is exactly how they work—fast, clean, no witnesses. They probably had her packed and gone within an hour." Hans runs his hand through his hair. "Boss, I'm sorry. If I'd gotten here sooner—"

"This isn't your fault." The words come out harder than I intend. "I should have moved faster. Should have taken her straight from the club instead of giving her time to go home first."

I know exactly who took her. More importantly, I know why they didn't just put a bullet in her head and leave her body for the police to find. Brutus wants to have some fun first. He wants to play with his food before he eats it.

The thought makes my vision go red around the edges. I know how Brutus operates because I used to operate the same way. Back when I was young and stupid and thought cruelty was the same thing as strength. Back when I claimed the Crow name and called Brutus mentor. Before I learned that there's a difference between killing for survival and killing for pleasure.

Before Peter Mitchell showed me a better way.

"Boss?" Hans's voice cuts through the haze of rage and memory. "What do we do now?"

"Get us to the airport," I tell Hans, settling back into the passenger seat. "We're going to Crowshaven."

He starts the engine, but I can see his massive hands grip the wheel tighter. "Boss, you sure about this? That's the heart of Crow territory. And it's just the two of us against all of them."

"They stole Sara," I say, watching the city lights blur past as Hans pulls into traffic. "And I know exactly how to steal her back."

"How can you be so sure?"

"Because the Crow won't be expecting me to come." I lean back against the leather seat, already planning. "I've been retired. Murder sober. Word spreads fast in our world, Hans. The fact that I haven't done anything to the Crow in retaliation for Peter's death tells them everything they need to know—that I won't."

Hans glances at me in the rearview mirror. "And now?"

"Now they're about to learn that some things are worth breaking sobriety for."

CHAPTER FIVE
SAYLOR

The first thing I notice is the sound of rain.

Heavy, persistent drumming against glass somewhere above me. Like the sky decided to empty itself all at once and won't stop until there's nothing left.

The second thing I notice is that I'm not tied up.

I keep my eyes closed while I take inventory. Wrists free. Ankles free. No gag in my mouth. Either these assholes are incredibly stupid, or they think I'm so harmless that restraints would be overkill. Both possibilities piss me off.

I'm lying on something that might generously be called a couch, though it feels more like a collection of springs wrapped in fabric that gave up hope sometime in the nineties. The smell hits me next— stale cigarettes, spilled beer, and unwashed bodies.

My father's compass rests heavy against my throat, and I focus on its weight to keep from hyperventilating. Peter Mitchell raised a survivor, not a victim. I will not give these fuckers the satisfaction of seeing Sara Mitchell cower. That scared little girl died the night they killed my father. They just don't know it yet.

I crack my eyes open just enough to see through my lashes, keeping my breathing steady and even.

"—should've been back by now." The voice comes from somewhere to my left, rough with impatience. "Caymans job was supposed to be simple. In and out."

"Brutus doesn't do simple." This voice is younger, casual in a way that makes my skin crawl. "Remember the senator's wife? He was supposed to make it look like an accident. Instead, we had to clean up body parts from three different counties." A laugh follows, like he's recounting a funny story from college. "Took us all weekend to find her head. Found it in a fucking tree, if you can believe that."

"At least he got creative with it," the rough voice says with what sounds like genuine appreciation. "Better than that boring shit we did in Phoenix. Three bullets, dump the body, collect the check. Where's the artistry in that?"

My blood turns to ice water. Fuck them. Fuck them for discussing murder like it's a weekend hobby.

"That was different. Personal." A third voice, older, with the weight of authority. "This one's business. Container manifest says the target was skimming from the cartel. Bad for business, bad for everyone involved."

"Still think he's having too much fun down there. Sun, sand, those little drinks with the umbrellas. Why the hell do we have to run operations out of this shithole when we could be somewhere warm," says the first voice I heard.

Through my barely open lashes, I catalog the room. Low ceiling, water stains spreading across yellowed plaster like abstract art painted in neglect. Heavy wooden beams that look original to whatever decade this place was built. The windows are small and set high, streaked with grime and years of neglect—that's where the relentless drumming is coming from. The glass is so dirty I can barely make out the gray sky beyond.

Three men visible from my position. The youngest one is tall and wiry, constantly moving. Tattoos crawl up his neck like black ivy. His hands never stop moving—fingers drumming against his thigh, foot tapping a rhythm only he can hear.

The second one is built like a linebacker. Massive shoulders, huge hands, and scars crisscrossing his knuckles. He's cleaning his fingernails with a knife, the blade nicked and worn.

The third one sits behind a table scattered with papers and photos. Salt-and-pepper hair, expensive watch, tailored suit. He carries himself like he's in charge.

"Crowshaven's perfect for our purposes," the man in the suit says, not looking up from his paperwork. "Close enough to Seattle for contracts, far enough out that nobody asks questions. Coast access for disposal. And the weather keeps the tourists away."

"Still hate the fucking rain," Twitchy mutters, lighting another cigarette despite the haze that already hangs in the air. "Makes my joints ache."

"Your joints ache because you're getting old," Granite Hands rumbles without looking up from his knife. "Rain just gives you something to blame it on."

The casual way they discuss their work makes my skin crawl. These aren't desperate men driven to violence by circumstance. These are professionals who've made murder their business.

The man in the suit shuffles through his papers, pulling out what looks like a photo. "Speaking of business, we've got another contract coming in. Witness protection dropout in Portland. Husband finally tracked her down."

"What's the timeline?" Granite Hands asks.

"Two weeks. Client wants it to look like a robbery gone wrong. Nothing complicated." The man in the suit sets the photo aside like he's filing tax returns. "Standard domestic violence cleanup. Thousand down, four thousand on completion."

My hands want to shake with rage, but I force them to stay still. They're talking about killing a woman who escaped an abusive marriage. Discussing her murder with the same tone they'd use to plan a grocery run. Some woman with a name, a life, a family who loves her.

Someone's daughter.

"What about this one?" Twitchy nods in my direction, and I squeeze my eyes tighter shut, fighting to keep my breathing even. "Sara Mitchell. Pain in the ass to track down, but here she is. What's the boss want us to do with her?"

"That depends on what mood Brutus is in when he gets back." The man in the suit's voice carries a note of anticipation that makes my stomach turn. "He's got particular feelings about the Mitchell family. Might want to take his time with this one."

"Lucky girl," Granite Hands says with a laugh that has no humor in it. "Brutus knows how to make things last."

"Can't say I blame him," Twitchy adds, and I feel his scrutiny on me even through my closed lids. "She's too pretty to waste with a quick bullet. Shame we can't have a taste first."

"Touch her and lose a hand," the man in the suit warns without heat. "She's spoken for until Brutus decides otherwise. You know the rules."

Spoken for. Like I'm a piece of property. Like I'm livestock waiting for slaughter. The rage builds in my chest, hot and bright, but I channel it into focus. Into planning.

I risk another glance through my lashes, scanning for escape routes and weapons.

I map the room in my mind, counting exit points and potential weapons. Two doors—one that probably leads outside based on the draft I can feel, another that might connect to interior rooms. The windows are too high and too small to be useful escape routes. But there are plenty of things that could be turned into weapons if I'm smart about it.

Twitchy's knife is in a sheath on his belt, easily accessible if I can get close enough. Granite Hands keeps his cleaning knife loose in his grip—overconfident, sloppy. The man in the suit has what looks like a gun in a shoulder holster under his expensive jacket.

The key is making them continue to underestimate me. Let them think I'm still the scared little girl who hid while her father died. Let them believe their own assumptions about frightened women and helpless victims.

They want Sara Mitchell? Fine. I'll give them Sara Mitchell, right up until the moment I show them who Saylor Mitchell really is.

"How much longer are we giving him?" Twitchy asks, stubbing out his cigarette on the arm of a chair that's seen better decades.

"Tomorrow, maybe the day after. Depends on how creative he got with the cartel guy." The man in the suit picks up another photo. "Client specifically requested that this one suffer before he died. Something about betraying trust."

"Brutus does love his work," Granite Hands observes, testing the edge of his knife against his thumb. A thin line of blood appears. "Maybe we should start charging extra for his enthusiasm."

"Already do," the man in the suit says with a laugh. "Premium service costs premium rates."

They continue discussing torture and murder like a book club debating character development. Each casual word drives the truth deeper: these men don't just kill for money. They enjoy it. They savor it. They've turned human suffering into an art form.

And they think I'm going to be their next masterpiece.

The rain intensifies against the windows, and I let the sound wash over me while I finalize my mental map of the room. Three men, multiple weapons, limited escape routes. Bad odds, but not impossible. I've survived worse.

I survived watching my father die. I survived five years of running and hiding and building a new life from nothing. I survived becoming someone stronger than the girl who used to cry herself to sleep every night.

My father's compass pulses against my throat with each heartbeat, steady and sure. North. Always north. Always toward whatever comes next, toward survival, toward becoming who I need to be.

But first, I'm going to show the Crow exactly what happens when you underestimate a Mitchell.

They want to wait for Brutus? Perfect. That gives me time to plan, time to learn their routines, time to figure out how to turn their own cruelty against them.

Let them think I'm still unconscious. Let them keep talking about their business, their murders, their sick fucking plans.

Every word they say is another reason to make sure none of them live to see sunrise.

CHAPTER SIX
BLUE

The safe house sits like a tumor in the Oregon wilderness with rotting wood and broken windows. It's tucked deep in Crowshaven's backcountry, miles from the main highway where tourists stop for coffee, clam chowder, and saltwater taffy. Most people never see this part—the logging roads that wind through dense forest, the compounds, and the numerous safe houses hidden behind walls of Douglas fir where the Crow run their operation.

It's easy to get lost in the maze of the Witchwood forest that separates Crowshaven from Grimlock. Crowshaven's a shithole. Grimlock's something else entirely. My town has character—old Victorian houses, narrow cobblestone streets, iron gates that look like they've been there forever. Even our graveyard has more class than most places.

Crowshaven just sprawls without giving a damn. But lucky for Grimlock, the forest gives a separation stronger than any stone wall or barbed wire fence could. The trees grow so thick they block out most of the daylight, turning everything underneath into permanent twilight. Deer paths branch off in every direction, some leading to abandoned camps, others just petering out into nothing. More than one hiker has gone in and never come back out.

But not me. I know every inch of Crowshaven and how it tries to utilize the mass of the Witchwood for its benefit. Five and a half hours. It took exactly as long as the flight from New York to Oregon on my jet to track down where the Crow dragged Sara after grabbing her from her apartment last night.

"Four heat signatures," Hans murmurs beside me, lowering his thermal scope. "Main room. They're not even trying to be smart about this."

Smart isn't in their vocabulary. Brutus took his A-team to handle some cartel business in the Caymans, leaving these bottom-feeders to play babysitter. Their mistake. My opportunity.

The intel came from Hans's network—someone spotted the black sedan heading into the mountains. Not exactly a sophisticated operation—more like amateur hour with delusions of competence.

"Remember," I tell Hans as we approach the building's rear entrance, "I don't kill tonight. You handle the wet work."

Hans raises an eyebrow. "Boss, are you sure? You seem very . . . tense."

Tense doesn't begin to cover it. My hands shake with the need to paint these walls with Crow blood, to make them suffer for every hour they've kept her captive. Three years of therapy, three years of Jay's breathing exercises and redirected aggression, and it could all disappear in the next ten minutes.

"I'm on the wagon," I repeat, as much to convince myself as Hans. "Can't risk falling off. Not now."

The back door hangs askew, held by one stubborn hinge that squeaks like a dying mouse. Hans oils it with spit and patience while I control my breathing the way Jay taught me. In for four, hold for four, out for four. Meditation that keeps reformed killers from relapsing.

The air inside hits like a slap—thick with smoke and the sour tang of men who've given up on hygiene. These idiots couldn't maintain a decent hideout if their lives depended on it.

Voices drift from the main room, unguarded. They're not expecting company.

"—should've heard him scream when Brutus started with the pliers. Sounded like a fucking opera singer hitting the high notes."

Laughter follows, blood-curdling and genuine.

"Wait here," Hans whispers, already moving toward the sound. "I make this quick."

Through the doorway, I watch Hans work. Three men clustered around a card table, playing poker with cigarettes as chips because they're too broke for actual money. And there, on a decrepit couch against the far wall, is Sara. Eyes closed, breathing steady, but I can tell she's awake. Smart girl—playing possum while gathering intelligence.

The first one dies mid-laugh, Hans's blade sliding across his throat like he's opening mail. The second one starts to stand, confusion replacing amusement on his face, but Hans is already there. The knife finds the sweet spot between ribs, puncturing the lung and heart in one efficient thrust.

The third man—younger than the others, with nervous eyes and shaking hands—actually manages to draw his gun. Almost manages to aim it before Hans's blade opens his carotid artery.

But Hans doesn't stop there. He drives the tip of his knife into the man's left eye socket with a wet pop, then twists the blade with deliberate slowness, stirring the contents like he's mixing cake batter. The eyeball bursts with a sound like stepping on a grape, and Hans actually hums a little tune while he works. The man's remaining eye stares up at nothing, blood and vitreous fluid running down his cheek in pink rivulets.

Even I have to look away, and I've seen some shit. There's excessive, and then there's whatever the hell Hans just did to that poor bastard's brain.

"You're just showing off," I tell him as he wipes the blade clean.

Hans grins, looking genuinely pleased with himself. "Boss, for years it's always been you leading the charge with that axe of yours. Now it's my turn to have some fun." He gestures at the bodies with mock pride. "Besides, when do I ever get to be creative? Usually I just follow your lead and clean up the mess. Where's the flair in that?" He toes one of the dead bodies on the ground. "They deserve it. Actually . . . they deserve worse."

Thirty seconds. Three bodies. One unnecessary eye socket violation. Zero survivors.

Sara's eyes are wide open, staring at the death scene. She sits up slowly, taking in the carnage, then her gaze finds mine across the room. Her skin has gone ghost-pale, making the bruise on her upper arm look even darker—dark purple against pale skin. The sight makes me want to resurrect these dead assholes just so I can kill them again.

Christ, she looks so young. So fragile sitting there surrounded by death and violence, trying to process what just happened. She shouldn't have to see this. Shouldn't have to witness grown men reduced to meat and blood.

"Blue?" Her voice cracks slightly on my name, those expressive eyes moving between relief and suspicion. "What the hell are you doing here?"

"Rescuing you, Sara." I step carefully around the bodies, hands visible, voice calm. The last thing she needs is another man making her feel trapped. "We're getting you out of here."

"How do you know that name?" Her voice wavers, shock bleeding through the words. "Nobody calls me Sara. Nobody even knows—" She stops, staring at me like I'm a ghost. "Who the fuck are you?"

"Sara, listen. We need to get you—"

"Don't call me Sara." The demand comes out sharp, desperate. "My name is Saylor. And rescue?" Her gaze darts to the bodies scattered around the room, to the blood pooling on the floor, to Hans wiping his knife clean. "This isn't rescue, this is—oh god, there's so much blood. They're all—are they all dead?"

Her breathing picks up, quick and shallow. She's spiraling, processing too much at once.

"You actually—I wanted them dead but I never thought—" She pushes herself up from the couch, swaying slightly. I can see the careful way she favors her left side. They roughed her up.

I move closer, needing to get between her and the carnage, to shield her from the worst of it. "Hey," I say softly, catching her attention. "Look at me, not them."

But her focus keeps drifting back to the bodies, to the blood spreading across the floor.

"Saylor." Her name puts her attention back on me. "These men were going to kill you. We stopped that from happening. But we need to go. Now."

She's looking around the room now, really taking it in—the blood, the bodies, the overturned chairs. "Jesus . . . it's like a fucking slaughterhouse in here."

She's right—this is exactly what it is. Her hands are shaking now, and I want nothing more than to wrap her in my jacket and carry her far away from this place, from this world, from everything that could hurt her.

"Why are you here? What do you want with me?"

"I was a friend of your father's." I keep my voice steady, calm. "I'll explain everything once we get to Grimlock. My home. Where you'll be safe."

"Safe from what? And what the hell is Grimlock?"

"We need to leave."

She processes this, stunning eyes studying my face like she's trying to read my thoughts. Smart. Too smart for her own good.

But I can see the fight building in her posture, the stubborn tilt of her chin that reminds me so much of Peter it hurts.

"I know this is a lot," I begin, but she cuts me off.

"A lot?" Her voice rises. "A lot is finding out your coffee shop raised their prices. A lot is getting a parking ticket. This is—this is fucking insane!"

She's right, of course. Completely, absolutely right. But we don't have time for a philosophical discussion about the nature of reality and how quickly it can turn to shit.

"I'm not going anywhere with two fucking strangers." Her voice rises, panic edging in. "I don't care if you knew my father. You just killed three people in front of me. You're clearly as dangerous as they were."

I take another step toward her, ignoring the way she flinches. "Saylor, listen to me—"

"No!" She backs away, her shoulder hitting the wall. "Stay away from me!"

The raw terror in her voice stops me cold. This isn't just about the bodies or the blood—it's about trust, about control, about a twenty-three-year-old woman who's been through hell and is now being asked to trust two more killers with her life.

I catch Hans's eye and nod toward the chloroform in his jacket pocket. She's going to fight this, and we don't have time for a lengthy negotiation. Every minute we waste here is another chance for more Crow to arrive.

"I'm sorry," I tell her, meaning it completely.

Hans moves behind her with surprising grace for such a large man. The chloroform-soaked rag appears in his hands like a magic trick, covering her nose and mouth before she can scream or run or throw something at my head.

Her eyes lock on mine as the drug takes hold, wide with shock and betrayal. She trusted me long enough to let her guard down, and I just violated that trust completely.

But she's alive. That's what matters.

"The steamer trunk in the corner," I tell Hans, pointing to the antique chest they probably used to transport her here.

Hans lifts her gently, placing her inside the trunk with more care than these assholes ever showed her. She looks impossibly small curled up in there, like a sleeping child.

"This still feels wrong, Boss," Hans mutters, securing the latches. "Like we are kidnapping her."

"We are kidnapping her." No point in pretending otherwise. "But we're kidnapping her away from people who would torture and kill her. Context matters."

"Will she see it that way?"

Probably not. She'll wake up angry, confused, and ready to murder me with whatever's handy. But she'll wake up alive, which is more than she can say if we'd left her with the Crow.

CHAPTER SEVEN
BLUE

My therapist's office is a library that had a nervous breakdown.

Dr. Jay Finch's domain is a masterclass in organized chaos—if you can call towers of psychiatric journals balanced on coffee-stained coasters "organized." Post-it Notes cover every surface like yellow confetti, each one scribbled with reminders that range from "pick up dry cleaning" to "research sociopathic tendencies in maritime professions." His desk is an archaeological dig of half-finished thoughts, fidget spinners, and a sandwich—based on the mold formed—from the Mesozoic Era.

"Blue!" Jay springs up from behind his fortress of academic debris, immediately knocking over a precarious stack of books. He doesn't bother picking them up. "Right on time! Well, technically seventeen minutes late, but who's counting? I've been thinking about our last session and—oh shit, you have that look. The 'I almost broke my sobriety' look. Please tell me you didn't kill anyone."

I settle into the leather chair across from his desk—the only clean surface in the entire office—and study the man who's supposed to be fixing my broken brain. Jay Finch is sixty-something with silver hair that reminds me of someone who stuck his finger in an electrical socket, wire-rimmed glasses perpetually sliding down his nose, and a nervous energy that makes you wonder if he's the patient here.

"I may have had a minor setback," I say, crossing my ankle over my knee.

Jay's face lights up like a kid on Christmas morning. "Ooh, setback! I love setbacks. They're so much more interesting than progress." He grabs a notepad from somewhere in the chaos, immediately drops it, picks up a different one, then stares at it like he's forgotten what it's for. "Define minor. On a scale of one to 'I broke three years of murder sobriety,' how minor are we talking?"

"I didn't kill anyone. But I wanted to. God, I wanted to."

"Okay, so that's actually huge progress." Jay pushes his glasses up his nose and they immediately slide back down. "Three years clean, Blue. Remember what happened last time? After Peter died?"

"Eighteen kills in two months."

"Right, right, the killing spree that made you realize you needed help. The one where you lost track of Peter's daughter because you were too busy painting the country red." Jay starts pacing behind his desk, stepping over books like they're landmines. "So, what triggered the urge this time?"

"I found Peter's daughter. The Crow had her. Grabbed her from her apartment, dragged her to some shithole cabin in the mountains. By the time Hans and I tracked them down, she'd been there for hours."

Jay stops pacing. "And you didn't kill them?"

I shift in my chair. "Hans handled it. I watched. Not completely innocent, I know. But at least I didn't kill. Counted breaths like you taught me. In for four, hold for four, out for four."

"Holy shit, you actually used the techniques." Jay grabs a stress ball from his desk, squeezes it twice, then tosses it up and catches it. "Blue, that's incredible. Three years ago, you would have redecorated that cabin with their entrails. What happened next?"

"I relocated her to a safer environment. In a steamer trunk."

"Oh, for fuck's sake." Jay slumps into his chair, which immediately starts spinning in slow circles. He doesn't try to stop it. "*Relocated.* That's what we're calling it now?"

"It sounds better than kidnapped."

"But you did kidnap her."

"Technically, yes."

"There's no 'technically' about trunk-based transportation, Blue."

"She's perfectly safe at Maison Rouge. Wren is taking excellent care of her."

"Wren, your housekeeper who used to help you dispose of body parts for fifteen years." Jay's chair has completed three full rotations. "Let me get this straight. You maintained your sobriety even when the Crow had Peter's daughter, but you still kidnapped her?"

"Relocated. The urge to kill them was . . . overwhelming. But I knew if I started again, I wouldn't stop. Just like last time."

"Right, the post-Peter murder bender. So you let Hans do the dirty work while you what, meditated in the same room?"

"Something like that."

"And then you decided the logical next step was to stuff her in luggage?"

"There's something else."

"Oh good, because this story needed more complications."

"We hooked up."

Jay blinks once. Twice. "You kidnapped a woman you slept with."

"She needed protection from the Crow."

"So naturally you put her in a trunk."

"It was a very nice trunk. Antique. Well-ventilated."

"Jesus Christ, Blue."

Jay stands up slowly, deliberately. "Blue, I've been treating you for three years. Three years since you came to me, covered in other people's blood, begging for help because you'd become the monster Peter would've hated. And you just told me you resisted the strongest trigger you've faced since then." Jay stops pacing and fixes me with a stare. "But this woman—what's her name again?"

"Saylor Mitchell."

"Saylor is going to wake up in your murder mansion and think you're a psychopath."

"I *am* a psychopath."

"A *recovering* psychopath! We've been working on this!" Jay grabs his stress ball from where he'd set it down, squeezes it until his knuckles turn white. "Here's what I'm hearing: You maintained your sobriety, but you're substituting one compulsion for another. You can't keep collecting damsels in distress like they're rare butterflies."

"They're not butterflies. They're people who need help. And she's not just anyone. She's Peter's daughter. The one person I swore to protect."

"Help, yes. Kidnapping and imprisonment, no." Jay sits back down, his chair immediately resuming its slow spin. "Tell me something. When you look at Saylor, what do you see?"

I think about her voice, smoky and seductive as she sang at the

White Note. The way she challenged me in the bar, unafraid. The compass necklace she wore—Peter's compass. Still wearing it after all these years.

"I see someone who's about to be very angry with me once she wakes up. And someone who doesn't know how close she came to disappearing forever. Which is why I relocated her. Why she needs to stay under lock and key. For her own good. I owe Peter that much."

"You're deflecting. This isn't about Peter anymore, is it?" Jay stops spinning and leans forward. "Blue, you're going to have to let her go."

"Not while the Crow are still a threat. Brutus doesn't leave loose ends."

"Then eliminate the threat without keeping her prisoner. Use those skills you've been redirecting. The planning, the strategy. Be the protector Peter believed you could be, not the killer—and *kidnapper*—you used to be."

"I can't protect her if she's not where I can see her."

Jay stares at me for a long moment, then reaches into his desk drawer and pulls out a flask. He takes a long pull, coughs, and offers it to me.

"It's Tuesday," he says.

"Your point?"

"My point is that it's Tuesday afternoon and I'm drinking shitty tequila because my patient just casually informed me he's kidnapped someone and doesn't plan to let her go." Jay takes another sip. "I need you to understand something. What you're doing isn't protection. It's possession."

"She's not a possession."

"Then prove it. Let her choose."

"Choose what?"

"Whether she wants your protection or not. Whether she wants to stay at Maison Rouge or leave. Whether she wants anything to do with you at all." Jay caps the flask and shoves it back in the drawer. "Because right now, you've taken that choice away from her, and that makes you the threat."

The words hit harder than I expected. I think about Saylor locked in the wing of my estate, probably trying to figure out how to escape, how to get as far away from me as possible. The same way any sane person would react to waking up in a stranger's house.

"She'll try to leave," I say finally.

"Probably."

"The Crow will kill her."

"Maybe. Or maybe you'll find another way to keep her safe without keeping her prisoner." Jay leans back in his chair. "Blue, do you want to be the man who saves her, or the man she needs saving from? Do you want to be the man Peter knew you could be, or the monster you became after he died?"

Before I can answer, my phone buzzes with a text from Wren: *She's awake.*

CHAPTER EIGHT
SAYLOR

Someone is humming Beethoven, and it's pissing me off.

The melody drifts through my skull like smoke, each note stabbing directly into the base of my brain, where a headache is throwing its own personal rave. My mouth tastes like I've been licking the inside of a chemistry lab, and every inch of my body feels like it's been wrung out and hung up to dry.

I'm folded into something that smells of lavender and old leather, my knees pressed against my chest in what I slowly realize is the same steamer chest from the safe house. Except now it's sitting in a room that looks like Versailles had a baby with a haunted mansion.

Everything screams wealth and old-world elegance. Deep sapphire velvet curtains hang from ceiling to floor, their fabric so rich it seems to absorb light. The walls are covered in damask wallpaper the color of dried blood, interrupted by oil paintings in heavy gold frames—aristocratic faces with pinched expressions that look like they're judging my life choices. A four-poster bed dominates the space, its carved mahogany posts twisted into spirals that reach toward a ceiling painted with cherubs and clouds.

"There we are, honey. Easy now."

A plump woman is helping me unfold from the chest as if this isn't her first time extracting a confused person from antique luggage. She's maybe sixty, with steel-gray hair pulled back in a bun so tight it could cut glass. Her black dress is perfectly pressed, her white apron spotless, and her bearing carries a maternal authority that makes you want to confess sins you haven't even committed yet.

"Wren," she introduces herself, steadying me as I try to climb out of what I'm now thinking of as my temporary coffin. "Welcome to Maison Rouge."

I step onto the marble floor, my heels clicking against the polished stone. I'm still wearing the same green dress I wore while singing, now wrinkled and reeking of chemicals, lavender, and the rank smell of that filthy couch from the last house.

"Where am I?" I sound like I've been gargling with broken glass.

"Blue's estate in Grimlock. You're safe here." Wren moves to a massive mahogany armoire and pulls out a simple sundress. "Let's get you out of those clothes and into something more comfortable."

"Safe?" The word comes out strangled. My brain is still catching up, memories filtering through the chemical haze. Years of hiding, and then they found me. Blue rescuing me from the safe house. Men with dead eyes in Crowshaven. Blood splattered across the walls. "He drugged me. He put me in a trunk."

"Yes. The travel arrangements were rather unconventional." Wren speaks with the same tone she might use to comment on the weather. "But you're here now, and that's what matters."

The casual way she dismisses my kidnapping makes my stomach lurch. Either this woman is completely insane, or this sort of thing happens here on a regular basis.

"I need to leave. Right now." I push past her toward what I hope is a door leading out, but the room tilts sideways and I have to grab the bedpost to keep from falling.

"I'm afraid that's not advisable in your current condition. The chloroform needs time to clear your system completely." Wren sets the dress on the bed with infuriating calm. "Blue has instructed me to ensure you're properly cared for."

"Blue can go fuck himself."

Wren's eyebrows rise slightly, but her face doesn't change. "I'll be sure to pass along your sentiments."

Anger cuts through the remaining fog in my brain with startling clarity. This isn't just about being kidnapped—although that's bad enough. It's the presumption, the casual dismissal of my choices, the way everyone seems to think they know what's best for me better than I do.

I straighten up, ignoring the way the room sways. "I'm leaving."

"Are you?"

The condescending tone in her question makes me want to scream. Instead, I head for the door—massive and made of dark wood with iron hinges that look like they belong in a medieval castle.

Wren doesn't try to stop me. She just watches with the patience of someone who's seen this movie before and knows exactly how it ends.

The door opens into a hallway that stretches in both directions, its length disappearing into shadows. The walls are paneled in dark wood, broken up by alcoves holding marble statues and ornate candelabras. The ceiling arches high overhead, supported by carved beams that create pockets of darkness between pools of warm light.

I choose left arbitrarily and start walking on the Persian runner that stretches down the center of the hall. Every few feet, I pass doorways—some open to reveal rooms draped in dust covers, others closed with heavy doors that could hide anything.

The hallway ends at a balcony overlooking what has to be the most dramatic staircase I've ever seen. It spirals down through the center of the house in a graceful curve, its wrought-iron banister twisted into patterns of thorns and roses. The steps are white marble veined with gold, and they seem to go down forever.

Stained glass windows line the stairwell, each one telling part of a story I can't quite piece together. There's a woman with long hair climbing a tower, a man in a boat surrounded by sirens, another woman dancing with a beast. The colored light they cast paints everything in jewel tones—emerald and sapphire and deep ruby red.

I start down the stairs, my hand trailing along the banister for support. The metal is cool under my palm, and I can feel the intricate details of the roses carved into it. Some of them have thorns sharp enough to draw blood if you're not careful.

Halfway down, the staircase opens onto the main floor, and I get my first real look at the heart of Maison Rouge.

The entry hall is enormous, its ceiling soaring up three stories to a dome painted with scenes from fairy tales. The floor is a mosaic of black-and-white marble arranged in intricate patterns that seem to shift and change as I move. Probably a result of being so overwhelmed, overstimulated, and still drugged as fuck. A massive chandelier hangs from the center of the dome, its crystal drops catching the colored light from the stained glass and throwing rainbows across the walls.

Furniture fills the space—not the kind you'd expect to see in a normal house, but pieces that would be in a palace. There's a grand-father clock that's easily ten feet tall, its face showing not just the time but the phases of the moon. Tapestries hang from the walls, their threads telling stories of knights and dragons and ladies in towers. A piano sits in one corner, its ebony surface gleaming under the chandelier light.

But it's the portraits that make me stop and stare. They line the walls between the tapestries—dozens of them, all women, all beautiful, all wearing visible emotions that range from joy to terror. Some are painted in a classical style, others look more modern, but they all have one thing in common: They're all staring directly at whoever's looking at them.

There's something unsettling about the collection, something that makes my skin crawl even though I can't put my finger on what it is.

"Quite a gallery," Wren says from behind me.

I spin around, my mind racing. She's followed me down the stairs with the silent grace of a cat.

Wren moves past me toward the front door, her keys jingling softly. She reaches the door and turns the key in the lock with a decisive click.

I'm frozen on the stairs, staring at dozens of painted eyes that seem to watch my every move while the housekeeper locks me in with them. This isn't real. This can't be real.

But the lock clicks shut with finality, and Wren is walking back toward me with the same pleasant smile she's worn since I woke up in a trunk. "Now then," she says, "shall we go back upstairs? I have a lovely dinner planned, and Blue should be home soon."

That breaks the spell. I bolt.

I run toward what I hope is a back door. The entry hall branches off into smaller rooms—a library with books stretching floor to ceiling, a dining room with a table that could seat twenty, a parlor with ornate furniture . . . palace-type furniture.

I find a door that leads to the kitchen, all gleaming copper and modern appliances that look strangely out of place in the gothic manor. Another door leads to a small pantry. A third opens onto a narrow staircase that probably goes to the servants' quarters.

Finally, I find what I'm looking for—a door with glass panels that shows trees and sky beyond. I grab the handle and pull, expecting it to be locked, but it opens easily.

The evening air hits my skin like a slap, cold and harsh with the trace of pine and ocean salt. I'm standing on a stone terrace that overlooks the most beautiful and terrifying landscape I've ever seen.

Maison Rouge sits on a cliff overlooking the Pacific, the ocean stretching to the horizon where it meets a sky painted in shades of purple and gold. The house itself is even more imposing from the outside—all towers and turrets and complex stonework that makes it look like something out of a fairy tale. Gothic windows climb the walls, their arched frames decorated with filagree and ivy.

Gardens spread out below the terrace in descending levels, each one more magnificent than the last. There are fountains and statues, hedges trimmed into fantastic shapes, and flowers in colors I don't have names for. Stone paths wind between them, disappearing into groves of trees that look massive and wild.

And surrounding it all is a wall.

Not just any wall—this one is at least twelve feet high, topped with iron spikes and built from the same dark stone as the house. It stretches as far as I can see in both directions, disappearing into the forest that surrounds the estate.

But there has to be a gate. There has to be a way out.

I run down the stone steps to the first garden level, my silk dress catching on rose bushes and my heels constantly getting trapped between the stones. The paths are gravel and stone, awkward to navigate in dress shoes, but I don't stop.

The gardens are bigger than I thought, stretching out in all directions like a maze. I follow what seems like the main path, passing fountains where stone nymphs pour water from urns and statues of women in flowing gowns seem to beckon me deeper into the maze.

The trees grow thicker as I move away from the house, their branches overhead blocking out more and more of the sky. The path splits and branches, and I take turns almost at random, just trying to find the wall, find the gate, find some way out of this beautiful prison.

When I finally reach it, I understand why Wren wasn't worried about me running.

The gate is massive—two curved sections of wrought iron that meet in an arch. But it's what's written there that makes me stop dead in my tracks.

The metal has been twisted and shaped to form words, their letters flowing and elegant against the darkening sky: "Once Upon a Time."

The gate is locked, of course. Not just with a simple latch, but with a complex mechanism that looks like it requires either a key or knowledge of some specific combination. The wall stretches away on either side, disappearing into the forest, and those iron spikes along the top suddenly seem a lot sharper than they did from a distance.

I grab the bars and shake them, but they don't budge. The metal is ice-cold under my hands, and when I look more closely, I can see that the decorative elements aren't just flowers and thorns—there are tiny skulls worked into the design, so small and delicate they're almost hidden.

"Beautiful work, isn't it?"

I spin around to find Blue standing behind me on the path, still in the same dark suit from the safe house but now with added splashes of blood on his shirt cuffs. His beard is as perfectly groomed as ever, that hint of blue catching the last light of sunset, and he's fixed on me with an intensity that makes me take a step back.

"The gate was commissioned by the original owner," he continues conversationally, as if finding me desperate at his locked gate is perfectly normal. "A man who believed that every story should have a proper beginning."

"Let me out." The words are steadier than I feel.

"I'm afraid that's not possible just yet." Blue takes a step closer, and I press back against the gate. "The men who killed your father are still looking for you, Saylor. Out there, you're vulnerable. Here, you're safe."

"Safe?" I laugh, but there's no humor in it. "I'm locked up with someone I don't even know, in a place I've never heard of. I don't know who you really are, what you do, if you actually knew my father, or what any of this has to do with me. How exactly is that safe?"

Blue's facial features don't change, but something glimmers in his eyes. He pulls out his cell and faces it toward me as I hear my father's voice on a message. I don't understand the context of everything being said, but I do hear this: *"You're the only one I trust to keep her safe. I owe you my forever gratitude."*

Tears form instantly, but I blink them away. I can't show weakness . . . I can't.

Okay, so he showed me proof, but that doesn't change the fact that— "And your charming housekeeper who locks doors and acts like kidnapping is just another Tuesday." I lift my chin, trying to appear brave. "So what's the plan? I have to stay here forever?"

"No." The word is quiet but certain. "I didn't kidnap you, Saylor. I rescued you. You're my guest."

"Guests can leave whenever they want."

"Not when leaving means dying."

We stare at each other across the growing darkness. Even covered in blood, even standing between me and freedom, Blue is magnetic in the most reckless way possible. But I've already been stupid once where he's concerned.

"I'll take my chances," I say.

"I won't."

"That's not your choice to make."

"Isn't it?" Blue steps closer, and now I can smell his cologne mixed with the metallic scent of blood that makes my stomach turn. "Your father asked me to protect you. That's exactly what I'm doing."

"My father is dead."

"Which is why someone needs to keep you alive."

The casual arrogance in his comments makes me want to scream. "And you've appointed yourself my guardian?"

"I've accepted the responsibility, yes."

"I didn't ask for your protection."

"You didn't ask for your father's death either, but here we are."

For a moment I can't breathe. The image of Dad's body, the blood, the way his eyes went wide with shock and pain—it all comes rushing back.

Blue's face softens slightly. "I'm sorry. That was cruel."

"You're a monster."

"Yes," he agrees easily. "But I'm a monster who's going to keep you alive."

He turns and starts walking back toward the house, clearly expecting me to follow. When I don't move, he stops and looks back.

"You can walk back with me, or you can stand here in the cold until you change your mind. But that gate isn't opening tonight." He glances up at the darkening clouds gathering overhead. "And I don't have an umbrella to offer."

I want to tell him to go to hell. I want to climb the wall, spikes or no spikes. I want to do anything except admit that he's right about one thing—I have nowhere else to go.

But my feet are already aching from running on gravel in heels, my dress is catching on every thorn bush, and the forest around the estate is making sounds that don't come from any animals I recognize. I'm clearly not in New York anymore, and this city girl is not up for roughing it.

"This isn't over," I say finally.

Blue's smile is as piercing as the thorns on his property. "I wouldn't expect it to be."

As we walk back through the gardens toward the house, me slipping and sliding on the gravel paths, I count the windows blazing with warm light, the towers reaching toward the star-filled sky, the impossible beauty of a place that's also a prison.

We're almost at the terrace when Blue calls over his shoulder without looking back.

"I'll make a deal with you. We start by agreeing you stay tonight. Have dinner. And I'll answer all the questions I'm sure you have."

He doesn't wait for my answer before disappearing through the glass doors, leaving me standing alone in the cold night air.

CHAPTER NINE
SAYLOR

Thirty-seven seconds is apparently how long it takes for dignity to lose a fight with hunger. I'm still standing outside those glass doors when my stomach decides to stage a rebellion. It growls loud enough to echo off the stone terrace, reminding me that I haven't eaten since . . . well . . . I don't even know when.

Fine. Dinner it is.

The dining room Blue leads me to is cozy but also intimidating. Dark wood paneling climbs halfway up the walls before giving way to deep green wallpaper. A table for twenty sits in the center, set for two with more silverware than any reasonable meal requires.

"Not quite what you expected?" Blue asks, pulling out a chair.

"It's very . . . formal." I settle into the chair, which is surprisingly comfortable despite looking like it was designed to make people sit up straight and confess their sins.

Wren appears from what must be the kitchen, carrying a silver soup tureen. She ladles something red into my bowl.

"Tomato bisque," she announces. "With cream and fresh basil."

I take a tentative sip. It's good. Actually good, which somehow makes this whole situation more irritating. If you're going to be held captive, the least your captor could do is serve terrible food.

"You look disappointed," Blue observes, settling into the chair across from me. "Were you hoping for gruel? Maybe some moldy bread to really sell the whole prisoner experience?"

"I was hoping for a way out of here."

"Hmm. Wren's many talents don't extend to lockpicking lessons." Blue starts on his soup. "Although she did suggest chloroform again if you became difficult."

"Charming." I focus on my soup, trying to ignore the way the candlelight flickers across his face. A crystal chandelier hangs overhead, but tonight Blue has chosen to dine by candles—candelabras scattered around the room casting everything in moving shadows.

It should feel romantic. Instead, it's like dining in a tomb. "Tell me something—do you always drug your guests, or am I special?"

"Oh, you're definitely special." His smile turns predatory. "Most of my dinner companions don't require quite such . . . creative transportation."

"Sure. Because most people probably come here willingly." I wave my spoon around the room. "Who wouldn't want to visit Castle Psychopath?"

Blue actually laughs at that, a genuine sound that transforms his whole face. "Castle Psychopath. I like that. Much better than what the locals call it."

"Which is?"

"You'll have to ask the locals when you meet them." He takes a slurp of his soup. "I'm sure they'll be happy to share all the town gossip about Maison Rouge."

Wren returns with the next course—a beautifully plated steak that's been pre-cut into bite-size pieces, accompanied by roasted vegetables that smell like heaven. There are no knives on the table. Not even butter knives.

"Afraid I'll stab you?" I ask, picking up my fork.

"House rules." Blue's casual appearance doesn't change as he picks up a piece of his own pre-cut steak. "When your usual dinner guests include people with anger management issues and homicidal tendencies, sharp objects at the table become a liability. I learned long ago that dinner parties go more smoothly when deadly objects are kept to a minimum."

"Dinner parties. Right." I try to picture it—this formal dining room filled with the people Blue considers friends. "What kind of people exactly?"

"The kind who need somewhere safe to eat a meal," he says, his tone taking on an almost wistful quality. "Grimlock attracts a certain type of individual." He pauses, swirling his wine. "They're all a little broken, a little strange, a little too much for the regular world. So we gather here, at my table, and for a few hours we're not the misfits. We're just . . . family." Something dark moves across his face. "For those of us who've lost ours, or never had one to begin with."

There is a sudden shift in his tone. For a moment, he sounds almost . . . sad.

"Like my father," I say quietly.

"Like your father." Blue nods. "Peter was one of the few people who could make me laugh. Did you know he once convinced an entire wedding party that he was the groom's long-lost twin brother?"

I nearly choke on my beef. "What?"

"Your father was working a case—needed to get close to the father of the bride who was being threatened by some very dangerous people. Peter was trying to help the man's family disappear before his enemies found them. But he showed up at the wrong church, different wedding entirely." Blue's face lit up with the memory. "Instead of leaving, he claimed he was the groom's twin who'd been raised separately after their parents' messy divorce. Spent the entire reception giving a heartfelt speech about how he'd searched the world to find his 'brother' on his special day."

I can picture it perfectly. Dad had this way of rolling with any situation, turning disasters into adventures. "Please tell me someone figured it out."

"The actual groom was six inches shorter and had red hair." Blue's smile is genuine this time, softer around the edges. "But your father was so convincing, so charming, that half the wedding party was in tears by the end of his speech." He takes a deep breath and smiles. "That was Peter. He could charm his way out of anything."

"Except whatever got him killed."

The lightness in Blue's eyes vanishes. "The Crow aren't a problem you can charm your way out of." He clears his throat and shifts in his seat. There's an awkward pause and then Blue finally adds, "I want you to know that I had no idea you were Peter's daughter when we . . . I didn't realize it the other night."

Wren refills our wine glasses—when did I start drinking wine?—and disappears again like a well-dressed ghost. The beef is perfect, practically melting on my tongue, but my appetite is fading.

"Tell me about them," I say, wanting to change the conversation away from our hook up. "The Crow."

Blue's fork pauses halfway to his mouth. He sets it down carefully, but doesn't lean back. Instead, he reaches for his wine glass, taking a slow sip while studying my face.

"Why ruin a perfectly good dinner?"

"You said if I stayed for dinner, you'd answer my questions." I lean forward slightly. "Well, here I am. And I have questions."

Blue is quiet for a long moment, swirling the wine in his glass. "Not all answers are ones you want to hear."

"Try me."

He sighs, a sound that seems to come from somewhere deep and tired. "What exactly do you want to know?"

"Everything. Who they are, what they want, why they killed my father." I set down my fork. "And don't give me some vague explanation about business. I want the truth."

Blue leans back in his chair. In the candlelight, his beard catches hints of that impossible blue color. "They're a crime syndicate. Started in Seattle about twenty years ago, spread down the coast like cancer. They specialize in making problems disappear."

"What kind of problems?"

"They kill people." His words are matter-of-fact, like he's discussing the weather. "They're very good at what they do. Very thorough. And they don't leave loose ends."

"Which is what I am. A loose end."

I stare at him across the table, trying to process this information. "I didn't even know what my father really did for a living. I thought he was an accountant. Some ordinary guy who helped people with their taxes and retirement plans." My voice gets smaller. "I thought my father was the most boring man on the planet. What exactly did he do? Who was he? What got him killed?"

"Peter was a pain in the Crow's ass and to the uppers that hired them." Blue picks up his wine glass. "He ran his own witness protection program for people who couldn't get help through official channels. When someone was marked for death by people like the Crow, Peter gave them new identities, new lives, safe places to hide. He saved dozens of people over the years."

"You mean he was one of the good guys."

"He was the best of the good guys. The kind of man who'd risk everything to save a stranger. Who'd spend his own money to keep families safe." Blue's expression grows darker. "The only thing he hated about the work was that it put you in danger. He knew the Crow would come for his family eventually, and it ate at him."

"That's insane."

"That's business." He takes a sip. "Peter tried to get out of the life before it was too late. That's why he asked me to look after you—he knew his past was catching up with him."

"He never mentioned you," I say. "In all these years, he never once said he had a friend named Blue."

"Peter was good at keeping secrets. He had to be, in our line of work."

Wren appears again, this time with dessert—some kind of chocolate tart that is fancy-five-star-restaurant worthy. She serves us both and vanishes without a word.

"And you were his partner?"

"I was his backup. When things got dangerous, when the Crow got too close to the people he was protecting, Peter called me." Blue's smile turns wicked. "I used to be very good at making dangerous things go away."

The way he says it makes my skin crawl. I remember the look he had at that cabin—not the calm control he's showing me now, but something hungry and barely restrained.

"Used to be?"

"I'm retired from that particular profession."

"And how do you plan to protect me if you don't . . . eliminate threats anymore?"

Blue's expression shifts to something I can't quite read. "I'm hoping it won't come to that."

"Hope isn't a plan." I set down my fork and look at him directly. "How many of them are there? The Crow in general?"

"Hard to say exactly. They operate in cells, keep things compartmentalized. Maybe thirty, forty active members along the coast."

"Do you know who they are?"

"Some of them, yes."

Something hot and vicious unfurls in my chest. "Good. I want them dead."

Blue blinks. "I'm sorry, what?"

"You heard me. I want them dead. All of them. Every single person involved in my father's murder." The words come out steady, sure, like I've been thinking about them for years. Because I have. "For five years, I've been dreaming about making them pay. For five years, I've been imagining what I'd do if I ever got the chance."

Blue studies me with new interest. "Saylor—"

"Don't." I hold up a hand. "Don't tell me that's not who I am, or that I'm too good for revenge, or that my father wouldn't want this. I know exactly who I am and what I want."

"And what's that?"

"Justice. For my father, for all the people they've killed, for everyone they're going to kill if someone doesn't stop them." I meet his stare across the table. "You said you used to be good at making dangerous things go away. How good?"

"Very good." His voice is careful, measured. "But I told you, I'm retired."

"Then teach me."

Blue stares at me for a long moment, his expression unreadable.

"You have no idea what you're asking for."

"Don't I?" I lean forward. "I'm asking you to teach me how to kill the people who murdered my father. I'm asking you to help me become someone who can make them pay for what they've done."

"You think you want revenge, but you don't understand—"

"I understand perfectly." I push my dessert away. "Can I have a pen and paper?"

Blue's eyebrows raise. "What for?"

"I want to write something down."

He nods to Wren, who appears with a fountain pen and elegant stationery, as if she's been expecting this request. I uncap the pen and start writing, the words flowing easily because I've carried this list in my head for five years.

"The one with the scar through his left eyebrow who smelled like cheap cologne and had these dead, cold eyes. The short one with the gold tooth who kept cracking his knuckles—nervous habit, like he was always ready for a fight. The tall one with the snake tattoo curling up his neck who wouldn't stop laughing at everything, even while they were . . . doing it. The heavy-set one with a pronounced limp who positioned himself by the door like a guard, watching for witnesses. And the one in the expensive suit with manicured nails who gave all the orders—clearly the man in charge." I look up at Blue. "Those are the five I remember from that night. The ones I watched from the closet while they killed my father."

Blue's face has gone very still. "Saylor—"

"There were others, weren't there? The one who gave the order. The one who planned it. The one who decided my father had to die." I add another line to my list. "I want all of them. Every single person involved."

I slide the paper across the table to Blue. He reads it slowly, his expression growing darker with each line.

"You know them," I say. "I can see it in your face. You know exactly who I'm talking about."

Blue sets the paper down carefully. "I have a pretty good idea . . . yeah."

"Good. Now you know exactly who I want dead."

"Killing them won't bring your father back."

"No, but it'll make sure they can't kill anyone else's father." I lean back in my chair. "You said the Crow multiply. That simply getting rid of these won't change anything."

Blue nods slowly. "They recruit constantly. Kill four, six more take their place."

"Good." I smile, and I know it's not a nice smile. "Let's kill them all."

The silence stretches between us for a long moment. Blue studies my face like he's seeing me for the first time.

"You're serious."

"Dead serious. No pun intended."

"You have no idea how to be a killer, Saylor. It's not something you just decide to do one day."

"That's why I need a teacher." I gesture to him. "And you're the best one I'm likely to find."

"I told you, I'm retired."

"From killing, yes. But not from teaching." I lean forward again.

"Show me how. Help me become someone who can end this. I stay here, which makes you happy, but I get what I want. A win, win."

Blue is quiet for so long I think he's going to refuse. When he finally speaks, it's barely above a whisper.

"Your father would hate this. Everything about it."

"My father is dead because he tried to save people the nice way. Maybe it's time someone tried the other way."

"And if I refuse?"

"Then I'll figure it out on my own. I'll make mistakes, probably get myself killed, and accomplish nothing except adding one more body to their count." I shrug. "But I'm going to try either way. The only question is whether you're going to help me do it right."

Blue picks up the paper again, reading over my list. "You understand what you're asking me to become again? What you're asking yourself to become?"

"I understand that these men killed my father while I watched, helpless. I understand that they're still out there, still killing, still destroying families." I meet his eyes. "I understand that if someone doesn't stop them, they'll keep doing it forever."

"And you want to be that someone."

"I want to be their nightmare. I want to be the thing they see coming in their last moments. I want them to know exactly why they're dying." The words come out harder than I intended, but I don't soften them. "Can you teach me how to do that?"

Blue folds the paper carefully and slips it into his jacket pocket. "We'll see."

"We'll see?" I stare at him. "That's what adults say to children when they want to placate them without actually committing to anything. I'm not a child, Blue."

"I know you're not."

"Then don't treat me like one." My voice hardens. "I'm twenty-three years old. I've been taking care of myself since I was eighteen. I watched my father get murdered and I survived it. I'm not some naive little girl who doesn't understand what she's asking for."

Blue is quiet for a moment, studying my face. "No, you're not," he says finally. "But you're young enough to think revenge is simple."

"And you're old enough to know it isn't?"

"I'm old enough to know it changes you in ways you can't undo."

"Good. I want to be changed."

Blue runs a hand through his hair, suddenly looking every one of his years. "Saylor, you have no idea what you're asking me to become again. What you're asking yourself to become."

"I know exactly what I'm asking for."

"Do you? Because once you cross that line, once you take a life with your own hands, you can't go back to being the girl who sang jazz in nightclubs and worried about rent money. That person dies the moment you become a killer."

"That person already died. The night they killed my father."

"No, she didn't. She's sitting right across from me, asking me to help her commit suicide."

"That's not what this is."

Blue sighs, the sound heavy with exhaustion. "It's been a long day. A very long day." He rubs his temples. "I'll think about it."

"When will you decide?"

"Tomorrow." He stands, offering me his arm. "After I've had time to think about what you're really asking for."

CHAPTER TEN
SAYLOR

Wren appears again, beginning to clear the plates. The meal has ended, and I still have so many questions. And Blue isn't going to agree to what I want . . . at least not now.

"This place," I say, gesturing around the dining room and needing a change of conversation. I don't want to end the meal with "oh hey, will you teach me how to kill people" and then turn in for the night. "This isn't exactly a normal house. And Grimlock—where exactly are we?"

"About twenty minutes from Grimlock," Blue says. "Maison Rouge is . . . private. Isolated." He pauses, considering his words. "But Grimlock itself—Grimlock is where people go when the regular world has no place for them. It's a sanctuary for the beautifully broken, the elegantly damned. A place where the villains of everyone else's stories come to write their own."

"Sounds charming."

"Oh, it is. Old money built on blood, older secrets buried in silk-lined coffins, and an atmosphere that welcomes anyone too dark, too twisted, or too hungry for revenge to fit anywhere else." His eyes meet mine. "It's a town full of misunderstood outcasts who refuse to apologize for who they are. You'll love it."

There's pride when he says it, genuine affection for this place and its people.

"Tomorrow, if you'd like, I can show you around. Let you get a feel for the place."

"You'd let me leave the estate?"

"With proper supervision, yes."

I stand on my own, but his offered arm from moments before still hangs in the air between us. "Proper supervision meaning you."

"Meaning me."

The gesture—formal, old-fashioned, gentlemanly—waits for my

decision. Every rational part of my brain screams that I shouldn't trust this man, shouldn't let him touch me, shouldn't ask for his help—and yet I did. But he was Dad's friend. Dad trusted him enough to ask him to protect me.

That has to count for something.

I take his arm, trying to ignore the way my skin burns where our bodies connect through the fabric of his suit jacket. The contact is electric—the second my fingers curl around his bicep, I'm transported back to that dressing room. His hands on my skin, the way he made me feel like I was coming apart at the seams, the way he tasted like whiskey when he kissed me.

He feels it too. I can tell by the way his muscles tense under my touch, the slight hitch in his breathing.

But instead of pulling away, I let my fingers tighten around his arm. Just slightly. Just enough to feel the solid warmth of him beneath his suit jacket. Just enough to remember what those hands felt like when they weren't being so careful, so controlled.

"I can walk back to my room on my own," I say, but I don't let go. My voice comes out breathier than I intended, and I curse myself for how easily he affects me.

Blue's smile is knowing, dangerous. "Of course you can." His voice drops lower, intimate. "But do you want to?"

I should say yes. I should drop his arm and pretend that night in the dressing room never happened. I should act like we're having a polite conversation about supervision instead of dancing around the fact that he had his mouth on me and we've barely acknowledged it.

Instead, I find myself stepping closer.

"Maybe not," I admit, the words slipping out before I can stop them.

We walk through the house in silence, our footsteps ricocheting off the floors. But it's a different kind of silence now. I'm acutely aware of every place our bodies almost touch, the way he adjusts his pace to match mine. The portraits watch us pass, their painted eyes following our progress through halls that seem to stretch forever. I try not to look at them, but it's impossible.

We climb the stairs in silence, the candelabras casting our shadows long and strange against the walls. Our shadows move together on the wall like dancers, intertwining and separating with each step. When we reach the door to my room, I stop.

"People will notice I'm gone."

"What people?" Blue asks gently. "Your employer at the jazz club who pays you in tips? The landlord who'll evict you for missing rent? The credit card companies who've already maxed out your accounts? The Crow cleaned out your apartment to make it look like you skipped town."

Each word is like a small slap, a reminder of how precarious my existence really was. "I had people . . ."

"Did you?" He leans against the doorframe, studying me.

I say nothing.

"You agreed to stay one night," Blue says when I don't answer. "Honor that agreement. Tomorrow we'll talk about what comes next." He pauses. "And we'll discuss your proposal."

I push open the door to my room, and whatever argument I was maybe planning dies in my throat.

The space has been transformed. Where before it was beautiful but impersonal, now it feels . . . lived in. My clothes from New York are hanging in the armoire—everything from my closet. My books are arranged on the nightstand. My jewelry box sits on the vanity, and when I open it, my mother's necklace is nestled safely inside.

"How did you—"

"Hans found the compound where the Crow had your stuff," Blue says from the doorway. "I thought you might want familiar things around you."

I pick up one of my books—a battered paperback copy of *Jane Eyre* that I've read probably twenty times.

"You brought everything."

"Everything that I believe mattered, but we put the bigger pieces of furniture in storage. If I missed something, let me know and I'll have Wren find it."

I set the book down and turn to face him. "I hate them. The Crow." I pound my chest. "The kind of hate that burns inside."

"I know." He reaches for my hand and I let him take it, his fingers warm and sure as they close around mine. His eyes are soft, understanding. "And we'll have that conversation tomorrow."

Before he can leave, I step closer. Close enough that I have to tilt my head back to meet his stare, close enough that if I wanted to, I could reach up and touch that perfectly trimmed beard, trace the strong line of his jaw.

"Blue," I say.

He goes very still. "Saylor."

For a moment, his careful control slips. I see the hunger, the way his gaze drops to my lips before snapping back up. The way his breathing changes.

Then he steps back, breaking the spell.

"Get some sleep," he says, but isn't quite steady.

The door closes behind him with a soft click, but I can hear him pause on the other side. Can picture him standing there, fighting the same battle I am. And I'm alone, surrounded by luxuries I never knew existed. The bed is enormous, piled high with pillows and covered in linens that probably have thread counts in the thousands. There's a fireplace with logs already laid, waiting to be lit. Fresh flowers in crystal vases. An attached bathroom with marble surfaces and gold fixtures.

I should hate this. I should be furious at the presumption, the way he's trying to buy my compliance with comfort and luxury. I should be planning my escape, figuring out how to get past Wren and her keys, over that wall with its cruel spikes.

But I'm not planning to escape anymore. I just asked a man to teach me how to kill. The words are still hanging in the air between us, impossible to take back. I told him I want to hunt down every single person who murdered my father. I laid out my plan for revenge like I was discussing the weather.

What kind of person does that make me?

I find myself sinking onto the bed, my body melting into a mattress that's like sleeping on a cloud. And all I can think about is the way Blue looked at me just now—like he wanted to consume me and protect me at the same time.

When was the last time I slept somewhere without worrying about the couple fighting next door? When was the last time I ate a meal that didn't come from a can or a takeout container?

When was the last time a man looked at me like that—like I matter?

The girl who worried about rent money never would have asked someone to teach her how to murder people. But maybe the person lying in this bed is someone else—someone who wants blood and doesn't feel guilty about it.

As I sink deeper into Egyptian cotton sheets and pull a luxurious down comforter around my shoulders, I can't help thinking about Cinderella. About what it might feel like to live in a world where money isn't a constant source of anxiety, where someone else worries about keeping you safe and fed and comfortable.

But I'm not Cinderella. And Blue isn't Prince Charming. He's something much more complicated, much more dangerous. And God help me, that only makes me want him more.

But maybe just for one night, I can pretend this is real. Maybe just for one night, I can let myself imagine what it would be like to not be alone.

The thought of letting down my guard should terrify me.

Instead, it follows me toward sleep, even as a warning bell keeps chiming in the back of my mind—persistent and urgent, telling me I'm in danger and the only way I can protect myself is by learning how to become the danger.

CHAPTER ELEVEN
SAYLOR

Some mornings you wake up in a four-poster bed with exquisite sheets and think, "Well, this is my life now."

Dad would have loved this place. Not the gothic mansion part—he wasn't really into displays of wealth—but the fact that someone was finally taking care of me.

Except now Dad's gone, and for the first time since I was eight years old, I'm actually considering taking his advice. Back then it was "Let me help you with your math homework, sweetheart." Now it's his voice in my head saying, "Stop being so stubborn and let someone take care of you for once."

Blue would let me leave—I feel that in my bones. Yeah, he technically kidnapped me, but underneath all the murder and mystery, he seems like a decent guy trying to keep his promise to a dead friend.

Jesus, toxic thinking much? "He kidnapped me but he's probably nice" isn't exactly the foundation for healthy decision-making.

But maybe, just this once, I'm going to listen to what Dad's telling me from the grave. I heard his final words to Blue. Maybe it's time to stop insisting I can handle everything alone. Maybe it's time to stop running and start fighting back.

I should be furious with my father. How did I not know what he really did for a living? Did he lie to me? Not exactly—I just assumed all that talk about "consulting" and "helping people with complicated situations" meant finance or something equally boring. Dad work. The kind of stuff that made my vision glaze over when he'd mention it over Sunday pancakes.

It's not like I asked a lot of questions. I was a teenager focused on school and friend drama. I figured it was spreadsheets and meetings, not whatever the hell the Crow are or places like Crowshaven or friends named Blue who do whatever it is Blue does.

How could I have missed all of this? How did I live twenty-three years thinking my dad was just some middle-aged guy with a nine to five, when apparently he had an entire shadow life I never even suspected existed?

I guess boring dad work was never as boring as I thought.

I'm lurking outside the dining room at 7 a.m., watching Blue through the doorway as he performs what's clearly a morning ritual. He's traded yesterday's funeral suit for a charcoal sweater that fits like it was made for him, paired with dark slacks that probably never wrinkle. His hair is damp from a shower, combed back but already starting to curl at the edges, and that blue-tinted beard frames a mustache with deliberate rockabilly curls at the ends that somehow make him look both vintage and untouchable.

He sits alone at a table built for entertaining, reading his newspaper . . . an actual newspaper. His coffee cup is so delicate I'm surprised it doesn't dissolve when he touches it. Even his toast has been cut into perfect triangles and arranged with a care most people reserve for surgery.

The man makes breakfast look uptight but sexy.

I'm still wearing yesterday's green dress because putting on the clothes the Crow stole from my apartment feels like surrender. The emerald fabric clings uncomfortably after a night of restless sleep, my hair has taken on a life of its own, and I'm about to walk into that dining room and ruin his perfect morning.

I walk through the doorway, my footsteps loud against the marble. "Morning."

Blue's newspaper crinkles as he looks up, and for half a second his composure slips. He wasn't expecting me. Or maybe he wasn't expecting me to look like a hot mess. But either way . . . Good.

"Saylor." He starts to stand, then thinks better of it. "You're awake early."

"Funny thing about being kidnapped—it messes with your sleep schedule." I drop into the chair across from him without waiting for permission, getting my first real look at the dining room in daylight.

It's completely different from last night's candlelit atmosphere. Morning sun streams through tall windows, illuminating walls lined with oil paintings of stern-faced people who probably owned this place generations ago. The table for twenty where we had dinner last night looks even more imposing in daylight, its dark wood surface polished to mirror brightness. Crystal glasses sparkle from an enormous chandelier overhead, and everything feels formal in a way that makes me glad I'm still in my wrinkled green dress instead of trying to live up to this level of elegance.

Wren materializes beside me with coffee and a place setting. The woman must have supernatural hearing. She pours from a silver service, the coffee so dark it's almost black and smelling like it could resurrect the dead. When I take my first sip, it fuels my system like liquid electricity. The coffee hits my bloodstream immediately, which is the first decent thing that's happened since I woke up.

"We need to talk," I say, setting down my cup with more force than necessary.

Blue folds his newspaper deliberately. "About?"

"About you teaching me how to kill people."

Blue pauses with his coffee cup halfway to his lips. "Before coffee? Really?"

"You said you'd think about it. I want an answer."

He takes a deliberate sip and sets down his cup. "I did think about it."

"And?"

"And I think you're serious about this, which is either impressive or terrifying."

"Both, hopefully." I lean forward, excitement building in my chest. "So? Will you teach me?"

Blue runs a hand through his hair, messing up that perfect styling. "You think you want revenge, but you don't understand what it actually costs—"

"I understand perfectly." I point my coffee cup at him. "I understand that the Crow killed my father and got away with it. I understand that they kidnapped me and were planning to torture me before you showed up. And I understand that you're the only person I've ever met who might actually be able to help me do something about it."

Blue goes quiet for a long moment, studying my face like he's looking for something. "You really think this is what you want?"

"I know it is."

"And if I say yes? If I agree to this insanity?" He leans back in his chair. "You'll do everything exactly the way I tell you to do it. No improvising, no going rogue, no deciding you know better than I do."

My heart jumps and I feel a Cheshire grin spreading across my face. "You're actually considering this?"

"I'm considering the fact that you're going to try to go after them with or without my help, and at least this way I can keep you alive while you do it." Blue picks up his coffee cup. "But we do this my way, at my speed. I'm not going to waltz you into Crowshaven with a knife in your hand and tell you to get at it."

"Crowshaven?"

"Where the Crow operate. About thirty miles south of here." His expression hardens. "And before you even think about hunting down Brutus and his A-team, you need to understand exactly how dangerous they are. Getting to them won't be easy, but it will happen. Just not the way you're probably imagining."

I can barely contain my excitement. "So you'll do it? You'll train me?"

"I'll teach you how to survive long enough to get your revenge, yes. But first"—he holds up a hand before I can interrupt—"we start small. Very small. The first thing you need to learn is just how deadly Brutus and his people can be when they're not distracted by other business."

"How small are we talking?"

"I bring them to you. One by one." His voice takes on an edge I haven't heard before. "Going after them all at once is suicide. But individually? That's manageable. I'll handle the hunting, the tracking, the logistics of separating them from the pack. Then I'll bring them here, like a gift, and teach you what to do next."

"Good. Then I'll learn to be better than they are."

Blue studies me again, and I catch something that might be approval in his expression. "You're serious about this."

"Dead serious." I grin at him. "And let me get this straight— you're going to hunt down murderers and bring them to me like some dark suitor offering deadly gifts? How romantic."

"Most women prefer flowers."

"Most women haven't had their fathers killed by a bunch of psychopaths." I lean back in my chair, practically bouncing with excitement. "So basically, you'll do all the hard work and I get to be the one who actually kills them?"

"That's . . . one way to put it."

"Best. Teacher. Ever."

"Then we have terms and conditions to discuss." He folds his hands on the table. "If you're staying here as my student instead of my . . . guest . . . we need ground rules."

"Naturally. Let me guess—no talking to strangers, no going out after dark, no breathing without permission?"

"I don't like dining alone." His tone is matter-of-fact. "Meals are more civilized with company."

I wasn't expecting that. "You want me to eat with you?"

"Breakfast and dinner, at minimum. Lunch if you're around." He spreads jam on his toast with careful attention. "It's a large house. Gets quiet."

I study his face, looking for the catch. "That's it? You want a dining companion?"

"And the third floor is off-limits."

There's a third floor? I think about the mansion's towering height, the way it seemed to stretch forever when I first saw it from the gardens. I've barely explored the first floor, and only my room on the second floor, and apparently there's an entire level above where I'm staying that I didn't even know existed. Just how big is this place?

"Why?"

"Because it's mine. Private." The finality in his statement brooks no argument. "Everything else in this house you're welcome to explore."

"And third?"

"You don't leave the property without me or security. Not until you're ready. Not until I'm sure you won't get yourself killed the first time you encounter a real threat."

"For how long?"

"Until I say you're ready." Blue pauses and studies me. "Could be weeks. Could be months. Depends how quickly you learn."

I consider this. The dining thing doesn't sound terrible, and one restricted floor hardly seems unreasonable. But the confinement . . .

"I need to be able to go into town. Alone sometimes. I can't be your prisoner while you're training me."

"Not until you can handle yourself."

"Then teach me to handle myself faster."

Blue's mouth twitches with what might be amusement. "Eager, aren't we?"

"I've been waiting five years for this chance. I'm not interested in taking it slow."

"Too bad. Patience is the first lesson." His voice takes on an instructional tone. "The Crow are still breathing because they're careful, methodical, and don't make mistakes. If you want to beat them, you need to be all of those things and more."

"Don't get ahead of yourself. Just because you're bringing me murder presents doesn't make you my daddy." I smirk and tease, "Unless you want to be my *daddy*." I give a playful wink.

The coffee cup halfway to Blue's lips stops moving. For a second, I think I've genuinely shocked him. Then he sets it down and covers his mouth with his hand, but I can see his shoulders shaking.

"Did I just make the big scary murderer laugh?"

"You have an interesting way of phrasing things," he manages, still fighting a smile.

"It's one of my many charms. Along with my stunning morning hair and my ability to make any situation awkward."

"I've noticed."

Blue stares at me for a long moment, and I can practically see him weighing the pros and cons in his head.

"You understand this isn't going to be like the movies? No montages, no dramatic moments where everything clicks into place. It's going to be ugly, methodical work. And there's a very good chance it will change you in ways you can't come back from."

"I'm counting on it."

"And you understand that once we start down this path, you'll never be the same person again?"

"Blue." I reach across the table and put my hand over his. "I've been walking this path since I was eighteen years old. The only difference is now I won't be walking it alone."

He looks down at our joined hands, then back up at my face. Something changes in his expression—a decision being made.

I grin at him, feeling lighter than I have in years. "When do we start?"

"Patience. Remember?"

I sigh and realize I shouldn't push it. I just got the man to agree to something that I in no way thought was possible.

"I've been thinking about your offer to show me around town," I say. "I'd like to go this morning."

Blue glances at his newspaper—something called *The Grimlock Gazette* with headlines about harvest festivals. This place even has its own newspaper. "I have an appointment, but . . ."

He stares at me across his perfect breakfast spread. I can practically hear the gears turning in his head.

"Hans will drive you," he says finally.

"Okay."

"He stays close."

"Define close."

"Close enough to help if you need it. Far enough away that you can pretend he's not there." Blue picks up his coffee cup. "Although Hans isn't exactly known for his subtlety."

I think about the giant German man who chloroformed me yesterday. "I noticed."

"There are parts of town you should avoid—"

"Nope." I hold up a hand. "If I'm free to explore, then I explore where I want. No banned zones, no helpful suggestions that aren't really suggestions."

Blue looks like I just asked him to juggle live grenades. "Some areas can be unpredictable."

"So can I."

We have a staring contest across the table. I win when he sighs and reaches for his pocket watch. A pocket watch . . . but then again . . . did I expect ordinary with this man? \

"How long do you need to get ready?" he asks, checking his watch.

"Thirty minutes." I stand up, smoothing my wrinkled dress. "I need to shower and change out of this outfit and look like someone who belongs in a small town instead of a crime scene."

Blue nods, although he still looks like I just asked him to let me go skydiving without a parachute. "Hans will meet you out front."

"Perfect." I head toward the door. "Oh, and Blue?" I pause at the doorway, suddenly feeling the weight of everything he's done. "Thank you. For saving me. For helping me save myself. I . . . I appreciate it."

Something in him changes direction, the careful mask slipping just enough to show surprise. "You don't need to thank me for that."

"Yes, I do." I meet his eyes directly. "I'll see you at dinner."

His smile is small but genuine. "I'll be here."

The way he says it makes my stomach flutter, and I'm not going there right now. "Don't get too excited. I'm terrible company in fancy situations."

"I'll take my chances."

I'm almost at the doorway when he calls after me. "Saylor?"

I turn back, and for a moment something vulnerable crosses his face.

"Don't worry, Blue. I promise not to get murdered on my first full day here."

"That's not as reassuring as you think it is."

"Wasn't meant to be."

CHAPTER TWELVE
SAYLOR

Hans drives like he's transporting nuclear waste instead of one moderately curious woman. His massive hands grip the steering wheel with white-knuckled intensity, his eyes constantly flicking between the road and the rearview mirror, where he can monitor my every breath. The sedan purrs along winding roads that appear designed to disorient anyone trying to find their way back to civilization, and I'm starting to understand why Blue felt comfortable letting me explore—there's literally nowhere to run.

"So, Hans," I say, breaking the silence that's been stretching between us for the past fifteen minutes. "How long have you worked for Blue?"

"Years and years, Miss," he replies in that thick German accent, his focus never leaving the road. "He is good boss. Very fair. Pays well."

"And what exactly does your job description include? Bodyguard? Driver? Professional kidnapper?"

Hans shifts uncomfortably in his seat. "I do what is needed to keep people safe."

I study his profile—the way his jaw keeps clenching and unclenching, how he keeps glancing at me like I might suddenly combust. "How many people has Blue 'kept safe' over the years?"

"This is not my place to say."

So, everyone in Blue's orbit seems to operate on a need-to-know basis, and apparently, I don't need to know anything.

The forest presses in on both sides of the road like something alive and breathing. Towering trees that Hans identifies as Douglas firs and western red cedars create a canopy so dense that only fragments of gray sky filter through, casting everything in perpetual twilight. Moss drapes from every branch like tattered velvet curtains, some strands so long they brush the car's roof as we pass beneath them. The understory is a jungle of sword ferns that reach as high as my waist, their fronds creating green tunnels that lead deeper into darkness.

Mushrooms sprout from fallen logs in impossible colors—bright orange, deep-sea blue, rich purple that looks almost black in the filtered light. They cluster in fairy rings around massive tree trunks whose bark is so thick with moss they look like they're wearing fur coats. Everything looks perpetually damp, a wetness that seeps into your bones even from inside the car.

Occasionally, I catch glimpses of something moving between the trees—a flash of white that could be a deer or something else maybe, a shape that's gone before I can focus on it. The deeper we go, the more the forest appears to be watching us back, ancient and patient and definitely hiding something. The locals call it the Witchwood Forest, according to the brief conversation I managed to extract from Hans before he clammed up.

"Tell me about Grimlock," I try again. "What's it like?"

"Is . . . unusual place," Hans says carefully. "Very old. Many stories."

"What kind of stories?"

"Stories that turn milk sour if spoken aloud on moonless nights."

Well, that's reassuring.

The road curves again, and suddenly we're descending through a break in the trees. Mist clings to everything like cobwebs, and the air through the car's vents carries the smell of damp earth and pine, but underneath there's something else—something that reminds me of old churches and forgotten graveyards.

And then I see it.

Grimlock sprawls along the coastline below us like a postcard that's been left too long in the rain. The town unfolds in tiers cascading down toward the harbor, connected by a maze of narrow cobblestone streets and shadowed alleyways that twist between buildings like arteries through a body. The Victorian houses and Gothic spires emerge from patches of mist that drift in from the ocean, their steep roofs and pointed gables creating a jagged silhouette against the gray sky. From this height, I can see the harbor with its weathered piers stretching into gray water, fishing boats bobbing like toys in a bathtub. The whole place has the cramped, layered feeling of Venice—buildings pressed so close together you could reach from one window to touch another, connected by stone bridges that arch over narrow canals where seawater flows in with the tide.

The first thing that hits me is how wrong everything looks. Not obviously wrong. If you squinted, you might mistake it for any other quaint Pacific Northwest town. Charming Victorian houses with gingerbread trim line tree-shaded streets. A town square with a massive clock tower. Shops with painted signs and flower boxes.

But the longer I look, the more the details begin to unravel the illusion.

The Victorian houses aren't painted in cheerful pastels. They're all variations of gray, from dove to charcoal to the color of storm clouds, broken only by the occasional house with scarlet red shutters or a crimson front door that looks like a splash of blood against the monochrome backdrop. The gingerbread trim that should be decorative and welcoming instead looks like carved teeth, shadows pooling in every curve and corner. Windows stare out like dead eyes, and I notice that many of them have iron bars or wooden shutters that may be more defensive than decorative.

The flower boxes I can see are there, but the flowers themselves are wrong. Even from this distance, I can see they're all deep purple-black, as if someone decided regular flowers weren't gothic enough for Grimlock's aesthetic.

"What kind of flowers are those?" I ask.

Hans follows my gaze. "Nightshade," he says matter-of-factly. "Very popular here. People say it keeps away unwanted visitors."

"Nightshade. As in, the poisonous plant."

"Ja. Is very effective."

We descend into the maze of the town proper, and I feel like Alice tumbling down the rabbit hole. The main road splits into three smaller streets, each one diving between buildings at different angles. Hans navigates the labyrinth like a man who has done this a million times, turning down alleyways barely wide enough for the sedan, past stone archways that frame glimpses of courtyards where laundry hangs like colorful flags between iron balconies.

The cobblestone streets are uneven, worn smooth in some places by thousands of footsteps, cracked and jutting in others where tree roots have pushed through from below. Water runs in narrow channels along the edges—not storm drains, but actual canals no wider than my arm, carrying seawater and rain through the town in patterns that must make sense to someone but look random to me.

And the people are . . . vibrant in ways I wasn't expecting. A woman in a flowing burgundy dress dances as she sweeps her porch, her movements so graceful she could be performing ballet with a broom. An elderly man sits on a bench feeding ravens—actual ravens, not pigeons—while having a full conversation with them, complete with hand gestures and pauses as if he's listening to their responses. A girl with wild curls bounces a yellow ball against a brick wall in complex patterns, her timing so deliberate it's like she's following some invisible choreography.

Three women with identical silver hair sit on rocking chairs outside the post office, knitting the same endless scarf in different shades of evergreen. A man with arms like tree trunks tends a garden where every single flower is a different variety of rose— red, white, pink, yellow—all blooming impossibly perfect. Near the stone fountain carved with mermaids and sea serpents whose tails intertwine around the base, a group of children chase soap bubbles that float far longer than physics should allow, their laughter gunning off the stone walls that close in around the small square.

Everyone appears completely absorbed in their own world, living their lives with an intensity and joy that makes my New York existence look gray by comparison. No one pays any attention to our car; they're too busy being magnificently themselves.

We wind through two more narrow streets before emerging into the main square, and I understand why Hans took such a circuitous route. The layout makes no logical sense. Streets branch off at odd angles, some ending in walls, others opening onto courtyards or disappearing under archways. It's designed like a puzzle box, meant to confuse anyone who doesn't know the secret.

The town square is dominated by a clock tower that should be the heart of the community but instead feels like its dead center. The structure is beautiful in a Gothic Revival way—all pointed arches and flying buttresses—but the clock face is wrong. The hands are frozen at midnight, and the numbers around the dial aren't standard. Instead of 1 through 12, they're symbols I don't recognize. Runes, maybe, or some kind of alchemical notation.

"How long has the clock been broken?" I ask.

"Is not broken," Hans says. "Is exactly right twice each day."

I can't help but laugh at that. Hans might be a man of few words, but when he does speak, he's got a point.

The buildings surrounding the square are a mixture of architectural styles that shouldn't work together but somehow do. There's a bakery with Gothic windows squeezed between two taller buildings, like a book pressed between bookends, next to a Tudor-style curiosity shop that leans so far over the street it nearly touches the medieval forge across from it. Each building leans slightly toward its neighbors, creating the impression that the entire square is slowly collapsing inward toward the clock tower.

The signs hanging from the buildings are hand-painted in script: The Upper Crust Bakery, Wonders & Oddities, The Iron Rose Forge. They're the kind of atmospheric names that fit Grimlock's mysterious vibe perfectly.

But it's the shop windows that really get to me. They're all lit from within by warm, golden light that should be welcoming. Instead, the glow illuminates displays that are just slightly off. The bakery window shows delicate cakes and pastries, but they're all decorated in shades of black and deep red. Wonders & Oddities' display features an eclectic collection of antique curiosities: ornate music boxes, vintage tarot decks, crystal balls on brass stands, and what appears to be a taxidermy raven wearing a tiny top hat. The forge window shows ornate metalwork—gates, door knockers, weathervanes—all depicting scenes that tell stories I'm dying to understand but can't quite decipher from a moving car.

"People actually live here?" I ask. "Like, raise families and go to PTA meetings and complain about property taxes?"

"Is home," Hans says simply. "People make homes where they can."

This place is . . . I need to get out and explore at a slower pace.

"Hans, can you drop me off somewhere? I want to walk around, maybe get a drink." I need out of this car and away from his nervous energy. "I promise I won't run away to join the circus or anything."

He checks his watch. "Is only ten in the morning, Miss."

"Hans . . . don't be the judgy judge. It hasn't been that long since I climbed out of an antique steamer trunk after being drugged and kidnapped. Cut a girl a break." I give him my best innocent smile. "Besides, mimosas are perfectly acceptable morning drinks. It's practically fruit juice."

Hans glances at me in the rearview mirror, clearly weighing his options. "There is good place. Local bar. Owners are friendly women."

He navigates us through another narrow alleyway, this one so tight I could touch the stone walls on both sides if I rolled down the windows. We emerge onto a street I haven't seen before. They all look different but somehow the same, like variations on a theme. He pulls over in front of a building that somehow manages to feel welcoming despite Grimlock's overall atmosphere of beautiful menace.

The sign reads Toil & Trouble Apothecary Bar in deep burgundy paint, and the building itself is a converted Victorian house painted in charcoal gray with black trim that makes it look like it's perpetually in shadow. Wind chimes hang from every available surface on the wraparound porch. Dozens of them in different sizes and materials, creating a constant chorus of soft, melodic chaos.

I climb out, immediately struck by the sound. The wind chimes create a symphony that's both soothing and unsettling, melodies that shift and change depending on which way you turn your head. Some are made of metal, others of bamboo, a few of glass or crystal. Together, they create a soundtrack that feels both magical and slightly sinister.

"I love the vibe," I say as we approach the front steps. "You don't see places like this in New York."

"The Dunsin sisters are the owners. Three of them—Duffy, Cate, and Inessa. Duffy works the day shift. She is the nice one, so you should be . . . safe." Hans pauses at the door, and there's something deliberate about that pause that makes me wonder what the other sisters are like. "She asks many questions, but questions come from curiosity, not suspicion."

"And that's unusual here?"

"In Grimlock, most questions come from suspicion."

The front door is painted deep crimson like so many others and decorated with a knocker shaped like a raven. As I reach for the handle, the wind chimes suddenly go silent, as if the building itself is holding its breath.

I push open the door, and I step into what can only be described as an apothecary's dream merged with a tavern keeper's vision. The walls are lined floor-to-ceiling with shelves holding hundreds of glass bottles in every shape and size imaginable. Amber, emerald, cobalt blue, and clear crystal, each filled with mysterious powders, dried herbs, tinctures, and things I can't begin to identify. Copper distillation equipment gleams from corner alcoves, and bundles of dried plants hang from the exposed ceiling beams like aromatic chandeliers. The bar itself is carved from a single piece of black walnut, its surface scattered with mortars and pestles alongside cocktail shakers and jiggers. Behind it, bottles of spirits mingle seamlessly with apothecary jars, creating a display that's equal parts magical and intoxicating.

This is a place where you could get both a masterfully mixed cocktail and a perfectly crafted poison, and somehow that feels exactly right for Grimlock.

"What can I get you? Poison or drink?" someone calls from behind the bar.

I turn to see a woman with wild auburn curls that cascade past her shoulders, with delicate silver threads woven throughout that catch the light. Despite the speckles of gray in her hair, she's close to my age, maybe twenty-six or twenty-seven tops, with green eyes and a mischievous smile. This must be Duffy, the "nice one" Hans mentioned. She has this effortless witchy chic thing going on— flowing black maxi dress that moves like water when she walks, layered with beaded necklaces and a fringed shawl that drapes over one shoulder. Her fingers are covered in silver rings, and her hands are stained with what could be ink, herbs, or something far more mysterious.

"Well, that's a hell of a greeting." I can't help but laugh. "I was hoping for the drink option."

"Smart choice. The poison pays better, but the drinks are more fun." She begins pulling bottles from both the spirit collection and the apothecary shelves. "I've got a lavender gin fizz that pairs beautifully with existential dread, or if you're feeling more optimistic, there's a blood orange old-fashioned that'll restore your faith in humanity."

I can't resist a smile. "The lavender gin fizz sounds perfect."

As she begins her cocktail ritual, measuring spirits with a jigger in one hand while adding what looks like actual lavender oil with a medicine dropper in the other, she glances up at me. "So what brings you to Grimlock? You don't look like our usual tourist demographic."

As she reaches up to pull a bottle from the highest shelf, her sleeve falls back to reveal an intricate tattoo that draws my attention immediately. Witchmoths spiral up her forearm in stunning detail, their wings spread wide to display the distinctive skull markings on their backs. The tattoo is done in deep blacks and grays, the moths appearing to migrate from her wrist toward her elbow in a haunting procession. Each moth is slightly different—some with wings fully extended, others caught mid-flight, their antennae delicate as spider silk.

"I'm staying with a friend," I say carefully. "Blue."

Her hands pause for just a moment before resuming their work. "Ahhh," she says, a knowing smile spreading across her face. "You're Saylor Mitchell. I didn't think I'd get to meet you until tonight at the party."

"What party?"

"Blue's throwing you a welcoming party," she explains, sliding the gin across the bar. "It's his way of trying to tell all of Grimlock that you can be trusted."

"And you all just take his word for it?"

"There's not a soul in this town that wouldn't die on the sword for Blue, so if he likes you . . ." she smiles warmly . . . "Welcome to Grimlock."

CHAPTER THIRTEEN
BLUE

The axe is calling my name from the trunk of my car, and I'm two seconds away from answering.

I'm sitting in Dr. Finch's waiting room like some kind of unhinged patient, which I suppose I am, bouncing my leg so hard the floor is probably developing stress fractures. The receptionist—a sweet elderly woman who definitely doesn't deserve to witness my mental breakdown—keeps shooting me concerned glances over her reading glasses.

"Blue?" she ventures carefully. "Dr. Finch can see you now."

I practically leap from the chair, nearly knocking over a potted plant in my haste. The familiar chaos of Jay's office should be comforting, but today it's sensory overload. Every scattered paper, every precariously balanced book stack, every abandoned coffee mug—it all screams disorganization while my brain demands control.

"Blue!" Jay looks up from where he's attempting to excavate his desk from an avalanche of patient files. "You look like hell. Also, you're early. Like, really early. I don't have another appointment for twenty minutes, which means—" He stops mid-sentence, taking me in from head to toe. "Oh. Emergency session. Got it."

I drop into my usual chair, my hands already twitching toward my pockets where I keep my knife sharpening stone. Old habits.

"I need to officially come out of retirement," I announce without preamble.

Jay blinks. Once. Twice. Then he very deliberately sets down the file he was holding and reaches for his emergency flask. It's not even noon.

"Okay," he says after taking a healthy swig. "Let's unpack that statement. What happened between yesterday and right now that made you decide to"—he gestures vaguely at me—"whatever this is?"

"I let her leave."

"Saylor? You let Saylor leave Maison Rouge?" Jay's eyebrows disappear into his hairline. "That's . . . that's actually progress, Blue. That's what we talked about. Letting her make choices."

"It was a mistake." I'm on my feet now, pacing the narrow space between his desk and the wall. "She's out there right now, wandering around Grimlock without protection, and all I can think about is systematically hunting down every single Crow until there's nothing left but feathers and blood."

"Systematic hunting." Jay jots something down in his notebook. "That's very organized thinking for someone having a breakdown."

"I'm not having a breakdown."

"You called an emergency therapy session because your houseguest went sightseeing. You're definitely having something." Jay caps his pen and leans back in his chair. "When you say you let her leave, what exactly do you mean?"

"I mean she demanded freedom to explore town alone, and instead of doing the rational thing—locking her in her room until the Crow are extinct—I agreed to let Hans drive her around." I rake my hands through my hair. "Hans, Jay. A man who once tried to comfort a crying witness by offering her his sandwich."

He claps his hands. "Congrats. You're actually making progress. You let her leave even though it makes you uncomfortable."

"Well . . . It's another reason I'm here visiting you," I admit. "I'm close enough that I could run to save her before you could make another cup of coffee." The heart of Grimlock is small.

"Hans seems competent enough when it comes to basic protection duties."

"Hans is competent at following simple instructions. 'Carry this body.' 'Drive here.' 'Don't let the witness escape.'" I stop pacing to face him directly. "He's not equipped to handle someone as smart and unpredictable as Saylor. She'll see right through any attempt to manipulate or control her."

Jay makes another note. "You seem particularly agitated by Saylor's . . . independence."

"I'm agitated by her complete disregard for personal safety. She has no idea what she's dealing with. The Crow aren't some abstract threat. They're real, they're hunting her, and they won't hesitate to torture her for sport before they kill her."

"But you took care of the immediate threat. The two men who came to her apartment—"

"Were scouts. Advance team. The Crow have at least two, maybe three dozen members, all of them trained killers, all of them patient enough to wait for the perfect opportunity." I resume pacing. "And I just handed them one by letting her wander around town like she's on vacation."

Jay watches me wear a path in his carpet, his expression transferring from concerned to calculating. "Blue, can I ask you something?"

"That's why I'm here."

"When was the last time you cared this much about someone's safety?"

I freeze mid-step. "I care about everyone's safety. That's the point of what I do."

"No, you care about justice. About eliminating threats. About protecting the innocent in general." Jay leans forward. "But when was the last time you personally, specifically, couldn't function because one individual person was potentially in danger?"

"This is different."

"How?"

"Because I promised Peter." The words taste like ash. "Because she's his daughter and I failed to protect him. Because—"

"Because you have feelings for her."

The accusation slices through my core. "That's ridiculous."

"Is it?" Jay pulls out a fresh notebook—apparently my psychological state requires additional documentation. "You've been agitated since the moment you brought her to Maison Rouge. You kidnapped her instead of finding literally any other solution to the protection problem. You're sitting in my office having a panic attack because she went shopping or whatever people do in small towns."

"I'm not having a panic attack."

"Blue, you're sweating through a merino wool sweater in sixty-degree weather."

I look down at myself. He's right. When did that happen?

"Even if—hypothetically—I had feelings for her, it wouldn't matter." I sink back into the chair, suddenly exhausted. "She's Peter's daughter. He trusted me to protect her, not to . . ." I trail off, unwilling to finish the thought.

"Not to what? Care about her? Connect with her? Potentially find happiness with her?" He's being gentle, which somehow makes it worse. "Peter is dead. He'd want his daughter to be happy. He'd want you to be happy."

"You don't understand." I grip the arms of the chair hard enough that the leather creaks. "We . . . before I knew who she was, we . . ."

"Had sex."

"Christ, Jay. And no, we didn't have sex." I look away. "I may or may not have gone down on her. And yes . . . I had every intention of fucking her the next night, but then all this shit went down and—" I take a deep breath. "But no, we didn't have sex."

"Oral sex counts as sex, Blue. You're allowed to acknowledge it." Jay sets down his pen and gives me his full attention. "So you two were intimate before you knew about her connection to Peter. That complicates things emotionally, but it doesn't make you a monster."

"Doesn't it?" The question comes out quiet. "What kind of man sleeps with his best friend's daughter? What kind of man then kidnaps her and holds her prisoner in his house?"

"The kind who's trying his best to navigate an impossible situation." Jay reaches for his stress ball, which is apparently hiding under a stack of medical journals. "You had no way of knowing who she was when you met her. And everything you've done since then—questionable methods aside—has been to keep her alive."

"That doesn't make it right."

"It makes it human." Jay squeezes the stress ball with both hands. "You know what's not human? Deciding that the only way to deal with this situation is to break your murder sobriety and go on a killing spree."

"It would be effective."

"It would be temporary. You kill the Crow, another organization takes their place. You become the monster again, and you know you won't be able to stop once you start." Jay hurls the stress ball at the wall with surprising force. "Or have you not thought that far ahead?"

"That's not what I'm worried about," I say. "Saylor isn't going to run from what I am. If anything, she wants me to embrace it."

"What do you mean?"

"She wants me to teach her how to kill people, Jay. Hands-on instruction in the fine art of making problems disappear permanently." I lean forward. "So technically, I wouldn't be breaking my murder sobriety. I'd just be . . . consulting."

Jay blinks slowly. "I'm sorry, come again?"

"She wants to hunt down her father's murderers and make them pay. And she's asked me to train her." I lean forward. "So technically, I wouldn't be breaking my sobriety. She'd be doing the killing."

Jay stares at me for a long moment, then reaches for his flask again. He takes a much longer pull this time, then sets it down and looks at me like I've just told him I'm opening a lemonade stand. "Let me get this straight. You're planning to become a homicide instructor for Peter's daughter so she can personally redecorate Grimlock with Crow entrails?"

"When you put it like that, it sounds—"

"Completely fucking insane?" Jay interrupts. "Because that's what it sounds like, Blue."

"She's going to do it with or without my help," I say defensively. "At least this way, she'll do it right. She'll survive."

Jay sets down his flask and looks at me with the expression of a man who's just realized his patient has found the most elaborate loophole in recovery history. "And you think this is . . . healthy?"

"I think it's what she needs. She's been carrying this rage for years. It's eating her alive."

"So you're going to teach her to be you."

"I'm going to teach her to be better than me." I lean forward. "She won't become what I became because she has something I never had."

"Which is?"

"A reason to stop."

Jay considers this, his fingers drumming against his desk. "You know what? This is actually . . . not the worst idea you've ever had."

I blink. "It's not?"

"Think about it. You stay clean. She gets her agency back. And when this is all over and the Crow are dead . . ." Jay's expression shifts into something that might be professional interest. "Well, I'll have a new client to work on her post-homicide adjustment issues."

"You're not horrified?"

"Blue, I've been treating killers for twenty years. A woman seeking justice for her father's murder? That's practically therapeutic compared to most of my clientele." Jay picks up his pen. "Besides, it keeps you from relapsing, which was my primary concern anyway."

"So you're . . . okay with this?"

"I'm okay with you finding a way to help her that doesn't involve you personally dismembering people." Jay makes a note. "Though I do think we should discuss healthy boundaries in mentor-mentee relationships that involve homicide instruction."

Jay starts to sit down, then immediately pops back up to rearrange three different pens on his desk. He picks up a paperweight, sets it down in a new spot, then moves it back. Finally, he settles into his chair, absently squeezing his stress ball while focusing on me again.

My phone buzzes with a text. I grab it like it's a lifeline, expecting an update from Hans.

Instead, it's a photo of Saylor standing outside Toil & Trouble— Grimlock's main watering hole. Hans's awkward attempt at surveillance photography has cut off half her body. She's changed out of the dress from this morning into something that's purely her—a fitted black dress with a cherry print, paired with a cropped leather jacket that's seen better days but fits her like armor. Her dark hair is styled in victory rolls with strategic pieces framing her face, and even from Hans's terrible angle I can see the red lipstick that makes her mouth look like sin itself. She's got one hand on her hip, studying the bar's entrance like she's deciding whether the establishment is worthy of her presence.

She looks like trouble in the best possible way. Like herself.

The relief is so intense I have to grip the chair to stay upright.

"Good news?" Jay asks, clearly reading my body language.

"She's fine. Hans sent a photo." I show him the screen. "She's outside Toil & Trouble."

"Toil & Trouble? The Dunsin sisters' place?" Jay fidgets with his glasses. "Huh."

"What do you mean, 'huh'?"

"Nothing. Just . . . the sisters are . . . protective of their space. They don't exactly roll out the welcome mat for newcomers." Jay's expression shifts to something more concerned. "Especially people they haven't had a chance to vet properly."

The image of the Dunsin sisters deciding Saylor is a threat, of them viewing her as someone who doesn't belong in their sanctuary, of them choosing poison over cocktails—fuck no. No fucking way.

"I need to go," I say, already standing.

"Blue, wait." His voice has lost its teasing edge. "But they wouldn't actually hurt her, right? I mean, they'd just . . . make her unwelcome?"

"The sisters aren't murder sober, Jay. They are the opposite when they feel justified. And they're wary of anyone they don't recognize. Until they get to know Saylor, until they understand she belongs here, she's just another potential threat."

Jay nods slowly, understanding. "Which is why you're worried."

"Exactly. But until then, she's a stranger in a town full of people who've learned not to trust strangers."

"Sit down," Jay says firmly. "We're going to talk through this like rational adults instead of letting your inner caveman take over."

"I don't have time for—"

"Make time. Because the alternative is you storming into Toil & Trouble, scaring Saylor, confirming every fear she has about you, and proving that bringing her to Grimlock was the worst decision you've ever made." Jay points to the chair. "Sit."

I sit, but every nerve ending in my body is coiled to spring into action.

"Here's what's going to happen," Jay says, his voice taking on the authoritative tone that means he's shifted into full therapist mode. "You're going to stay here for the rest of our session. You're going to work through these feelings like a mature adult. And then you're going to go home and wait for Saylor to return on her own terms."

"And if she doesn't return?"

"Then you'll deal with that when it happens. But Blue?" Jay leans forward, his energy shifting to serious. "If you want any chance of this working—whatever 'this' turns out to be—you need to prove you trust her judgment. Starting right now."

My phone buzzes again. Another photo from Hans—this one showing Saylor sitting at the bar, laughing at something Duffy is saying as she slides one of her foo-foo crafted cocktails across the polished wood toward her. The warm lighting of Toil & Trouble makes her skin glow, and even through Hans's terrible photography skills, I can see the genuine smile on her face. She looks relaxed for the first time since I've known her. Happy.

Something cold puts down roots in my chest, but it's not about Duffy this time. It's instinct. The same sixth sense that's kept me alive through fifteen years of dancing with death.

I go back and zoom in on the first photo Hans sent, the one of her standing outside the bar. My blood turns to ice.

There, in the background behind a lamppost decorated with iron roses, partially obscured by shadow but unmistakably familiar, stands a figure I hoped never to see again. Tall and lean with silver hair slicked back, wearing a charcoal coat that screams money and power. Even in Hans's grainy surveillance photo, I can make out the calculating smile that's gotten him into more high-society events than any criminal has a right to attend.

Samuel "Sly" Crow. The Crow's intelligence gatherer. Their eyes and ears, their master manipulator who can charm state secrets out of senators' wives and assassination targets out of their own bodyguards.

If Sly is in Grimlock, it means the Crow know exactly where Saylor is.

I stand up so fast the chair tips backward, crashing into Jay's filing cabinet.

"Blue, what—"

"It's decided." I'm already moving toward the door, my hand instinctively reaching for my phone to call Hans. "I need to get her out of there. Now."

The axe is calling, and I'm going to try my damnedest to ignore it.

CHAPTER FOURTEEN
SAYLOR

Duffy Dunsin has the smile of someone who can see your future and finds it amusing.

I'm three sips into Duffy's lavender gin fizz—which tastes like drinking liquid starlight with a hint of garden party—when she starts casual conversation that feels anything but casual.

"So what's your story?" she asks, wiping down glasses that already look spotless. "Jazz singer from the big city, right? Must be quite the change, going from New York nightlife to . . . well, whatever this is."

"Whatever this is seems pretty charming so far." I gesture around the bar. "Although I'm starting to think 'charming' might be Grimlock's specialty."

"Oh, we're full of charm here. Sometimes too much for our own good." Duffy's smile is easy, but there's something watchful in her eyes.

"Well, let's see." I take another sip of my gin fizz, buying time to come up with the perfect response. "You're probably going to think I'm completely insane."

"I run an apothecary bar in Grimlock," Duffy says with a dry laugh. "There's nothing you could tell me that I haven't heard before. Trust me."

Her matter-of-fact tone gives me the courage to continue. "Jazz singer gets her father murdered in front of her, gets kidnapped by the Crow, then gets drugged and kidnapped *again* by her father's mysterious best friend, then gets stuffed into a steamer trunk for transport, then wakes up in a Gothic mansion where the housekeeper acts like kidnapping is just a typical day. I tried to escape but discovered I'm trapped on an estate surrounded by a twelve-foot wall in a town I've never heard of—and I may have been terrible at geography, but I'm pretty sure I would have remembered a place called Grimlock. Now I'm drinking gin before noon on a Wednesday because apparently this is what my life has become. So basically, I've had a week that makes you reevaluate your life choices."

I vomit out the truth, not expecting her to believe me. To laugh and say "yeah right" or something of that nature. No way would anyone think all of what I just said really happened, and if they did, they'd be calling the police right away.

Duffy nearly drops the glass she's polishing. "Jesus. I'm sorry about your father."

Her straightforward response, without questioning the kidnapping part, tells me everything I need to know about what passes for normal conversation in Grimlock.

"Thanks. I have to say, the accommodations here are a significant upgrade from my New York shoebox apartment. Nothing says 'your life has taken an unexpected turn' like waking up in a four-poster bed after being transported in antique luggage."

"You're handling this remarkably well for someone who just described getting kidnapped. Twice."

"What's the alternative? Hysterics? I considered it, but crying into Egyptian cotton sheets felt a little too dramatic, even for me." I shrug. "Besides, between you and me, I was one missed rent payment away from eviction anyway. At least now someone else is worrying about the bills."

Duffy arranges bottles behind the bar with the careful attention of someone buying time to think. "How are you finding Maison Rouge? Must be quite the step up from city living."

"It's . . . grand. Very grand. Like living inside a Gothic novel where the protagonist hasn't figured out she's in danger yet."

"Blue does like his nice things. Always has, as long as I've known him." Duffy stays focused on her bottles, but there's something almost reverent in her tone. "He's got excellent taste in houseguests too. I have to say, you're a bit different from his usual . . . visitors."

Her tone makes me set down my glass. "Different how?"

"Well, for starters, you're here. In town. Talking to people." Duffy stays light, conversational. "Most of Blue's lady friends tend to be more . . . reclusive. Prefer the estate to mingling with us common folk."

"Lady friends?" A laugh bubbles up before I can stop it. "Duffy, I think you might have the wrong idea about—"

"Do I?" She leans against the bar, close enough that I can smell her perfume—something with vanilla and spice. "Because in all the years I've lived here, I've seen Blue with quite a few beautiful women. And they all had that same look you've got right now. Like you're not sure if you're living in a fairy tale or a nightmare." She leans closer, and instead of warning, there's something like excitement in her voice. "The rumors say Blue's had seven wives, Saylor. Seven."

The words hit me like ice water. "Seven wives?"

Duffy glances around the empty bar, checking to make sure we're truly alone before her easy smile turns knowing. "People love their dramatic stories about Blue systematically murdering his way through beautiful women."

"And you don't think he does?"

"Oh, I think Blue's perfectly capable of murder—we all are around here." Duffy shrugs, completely unbothered by the concept. "But wife-killing? That's not his style. Blue's the type who kills to protect what's his, not destroy it. The man's got his flaws, but harming someone he loves isn't one of them."

My stomach churns, not because I'm shocked that Blue might be capable of murder—I already know what he is—but because hearing Duffy dismiss the wife-killing rumors so easily attacks my inner core harder than I expected.

I think about the forbidden third floor of Maison Rouge, the one Blue specifically asked me to avoid. *Private,* he'd said when I asked about it. *Mine.* What secrets is he keeping up there?

"And you're telling me this because . . . ?"

"Because I like you." Duffy shrugs, going back to organizing her bottles. "Blue's brought women here before, but they never last long in town. Too nervous, too scared of the locals. You? You walked into an apothecary bar and asked for poison advice like you were ordering coffee."

"I didn't ask for poison advice."

"Not yet." Duffy grins. "But you will. This place has a way of bringing out what people really are underneath all the pretending."

I study her face, trying to read between the lines. "And what if I did want some? Hypothetically."

Duffy's eyes light up with genuine interest. "Well, that would depend on your style. Some people prefer the dramatic flair of immediate results. Others like to sit back and watch the slow burn."

The casual way she discusses murder methods should horrify me. Instead, I find myself leaning forward. "What would you recommend for—"

Before I can finish the question, Duffy freezes, her gaze fixed on something behind me. She carefully sets down the bottle she's holding, and a knowing smile spreads across her face.

"Well," she says quietly, "speak of the devil."

I turn to find Blue filling the doorway like an avenging angel who's had a rough morning. His charcoal sweater is immaculate except for a few dark spots across the left shoulder that could be wine stains if you're feeling optimistic. His hair looks like he's been running his hands through it, and there's something predatory in the way he scans the room before his eyes lock onto mine.

He moves directly to Hans, who's been lurking near the entrance trying to blend in with the decor. Blue whispers something in Hans's ear—something urgent, judging by the way Hans's eyes widen. The big German nods once and disappears through the front door like smoke.

The atmosphere in Toil & Trouble shifts immediately, the air itself seeming to thicken with tension. The moment he sees me sitting at the bar with Duffy, something dangerous settles into his features. Not anger exactly, but something deeper. More primal.

"Saylor." My name carries across the sudden quiet, and there's something in the way he says my name that makes my pulse skip. "Having a good morning?"

"Fantastic," I say, lifting my glass in a mock toast. "Duffy here was just telling me about your colorful romantic history."

Blue approaches the bar with the fluid grace of someone who's never had to wonder if a room contains enemies that will kill him . . . which I know is not true. Up close, those dark spots on his sweater are definitely not wine. When he reaches us, he doesn't sit.

Instead, he stands behind my barstool, close enough that I can feel the heat radiating from his body.

"Duffy." Blue nods to the bartender, who's already reaching for the whiskey without being asked.

"Blue." Duffy's easy charm has shifted to something more respectful, but not fearful—more like the careful attention someone pays to a celebrity. "Whiskey neat?"

"Please."

Blue's hand rests on the back of my chair, his fingers brushing against my shoulder blade. It's a casual gesture that feels anything but casual.

I reposition my body to study the crimson spots on Blue's shoulder. "Rough morning shaving?"

Blue follows my gaze and touches the stains with the casual air of someone discovering ketchup on their shirt. "Small accident with the razor. You know how it is."

"Not really. I don't typically bleed that much when grooming." I take another sip of my gin fizz. "Must have been quite the close shave."

"I'm very thorough in my personal hygiene."

Duffy slides the whiskey across the bar, and I notice her hands are steady, but there's an energy about her that suggests she's watching everything with keen interest. "So, Blue, what brings you to town? Besides collecting Saylor, I mean."

"Just making sure she's settling in well." His attention ping-pongs between Duffy and me, and I can practically feel him cataloging every detail of our interaction. "Grimlock can be overwhelming for newcomers."

"Duffy's been an excellent source of info," I say sweetly. "Very informative about local customs and folklore."

Blue's hand comes to rest on the back of my chair, his fingers brushing against my shoulder blade. "Has she?"

He reaches for my gin fizz and brings it to his nose first, inhaling deliberately. Duffy watches with growing amusement as he takes a careful sip, his eyes locked on hers the entire time.

"Really, Blue?" Duffy's smile is equal parts fond and exasperated. "Gin is gin."

He sets the glass down, but keeps his fingers wrapped around it. "Can't be too careful."

"If that was the plan, it would have happened by now." Duffy shakes her head, clearly entertained by his paranoia. "Besides, you know I wouldn't let you drink it if it was actually poisoned."

"I know." Blue's posture relaxes slightly. "But I had to be sure."

Duffy gives me a warm look. "I like this one too much to waste good gin on." She glances between us, then starts gathering empty bottles from behind the bar. "I should go check on my distillation setup in the back. Take your time, you two."

She disappears through a door marked Employees, leaving us alone with the soft ringing of wind chimes from outside.

Blue throws back his whiskey in one smooth motion, finally releasing my glass. The silent conversation between them seems to be over, whatever test he needed satisfied.

"Testing my drink for poison? Really?" I shake my head, though I'm oddly touched by the protective gesture. "What's next, a food taster?"

"Don't give me ideas." His smile is mischievous beneath that curved mustache of his. "But Duffy's right. If she wanted you dead, you'd already be dead."

"Comforting," I say dryly.

"I thought so."

Blue reaches for the whiskey bottle behind the bar, helping himself to another pour. His movement forces him to lean across me, and I catch his scent. Jesus the man smells good. "What exactly was Duffy telling you about our local folklore?"

The way he emphasizes *folklore* tells me he knows exactly what Duffy was discussing.

"Oh, you know. The usual small-town gossip." I watch his face carefully. "Apparently you're quite the romantic."

Blue's hands slide from my shoulders to the arms of my chair, effectively caging me in. "Whatever Duffy told you—"

"Seven wives, Blue." I meet his gaze directly, then laugh. "Seven! That's quite the resume."

For a moment, something raw passes across his features. Then the mask slides back into place, and he almost smiles.

"Small towns love their stories," Blue says.

I shake my head in amusement.

"You find it funny."

"I find it ridiculous." I grin up at him.

Blue stares at me for a long moment, and I can see something settle in his face—relief, maybe. Finally, he straightens, pulling out enough cash to cover both our drinks plus a tip that will make Duffy weep with gratitude.

"Come on," he says, giving me space to stand. "If you want to explore Grimlock, I'll show you the parts worth seeing."

I want to argue, to insist I can handle my own exploration without a murderous escort. But the way Duffy talked about Blue, with that mixture of fondness and respect, tells me there's more to him than I understand. And honestly? After watching my father die in front of me and knowing the Crow are still out there, having that kind of protection might not be the worst thing in the world.

"Fine," I say, sliding off my barstool. "But I want to see everything. The real Grimlock, not some sanitized tourist version."

"Trust me," Blue says, offering his arm in that old-fashioned gesture that melts all the feminist-fuck-all-men energy I've nursed my whole adult life. "Grimlock doesn't have a sanitized version."

CHAPTER FIFTEEN
SAYLOR

We step out into the gray afternoon, and I'm immediately struck by how different the town feels with Blue beside me. People don't just notice us, they acknowledge our movement with genuine warmth. An elderly woman spinning yarn on her porch gives Blue a respectful nod. Three teenagers smoking behind the fountain wave cheerfully and call out greetings. A man walking a dog the size of a small horse crosses toward us with a friendly smile and tips his hat.

"They really like you," I observe.

"We look out for each other here," Blue says simply.

"So about this party Duffy mentioned," I say as we start walking. "Should I be concerned that I'm apparently the guest of honor at an event I knew nothing about?"

Blue's hands are tucked into his pockets, his stride unhurried as people go about their daily routines around us. "I host them regularly. It's better to control the narrative than let it write itself."

"Control the narrative?"

"You've been in Grimlock for less than twenty-four hours and already people are curious about us." Blue glances down at me, his eyes wry. "By dinner tonight, that story will have grown into a full romance novel with elaborate backstories about how we met."

I can't hold in the laugh. "So you're putting me on display to satisfy their curiosity?"

"I'm introducing you to the community before they decide you're either my next girlfriend or my secret accomplice." He pauses beside a shop window filled with clockwork contraptions that tick and whir in hypnotic patterns. "Grimlock is a community of people with . . . complicated pasts. They need to know you're one of them before they'll truly accept you."

"One of them? What does that mean?"

"You'll see," Blue says, his tone suggesting he has something specific in mind. "I have my ways of making things clear."

"Why do you care if they accept me?"

The question seems to catch him off guard, and Blue goes very still beside me. For a moment, the only sounds are the mechanical symphony from the clockmaker's window and the soft murmur of conversation drifting from nearby shops.

"Because I want you to have the option to stay," he says finally. "But that's a conversation for after you've given this place a real chance."

His tone makes me look at him more carefully. There's a tension in his shoulders that wasn't there before, a tightness around his eyes.

We continue walking, and I become aware of how seamlessly Blue navigates Grimlock's maze-like streets. Where I would be completely lost without Hans's guided tour, Blue moves with the confidence of someone who knows every shortcut, every hidden alley, every building's history. When he nods to the woman tending a garden of black roses, she beams back like he's just made her day. When he raises a hand to the man repairing ornate ironwork outside a Victorian townhouse, the gesture is returned with obvious respect.

"You really do know everyone here," I observe.

"Small town. Everyone knows everyone eventually." Blue steers us down a side street I haven't seen before, this one lined with workshops where the sounds of hammering and grinding drift through open doors. "Besides, most of the people who end up in Grimlock are here for similar reasons."

"Which are?"

"They needed somewhere that doesn't ask too many questions about where they came from."

The comment hangs between us as we pass a forge where sparks fly through the doorway and the smith inside waves a gloved hand at Blue. Next door, a woman with silver hair braids leather into intricate patterns while humming something that sounds like a lullaby written in a minor key.

"Including you?" I ask.

Blue grins. "Especially me."

We turn another corner and emerge onto a street that looks

designed by someone who collected postcards from European villages and decided to re-create them all in one place. Narrow buildings with steep gables press against each other in a rainbow of weathered colors—sage green next to dusty rose next to deep amber. Flower boxes overflow with herbs that perfume the air with scents I can't identify, and hand-painted signs creak gently in the ocean breeze.

"This is the artisan quarter," Blue explains as we pass studios where painters work at easels visible through tall windows and a weaver's shop displays tapestries that seem to tell stories in thread and color. "Most of Grimlock's artists live and work here."

"It's like a whole creative community," I observe, watching a potter shape clay through her window.

"Painters, sculptors, musicians, writers. People who make beautiful things." Blue pauses outside a studio where a man with paint-stained fingers is working on a canvas that shows Grimlock's harbor during a storm, the waves captured mid-crash with such detail I can almost hear the thunder. "They come here because Grimlock doesn't care if you're successful by conventional standards. It only cares if you're authentic."

The word *authentic* sits heavy between us. I think about my jazz singing, how it felt like the only genuine thing in my life before everything went to hell. How performing at the White Note was the closest I ever came to feeling like myself.

"Is that why you came here? Because Grimlock accepts what you are?"

Blue considers the question while we watch the painter add another layer of storm clouds to his canvas. "I stayed because Grimlock accepts what I am without expecting me to become something else."

"And what are you?"

His laugh is dark. "That's still under investigation."

We continue through the artisan quarter, past a glassblower's shop where rainbow light refracts through the windows and a pottery studio where clay figures seem to watch us from their shelves. Blue points out details I would have missed—the way each building's architectural style reflects its owner's personality, how the studios are arranged to catch different qualities of light throughout the day, the reason certain shops cluster together while others stand alone.

"The silversmith and the jeweler share customers but compete on craftsmanship," he explains as we pass two shops whose windows display intricate metalwork and fancy necklaces. "The fiber artist and the dressmaker collaborate on custom pieces. The woodcarver makes frames for the painters and sculptures for the gardeners."

"It's like a whole ecosystem."

"Exactly." Blue seems pleased that I understand. "Everyone here has something they need, and something they can offer. It creates . . . balance."

The way he says *balance* makes me think he's talking about more than just commercial relationships. As if Grimlock itself is some kind of carefully maintained equation where every element serves a purpose.

We emerge from the artisan quarter onto a broader street that leads uphill toward Grimlock's residential area. The houses here are larger, more ostentatious, set back from the street behind iron gates and gardens that look like they require full-time maintenance. Gothic Revival mansions stand next to Victorian painted ladies, with the occasional Tudor cottage tucked between them like punctuation marks.

"The old families live up here," Blue says, following my gaze toward a particularly imposing mansion whose turrets and gargoyles make it look like it belongs in a horror movie. "People whose great-grandparents founded Grimlock, or whose money built half the town."

"Do you qualify as old family or new money?"

"Neither. I'm useful family." Blue's tone is matter-of-fact. "I solve problems that the old families prefer not to acknowledge and the new money isn't equipped to handle."

Before I can ask what kind of problems require Blue's particular skill set, he guides us onto another side street.

We make our way back toward the town center, but Blue chooses yet another route, this one leading us past Grimlock's cemetery. The wrought-iron gates stand open, revealing rows of headstones and monuments that speak to the town's long history. Some of the graves are recent, marked with fresh flowers and polished stone. Others are aged, their inscriptions worn smooth by weather and time.

In the distance, a figure moves between the headstones. A man with weathered features and dirt-stained clothes, methodically digging a fresh grave with an actual shovel. The steady thunk of metal hitting earth carries across the quiet cemetery, punctuated by the scrape of dirt being tossed aside. Even from here, I can make out the intricate tattoos covering his arms, symbols I can't quite make out but that definitely aren't your typical tribal bands or barbed wire. Do people even use shovels anymore? I think everything is done with machines these days. But this guy works like he's done this a thousand times before, no rush, just muscle memory.

"Grimlock takes its history seriously," Blue observes as we pass the entrance. "Death is just another part of the community here."

"Cheerful."

"Reality." Blue glances at the cemetery with something that might be fondness. "People here understand that everything ends eventually. It makes them appreciate what they have while they have it."

The comment feels loaded with meaning, but before I can pursue it, we stop in front of a bakery. The building itself is narrow and tall, wedged into a space that barely looks wide enough to hold it. The facade is painted in alternating stripes of deep purple and gold, with windows outlined in white gingerbread trim that's definitely not regulation. Above the door, a hand-painted sign reads The Upper Crust in flowing script, surrounded by painted roses that seem to melt when you're not looking directly at them.

"This is where Wren sources her favorite desserts," Blue explains as his hand presses against the small of my back. The touch is light, automatic, but it sends heat racing up my spine. "The Cupp brothers took special requests for tonight's party, and I want to make sure Wren has her favorites."

The gesture is unconsciously protective, casually courteous, and I find myself wondering if Blue realizes he's doing it. There's something old-fashioned about the way he moves through the world. Like he was raised by people who believed in opening doors and treating women like they were made of something precious.

"Smart man. Never anger the person who controls your food supply."

The front windows display the most elaborate pastries I've ever seen—three-tiered cakes decorated with sugar flowers in impossible colors, éclairs filled with what resembles liquid gold, croissants shaped like tiny works of art. But it's the attention to detail that takes my breath away. Every sugar rose has individual petals, every éclair is perfectly glazed, the croissants are identical to one another, showing obsessive care. Nothing on display is flawed.

A bell above the door chimes a complex melody as we enter. Not the simple ding of most shops, but an actual composition that could be mistaken for wind chimes caught in a gentle breeze. I step into what can only be described as a curiosity shop that happens to sell pastries.

The bakery is crammed floor to ceiling with treasures that have nothing to do with baking. Mismatched chairs surround tiny tables set with delicate china tea services. Shelves line every available wall space, displaying teapots shaped like fantastical creatures, vintage books with cracked leather spines, pocket watches that tick at different rhythms, and an extensive butterfly collection in glass cases that throw rainbow patterns across the walls when sunlight hits them.

But it's the man behind the counter who makes everything else look ordinary by comparison.

Elliott Cupp moves like he's conducting an invisible orchestra, his hands dancing through the air as he arranges sugar flowers on a cake that defies several laws of physics. He looks about forty, but his hair is completely gray. He's wearing a pristine white baker's apron over a three-piece suit in blue velvet that makes Blue's beard look subtle. His hair is Einstein-wild, and his pale green eyes have the unfocused look of someone who's always listening to something just out of earshot.

"Elliott," Blue calls gently. "I've brought someone to meet you."

Elliott looks up, and for a moment his eyes snap into laser focus.

"Blue! Perfect timing, my dear boy," he says, his voice carrying the faint warmth of somewhere farther south. "Been expecting you."

A man emerges from the kitchen, and I have to work to keep my appearance unemotional. He's tall and lean with a build that indicates an intense exercise routine—broad shoulders that fill out his cream linen shirt perfectly, sleeves rolled to reveal forearms decorated with intricate tattoos that look like botanical illustrations. Dark auburn hair catches copper highlights where flour dust has settled, and when he looks up from wiping his hands on a towel, storm-gray eyes assess me with attention that makes me think he's cataloging everything about me in seconds.

"Ash Cupp," he says, extending a flour-dusted hand. His voice has that same subtle warmth as Elliott's, like honey over steel. "I knew your father, ma'am. I'm sorry for your loss. Peter was . . . I liked him."

The words carry genuine grief, and I can see that his sympathy is real rather than polite. But there's something else in the way he stands—perfectly positioned between Elliott and the rest of the room, like he's protecting his brother without making it obvious. His hands are gentle when he touches Elliott's shoulder, but I catch a glimpse of scars on his knuckles that suggest they've seen violence.

"Blue," Ash continues, his attention morphing completely to business. "I was hoping to see you before the party. There's a lot of chatter going down right now. Not good chatter. The Crow are gathering—more than usual. And they're not just asking about Saylor anymore."

My stomach drops. Blue's hand on my back doesn't move.

"They're putting a price on your head now too," Ash says, glancing at me apologetically. "Seems you made quite an impression."

Blue shrugs, completely unbothered. "Good. Message received."

The casual dismissal of what sounds like a death sentence makes me stare at him. Who reacts like that to news that people want to kill you?

Elliott continues his decorating, humming softly. "Oh, they're all atwitter about it," he says dreamily. "Did you know that a flock of crows is called a murder? How fitting." He pauses in his work, those pale green eyes focusing on Blue with sudden clarity. "Off with his head, they're saying. Quite dramatic, really."

Blue actually smiles. "Let them come."

"At least a dozen confirmed," Ash continues, his jaw tight as he absently checks a silver pocket watch. "Maybe more on the way. They're not playing games anymore, Blue. They want both of you dead, and they're bringing enough firepower to level half of Grimlock if they have to."

Blue nods, completely unsurprised. "Good. About time they stopped playing games."

Ash fidgets uncomfortably, positioning himself slightly closer to Elliott. "They're bringing heavy artillery. Military-grade weapons."

"Like I said . . . good." Blue grins like Ash just told him Christmas is coming early. "I've got plenty more messages to send."

I stare at him, trying to process what I'm hearing. The man who puts his hand on my back to guide me through doorways and who is worried about Wren's pastry preferences is standing here shrugging off the threat of heavy artillery. There's something almost eager in him, like he's been waiting for this excuse to let loose whatever he keeps carefully contained.

Elliott begins humming again, something that sounds vaguely funeral-esque. "We're painting the roses red," he murmurs dreamily, adding copper touches to his sugar flowers. "All the pretty roses red."

I want to shake both of them. How can they be so calm about this?

Blue pays for a box of pastries that Ash wraps with the careful attention of someone packaging explosives, and we prepare to leave as if we didn't just have the most bizarre—even terrifying— conversation possible. But the afternoon has given me a better sense of how Grimlock works, and more importantly, how Blue fits into it.

It seems as if death is . . . casual here.

As we prepare to leave, Elliott looks up from his work again. "Saylor," he says, more focused than before. "Tonight will be . . . revealing. Grimlock parties usually are."

"Revealing how?"

"You'll see," Elliott says simply, then returns to his decorating as if the conversation never happened.

Outside the bakery, I ask Blue, "What did he mean about revealing?"

"Elliott has a way of seeing patterns other people miss," Blue says as we walk toward the main square. "He's usually right about social dynamics."

"That's not really an answer."

"Because I don't have one yet," Blue admits. "But Elliott's rarely wrong about these things."

"What's their story?" I ask as we walk away from the Upper Crust. "There's something about Ash—the way he watches everything, positions himself to protect Elliott. And those tattoos . . ."

Blue glances back at the bakery. "Elliott's got early-onset dementia. Started showing signs about three years ago. Ash gave up everything to take care of him."

"Gave up what?"

"He used to work for the Crow. Intelligence gathering, mostly. They called him the Collector. Word is something went very wrong on his last job, and he realized he had to choose between his brother and that life."

"And he chose Elliott."

"Without hesitation. The Crow consider him a traitor now, but he knows too many of their secrets for them to move against him directly." Blue's face grows thoughtful. "Ash is probably one of the most dangerous men in Grimlock, but he channels all that energy into keeping Elliott safe and happy. Makes the best coffee in town too. Learned it during surveillance work where he had to stay awake for days."

I think about the protectiveness in his positioning, his voice. "That's why he warned you about the Crow gathering. He's still got sources."

"Exactly. And if Ash is concerned enough to warn me, it means they're finally bringing a real fight." Blue's smile turns predatory. "Now the real fun can begin."

We reach the car where Hans waits, engine idling. He spots us approaching and immediately gets out to open my door.

"All good, Boss?" Hans asks Blue while helping me into the passenger seat.

"All good. Any issues while we were gone?"

"Everything is clean. Quiet afternoon." Hans closes my door and circles to the driver's side.

As we settle into our seats, I realize that the afternoon has shifted something between Blue and me. Understanding, maybe. I'm starting to see how Grimlock works, how Blue fits into it, why people respect him and genuinely care about him. But more importantly . . . I'm really starting to like the guy. He's charming. He's a gentleman. He's . . . yeah, so maybe he's a killer, but he's also . . . genuine.

"Ready to head back?" Blue asks.

"I should probably figure out what to wear tonight at this party."

"Wren will have thoughts about that," Blue says with a slight smile.

"Should I be worried about her thoughts?"

"Only if you're planning to wear something she considers inappropriate for the occasion." Blue's tone hints this is a real possibility. "Wren takes parties very seriously."

"More seriously than kidnapping, apparently."

"Different skill sets," Blue says without missing a beat.

As Hans drives us back through Grimlock's winding streets, I watch the town pass through the windows and realize I'm not thinking about escape anymore. I'm thinking about tonight, about meeting these people properly, about what Elliott meant when he said the evening would be revealing.

For the first time since Dad died, I'm curious about what comes next instead of just trying to survive it.

CHAPTER SIXTEEN
SAYLOR

Wren's hands are steadier than mine will ever be, and I'm trying not to blink because apparently that ruins everything.

"Stop twitching," she says, dabbing tiny silver stars along my lower lash line. "You're making this harder than it needs to be."

She's been working on my face for the past hour, transforming me into something that belongs in a fantasy novel. The eyeshadow shifts from shimmery copper to deep bronze, and the eyeliner extends beyond the corners of my eyes in delicate swooping lines that trail down my cheekbones like cosmic tears. Little flecks of glitter catch the light every time I move, and the stars she's adding make my eyes look celestial.

"This is insane," I mutter. "It's just a dinner party."

"Honey, this is not just a dinner party." Wren steps back to examine her work. "Blue invited all of Grimlock. The whole damn town is coming to meet you."

My stomach drops. "The whole town?"

"Every last soul." She picks up another brush. "When Blue throws a party, people show up. Trust me on this."

The burnt orange dress she picked out for me is hanging on the wardrobe door, and just looking at it makes my chest tight. It's beautiful silk, something I could never afford on a jazz singer's tips. Dad would have loved seeing me dressed up like this.

The thought steals my breath. And here I am, letting Wren paint my face like I'm going to prom.

"I can't do this," I say suddenly. "I can't go to a party and pretend to be normal when his killers are still breathing."

Wren pauses, her brush hovering near my cheek. "And what exactly would staying locked in this room accomplish?"

"I should be hunting them down. Planning their deaths. Not worrying about whether my eyeliner looks good."

"And then what?" Wren sets down her brush. "Storm into Crows-haven alone with nothing but rage and a death wish? Get yourself killed before you can make them pay?"

I want to say yes, because that's what feels right. What feels honest. I've spent five years building a life in New York, but underneath every smile, every song, every normal moment, the fury has been growing. Festering. Turning into something dark and hungry that demands blood.

"I should be doing something," I whisper. "Anything other than playing dress-up."

Wren comes around to face me, her eyes sharper than I've ever seen them. "You think your father would want you to waste the chance Blue's giving you? The training, the resources, the connections? You think he'd want you to throw away your shot at real revenge for some half-cocked suicide mission?"

"I want them to suffer," I say quietly. "All of them. I want them to know exactly who's killing them and why."

"Good," Wren says simply. "But first, you need to be smart about it. You need allies. You need to understand how this world works." She picks up her brush again. "And tonight, you're going to meet every person in this town who can help you destroy the Crow properly."

I should probably be horrified by this. Instead, I feel something that might be hope.

"Now hold still," Wren continues, returning to my makeup. "We're going to make you so gorgeous that every person in that room remembers exactly who Saylor Mitchell is. And when word gets back to the Crow that Peter's daughter is alive and thriving under Blue's protection, they're going to shit themselves."

This time I do smile. "You really think so?"

"I know so." She adds the final touches to my face. "Your father was proud of you, honey. He talked about you constantly when he'd visit. How smart you are, how talented, how you could make a room full of strangers fall in love with you just by singing." She meets my eyes in the mirror. "Tonight, you show this town exactly what those bastards took from the world when they killed Peter Mitchell."

"Tell me about the version of my father you knew," I say suddenly.

Wren's hands still. "Peter was genuine. Complicated, but genuine. He'd come here maybe four times a year, always bringing Blue some new problem to solve."

"Problems I clearly was never made aware of."

"Good, because they kept Blue awake at night." Wren sets down her brush. "People in trouble. Women mostly, running from bad situations. Peter would find them, bring them to Blue, and between the two of them they'd figure out how to make the danger disappear."

I think about Dad's vague explanations of his work, the way he'd brush off questions about his trips. "He never told me any of this."

"He was protecting you. The less you knew, the safer you were." Wren turns to face me fully. "Your father loved you more than his own life. Everything he did was to keep that love pure, untainted by the darkness he dealt with."

I look at my reflection and barely recognize myself. The woman staring back at me looks fierce, untouchable. Like she could walk into any room and own it completely. Like she's never been afraid of anything in her life.

I look like someone worth killing for.

The thought should scare me. Instead, it makes me feel powerful.

"Wren," I say as she helps me into the dress, "do you think Blue will really help me go after them? The Crow?"

"Honey, Blue's been wanting to destroy them for five years." She zips up the back of the dress. "Now that he knows what you want, the only question is whether you'll make it quick or take your time."

A knock at the door interrupts us, and Wren opens it to reveal Blue. He's wearing a three-piece suit in onyx black with subtle pinstripes that nearly glow like captured starlight. The vest is cut perfectly to emphasize his lean build, and his pocket watch chain glints silver against the dark fabric. His shirt is crisp white with a high collar and onyx cuff links that match the single black rose pinned to his lapel. But it's the details that make him look like he stepped out of a Gothic fairy tale. The way his dark hair is slicked back with just enough wave to soften the severity, how his blue-tinted beard is groomed to aristocratic perfection, and the mustache that frames his mouth like calligraphy.

When he sees me, his entire persona shifts from controlled

composure to something raw and hungry that makes my pulse pick up speed even though I'm trying everything I can to not allow it.

"Jesus," he breathes.

"Is that good or bad?" I ask, smoothing the dress nervously.

"That's dangerous." His statement is rougher than usual. "You look like the type of woman men start wars over."

Wren makes a satisfied sound behind me as she gathers her stuff. "I told you I do good work." She then leaves the room so it's now just the two of us.

Blue steps fully into the room, and suddenly I'm hyperaware of everything. The way he fills the space, the sound of my own heartbeat, the warmth radiating from his body. "Are you ready to meet all of Grimlock?"

My stomach does a little flip. "How many people is that exactly?"

"Every soul in town. Shopkeepers, artists, the old families up on the hill, even Jasper from the cemetery." Blue straightens his cuff links, the movement casual but somehow deliberate. "When I send out invitations, people show up."

"Why does that sound ominous?"

"Because it is." His smile turns wicked. "Tonight isn't just a party, Saylor. Everyone's going to see exactly where you stand in this town."

"And where exactly do I stand?" I ask, turning to face him fully.

Blue's smile is enigmatic. "That depends on how you handle tonight."

"Handle what, exactly? Small talk and hors d'oeuvres?"

"Questions. Lots of them. Grimlock's residents will want to know who you are, why you're here, how long you're staying." His eyes travel slowly from my face down to my feet and back up again, lingering on the way the silk hugs my curves. When his gaze meets mine again, there's heat there that makes my skin flush. "They'll be polite about it, but persistent."

"Should I be worried?"

"No." Blue straightens, offering his arm. "You should be yourself. That's always enough."

As we prepare to leave the room, I catch sight of myself in the full-length mirror one more time. I look like someone who could survive in Blue's world. Someone who deserves whatever protection he's offering.

Most importantly, I look like someone the Crow should be very, very afraid of.

"Ready?" Blue asks, offering his arm.

I think about Dad, about how proud he'd be to see me holding my head high instead of hiding in my room. I think about the Crow, and how satisfying it will be when they realize they picked the wrong family to destroy.

"Let's go show them what a Mitchell looks like," I say, taking Blue's arm.

I can hear voices and laughter drifting up from downstairs, the sound of a party in full swing. My party. A celebration of the fact that I'm alive, that I survived, that I'm here to stay.

When we reach the top of the grand staircase, I stop completely. The main floor has been transformed into something that belongs in the most exclusive gothic nightclub in Manhattan. Hundreds of candles flicker from candelabras, mantelpieces, and even the windowsills, their flames creating a living tapestry of light and shadow that casts across the dark wood paneling. The massive chandelier overhead has been dimmed to amber, bathing everything in honey-colored warmth that makes the floors gleam and that turns every guest into a figure from a romantic oil painting.

Musicians have claimed strategic corners. A violinist near the fireplace draws haunting melodies from her instrument while a pianist at the black Steinway weaves jazz standards into something darker, more seductive. The bass notes seem to vibrate through the floor itself, creating a pulse that matches my heartbeat. Servers in crisp black uniforms move between clusters of guests, offering champagne in crystal flutes and delicate hors d'oeuvres arranged on silver platters.

The guests themselves are a study in elegant darkness. Women wear rich jewel tones—emerald velvet, sapphire silk, deep burgundy that looks almost black in the candlelight. Men sport perfectly tailored suits in charcoal and haunting blue, their pocket squares and cuff links catching the light. Everyone moves with the unhurried grace of people who know they belong exactly where they are, their conversations creating layers of sound that rise and fall with the music.

It's beautiful and mysterious and exactly the kind of place I would have killed to perform in back in New York.

"It's perfect," I breathe.

Blue's smile is pleased, almost proud. "I thought you might appreciate the atmosphere."

"Did you do all this just to impress me?"

"Maybe." He adjusts his tie with deliberate nonchalance. "Did it work?"

"I'm standing here in a designer dress about to meet an entire town full of strangers who probably think you've lost your mind." I glance down at the elegant crowd. "So yeah, I'd say you've made an impression."

"Good. Because once we walk down there, there's no taking it back."

"Taking what back?"

Blue's eyes meet mine, serious for a moment. "The fact that you're mine to protect."

Before I can process what that means, he's offering his arm again. "Ready to make an entrance, Miss Mitchell?"

"As ready as someone can be to meet an entire town of strangers in silk and heels."

"That's all anyone can ask for."

CHAPTER SEVENTEEN
SAYLOR

I'm starting to think Blue's definition of *party* and mine are fundamentally incompatible. What I pictured: cocktails, small talk, maybe some light interrogation about my intentions toward Grimlock's most eligible bachelor-slash-serial-killer.

What I'm getting: a receiving line that stretches across the entire main hall, with every single resident of Grimlock queued up like I'm royalty holding court.

"Is this normal?" I whisper to Blue as we pause at the bottom of the staircase.

"Define normal."

"People lining up to meet your houseguest like she's the Queen of England?"

Blue's smile is almost apologetic. "You're the first woman I've brought to a party in . . . well, ever. They're curious."

Before I can ask what that means for my social survival, the first wave hits.

"Saylor!" A woman with silver hair piled into a classic updo glides toward us, her emerald dress rustling like autumn leaves. "I'm Dame Gothel. Welcome to Grimlock, darling. So lovely to finally meet you."

Dame Gothel. Even her name sounds like it belongs in a fairy tale. She looks like she stepped off the pages of *Vogue* at seventy with an elegance that makes me immediately curious about her story.

"Of course," I manage, accepting her gloved hand. "Thank you for coming."

"Darling, I wouldn't miss it." Her eyes sparkle with something that might be mischief. "Blue throws such interesting parties. Always full of surprises."

Before I can ask what she means by that, another voice cuts through the crowd.

"Miss Mitchell!" A distinguished older man wearing wire-rimmed glasses appears at my elbow, his kind eyes warm with genuine concern. "I'm Dr. Finch. How are you settling into Grimlock?"

"It's been . . . eye-opening," I say carefully.

"I'm sure it has." His smile conveys that he knows exactly how revealing it's been. "Blue's given you the full tour, I take it?"

"The highlights, anyway."

"Ah, well, there's always more to discover." Dr. Finch glances around the crowd. "Grimlock has layers. Like an onion, but with more secrets and less tears."

A man with dirt under his fingernails and tattoos covering his forearms steps forward—the gravedigger from the cemetery we passed earlier, although he's cleaned up remarkably well for the evening. His black suit fits him perfectly, and his dark hair is slicked back in a way that gives him an old-world elegance—like a Victorian gentleman who just happens to spend his days six feet underground. The whole room has this vibe, actually. Pocket watches and perfect posture, like everyone walked out of a period drama but forgot to mention it.

"Jasper Crane," he says, offering a calloused hand. "Sorry for your loss. Your father was an honest man. Fair in his dealings."

"Dealings?"

"He helped my sister when she needed it. Got her somewhere safe." Jasper grows more serious. "Family don't forget debts like that."

I want to ask what kind of help Dad provided, but a younger woman bounces over with the enthusiasm of a golden retriever who's just discovered tennis balls.

"Saylor! Finally!" She's maybe twenty-five with wild curls barely contained by a hot-pink hair tie and a smile that could power the entire electrical grid. "I'm Luna Bright. I run the flower shop, and oh my god, your dress is absolutely stunning. That color is perfect with your skin tone, and the way it moves—"

"Luna," Blue interrupts gently. "Let her breathe." He gets pulled away with another guest but makes quick eye contact first and I nod that I'll be fine.

Luna laughs, completely undeterred. "Sorry, I get excited. It's just so nice to have new people in town, especially someone with such exquisite taste in fashion. And speaking of taste"—she leans in conspiratorially—"the whole town's been buzzing about when you two are getting married."

I nearly choke on the champagne someone just handed me. "Married?"

"Well, yes! Blue's never brought a woman to one of his parties before. Not as his guest, anyway." Luna's eyes sparkle with gossip-hungry delight. "Everyone's taking bets on whether it'll be a spring or summer wedding."

"There's not going to be a wedding," I say quickly, very aware that our conversation is drawing interested glances from nearby guests. "Blue was just a friend of my father's. He's helping me get back on my feet after"—I struggle for words that explain kidnapping and murder without actually saying kidnapping and murder—"after everything that happened."

Luna's expression changes, her enthusiasm dimming to something more understanding. "Oh, I'm sorry. I didn't realize you'd been through something difficult."

I'm about to respond when a distinguished man with salt-and-pepper hair and a perfectly groomed goatee joins our growing circle. "Arthur Bearskin," he introduces himself with a refined accent indicative of private schools and old money. "I own the bookshop downtown. Your father mentioned you were a singer?"

"Jazz, mostly. Swing. Some rockabilly." I'm grateful for the change of subject. "Although I'm between venues at the moment."

"We'll have to remedy that," Arthur says with genuine enthusiasm. "Grimlock appreciates good music. Perhaps we could arrange something at the Haunted Windchimes? It's our local music venue— intimate space, perfect acoustics, and a crowd that actually listens to the music rather than just talking over it."

"That would be wonderful."

More introductions follow in a blur of names and faces. Elliott appears again with his wild gray hair and striped blue suit, this time carrying a plate of pastries and still talking like he's narrating a dream. Twin sisters, who own competing fabric shops and finish each other's sentences with the synchronized precision of people who've been doing it for seventy years, say hello.

Everyone wants to talk about Dad. Tales from his visits to Grimlock, whether I inherited his sense of humor or his stubborn streak. They share stories I've never heard—Peter teaching Jasper's younger brother to whittle, Peter helping Dame Gothel's daughter through a difficult divorce, Peter playing poker with the old men who gather at the barbershop every Monday when he was in town.

It's like discovering my father lived an entire second life without me knowing.

"He talked about you constantly," says a woman with intricate braids and paint-stained fingers who introduced herself as Maya, the town's muralist. "Always so proud. 'My Saylor's got a voice that could make angels weep,' he'd say."

Something warm and painful blooms in my chest, and I have to blink back sudden tears. "He said that?"

"Every time he visited. Which was more often in the months before he died." Maya appears more thoughtful. "He seemed worried about something, but whenever anyone asked, he'd just say he was making sure all his affairs were in order."

Affairs. Like he knew something was coming.

I continue to be approached by what quite possibly could be every resident of Grimlock, each one eager to welcome me personally. The whole evening is like being embraced by a community I didn't know existed—people who cared about Dad and who seem determined to care about me by extension. It's overwhelming and comforting at the same time, like being wrapped in a blanket I didn't know I needed.

"Ladies and gentlemen!" The words carry across the crowd, drawing everyone's attention. Blue's standing near the entrance to another room, looking every inch the perfect host. "If you'd join me in the ballroom, dinner is served."

The crowd begins moving toward Blue, conversations shifting to anticipation about the meal. I let myself be carried along with the flow, grateful for the chance to process everything I've just learned about Dad's secret life in Grimlock.

Blue catches my eye across the moving crowd and nods toward

the ballroom doors. There's something in his eyes I can't quite read—anticipation, maybe, or nervousness. Like he's been waiting for this moment all night. Like there's something specific he needs me to see.

As we approach the ballroom entrance, I can hear the haunting strains of dark folk music drifting from behind the closed double doors. A bass line so deep it vibrates through the floor, violin melody that sounds like it's mourning something beautiful, and the distinctive twang of a banjo weaving through it all. It's southern gothic at its finest, the type of music that belongs on my "murderfolk" playlist. How could Blue possibly know about my secret obsession with songs about love and death and all the beautiful violence in between?

Blue opens the doors with a flourish, and I step into my aesthetic heaven.

If the main hall was gothic elegance, the ballroom is pure dark cottagecore fantasy. The room has been transformed into an enchanted forest clearing, complete with strings of warm Edison bulbs woven between artificial branches that span the ceiling like a canopy. Moss covers every available surface—real moss, judging by the earthy scent that fills the air. Wildflowers in deep purples and ocean blues spill from rustic wooden planters placed throughout the room, and vintage mason jars filled with flickering candles cast dancing shadows across walls draped in flowing cream fabric.

The buffet setup is nothing short of magical. Long wooden tables that look like they were hewn from time-worn trees display an abundance that would make a medieval feast jealous. Roasted meats carved and arranged on slate platters, artisanal cheeses paired with honeycomb still dripping golden nectar, crusty bread loaves that smell like they came straight from a fairy tale oven. Glass cloches protect delicate pastries that look too beautiful to eat, and copper serving pieces catch the candlelight like captured sunset.

But it's the attention to detail that takes my breath away. Vintage books used as serving platforms, antique teacups repurposed as individual dessert vessels, fresh herbs scattered artfully around each dish like nature decided to help with the presentation. Everything seems to have grown organically from some magical forest where woodland creatures learned to cater.

"This is incredible," I breathe, taking in the scene. "It's like stepping into a storybook."

"I thought you might appreciate the aesthetic," Blue says, appearing beside me with two glasses of mulled wine garnished with cinnamon sticks and star anise.

"Appreciate it? I want to live in it." I accept the wine gratefully, inhaling the warm spices. "How did you put this together so quickly?"

"Grimlock has its resources. And Wren has very strong opinions about proper entertaining."

The crowd spreads throughout the ballroom, everyone moving with the relaxed enthusiasm of people who know they're in for a good time. Conversations resume as guests begin filling their plates, the atmosphere warm and convivial despite the elegant setting.

I'm laughing at a story about Dad attempting to help Elliott with a particularly stubborn batch of sourdough starter when I finally look up and really take in the center of the room.

One step closer.

Two steps . . .

That's when I see him.

At first, my brain refuses to process what I'm looking at. The buffet tables are arranged in a large circle around something that's been decorated with trailing ivy and those gorgeous midnight-blue flowers that seem to be Grimlock's signature botanical choice. More candles, more fairy lights, more of that magical forest atmosphere that's been enchanting me all evening.

But underneath the beautiful, whimsical decorations is a man.

A dead man.

A very, very dead man whose torso has been split open in a grotesque flower arrangement that's both horrifying and impossibly elegant.

He's laid out like some macabre centerpiece, his body positioned with the careful attention of someone arranging a formal dinner setting. His chest has been split wide open, the jagged wound filled with the most beautiful blue flowers I've ever seen. They spill from the gaping cavity like some twisted corsage, their petals a shade of midnight that matches Blue's beard perfectly. More flowers cascade from his hands, which have been positioned to look like he's offering bouquets to the dinner guests. Ivy winds around his arms and legs, and someone has even woven a crown of those blue flowers through his hair.

But it's the tattoo on his neck that makes my breath catch—a small black crow in flight, its wings spread wide. One of them. One of the men on my list who killed my father with that cruel smile I'll never forget, delivered to me on a literal silver platter.

The realization stops me cold. One of them. One of the men who killed my father is here, dead, turned into some twisted centerpiece.

My stomach lurches, but not with revulsion. With something that feels dangerously close to relief.

I scan the room, looking for someone—anyone—who seems bothered by the fact that we're having dinner around a murdered man who's been turned into a botanical display. Dame Gothel is discussing the merits of the herb-crusted lamb with Maya the muralist, neither of them so much as glancing at the corpse center-piece. Arthur Bearskin is examining the selection of cheeses while standing close enough to the body that he could probably identify the exact species of flowers growing from the chest cavity. Elliott is humming while he arranges pastries on his plate, occasionally pausing to admire the way the candlelight plays across the dead man's ivy-crowned head.

Everyone is acting like this is completely normal.

Like casual murder-as-decoration is just another charming Grimlock tradition.

And somehow, the most disturbing part is that I'm not running. I'm not screaming or demanding to know what kind of psychopath decorates with dead bodies. I'm standing here wondering if this is what Blue expects from me—to handle this kind of scene without flinching. To become someone who could create this kind of scene.

I catch Blue's eyes across the room, and he's watching me with the intensity of someone waiting for a verdict. He's been pulled into a conversation with Hans about something that requires serious nodding and occasional gestures, but his attention keeps drifting to me. Checking my reaction. Measuring my response to his test.

The message is becoming clear: This is what your future looks like. This is what I'm going to teach you to do. But first, I need to know if you can even handle seeing it.

I look back at the corpse, and this time I notice details that make me stare despite myself. The way his mouth has been positioned in an almost serene smile, as if he's peacefully sleeping despite the gaping wound in his chest. How his fingernails have been cleaned and buffed, his hair carefully combed and styled with that floral crown. The careful way his clothing has been pressed and arranged so he looks dignified even in death—a twisted form of respect that's somehow more disturbing than outright desecration.

It's a statement piece, but not just Blue showing off. He's making sure every person at this party knows exactly what happens to people who cross him. And he's showing me what I'll be capable of once he's done training me.

But there's something else here. Something that makes my chest tighten with an emotion I can't quite name. He did this without asking me. Without warning me. Is this how he plans to handle my education—surprising me with tests I didn't know I was taking?

The thought hits me so suddenly I actually take a step backward. I'm not just being shown a dead body—I'm being evaluated. My reaction right now is determining something about how Blue sees me, what he thinks I'm ready for.

When did murder become a pop quiz?

But beneath the unease is something darker. Something that whispers that this is exactly what I wanted to see. That I've been fantasizing about these men dead for years, and now one of them actually is. The only thing missing is that I didn't get to do it myself.

Is that the point? Is he showing me what I'm missing out on by letting others handle my revenge?

I look across the room at Blue, who's watching me with those dark eyes that seem to see straight through to my soul. He's not just protecting me or taking over my revenge—he's testing whether I'm ready to claim it myself.

In front of the entire town. With a corpse as his teaching aid.

And God help me, I think I'm passing.

CHAPTER EIGHTEEN
BLUE

Death has its own magnetism, and Saylor is caught in its pull.

She circles Samuel "Sly" Crow's corpse with the deliberate hunger of a predator examining prey, her copper silk dress whispering against the moss-covered floor as she moves. Each step brings her closer to the truth I've laid bare for her—not just Sly's eviscerated chest blooming with midnight flowers, but the careful choreography of violence I've orchestrated in her honor. The violence Hans executed while I held myself back, counting breaths and fighting every instinct that screamed at me to be the one wielding the blade.

My conversation with Hans dies mid-sentence as I watch her lean forward, close enough that the candlelight catches the silver stars Wren painted along her lash line. She's not recoiling from death's embrace. She's welcoming it, breathing it in like expensive perfume.

This is the moment that separates the survivors from the casualties in my world. The instant when civilized masks slip away and reveal the teeth underneath. I've seen grown men weep at far less provocative displays, watched seasoned criminals lose their nerve when confronted with my particular brand of artistic expression. Or rather, Hans's execution of my particular brand of artistic expression.

Saylor does something that stops my heart.

She smiles.

It's not the smile of someone trying to appear brave or sophisticated. It's the slow, satisfied curve of lips that have just tasted something exquisite. She reaches out—actually reaches out—and her fingertips hover just above the crown of blue flowers Hans wove through Sly's silver hair. Close enough to feel the residual heat bleeding from his cooling flesh, close enough to disturb the careful arrangement if she wanted to claim a souvenir.

The gesture is intimate. Proprietorial. Like she's already thinking of him as hers rather than mine.

Conversations murmur somewhere behind me, but the voices sound like they're coming from underwater. The entire ballroom might as well be empty except for the woman tracing the architecture of death with her eyes, memorizing each detail of Hans's handiwork with the focus of someone committing a lover's body to memory.

A familiar voice cuts through my concentration. "That was quite the statement."

I turn to find Ash Cupp standing beside me, his calculating gaze fixed on the flower-adorned corpse. He's holding a crystal tumbler of whiskey, and there's something different in his posture—less protective baker, more dangerous strategist.

"Ash." I nod. "Enjoying the party?"

"Elliott's been charming the ladies with stories about his butterfly collection." Ash takes a sip of his whiskey, then meets my gaze directly. "But we both know tonight wasn't about hospitality. You just painted a target on your back in front of the entire town."

The words settle between us like stones dropping into still water. Ash understands exactly what I've done here—not just arranged for Sly Crow to be killed, but made it public, taunting, impossible to ignore.

"They're going to be furious," he continues, his tone dropping to something that reminds me of the man he used to be. "Pissed-off Crows can either be extremely lethal or they can make stupid mistakes. Depends on how much you've gotten under their skin."

"I'm banking on stupid mistakes."

Ash's smile is as lethal as any blade I've ever wielded. "Good. Because if you need another general in your army, I volunteer." He raises his glass slightly, a toast to violence yet to come. "The Collector may be retired, but he remembers every trick they taught him. And he has some scores of his own to settle."

The offer solidifies between us like a pact written in blood. Ash isn't just offering to help. He's declaring his loyalty, choosing sides in a war that's about to consume Grimlock.

"What about Elliott?" I ask.

"Elliott will be protected. But these bastards killed Peter, and Peter saved my brother's life." Ash's grip tightens on his glass. "Some debts can only be paid in blood."

The pact between us feels sealed without another word. Ash melts back into the crowd as silently as he appeared, leaving me to turn my attention back to the woman still circling my gift.

When she finally looks up and catches my eye across the room, there's something in her look that makes my cock hard. Not fear. Not disgust. Something deeper, darker, utterly captivating.

Recognition.

She sees what I've done for her, and she understands exactly what it means.

I excuse myself from the conversation and make my way through the crowd, accepting compliments on the evening's ambiance while keeping my focus locked on Saylor. She hasn't moved from her spot, hasn't looked away from my gift. When I finally reach her side, she doesn't startle or step back. She just continues studying Sly's lifeless face.

"Nice flower arrangement," she says, like we're discussing weekend hobby projects instead of the results of my latest orchestrated murder. "The blue really brings out his eyes."

"I had a feeling you'd appreciate the attention to detail." I move closer, catching her fragrance over the moss and death. "Color coordination is important in any good centerpiece."

"A Crow decorated with flowers." She tilts her head, considering. "There's definitely some irony there. Very Martha Stewart meets Edgar Allan Poe."

"I do try to keep things thematically appropriate."

When she turns to face me, her eyes hold something that makes my chest tighten. No horror, no demands for explanations. Just genuine interest, like I've finally done something worth her attention.

"So is this your usual party trick?" she asks. "Corpse as conversation starter?"

"Only for special occasions." I let my hand drift close to hers on the table's edge. "Only when I really want to make an impression."

"And what exactly are you trying to impress upon me?"

I lean in, voice dropping low enough that the nearest eavesdropper would have to strain. "That anyone stupid enough to threaten you gets promoted to table decoration. Consider it my version of a strongly worded letter."

The way her breath halts tells me she understands the implication. This isn't just about protection—it's about possession. About making it clear to everyone in this room that Saylor Mitchell belongs under my care, and anyone who threatens that arrangement will become my next decorating project.

"How many more are there?" she asks, her gaze drifting back to the corpse. "Crows, I mean."

"Eleven confirmed had a part in your father's death."

"Eleven." She traces the edge of a flower petal with one finger, her touch gentle against the dead man's chest. "That's a lot of future gifts."

Ravaging satisfaction settles into my bones at her phrasing. She's not asking me to stop. She's calculating how many victims I'll be bringing her.

"As many as it takes," I promise. "Every last one of them will pay for what they did to your father."

Saylor is quiet for a long moment, still studying Sly's peaceful expression. When she speaks again, her voice is so soft I have to strain to hear it over the ambient music and conversation.

"I thought you were murder sober."

"I am," I say carefully. "Hans did the actual killing. I just . . . detained Sly. Made sure he couldn't escape."

Her head snaps up, eyes flashing with something between surprise and anger. "Hans killed him?"

"I couldn't risk falling off the wagon. Not when you need me steady." The admission tastes like failure on my tongue. "But I made sure Sly understood exactly why he was dying."

Her jaw tightens, and I can see her mind working through the implications.

"I'm jealous," she says finally, her voice carrying an edge that sends heat racing through my veins. "It should have been me. I don't want Hans doing all the killing for my revenge."

The raw honesty in her confession . . . She's not horrified by the violence—she's frustrated she wasn't the one wielding it.

"The next one," I promise, stepping closer until I can see the gold flecks in her dark eyes, "will come to you alive. Completely at your mercy. Whatever you want to do to them, however long you want to take—that kill will be yours."

Her breath catches, pupils dilating as she processes what I'm offering her.

"When?" she asks, and there's something hungry in her voice that makes my blood sing.

"Soon."

The way she looks at me then—like I've just offered her the keys to salvation itself—makes something primal and possessive roar to life in my chest. I've never been so fucking turned on by anyone in my life.

For a moment we just stare at each other across the space between what's proper and what we both actually want. The weight of what I've just offered her—and what she's accepted—hangs between us until the sound of laughter from nearby guests reminds me we're not alone. We're standing beside a corpse making promises about death while fifty people eat dinner around us.

"We should probably rejoin the party," I say, although the last thing I want is to share her attention with anyone else.

"Probably," she agrees, but neither of us moves.

Before either of us can say anything else, the band's music changes, taking on a more prominent role as the room's energy shifts. A woman with dark hair pulled back approaches with a guitar in her hands, her smile warm and inviting.

"Saylor," she says, offering the instrument. "We heard you're a singer. Any chance we could convince you to join us for a song?"

I watch Saylor's energy shift from dark satisfaction to something lighter, more playful. She glances at me, then at the small stage area where the band has set up their instruments—a double bass, violin, banjo, and mandolin arranged in a semi-circle with space for a vocalist at the center.

"I don't know if my style matches yours," she says, but there's interest.

"Try us," the woman encourages. "We're pretty adaptable."

The crowd has started to notice the exchange, conversations dying down as people turn their attention toward us. I can see the expectation building, the way Grimlock's residents are settling in for what they clearly hope will be entertainment.

"What do you say?" I ask Saylor, nodding toward the instruments. "Let them hear what Peter Mitchell's daughter can do."

Her chin lifts slightly at the mention of her father—pride, maybe, or determination. She takes the guitar from the woman with steady hands.

"One song," she agrees. "But don't blame me if I scandalize your dinner party."

"I'm counting on it," I say, following her toward the stage area.

The band members nod respectfully as Saylor positions herself in their center, quickly conferring about key and tempo. I find myself a spot near the edge of the crowd where I can watch her face, where I can catalog every look that crosses her features as she prepares to sing.

When the opening notes ring out—a haunting bass line that seems to rise from the earth itself—the entire room goes silent. The violin joins next, weaving a melody that sounds like mourning and celebration wrapped together. Then the banjo and mandolin create a complex harmony that transforms the ballroom into something haunting and wild.

But it's when Saylor opens her mouth that the world stops.

Her voice pours out rich and dark as aged whiskey, carrying notes that seem to bypass the ears and sink directly into bone and bloodstream. She's chosen something that sounds like a traditional folk ballad but with lyrics that speak of love and loss and the beautiful violence that connects them. The melody rises and falls like breath, like heartbeat, like the rhythm of skin against skin in the darkness.

She moves as she sings, her body swaying with the music in ways that make my blood run hot and my hands clench into fists. The copper silk dances and flows around her curves, and the way the candlelight catches her face makes her look like some goddess of war and desire. Her eyes are closed, her head tilted back, completely lost in the music she's creating.

My throat goes dry watching her. Every movement, every note, every breath she takes seems designed to unravel what's left of my self-control.

When she reaches the chorus—something about drinking from the cup of vengeance and finding it sweeter than wine—her voice takes on an edge that makes every person in the room lean forward. There's something primal in the sound, something that speaks to the part of humanity that remembers when survival meant being willing to kill or be killed.

The song builds to a crescendo that seems to shake the walls themselves, Saylor's voice soaring over the instruments with power that makes my cock throb harder. God help me, it does.

She's not just singing. She's casting a spell, weaving magic that transforms the ballroom into something wild and raw and impossible to resist.

When the final notes fade away, there's silence for several heartbeats before applause erupts that sounds more like worship than appreciation. But I'm not clapping. I'm staring at the woman on the stage who just proved that everything I suspected about her darkness was true.

Saylor opens her eyes and finds mine across the crowd, and the smile that curves her lips is pure sin. She knows exactly what she just did to me, exactly how completely she just destroyed any remaining boundaries between us.

She hands the guitar back to the woman and makes her way through the crowd toward me, accepting congratulations and compliments with gracious smiles that don't quite hide the satisfaction in her eyes.

When she reaches me, she rises up on her toes to speak directly into my ear, her breath warm against my skin.

"How was that for scandalizing your dinner party?"

"Perfect," I manage. "Although I think you just made every person in this room want to ravage you."

"Every person?" She pulls back to look at me directly, her dark eyes dancing with something wolfish. "Or are you talking about someone specific who's been undressing me with his eyes all night?"

The question hangs between us like a challenge, and we've definitely crossed some invisible line tonight.

And as she stands there waiting for my answer, her lips curved in that knowing smile while a dead man serves as our witness, there's no going back from this moment.

"Just one," I admit quietly. "And it's not just because of your singing."

Her smile widens, and for the first time since Peter died, I allow myself to imagine what it might be like to have something worth protecting that isn't just duty or obligation or guilt.

Something worth killing for. Something worth dying for.

Something worth burning the whole fucking world down for, if that's what it takes to keep her looking at me like I'm salvation and damnation wrapped in the same beautiful package.

CHAPTER NINETEEN
BLUE

"God, I'm exhausted," she says suddenly, pressing her fingertips to her temples. "It's like this day has lasted about three years. I hate to leave the party, but I think I need to call it a night."

The admission reminds me that less than twenty-four hours ago, she was being hunted by the Crow and getting chloroformed into a trunk. Today she met an entire town, accepted my promise to deliver her father's killers, and just seduced a room full of strangers with her voice. No wonder she's running on fumes.

"Come on," I say, offering my arm. "I'll walk you up."

We make our way through the crowd, Saylor accepting final compliments on her performance with tired but genuine warmth. Hands reach out to squeeze hers, voices murmur praise and promises to see her again soon. She nods and smiles through it all, but I can see the exhaustion pulling at the corners of her eyes.

The house feels different as we climb the grand staircase, the party sounds fading to a distant murmur below us. Our footsteps echo softly against the stone, creating an intimate bubble of silence that makes me hyperaware of her presence beside me. The way her hand rests lightly on my arm, the whisper of fabric as she moves, the lingering scent of her perfume mixed with wine and warmth.

When we reach her door, she turns to face me, leaning back against the dark wood. The hallway is lit only by a few scattered candelabras, casting everything in warm golden light that makes her skin glow.

"Thank you," she says quietly. "For today. For showing me Grimlock, for the party . . ." Her gaze drifts toward the staircase where the sounds of celebration continue below. "For the gift. And for what you promised me."

The way she says *gift* makes my blood heat. She's not talking about hospitality or party planning. She's talking about Sly's corpse, about the message Hans and I wrote in blood and flowers.

"Saylor—"

But before I can finish whatever I was going to say, she steps closer and rises on her toes, her hands sliding up my chest to rest against my shoulders. Her lips brush against mine, soft at first, testing. Then her mouth opens under mine and the kiss deepens into something that makes my vision blur.

She tastes like spice and sin, like everything I've been craving without realizing it. Her tongue slides against mine with deliberate intent, and when she bites gently at my lower lip, I have to grip the doorframe to keep from pushing her back against the wood and taking this exactly where my body wants it to go.

Her fingers find the hair at the nape of my neck, tugging just hard enough to make me groan against her mouth. The sound seems to please her because she smiles against my lips, the curve of her mouth wicked and knowing.

When she finally pulls back, we're both breathing hard. Her lips are swollen from kissing, her eyes dark with something that makes my head spin.

"Come inside," she whispers, her fingers trailing down my chest, finding the buttons of my shirt. "I don't want this night to end yet."

The invitation hangs between us like a loaded gun, and every cell in my body screams yes. I want nothing more than to follow her into that room, but the rational part of my mind—the part that remembers what Peter meant to me—knows this is exactly what I can't do.

"Saylor." I catch her hand, stilling her fingers against my chest. "You don't know what you're asking for."

"I know exactly what I'm asking for." Her eyes flash with something between challenge and frustration. "I'm not some innocent little girl who needs protecting from the big bad wolf. I can handle whatever you think you might do to me."

But that's exactly what she is, whether she realizes it or not. Peter's little girl, twenty years younger than me, standing in a hallway asking me to take something I have no right to take. She thinks she understands the darkness in me, but she's spent her whole life around good people. Normal people. She has no idea that I don't know how to be gentle, that everything in me would want to own her completely if I let myself have her.

"You deserve someone who can give you flowers and poetry," I say quietly, my thumb tracing across her knuckles. "Someone who'll hold you like you're precious instead of . . ." I trail off, unable to finish the thought.

"Instead of what?" she asks, stepping closer, eliminating the space I'd tried to put between us. Her eyes darken with something that looks like interest—or maybe recognition of exactly what I meant.

Instead of taking you like the killer I am. Instead of leaving marks on your skin and shadows in your eyes. Instead of turning you into something as twisted as me.

"Instead of doing what every instinct tells me to do," I say finally. "You deserve better than what I am."

"What if I don't want better?" Her voice carries an edge that makes my blood heat even as it terrifies me. "What if I want exactly what you're afraid to give me?"

"Then you don't understand what you're asking for." I force myself to step back, breaking the spell of her proximity. "You're twenty-three years old. You should be falling in love with some nice boy your own age who'll take you dancing and treat you like a princess. Not standing in a hallway asking a man old enough to be your father to—"

"To what?" she challenges. "To want me? To stop pretending you don't?"

I close my eyes for a moment, trying to find the strength to do what's right. "You deserve someone who can love you the way you should be loved. Soft and sweet and safe. I don't know how to be any of those things."

"Then I don't need them." Her voice is barely above a whisper, but it cuts through me like a blade. "I'd rather have what you can actually give me than some fantasy about what I should want. I want your cock, Blue. Not flowers and sweet compliments."

"Tomorrow," I say, forcing myself to step back, to break contact before I lose the ability to think clearly. "Tomorrow is going to be a very long day, and you're going to need all your strength for what's coming."

"You're afraid of me."

"I'm afraid of what I'll turn you into," I admit. "In one night, I could destroy everything beautiful about you and twist it into something dark and hungry and broken."

Something shifts in her expression—not hurt anymore, but understanding. She steps forward and places her palm flat against my chest, over my heart.

"What if I'm already broken?" she asks quietly. "What if watching my father die already took away everything soft and sweet and safe about me? What if the person you're trying to protect is already gone?"

The words land hard, and I know she's right on some level—I can see it in the way she smiled at Sly's corpse, in how easily she accepted the promise of more bodies to come.

"Then maybe we're both already lost," I say, covering her hand with mine.

For a long moment, we just stand there in the candlelit hallway, her palm pressed against my chest, my hand covering hers. I can feel the warmth of her skin, the slight tremor in her fingers that betrays how affected she is despite her bold words. She's not backing down, not retreating from what she wants.

"You're going to make me wait," she says, and it's not a question.

"I'm going to try to do the right thing," I say, though we both know how flimsy that sounds.

Her eyes flash with something between frustration and amusement. "The right thing for who?"

I don't have an answer for that, and she knows it. She rises up on her toes one more time, her lips brushing against my ear.

"When you're lying in your bed tonight with your hand on your cock, thinking about what I offered," she whispers, "remember that I'm just down the hall. And I'd do it better than you can." Her lips curve into a smile that's pure temptation. "Goodnight, Blue. I'll see you at breakfast."

She slips inside her room and closes the door with a soft click, leaving me standing in the hallway with my blood on fire and my dick throbbing.

I press my palm flat against her door, fighting the urge to follow her inside and finish what she started. My cock will be hard for hours from that kiss, from the way she looked at me like she wanted to devour me whole, from the invitation she offered and the way the girl says exactly what she wants.

I stay there for another minute, listening to the sounds of her moving around inside—the whisper of silk hitting the floor, the soft pad of bare feet on stone. Every sound makes my blood burn hotter.

Tomorrow I'll see her at breakfast and pretend I'm not thinking about backing her against the nearest wall. Pretend I'm not already planning which Crow to hunt down next, how to capture them alive and deliver them to her like some twisted courtship offering. Pretend I can't still taste her on my lips or feel the phantom heat of her fingers trailing down my chest.

Tomorrow I'll have to acknowledge that everything changed tonight—not just with the message we sent the Crow, but with how badly I wanted to finish what we started in that dressing room. The line we crossed once. The line I'll spend the rest of my life wanting to cross again.

Just another taste like we had at the White Note.

One more lick . . .

Peter's daughter!

One more kiss . . .

Peter's daughter!

The way she . . .

Peter's fucking daughter!

But that kiss she just gave me was a declaration of war against my self-control. And her invitation into her bedroom was a promise that this battle is far from over.

She's already winning.

CHAPTER TWENTY
SAYLOR

There's something perversely therapeutic about applying winged eyeliner when you're planning to commit your first murder. I stand in front of the vanity mirror at 6 a.m., drawing liquid black lines with the same careful attention I imagine goes into slitting throats. Today calls for armor, and mine happens to be a fitted black dress with white polka dots, victory rolls that could survive a hurricane, and red lipstick dark enough to hide bloodstains.

If I'm going to ask a man to teach me how to kill people, I'm damn well going to look like I deserve the lesson.

The walk downstairs feels different this morning. My Mary Janes click a steady rhythm against the floors, but instead of nerves, I feel something closer to anticipation. Yesterday I was a grieving daughter playing dress-up in a world I didn't understand. Today I'm someone who kissed a killer and asked for seconds.

Blue is already at the breakfast table, wearing a burgundy velvet smoking jacket that makes him look like he stepped out of a Sherlock Holmes story. His dark hair is perfectly styled, that blue-tinted beard groomed to aristocratic polish, and he's reading stock reports instead of his usual newspaper.

When he looks up and sees me, something alters in his face. His eyes travel from my hair down to my patent leather shoes and back up again, lingering on the way the dress hugs my waist.

"Well," he says, setting down his papers. "Someone's ready to take on the world."

I slide into my chair, accepting coffee from Wren with a grateful smile. The silence stretches between Blue and me, filled with everything we're not saying. The kiss. The promise. The way he looked at me when I asked him to let me kill them myself.

Wren pours Blue's coffee with the careful attention of someone who's witnessed awkward morning-afters before. "Eggs Benedict this morning, dear?"

"Perfect," I manage.

She disappears into the kitchen, leaving Blue and me alone with our newspapers and coffee cups and the weight of last night hanging between us like expensive perfume.

"Sleep well?" Blue asks finally.

"Fine." I take a sip of coffee, savoring the way it burns down my throat. "You?"

"Well enough."

We eat breakfast like civilized people discussing civilized things. Blue mentions the weather forecast. I ask if Dame Gothel enjoyed herself last night. He mentions how impressed Elliott was with the floral arrangements. We discuss the band's performance, and Blue tells me that Maya asked if I'd consider singing at the autumn art show. Surface-level conversation that skips over the fact that I spent half the night replaying that kiss, and the other half wondering what it would feel like to watch someone die by my own hand.

But underneath the polite chatter, there's electricity. Every time Blue looks at me, I remember the way his mouth felt against mine. Every time I reach for my coffee cup, I think about his hands arranging flowers in a dead man's chest cavity, turning murder into dinner décor.

Every time our eyes meet, I catch something that looks like guilt flickering across his features, like he's already regretting what he's about to teach me.

Finally, Blue sets down his napkin and checks his pocket watch. "There's something I want to show you."

"Oh?"

"Something you asked for last night."

He leads me through the house to a door I haven't noticed before, heavy and dark and tucked beneath the grand staircase. When he opens it, stone steps disappear into shadow.

"Basement," he says, flicking on lights. "Time for that lesson you wanted."

He pauses at the top of the stairs, his hand on the light switch. "Saylor . . . there's no shame in changing your mind. You're still so young, still—"

"I'm not changing my mind," I interrupt, though something in his tone makes my stomach flutter with nerves I wasn't expecting.

I follow him down the worn stone steps, the sound of my footsteps bouncing off the narrow walls. The air grows cooler with each step, carrying scents of earth and something metallic that makes my stomach uneasy.

At the bottom, Blue opens another door, and I step into what can only be described as a gentleman's torture chamber.

The space is larger than I expected, with stone walls that arch overhead and wine racks lining the far wall. But it's the center of the room that makes my breath catch.

A man sits tied to a chair, duct tape over his mouth, dark hair falling across his forehead. He's maybe thirty, with the lean build of someone who knows how to run fast and fight dirty. When he sees me, his eyes widen with the particular alarm of someone realizing his day just got significantly worse.

"Julian Crow," Blue says conversationally. "One half of the Shadow Twins assassination team. He was kind enough to volunteer for today's demonstration."

"Julian Crow," I repeat, frowning. "Why do they all have the same last name? Is it like . . . a family thing?"

Blue's expression darkens slightly. "The Crow isn't just what they do. It's who they are. When you join them, you take the name. Julian Crow, Victor Crow, Leroy Crow. You become part of the murder of crows, literally."

"Murder of crows," I say, the phrase clicking. "That's poetic."

"Brutus thought so." Blue's voice carries an edge. "It's also practical. Makes them harder to track when everyone shares the same last name."

Julian makes muffled sounds of protest behind his gag.

"I know, I know," Blue continues. "You didn't technically volunteer this demonstration. But you did hold the knife that slit Peter's throat while your partner carved his initials into his chest. You laughed while he bled out, Julian. You filmed it for Brutus. That makes this educational opportunity well-deserved."

My stomach does a little flip at the casual mention of Dad's name, but it's not nausea. It's something darker, hungrier. This is one of them. One of the men from my list—the tall one with the snake tattoo curling up his neck who wouldn't stop laughing while they killed my father.

Blue moves to a table covered with black cloth. When he pulls it away, I see an array of knives that could have come from a serial killer's wet dream. Each blade is polished to mirror brightness, arranged with the same care Wren uses for formal dinner settings.

"I thought you might prefer something easier to handle than my axe," Blue explains, running his finger along the edge of a particularly wicked-looking dagger. "These are designed for finesse rather than brute force."

I stare at the display, my mouth suddenly dry. "This is really happening."

"Only if you want it to." His voice is gentler than usual.

Blue reaches out to steady me, his hand brushing my shoulder, and I flinch away from the contact before I can stop myself. The involuntary movement gives away everything—the nerves I'm trying to hide, the fear I don't want to admit to.

"Maybe we should start with something else," Blue continues, and there's something protective in his tone that makes me bristle. "Some target practice. Work up to—"

The offer should be comforting, but instead it makes something stubborn flare in my chest. I asked for this. Demanded it. Last night I told Blue I wanted to kill my father's murderers myself, and I meant every word.

"Remove his gag," I say, surprised by how calm I sound.

Blue hesitates, studying my face like he's looking for cracks.

"Remove his gag," I repeat, lifting my chin.

Blue raises an eyebrow but complies. The moment the tape comes off, Julian starts talking.

"What the fuck is this? Who is this bitch in the vintage pin-up costume?"

"Language," Blue says mildly. "You're in the presence of a lady."

"A lady?" Julian looks me up and down with obvious confusion. "She looks like she should be serving pie at a diner, not standing in a murder basement."

"Saylor, meet Julian Crow," Blue continues. "Julian, meet Saylor Mitchell. Peter's daughter."

Julian's face goes white. "Oh. Shit."

He knows he's going to die.

"There's that mouth again." I pick up one of the smaller knives, testing its weight in my palm. "Tell me something, Julian. How long did it take my father to die? Did you time it while you cut him?"

Julian's cocky demeanor falters for just a moment. "Look, your dad fought hard. Gave us more trouble than most. Gutsy bastard, I'll give him that."

"That's not what I asked." My voice sounds steadier than I feel. "I asked if you timed it."

"Three minutes," Julian says, his eyes growing cold. "Three minutes from the first cut to when he stopped making noise. Would have been faster, but Brutus wanted to make it last."

The casual cruelty of it—the way he talks about my father's death like it was a game—makes rage bloom hot and bright in my chest.

"Look, lady, I don't know what kind of revenge fantasy you're playing out here, but maybe let the professional handle this?" Julian jerks his head toward Blue. "At least he knows what he's doing." His acceptance of his impending death is surprising, but I guess in his line of business this is normal.

"The whole point is that I do it myself." I raise the knife, studying how the basement lights catch on the blade. "You killed my father. I kill you. Simple math."

Julian stares at the knife in my hand, then at my face, clearly trying to reconcile my pin-up appearance with my apparent homicidal intentions. "You're shaking."

He's right. My hands are trembling so badly the knife wavers in the air like I'm conducting an invisible orchestra.

"First-time nerves," I say, trying to sound confident. "Blue, where exactly do I put this?"

Blue moves closer, and I can feel the heat of his body behind me. When he speaks, it's low, meant only for me. "You don't have to do this, sweetheart. I can handle Julian. You can watch if you want to see him die, but you don't have to—"

"Stop protecting me," I whisper back, not turning around. "I need to do this myself."

"Wherever feels right," Blue says finally, resigned. "Trust your instincts."

I step closer to Julian's chair . . . so close. This is it. This is justice for Dad. All I have to do is push the blade into his neck and watch him bleed.

So why do I feel like I'm about to throw up?

"Come on," Julian says, sounding almost bored. "If you're going to do this, do it. Stop standing there looking like you're about to cry."

"I'm not going to cry." Even though my eyes are definitely watering. "I'm just figuring out the best approach."

"The best approach is to get it over with. Some of us have places to be."

He sighs loudly and then again over-dramatically.

"Look, Blue," Julian says, turning his attention away from me. "Can't you just step in here? Put me out of my misery? At least let me die with some dignity by the hands of the infamous Blue instead of whatever this amateur hour bullshit is."

Blue's response comes out strained, like the words are fighting their way past his throat. "Sorry, Julian. I'm retired. This is Saylor's show now."

"Your retirement is going to get me tortured to death by someone who can't figure out which end of a knife is sharp," Julian says with genuine disgust.

I can feel Blue's tension radiating from across the room, can practically hear him reconsidering this entire plan.

I raise the knife again, aiming for his throat because that seems efficient. But as I bring the blade closer to his skin, my stomach revolts. The metal is maybe two inches from his neck when I freeze completely.

"Jesus Christ," Julian mutters. "Just push it in. It's not complicated."

"Stop talking. You're making this harder."

"How am I making it harder? You point the pointy end at me and apply pressure. My little nephew could figure this out."

I press the tip of the blade against Julian's throat, barely touching skin. The contact makes him stiffen, but he doesn't make a sound. I can see where the knife point has just barely pierced him, the tiniest drop of blood welling up like a scarlet bead.

"Ow," Julian says dryly. "That really stings. Are you planning to kill me one cell at a time?"

I grit my teeth and press harder, trying to coach myself through it. It's just like cutting into a steak, I tell myself. Just meat. Just flesh. People do this at dinner tables every night without puking all over themselves. The blade sinks in maybe a quarter inch, and suddenly there's more blood—a thin red line trickling down his neck like some grotesque necklace.

Julian hisses. "Well, that's slightly more progress. At this rate, I'll bleed out sometime next Thursday."

The sight of that crimson trail makes my stomach clench violently. My vision starts to tunnel, and I can taste bile rising in my throat. I pull the knife back, waving it around wildly as panic sets in.

"I can't do this," I gasp, flailing the blade through the air as I pace. "This is insane. I can't actually—"

"Jesus, watch where you're swinging that thing," Julian says, trying to lean his chair away from my erratic movements.

"I thought I could do it but I can't!" I'm gesticulating frantically now, knife cutting through the air in wide arcs as the words tumble out. "This is crazy. I'm not a killer, I'm a jazz singer from New York who can barely kill a spider without calling my neighbors for help!"

"Could you maybe put the knife down while you have your breakdown?" Julian suggests with the weary patience of someone who's dealt with hysterical amateurs before.

"This is supposed to be easy!" I cry out, slashing the air with wild, exaggerated motions. "You just stab, or slice, and—" I demonstrate with frantic gestures, the razor-sharp blade cutting dangerous arcs through the air.

"I wanted to be strong enough," I continue, gesticulating emphatically as I talk. "I wanted to prove that I could—"

The knife slices through the air in a wide arc as I wave my hands, and suddenly Julian's complaining stops. His eyes go wide, then confused, then oddly peaceful as a thin red line opens across his throat like a zipper.

For a moment, we all just stare at each other.

"Huh," Julian manages to say, blood bubbling from his lips. "Well, that's one way to—"

And then he's gone.

I look down at the knife in my hand, then at Julian slumped in his chair, then back at the knife.

"Oh god," I whisper. "Oh god, oh god, oh god."

Blue moves to my side, and I can feel his hand hovering near my shoulder, like he wants to comfort me but isn't sure I'll let him. When he speaks, his words carry the faintest trace of what might be amusement. "Well. That was . . . unexpected."

"I killed him," I say, my voice climbing toward hysteria. "I killed him by accident. Who does that? Who accidentally murders someone?"

"Technically, you still murdered him," Blue points out helpfully. "The method was just . . . unconventional."

My stomach chooses that moment to revolt completely. I drop the knife and barely make it three steps before Wren's perfect breakfast comes back up in violent waves.

"This is harder than it looks," I say weakly, wiping my mouth with the back of my hand.

"Most first kills are," Blue says, and I can't tell if he's trying not to laugh. "Though I'll admit, I've never seen one accomplished through interpretive dance."

My stomach lurches again at the sight of Julian's lifeless form, and I press my hand to my mouth. "Oh god, I think I'm going to be sick again."

I stumble up the stone steps, leaving Blue and Julian's very dead body behind. By the time I reach my room, I'm running. I slam the door and lock it, then collapse onto the four-poster bed still wearing my perfect polka dot dress.

I killed him. I actually killed him.

By accident.

While having a panic attack.

This is either the most pathetic victory in the history of revenge, or the most ridiculous tragedy in the history of murder. I'm not sure which is worse.

But lying there staring at the painted ceiling, I can't shake the image of Julian's surprised expression when he realized he was dying, or the way his blood looked so much redder than I'd expected.

I did it. I killed one of my father's murderers.

Even if I did it completely by accident while waving a knife around like a deranged conductor.

God, what must Blue think? I was supposed to be some dangerous femme fatale, not a disaster who accidentally murders people and then pukes everywhere.

And with that thought . . . I bolt for the bathroom.

CHAPTER TWENTY-ONE
BLUE

The sound of running water from Saylor's bathroom tells me she's trying to wash away what happened in the basement. I stand outside her door for a full minute, listening to the rhythm of her movements through the heavy wood. Toothbrush against porcelain. Faucet turning on and off. The soft thud of a glass being set down with more force than necessary. She's angry at herself, which is exactly what I expected and precisely what I need to address before it festers into something that drives her away from what we both want.

But fuck, the way she threw up and ran—that's on me. I've been killing people for so long I forgot what it looks like to someone who hasn't had their soul scraped hollow by necessity. Peter would probably haunt my ass for even letting her near Julian, let alone handing her a blade and saying "have at it." What kind of friend puts his best mate's daughter in a basement with a tied-up psychopath and expects her to carve him up like Sunday dinner?

The truth is, watching her try to work up the nerve to slide steel into Julian's throat did something twisted to my insides. Part of me wanted her to do it—wanted to see that spark of darkness catch fire that I know lives in her. But a bigger part wanted to shield her from ever having to cross that line. Peter raised her to sing jazz and worry about rent money, not to develop a taste for arterial spray.

I knock gently. "Saylor?"

"Go away." It's muffled but clear enough to hear the embarrassment threading through the words. "I'm busy contemplating my complete failure as a human being."

"You're not a failure."

"I threw up on your basement floor and then ran away like a child." The bathroom door falls opens and I hear her footsteps crossing the room. "I'm pretty sure that qualifies as failing."

When she appears in the doorframe, she's got a toothbrush

sticking out of her mouth, foam dotting her lips, and somehow she still manages to look like something worth burning cities for.

"Throwing up just means you're still human," I say, leaning against the doorframe. "First time I killed someone, I puked for an hour and then couldn't eat meat for a week. Perfectly normal response to crossing that particular line."

She removes the toothbrush long enough to glare at me. "Yeah, well, most people don't have their first kill watched by someone who's apparently a professional at it."

"Most people don't have a very good reason to want someone dead. You do." I watch her face carefully. "And you got what you wanted. Julian's dead by your hand."

"Did I?" She disappears back into the bathroom, and I hear more aggressive tooth brushing. "Because from where I'm standing, that wasn't supposed to happen by accident. It's not how I pictured it at all."

Christ, I'm not used to this—giving pep talks to someone who's upset about how their first kill went down. In my world, people either kill or get killed. There's no middle ground, no hand-holding through the emotional aftermath. But here I am, trying to figure out how to comfort someone who accomplished exactly what she wanted, just not how she expected.

When she emerges again, her mouth is clean but her entire being is thunderous. She's working herself into a spiral, and I know from experience that spirals lead nowhere good.

"Walk with me," I say, stepping back to give her space.

"I don't want to walk anywhere. I want to hide in this room until everyone forgets I exist."

"Hiding never solved anything. Trust me, I've tried." I straighten my cuff links, a gesture that's become automatic when I'm trying to appear calm. "Besides, there's something I want to show you. Something that might help you understand me better."

"If it's another dead body, I'll probably faint."

"Something alive for a change. Revolutionary concept, I know."

Saylor considers this, her fingers worrying the fabric at her waist. "Will you answer questions while we walk? Honest answers, not your usual cryptic bullshit?"

"Depends how uncomfortable the questions make me feel. But I'll try."

"Fine." She grabs a black cardigan from the wardrobe. "But if I start crying or throwing up again, you're obligated to pretend it didn't happen."

"Deal."

We make our way downstairs, and I can feel the tension radiating from her with each step. She's building walls again, protecting herself from what she sees as weakness. The Saylor who asked me to teach her killing has retreated behind the Saylor who thinks she's not strong enough for this world.

Both versions are wrong about what strength actually is. But maybe that's my fault for throwing her into the deep end without teaching her how to swim first.

As we approach the front entrance, Hans appears around the corner of the house, dragging Julian's body wrapped in black plastic. Julian Crow, making his final exit from Maison Rouge.

Saylor stops dead, her eyes tracking Hans's progress across the garden path.

"Do you regret it?"

She's quiet for a long moment, watching Hans disappear behind a grove of apple trees. "No. But I'm not sure how I feel about it. And I hate that I'm not sure."

"Uncertainty means you're not a psychopath. Most people would feel conflicted after their first kill, even when it's justified."

"How do you do it?" The question comes out softer than her previous words. "How do you just . . . end someone and then go about your day like nothing happened?"

The honest answer? Years of practice and a conscience that's been scraped raw by doing what needs to be done. But she doesn't need to hear that.

"You learn to compartmentalize. Put the violence in a box, lock it away until you need it again." The morning light filters through trees, casting everything in dappled shadows. "The trick is remembering why you're doing it. Julian deserved what he got. Your father didn't."

"That's very philosophical for a murder."

"Killing without philosophy is just butchery. I prefer to think of myself as more selective than that."

Despite everything, her mouth twitches with what might be amusement. "Selective assassination. That's definitely going in my vocabulary."

The path winds between sculptures that weren't designed to soothe—stone angels with faces twisted in grief, fountains where water pours from stone hearts. Dark as hell, which suits my mood most days.

"These are cheerful," Saylor observes, pausing beside an angel whose hands are pressed to her face in a gesture of absolute despair.

"What can I say? I'm not really a garden-gnomes-and-happy-little-fountains kind of guy." I lead her past the fountain.

We move through the manicured sections into older territory, where pines spread their branches overhead and the forest floor is alive with mushrooms pushing up through the damp earth, slugs trailing silver across fallen logs, and moths fluttering between patches of shadow. Stone monuments emerge from the undergrowth like forgotten memories—weathered headstones and mausoleums that tell stories of lives cut short.

"Is this a cemetery?" Saylor asks, running her fingers along a headstone decorated with carved roses.

"Memorial garden. For people who needed to be remembered." I pause beside a monument topped with a stone raven. "Not all of them are buried here, but they all deserved acknowledgment."

"People you killed?"

"People who died because of choices I made." The distinction matters, although I'm not sure I can explain why. "Some were bastards who had it coming. Others were just in the wrong place when everything went to hell."

The weight of those deaths sits heavy in my chest—especially the innocent ones. The witnesses who saw too much, the bystanders caught in crossfire, the people who died because I wasn't smart enough or fast enough to save them. Each headstone in this garden represents a life that ended because of me, and some nights that knowledge feels like drowning.

Saylor traces the carved letters of a name I can't quite make out from this angle. "Do you regret any of them?"

"Every single innocent." The admission comes out rough. "The guilty ones? No. The world's better without them breathing. But the others . . ." I trail off, thinking about Peter and how his death still haunts me. "Those are the ones that follow you home."

The path curves ahead toward a structure I haven't shown anyone in years. The greenhouse rises from the garden like something conjured from shadow and light—all glass and twisted iron that catches the morning sun and throws it back in fractured rainbows.

Through the glass, I can see what five years and an obscene amount of money bought me. Orchids that shouldn't exist climb steel supports, their colors bordering on unnatural. Trees heavy with fruit that looks wrong—silver where it should be red, gold where it should be green. Vines wrap around columns in patterns that took three years to train properly.

And everywhere, absolutely everywhere, are roses. Roses in every color imaginable and several that shouldn't be possible. Blood-red roses the size of dinner plates, white roses so pure they seem to glow, black roses that absorb light rather than reflect it. Some climb the walls in cascading waterfalls of petals; others emerge from carefully tended beds in perfect geometric patterns.

In the heart of the greenhouse, a gazebo built from living trees creates a perfect circle of green walls and a flowering roof. The branches have been trained and woven together over years of careful tending, creating a structure that's both architectural and organic. Roses climb every surface, their blooms creating a canopy of color overhead, while the floor is carpeted in moss, thick like nature's own velvet.

"How is this possible?" Saylor breathes.

"Money, patience, and a very talented botanist who doesn't ask questions about my other hobbies." I push open the greenhouse door, and the scent of growing things washes over us in waves. "Welcome to the one place on the estate where nothing dies unless it's supposed to."

We step inside, and the temperature difference is immediately noticeable. The air is warm and humid, heavy with the perfume of a thousand different flowers and the green smell of things growing wild and free. Our footsteps are muffled by the moss that carpets the stone pathways, and everywhere we look, life explodes in patterns too beautiful to be accidental.

"This is insane," Saylor says, reaching out to touch an orchid whose petals seem to shimmer with their own inner light. "How long did this take to build?"

"Five years for the structure, another three to get the ecosystem balanced." I watch her explore with the fascination of someone discovering a new world. "It's my meditation space. When the killing gets too loud in my head, I come here and remember that I can create things as well as destroy them."

She pauses beside a tree whose branches are heavy with fruit that looks like crystallized honey. "Can I . . . ?"

"Everything in here is safe to touch. Most of it's safe to eat, although I'd avoid the silver berries unless you want to spend the next six hours seeing colors that don't exist."

Saylor laughs, the sound bright and genuine for the first time since this morning. "Hallucinogenic garden fruit. Of course you'd have hallucinogenic garden fruit."

"The botanist has a sense of humor."

We make our way toward the living gazebo at the center of the greenhouse, passing a fountain carved from a single piece of jade where water trickles down in patterns that seem to defy gravity. Butterfly bushes where actual butterflies rest in perfect stillness, their wings iridescent in the filtered light. A section where every plant glows with soft bioluminescence, creating an underwater feeling despite being surrounded by air.

When we reach the gazebo, Saylor stops just outside the entrance, her hand resting on one of the living posts. The roses growing here are unlike anything else in the greenhouse—deep blue petals that match my beard exactly, their blooms so perfect they look carved rather than grown.

"You grew roses that match your hair," she says, wonder threading through her voice.

"I had help. But yes." I watch her lean closer to inhale. "They don't exist anywhere else in the world."

"Just like you."

The comment hangs between us, and I'm not sure what to do with it. We step inside the gazebo, where the living walls create perfect privacy and the rose canopy overhead filters the remaining sunlight into something magical. The moss beneath our feet is so thick it's like walking on clouds, and the air itself seems to glitter with magic.

"This is where you bring women, isn't it?" Saylor asks, but there's no judgment in the question. "I mean . . . it's fucking impressive. I wouldn't blame you."

"I've never brought anyone here." The admission comes out before I can stop it. "You're the first."

She turns to face me fully, her dark eyes wide with something that might be surprise. "Ever?"

"Ever."

I step closer. "I created this place thinking I'd never want to share it with anyone. And then you came, and well . . ."

Her breath catches. "Blue . . ."

"I've never wanted to protect someone the way I want to protect you." I reach out to touch one of the blue roses, its petals soft as silk beneath my fingers. "I've never wanted to claim someone the way I want to claim you."

Understanding flares in her eyes, and when she steps closer, I can smell her perfume mixed with everything around us.

"Then claim me," she whispers.

I take a step back. "It's the killing talking."

"What?"

"This feeling—the need to fuck after violence. It happens every time you kill someone who deserves it." I run a hand through my hair, trying to create distance between us. "Your blood is still running hot from what happened in the basement. You think you want this, but it's just adrenaline."

She steps closer, closing the gap I tried to create. "Don't tell me what I'm feeling."

"Saylor—"

"No." Her voice is firm, her dark eyes blazing. "Don't you dare use my inexperience against me. Don't patronize me by saying I don't know my own mind." She reaches up, her fingers grazing the edge of my jaw. "I wanted you before I killed Julian. I wanted you ever since I saw you watching me at the White Note. And I wanted you last night when we kissed outside my bedroom door. This isn't about violence—it's about you."

I catch her wrist, but I don't pull her hand away. "Stop protecting me from what I want." Her thumb brushes across my bottom lip, and I feel my resolve cracking. "Stop protecting me from you."

The last of my self-control snaps.

Instead of answering with words, I cup her face in my hands. Her skin is warm beneath my palms, and when she tilts her head up to meet my gaze, I can see myself reflected in her dark eyes.

The space between us disappears as I lean down and she rises up on her toes, our mouths meeting in a kiss that tastes like forgiveness and promises and of hunger that's been building since the moment I first saw her sing. Her lips are soft and demanding, and when she makes a small sound of pleasure against my mouth, something in my chest ruptures open.

This kiss is different from last night's desperate collision outside her bedroom door. This one is deliberate, exploring, a conversation conducted through touch and breath and the way she threads her fingers through my hair.

When we finally break apart, we're both breathing hard, and I can see in her eyes the same hunger that's been eating me alive since she asked me to teach her violence.

"Tell me what you need," I say against her ear, my hands sliding down to rest at her waist.

"You," she says. "But not the gentleman who's been so careful with me. I want the man who wields the axe. I want you to stop holding back and fuck me like you mean it."

The rose petals fall around us like rain as I kiss her again, deeper this time, with all the control I've been holding on to finally slipping away.

In a greenhouse full of impossible flowers, with rose petals falling around us like blood-red rain, I can see the exact moment Saylor stops being the good girl who ran from violence.

And becomes the woman who's going to let me destroy her completely.

CHAPTER TWENTY-TWO
SAYLOR

When Blue kisses me, it's like tasting lightning and wildfire, and I want to burn from the inside out.

His hands slide down to my waist, fingers digging in with just enough pressure to remind me he's done this before and that this is the same man who would kill men without hesitation. The gentleman who's been so careful with me is nowhere to be found, and thank god for that because I'm done pretending I want soft touches and sweet words.

I want the psychopath who ordered his man to split open a corpse and stuff it with flowers like some twisted bouquet.

"If we do this," he says against my neck, "there's no going back. You understand that? I don't do the typical boyfriend and girlfriend. I don't do sweet and normal. I don't do vanilla in anything I do."

Instead of answering, I grab his shirt and pull him deeper into the gazebo, where the living walls close around us like a confession booth made of roses and shadows. The moss beneath my feet is thick enough to cushion anything, and when Blue's eyes go dark with understanding, I know he's thinking the same thing.

"I told you to stop holding back," I say, my hands already working at the buttons of his shirt. "I meant it."

I see something different . . . the last of his control cracking like ice under pressure. When he kisses me again, there's nothing gentle about it. His teeth catch my lower lip, his tongue claiming my mouth with an intensity that makes my knees weak. This is what I wanted. Not the careful guardian who's been protecting me, but the predator who kills without hesitation.

His hands are everywhere at once, fingers tangling in my hair to tilt my head back so he can trace his mouth along my throat. When his teeth graze the sensitive spot where my pulse hammers, I make a sound that would embarrass me if I cared about dignity anymore.

His hands find my zipper, and the sound of it sliding down

seems impossibly loud in the quiet of the gazebo. When he pauses, I grab his wrists and guide them back to my skin.

"Don't you dare stop," I whisper against his mouth, gripping his hard cock tenting his pants.

The sound he makes is purely animal . . . raw. It rakes through my insides and blots out the sky. I cling to him and let the dress fall to my hips.

Blue drops to his knees and runs his hands up my thighs, burying his face in my pussy and inhaling as his tongue licks a long line from my clit to my needy entrance. I gasp, my hands finding his shoulders for support as his tongue delves deeper, exploring every fold and crevice with a hunger that leaves me reeling.

He looks up at me, his eyes reflecting the muted light filtering through the rose petals, and the sight of him kneeling before me, his face buried in my most intimate place, sends a shockwave through me. It's not just the physical sensation, but the sheer intensity of his gaze, the unapologetic desire I see.

I feel like I'm falling, spiraling into an abyss where only Blue and this consuming need exist.

He grips my hips, his fingers digging into my flesh as he pulls me closer, his tongue delving deeper, setting off sparks behind my eyelids. I can barely breathe, my heart pounding so hard it might burst. When he focuses his attention on my clit, sucking and licking with a skill that leaves me gasping, I know I'm lost.

I tangle my fingers in his hair, holding him against me as I grind against his mouth, chasing the release that hovers just out of reach. His growl vibrates against my skin.

"Blue," I manage to gasp.

He knows what I need, and he doesn't make me wait. He slides two fingers inside me, curling them to hit that perfect spot, and I shatter.

"Look at me as you cum around my fingers," he orders.

My orgasm rips through me, leaving me a trembling, breathless mess. But I'm greedy and I want more. So much more.

"Fuck me, Blue. Fuck me."

He stands, wipes his mouth on the back of his hand, and looms over me, pupils blown wide and face greedy and unrepentant, the way only men like Blue can be. He shoves his slacks down just enough to free himself, and it's almost obscene how ready he is, how the shine on his lips matches the precum wetting the head of his cock.

He pulls out his wallet, then a condom, and within seconds we are both on the ground, him on top of me.

He grabs my thighs, spreads them, and when he thrusts inside it's slow at first, almost mocking, as if he's enjoying my helpless squirming. He leans in, bracing himself with a hand on the moss, the hollow of his throat damp with sweat, a vein pulsing in time with the force that builds inside us both.

"Mine," he mutters, lips flaring hot just above my ear. "Fucking mine."

The word tears something open in me. I can't think, can't breathe. I want to claw at his shoulders but I settle for digging my nails into his back, drawing him deeper, urging him to use me up.

He does exactly that.

He abandons that civilized cadence, gives himself over to the rhythm the animal in him demands—hard, urgent, like he could fuck the world apart and remake it from scratch.

There's a brutality to the way he moves, to the way neither of us is even pretending to care about the dirt, the stains, or how my ass is probably turning green from the friction on the moss.

He presses his lips to mine, biting more than kissing, and I taste blood, maybe mine or his, who cares. All I know is the way he fills me, how every thrust is like a dare—how far will I let him go, how much of myself am I willing to give up to this man.

He wraps an arm under my shoulders and slams in deeper, dragging my body up against his. I arch up, helpless, boneless, skin heated from the humid air and the warmth of his mouth at my jaw. The roses are everywhere, and dirt grinds into my back where my dress bunches at my waist, but all I see is the dark chaos of his eyes right above me.

All I want is this endless burn of his hard cock as he fucks me through the next orgasm, and into a third.

"This pussy is mine," he growls, shoving even deeper than I thought possible.

Again and again, he pounds into me, hips snapping as the gazebo seems to tremble with our violence. My pleasure doubles, then fractures into shards of raw sensation. I've never been fucked so hard in my life but I'm loving every painfully erotic second.

The world blurs at the edges. All I know is Blue, the shadow and weight of him above me, the taste of his name in my mouth when I beg for more. He gives it, relentless, until I can barely see through the pulsating in my temples. Until my legs lock around his hips and I scream into the moss, uncaring that someone—anyone—could be listening.

He bites down on my shoulder, not breaking skin but so close I'll carry the bruise for weeks. The thought thrills me. I want to be marked, to be claimed. I want everyone in Grimlock to see what Blue has done to me.

He shudders through his own climax, hips driving so deep and so hard I swear I feel every inch of him in my stomach, my throat, everywhere. He curses hot against my skin, throbbing inside me and spilling heat, the sound almost a growl.

"Fuck," he pants. "Fuuuuuck."

Blue collapses on top of me, and for a minute we just breathe.

I'm pretty sure I have moss in my underwear. Well, what's left of my underwear. Also rose petals stuck to places that are going to be awkward to explain to Wren if she does my laundry.

"Well," I say when I finally catch my breath, "that was definitely not vanilla."

His laugh rumbles through his chest, vibrating against me. "I did warn you."

"You did. Although I feel like there should have been a more detailed disclaimer. Something about potential moss stains and the risk of being permanently ruined for all other men."

"Permanently ruined?" He lifts his head to look at me, and there's something almost boyish in his satisfaction. "Good."

I trace my finger along his jaw, feeling the roughness of his beard. "You know, most people have sex in beds. Like civilized humans."

"Most people are boring." He presses a kiss to my throat, right where he bit me. "Besides, you're the one who told me to stop holding back."

"Fair point. Although I'm pretty sure I have dirt in places that should never see dirt."

"I'll help you wash it off later." The way he says it makes me want him again, which should be impossible given what we just did.

"Later?" I raise an eyebrow. "Already planning round two?"

"Round two, three, four . . ." He grins against my skin. "I'm a very thorough man, Saylor. When I claim something as mine, I make sure it stays claimed."

The possessiveness in his voice makes me clench my thighs together. "Territorial bastard."

"Guilty as charged."

He rolls off me finally, but the air in here is so thick and humid that my skin stays slick with sweat. I sit up, trying to assess the damage to my dress while Blue deals with the condom and adjusts his clothes. My hair has definitely seen better days, and there are definitely going to be some interesting bruises tomorrow.

"I look like I got in a fight with your garden and lost," I observe, attempting to finger-comb rose petals out of my hair.

"You look perfect." Blue's voice is rough with sincerity. "You look exactly like what you are."

"Which is?"

"Someone who just figured out she likes getting dirty."

Before I can respond to that loaded statement, his phone starts ringing. The sound is jarring in our rose-scented bubble, dragging us back to reality with all the subtlety of a fire alarm.

Blue glances at the screen and frowns. "I should—"

"Take it," I say, still working on my hair situation. "Don't mind me."

He declines the call and helps me to my feet instead, his hands gentle as he checks me over for any actual damage. The phone immediately starts ringing again.

"Popular man," I tease, but there's something in Blue's energy that makes my stomach tighten.

He declines again. The ringing stops for maybe ten seconds before starting up once more.

"Jesus Christ." Blue's jaw clenches as he looks at the screen. "Hans doesn't call unless—" The phone keeps ringing. "I'm sorry, I have to take this."

"Hans?" he answers, and even from where I'm standing I can hear the rapid-fire German coming through the speaker. Blue's entire demeanor morphs, the satisfied post-sex contentment draining from his face like water through a sieve.

Whatever Hans is saying, it's not good news.

"How many?" Blue asks. More rapid German. "When?"

I watch Blue's face darken with each word, his free hand clenching into a fist at his side. The man who was just worshipping my body with his mouth has disappeared, replaced by someone calculating and deadly.

"No, don't engage. Pull back and wait for me." Blue runs his hand through his hair, suddenly looking like he's juggling a dozen different worst-case scenarios. "How long do we have?"

Hans says something that makes Blue curse under his breath.

"Pull the car around," Blue says finally. "I'll be there in a minute."

He ends the call and turns to me, his expression apologetic but grim. "I'm sorry. I have to go."

"What's wrong?" The question comes out like I'm a damsel in distress and I hate it.

"Nothing you need to worry about, but I need to handle it personally." He cups my face in his hands, thumbs stroking my cheekbones. "I'll probably miss dinner. Make yourself at home. There's a library on the second floor, the kitchen's always open. Wren will take care of whatever you need."

"Blue—"

"I'll be back as soon as I can. I promise." He kisses me, hard and quick, like he's trying to memorize the taste of me. "Don't wait up."

And then he's gone, striding through the greenhouse like he's already forgotten I exist.

I stand there trying to process the whiplash. Five minutes ago he was inside me, and now he's running toward whatever emergency Hans just dropped in his lap.

CHAPTER TWENTY-THREE
SAYLOR

I've been alone in this house for exactly forty-three minutes, and I'm already losing my mind. I'm sitting at the black Steinway in the main hall, my fingers finding random keys like they're searching for something familiar in all this ridiculous grandeur. The notes echo off the vaulted ceilings and disappear into corners I can't even see, swallowed by a house too big for any reasonable person to call home. Each chord I play sounds like a ghost trying to communicate, which is exactly the kind of melodramatic bullshit my brain doesn't need right now.

The piano bench creaks when I shift my weight, and even that small sound gets amplified and twisted by the acoustics until it sounds like the house itself is complaining about my presence. I try a few bars of "Summertime," but the melody gets lost in all that empty space, turning sultry jazz into something that belongs in a horror movie soundtrack.

"This is ridiculous," I mutter, closing the piano lid with more force than necessary. The bang reverberates through the hall like a gunshot, making me jump at my own dramatic gesture.

I need to find somewhere smaller. Somewhere that doesn't make me feel like I'm performing for an audience of painted eyes and stone statues.

The library seems like a logical choice. What self-respecting Gothic mansion doesn't have a cozy library with leather chairs and a crackling fireplace? But when I push open the heavy doors, I realize I've made a serious miscalculation about what constitutes *cozy* in Blue's world.

The library is fucking enormous. Not just big—cathedral enormous, with shelves that stretch up three stories and a ceiling painted with scenes of angels and demons locked in eternal combat. Rolling ladders on brass tracks provide access to books so high up they might as well be in orbit, and the whole space is lit by chandeliers that cast more shadows than actual light. It's beautiful in the same way that thunderstorms are beautiful. Impressive as hell but not exactly inviting.

A massive fireplace dominates one wall, its mantelpiece carved with thorny roses and ravens that seem to watch me move through the room. The hearth is cold and empty, no wood in sight, and I have zero idea how to build a fire anyway. The whole space feels like it's about ten degrees colder than the rest of the house, which is already approaching arctic.

I pull my cardigan tighter and wander between the stacks, running my fingers along leather spines that look older than American democracy. First edition classics mixed with books written in languages I don't recognize, their titles embossed in gold that catches the dim light. Everything smells like old paper and expensive leather and money that gets passed down through generations.

But it's too quiet. Too big. Too much like being alone in a museum after hours.

I give up on the library and drift back toward the main hall, my footsteps ringing against floors that probably came from some Italian quarry where they carved headstones for princes. The sound follows me like a lonely echo, reminding me how completely alone I am in this beautiful, haunting place.

Halfway down the grand staircase, I stop.

The portraits are watching me again. All those beautiful women with their knowing eyes and mysterious smiles. But this time, instead of hurrying past like I did when I was trying to escape, I actually look at them. Really look.

The first one shows a woman maybe five years older than me with platinum blonde hair pulled back in an elegant updo. She's wearing a flowing emerald dress that looks expensive, and her smile is radiant—genuine in a way that reaches her eyes. The nameplate reads "Cordelia."

Next to her, a brunette, her hair in loose waves, wears a simple cream blouse and dark jeans, casual but polished. She's holding a single blue rose—one of those impossible blooms from Blue's greenhouse—and her smile is small but warm. "Margaret."

The pattern continues down the wall. "Eleanor" in a soft pink sweater that brings out the warmth in her brown eyes, her smile quiet but real. "Vivian" with her dark hair styled in modern layers, wearing a burgundy blazer over dark pants, looking directly at the camera with steady confidence. "Catherine" with long blonde hair cascading over one shoulder, dressed in a flowing bohemian-style top, her eyes bright and clear. "Sophia" in a tailored navy jacket that screams professional success, her posture straight, chin lifted slightly.

All recent, from the look of the clothing. All holding single blue roses. All with natural, unforced smiles.

"Holy shit," I whisper to the empty hallway.

Duffy's warnings echo in my memory: "The rumors say Blue's had seven wives, Saylor. Seven."

I had dismissed it as gossip. Small town rumors about the mysterious rich guy with the Gothic mansion. But here are seven portraits of beautiful women, all with that same kind of smile, all holding his signature blue roses.

Blue never said much when Duffy mentioned the wife rumors. When I'd laughed about it and called the whole thing ridiculous, he'd just said, "Small towns love their stories," with that unreadable expression of his.

My mouth goes dry as I count them again. One, two, three, four, five, six, seven. Exactly seven, just like the rumors said. Seven women who all look content in a way that's hard to define.

But what happened to them? And why do the rumors insist they were wives?

And Blue's one rule about the house: The third floor is off-limits. Private. His.

What could he be keeping up there that requires such secrecy?

The thought makes me restless, making my palms go clammy. Blue specifically asked me to avoid the third floor. Said it was private, like he was protecting his personal space. But what if he wasn't protecting his privacy? What if he was protecting his secrets?

I shouldn't go upstairs. I know I shouldn't. Blue asked me to respect his one boundary, and given everything he's done for me, I owe him that much trust.

But doubt is a poison that spreads through every rational thought. I can't stop staring at Margaret's face, at the way she looks so young and hopeful. Can't stop wondering what happened to her, to all of them.

I can't stop thinking about the way Blue looked at me in the greenhouse, possessiveness when he said I was his to claim.

What happens when he gets tired of claiming me? When the novelty wears off and I become just another beautiful thing he wants to keep forever?

My feet are moving before my brain catches up, carrying me up the remaining stairs, past the second-floor landing, toward territory I've never explored. The hallway that leads to the third floor is different from the rest of the house—narrower, with lower ceilings that make everything feel more intimate and claustrophobic.

At the top of the stairs, I find a door I haven't seen before. Heavy wood painted deep midnight blue, with an ornate iron handle that's cold beneath my palm. When I turn it, the door opens with the smooth silence of expensive hinges and regular maintenance.

The sight beyond stops me completely.

The hallway stretches ahead like a city block, lined with doors on both sides like the world's most elegant hotel corridor. But it's what hangs from the ceiling that makes my breath catch. Hundreds of skeleton keys suspended on nearly invisible wire, creating a curtain of brass and iron that sways gently in air currents I can't feel. They range from tiny delicate things no bigger than my thumb to massive medieval-looking contraptions that could unlock castle gates.

Each key catches the light from wall sconces positioned between the doors, creating patterns of shadow and gleam that shift and dance with every slight movement. The whole thing gives me the creeps, but I can't stop staring.

And the doors. Jesus, the doors.

Each one is different. Some painted in rich jewel tones, others natural wood polished to mirror brightness, a few that look like they're covered in fabric or leather. But they all have one thing in common: intricate keyholes that seem to beckon like dark, judging eyes.

I move deeper into the hallway, my footsteps muffled by a runner carpet so thick my heels sink into it with each step. The keys hang just low enough that I have to duck slightly to avoid them, their metal surfaces catching the light as I pass beneath. Some of them look newer than others, like they've been polished recently.

The first door I try is painted deep burgundy with a keyhole shaped like a heart. The handle turns under my hand, but the door doesn't budge. Locked, just like I somehow knew it would be.

The second door, this one covered in blue velvet, is also locked. As is the third, painted silver with a keyhole surrounded by carved roses.

Every door I try stays stubbornly closed, their keyholes dark and secretive. But one of those keys hanging overhead has to fit each lock. That's the only reason for such a display. Blue hasn't just locked these rooms; he's turned the whole process into some kind of elaborate puzzle.

The hallway seems to stretch forever, with more doors than any reasonable person could need. What could possibly require this much secured storage space? Art collection? Wine cellar? Historic artifacts?

Or seven wives who asked too many questions?

Christ, listen to me. I'm starting to sound like one of those true crime podcasts.

I'm halfway down the hallway when curiosity finally wins over common sense. I kneel beside a door painted the color of dried blood, pressing my eye to the keyhole like some Victorian gossip trying to spy on the neighbors.

It's too dark to see anything clearly, but there's definitely a room beyond the door. And something pale that might be fabric. Or skin. Or—

"I told you not to go to the third floor."

I jump so hard I nearly fall backward onto the carpet. I scramble to my feet, adrenaline spiking through my system as I turn to face him.

Blue's standing at the other end of the hallway, still wearing the clothes he left in, but now they are rumpled and stained with something dark across his shirt front. His hair is disheveled, like he's been in a fight, a storm, or both, and there's something in the way he looks at me that makes every instinct scream at me to run.

But there's nowhere to go except past him, and something tells me that's not happening.

"You're back early," I say, trying for casual and missing by about a mile. "I thought you'd miss dinner."

"Plans changed." He starts walking toward me, his footsteps silent on the thick carpet. "Care to explain why you're kneeling in front of doors you have no business opening?"

"I wasn't—I mean, I didn't open anything." The words tumble out too fast, making me sound exactly as guilty as I am. "I was just curious about the keys. They're beautiful. Very . . . decorative."

Blue stops about six feet away, close enough that I can see the muscle jumping in his jaw but far enough that I can't read his face clearly in the dim light.

"Curious," he repeats, his tone suggesting curiosity might be a capital offense in his world.

"I'm sorry. I know you said the third floor was private, but I was alone in this enormous house and I got bored and started wandering and—" I'm babbling now, words spilling out like I can somehow explain away the fact that I'm obviously snooping through his most personal space. "I didn't actually go into any rooms. I tried the handles but they're all locked anyway, so really I was just looking at the hallway, which is honestly very impressive from an interior design perspective—"

"Saylor."

The way he says my name makes me stop mid-sentence.

"We have dinner guests waiting downstairs," he says. "We can talk about this later."

Dinner guests. Right. Because nothing says "I'm definitely not hiding seven dead wives in my coffin manor," like hosting a dinner party immediately after catching your current girlfriend snooping around locked doors.

"Dinner guests?" I repeat. "Right now?"

"They're waiting downstairs." His tone shows this isn't up for negotiation.

"Blue, about what just happened—"

"Later." He steps aside, gesturing toward the stairs with exaggerated politeness that feels more like a threat. "After you."

As I walk past him toward the staircase, trying to project confidence I definitely don't feel, I catch a glimpse of his glare in my peripheral vision.

He's not angry.

He's calculating.

And somehow, that's infinitely worse.

CHAPTER TWENTY-FOUR
BLUE

Wren has truly outdone herself with tonight's table setting. The crystal gleams, the silver is polished to mirror brightness, and our three dinner guests are tied so expertly to their chairs that they could pass for enthusiastic participants if you ignored the duct tape.

I guide Saylor into the dining room with my hand at the small of her back, feeling the tension radiating through her body as she takes in the scene. Leroy "The Prince" Crow sits to the immediate right of where Saylor normally sits, his refined features twisted with fury despite the gag. Jack "The Knife" Crow occupies the chair across from him, while Victor "The Veteran" Crow, the old-school gangster with the cane sword, completes our dinner party triumvirate.

"Gentlemen," I say pleasantly, pulling out Saylor's chair next to Leroy with the courtesy of a perfect host. "So pleased you could join us for dinner."

"What the hell?" Saylor whispers as I guide her into the seat.

Leroy makes muffled sounds of outrage behind his gag. I wave dismissively.

"Please, no need to thank me for the invitation. It's my absolute pleasure."

Hans stands at attention near the sideboard, looking like a bouncer at the world's most exclusive restaurant. His black suit is immaculate, his posture perfect, and he's eyeing our guests as if he's calculating exactly how many seconds it would take to snap their necks if things go sideways.

"Wren has prepared something special tonight," I continue, settling into my chair. "Braised short ribs with seasonal vegetables. I do hope you're hungry."

I catch Saylor's eye and nod almost imperceptibly toward the large carving knife positioned next to her place setting. It's a beautiful piece—German steel with an ebony handle, sharp enough to split hairs. Or fingers. Or whatever else might need splitting.

The way her gaze flicks between the knife and Leroy tells me she understands exactly what I'm offering her.

Wren appears with the first course, serving soup with the same unflappable grace she'd use for a state dinner. She doesn't bat an eye at our bound guests, though she does pause to straighten Leroy's napkin with motherly care.

"Butternut squash bisque," she announces. "With brown butter and sage."

"Smells divine," I say, lifting my spoon. "Doesn't it smell divine, gentlemen?"

Jack glares at me over his gag. Victor tries to lean forward aggressively but only manages to make his chair groan under the strain.

"Oh, right," I say, as if just remembering. "You can't exactly participate in dinner conversation at the moment. Hans, would you mind helping our guests with their dietary restrictions?"

Hans approaches Leroy first, removing his gag with the careful attention of someone defusing a bomb. The moment his mouth is free, Leroy starts talking.

"You're fucking insane if you think—"

"Language," I interrupt mildly. "We're at dinner. There are standards."

Leroy's aristocratic features contort with rage. "You can't just kidnap us and play house. The Crow know where we are. They'll come looking."

"I'm counting on it." I take a delicate spoonful of soup. "More guests for future dinner parties."

Hans moves to Jack next, peeling away the tape with surprising gentleness. Jack immediately spits a stream of curses that would make a sailor blush.

"Hans," I sigh. "Perhaps you could help our guests remember their manners?"

Without hesitation, Hans picks up Leroy's soup spoon and shoves a generous portion of bisque into his mouth. Leroy sputters and chokes, but Hans holds his jaw firmly until he swallows.

"Jesus," Leroy gasps once he can breathe again. "That's actually fucking delicious."

"Wren will be so pleased you approve," I say warmly. "She takes great pride in her cooking."

Hans moves on to Jack, who tries to turn his head away but gets a spoonful of soup anyway. His eyes widen with surprise before he can stop himself.

"Damn," Jack mutters. "What's in this?"

Hans removes Victor's gag last, and the old gangster immediately works his jaw like he's testing for damage.

"Family recipe," Wren calls from the kitchen. "Roasted bones for the stock."

"What kind of bones?" Victor asks, then immediately looks like he regrets speaking.

"Best not to ask too many questions about Wren's ingredients," I advise. "She's very creative with her sourcing."

Victor clears his throat pointedly. "So, Blue. Heard you were retired. What's all this then? Midlife crisis?"

"Something like that," I agree pleasantly, tearing my bread roll in half. "Turns out retirement doesn't suit me."

"You're completely fucking insane," Jack states with the confidence of someone making a weather observation.

"Guilty as charged," I say, raising my wine glass in a mock toast. "Thank you for noticing. I do try to maintain professional standards."

Leroy snorts. "Professional standards? You've kidnapped three people and are serving us soup like we're old friends catching up."

"Are we not?" I ask with genuine surprise. "I thought we were having a lovely time. Hans, are we not having a lovely time?"

"Is very nice dinner party, Boss," Hans confirms while straightening the napkins. "Very civilized conversation."

"See? Hans agrees. We're practically family now."

Saylor has been quiet through this entire exchange, mechanically eating her soup while shooting glances at the carving knife. I can see the wheels turning in her head, weighing options, building courage.

I catch her eye and nod almost imperceptibly toward Leroy, then glance meaningfully at the knife. *Do it,* I mouth silently when the others aren't looking. *Take it.*

She looks uncertain, so I try again. *For your father*, I mouth, attempting to be encouraging.

"So," Leroy says, apparently deciding to try charm over aggression. "Saylor, right? You're even prettier than your photos suggested. Peter talked about you constantly."

Saylor's spoon freezes halfway to her mouth. "Oh really? You knew my father?"

There's my girl. I can see she's starting to toy with him.

"Knew him? Hell, I was there when we killed him." Leroy's smile is pure cruelty. "Watched him bleed out like the pathetic waste of space he was."

The temperature in the room drops about ten degrees. I set down my spoon very carefully.

"That's an interesting dinner conversation choice," I observe.

But Leroy is warming to his theme, apparently mistaking Saylor's silence for weakness. "Poor bastard." His laugh is like broken glass. "Should have seen his face when he realized he was going to die."

Saylor's knuckles are white around her spoon. I shift slightly in my chair, ready to intervene if necessary, but something in her actions—or lack of actions—tells me to wait.

"You want to know what his last words were?" Leroy leans forward as much as his restraints allow. "He said—"

The carving knife is in Saylor's hand before Leroy finishes the sentence.

"I know what he said," she says with deadly calm. "I was there when you killed my father."

She drives the blade straight through Leroy's hand, pinning it to the armrest with a wet thunk that booms through the dining room. Blood spurts immediately, painting the white tablecloth in abstract patterns that would make an amateur painter jealous.

Leroy's scream tears through the dining room, all his aristocratic composure cracking like expensive china. The sound bounces off the chandelier and seems to multiply, filling the room with harmonic agony.

"Oops," Saylor says conversationally, but her face has gone completely white. "That looks like it hurts."

She's gripping the edge of the table now, her knuckles white as she stares at the blood still pumping from Leroy's impaled hand. Her throat works like she's trying to swallow something back down, and I can see the exact moment nausea hits her.

Come on, love, I think, watching her jaw clench with determination. *You can do this. Fight through it.*

She takes a shaky breath, closes her eyes for a second, and I think she's got it under control. *Good girl. That's it. Show them what you're made of.*

But then Leroy jolts in his chair, and the movement sends a fresh spurt of blood across the white tablecloth. Saylor's eyes snap open, focus on the crimson spreading like spilled wine, and her face goes from pale to green.

"Oh shit," she whispers.

I'm already lunging forward when she starts to topple, catching her just before she can plant her face in the butternut squash bisque.

"Hans," I call, lifting Saylor into my arms. "Keep our guests company. I'll be back shortly."

"What about his hand?" Jack asks, staring at the blood still dripping from Leroy's impaled appendage.

"What about it?" I adjust my grip on Saylor, her head lolling against my shoulder. "Consider it an appetizer."

I carry her from the dining room while Leroy continues screaming things like, "You fucking psycho bitch!" and "I'll shove that knife so far up your ass you'll taste steel!"

Hans's voice follows us up the stairs as he tries to console our guests. "Is not so bad," he's saying in his thick accent. "Lots of blood makes everything look worse than it is. Here, try some bread. Very good bread. Wren makes from scratch."

The screaming stops abruptly, replaced by muffled sounds of appreciation.

"See? Much better when mouth is full of carb."

I push open the door to my bedroom with my shoulder, carrying Saylor across the threshold like some twisted version of a wedding night. She's starting to stir in my arms, her eyelashes fluttering against her pale cheeks.

My bedroom is the one space in Maison Rouge that's purely mine—no guest accommodations, no consideration for anyone else's comfort. The walls are painted deep charcoal, the furniture is all mahogany and leather, and the massive four-poster bed dominates the space like an altar to hedonism.

I settle Saylor onto the black silk sheets, smoothing her hair away from her face as she slowly returns to consciousness. When her eyes finally focus on mine, there's something new there. Something darker.

"Did I really stab him in the fucking hand?" she asks quietly.

"You sure did. I'm proud of you."

"I think I'm going to be sick again."

"Perfectly normal reaction. Violence takes practice." I brush my thumb across her cheekbone. "How do you feel about it? The stabbing, not the nausea."

She considers this with the serious attention the question deserves. "I think knives might not be my thing," she says finally. "All that blood. God, what kind of wannabe killer says blood isn't their thing?"

She sounds genuinely annoyed with herself, like she's failed some sort of basic life skill.

"It's honest." I lean down to press a kiss to her forehead. "And Leroy deserved every inch of that blade. Every killer has their own way, love. I choose the axe, some choose a gun, some choose—"

"No gun," she says quickly. "I actually want the kill to be drawn out."

"See? You already know what you don't want. We'll figure out exactly what your style is. No need to rush it."

"I feel like the worst student," she says with a frustrated sigh. "Like I'm getting an F in murder."

"At least a solid C+," I assure her. "You did pin his hand to the chair on your first try."

I've never found a woman sexier than she is right now—hair mussed, cheeks flushed, still holding the memory of how perfect that knife looked in her grip. The way she wielded that blade, the deadly calm in her voice . . . she's speaking my love language.

From downstairs comes the sound of Hans attempting to maintain dinner conversation with three hostile dinner guests, one of whom is still bleeding on my antique chairs.

"Should we go back down?" Saylor asks, but she makes no move to sit up.

"Not unless you want to experiment more tonight." I trace the curve of her jaw with my fingertip. "But you've had enough for one evening. I'll have Hans store them on ice for later—no need to act now." I reluctantly pull away from the bed. "Rest here. I'll handle the cleanup and be back shortly."

"Blue?" She catches my hand before I can leave. "Thank you. For letting me be the one to hurt him."

"You're welcome," I say simply. "Baby steps."

As I head back downstairs, Leroy is still making pathetic noises about his hand.

Just another evening at Maison Rouge.

Leroy's still screaming.

And I'm already planning tomorrow's lesson.

CHAPTER TWENTY-FIVE
SAYLOR

The last thing I remember before sleep claimed me was Blue's hand smoothing my hair back from my face, promising he'd handle the cleanup downstairs. I wake up disoriented in a bed that's definitely not mine, sinking into a mattress so soft it's like floating on toasted marshmallows. The sheets beneath me are actual silk, not the cheap knockoff stuff from discount stores. Heavy burgundy curtains block most of the light, and I have no idea if it's evening or the middle of the night. A fireplace crackles across the room, throwing shadows on walls covered with oil paintings of shipwrecks and ravens. Everything about this space screams expensive but also mysterious.

How long was I out? The last clear memory I have is driving a carving knife through Leroy Crow's hand and watching his blood paint the white tablecloth. Then my stomach decided to stage a rebellion, and apparently my brain followed suit by shutting down completely.

The shower is running in the adjoining bathroom, steam drifting through the partially open door along with the sound of water against tile. I sit up slowly, testing my stomach's current stance on being vertical. Better. Still shaky, but no immediate threat of losing whatever's left in my system.

My dress is wrinkled but still intact, my hair probably resembles a bird's nest, and I can still taste that metallic tang of adrenaline on my tongue. But I'm alive, conscious, and Leroy Crow is hopefully still bleeding somewhere in this house.

The water shuts off with a decisive click, followed by the rustle of towels and Blue's low humming. Something that sounds vaguely eerie but in a way that's oddly soothing. Steam billows out as the bathroom door opens wider, and then Blue emerges wearing nothing but a towel wrapped around his waist and water droplets that catch the lamplight.

Jesus Christ.

I've seen him partially undressed before. Felt his hands on my skin, tasted the salt of his sweat. But this is different. This is Blue in his natural environment, completely at ease in his own skin, and the sight of him makes my mouth go dry.

His chest is a masterpiece of controlled power, lean muscle and definition without being overly bulky. The tattoos I glimpsed in my dressing room cover his torso in intricate patterns that seem to tell stories I'm dying to read with my fingertips. Dark ink swirls across his ribs, over his shoulders, down his arms in patterns that make me want to lick every single one. Water beads along his collarbone and trails down paths between muscles, and I find myself following those droplets with my eyes. His hair is slicked back and darker when wet, making his bone structure appear even more defined.

The way he moves around the room is casual, confident. Completely at ease.

"You're awake," he says. "How are you feeling?"

"I just stabbed someone in the hand and then passed out with all the dignity of a Victorian lady with the vapors." I pull my knees up to my chest, wrapping my arms around them. "Very dignified. I'm sure Leroy was impressed by my follow-through."

Blue's mouth curves into what might be amusement. "Leroy is more concerned with his hand at the moment. Hans had to call in reinforcements to stop the bleeding."

"Good." The vicious satisfaction in my voice surprises me, but I don't try to hide it. "I hope it hurts."

"Well, about that . . ." He moves to the dresser, water still dripping from his hair onto those incredible shoulders. "They're currently enjoying the hospitality of my basement. All three of them." Blue says this like he's discussing the weather. "Turns out they weren't quite ready for the evening to end."

I should feel something more than satisfaction. Horror, maybe. Guilt. These were human beings, and now they're locked in a basement because of choices I made. Because I picked up that knife and drove it through Leroy's hand.

But all I feel is relief. They can't hurt anyone else now. Can't kill another father in front of his daughter.

"Is that where you went?" I ask. "To get them?"

"Just the three who joined us for dinner. Leroy, Jack, and Victor." Blue opens a dresser drawer, rifling through whatever's inside. "Hans got word on where they were hiding. After what happened in the greenhouse, I thought the least I could do was bring you a gift."

Three of the five from my list. Leroy with his gold tooth. Victor with his limp. And Jack in his expensive suit—the one who gave all the orders that night.

"And the others? The rest of the Crow?"

"Still breathing, unfortunately. But not for long." He glances at me over his shoulder. "One problem at a time."

The matter-of-fact way he discusses hunting down the remaining members of a criminal organization should probably worry me. Instead, it makes me feel safer than I have since Dad died.

"Blue, about earlier." I start, then stop when I realize I'm not sure which earlier incident needs to be addressed first. The snooping through his private floor, the sex, the stabbing, or the fainting. "I mean, about the third floor. I'm sorry I went up there when you specifically asked me not to."

He pauses in his search through the dresser drawers, his back still to me. "Are you?"

"Am I what?"

"Sorry." He turns to face me. "Because breaking into locked areas of my house means you're either not sorry at all, or you're sorry you got caught."

The distinction shouldn't matter, but somehow it does. "I was curious. I was exploring this massive place and . . . well, I've never been good at being told no."

"And what exactly did you discover during your unauthorized exploration?"

"A lot of locked doors and a serious addiction to decorative keys." I try for lightness, but his stare is too intense. "I didn't actually get into any of the rooms."

"No, you didn't." His tone is conversational, but there's steel underneath. "Although not for lack of trying."

Heat floods my cheeks. "I said I was sorry."

"You did." Blue opens another drawer, his movements deliberate. "But breaking rules has consequences, Saylor. And a punishment is in order."

"Punishment?" I let out a short laugh. "You're joking, right?"

Instead of answering, he reaches into the drawer and pulls out something that makes my brain stutter to a complete stop.

Handcuffs.

Not toy handcuffs from some novelty store, but real ones. Heavy steel with chain links. He holds them casually, testing the weight in his palm.

"Wait, what?" I scramble backward on the bed until my spine hits the headboard. "What are those for?"

"Your punishment."

"For examining locked doors?"

"For disobeying a direct request when I specifically asked you to stay away." Another step closer. "For breaking into areas of my house that are explicitly off-limits."

"I didn't break into anything. I just examined . . ."

"You tried every door handle in that hallway." His voice drops lower. "You knelt down to peer through a keyhole. You invaded my privacy after I specifically asked you not to."

Guilt and arousal war in my chest, creating a cocktail of emotions. He's right. I did exactly what he's accusing me of, and I'd probably do it again given the chance.

"What are you going to do with those?" I nod toward the handcuffs, my mouth suddenly dry.

"Whatever I want." The promise makes me clench my thighs together. "I warned you I don't do gentle. I'm not the vanilla, strawberries-and-champagne-by-candlelight kind of guy. The question is whether you're going to make this easy or difficult."

I stare at him—standing there half-naked with handcuffs, having just captured three people—and realize I'm not afraid. An ordinary girl would be scared shitless, but what I feel is anticipation.

"That depends," I say. "Are you planning to hurt me?"

"Only in ways you'll enjoy."

The way he says it makes something clench deep inside me,

urgent and needy and completely at odds with any rational response to this situation.

"Blue . . ."

"Hands," he commands, moving close enough that I can smell his shower soap mixed with something I desperately want to lick off him.

I don't hesitate, not really. I flatten my palms together, wrists daintily crossed and held out in front of me like a damsel or a saint awaiting the sword.

The metal is icy against my skin, biting down when he clicks the restraint shut.

"Up," Blue says, and hooks his fingers under my chin. The mood in his eyes is menacing, but I don't look away.

Then his towel is gone, peeled off and tossed to the floor. His cock is impossibly thick and hard already, flushed at the tip, and the sight of him standing over me, fully naked and utterly in control, flips some secret breaker in the caveman part of my brain.

The world goes soft at the edges. He sits on the bed and pulls me into his lap, my cuffed arms caught between our chests. My knees straddle his hips, the fabric of my dress riding up so far it's practically a belt. Blue pushes the hem even higher, rough hands sliding under to find bare skin at the backs of my thighs.

"You didn't obey," he says, mouth against my ear. "You're going to pay for it."

"Yeah?" I want what's coming so badly my body aches. "How?"

He reaches behind me, finds the zipper. One tug and my dress peels open, the angle awkward with my arms stuck in front of me. He yanks the straps off my shoulders and exposes my bra, black-and-lace, probably twisted and misshapen from the night's misadventures. The way he stares at my chest makes my nipples pebble beneath the thin mesh.

He tugs the straps down, pulls the cups lower, palms my tits like he's weighing them for a recipe. Grazes his thumb over the nipple until I gasp. Then pinches. Hard.

"Ow," I say, and squirm, but my hips roll into his lap on instinct.

His teeth are at my throat, scraping gently, then sinking in. "You'll take exactly what I give you."

His hands work the dress and bra off me, tearing what's left to get over the handcuffs. He makes a sound deep in his chest, a little snarl, then flips me flat onto the mattress, face-down, ass high in the air.

He kneels over me, tugs my hips back, and bites a line up the inside of my thigh. My body's gone boneless, floating in endorphin soup already. Blue presses a warm palm to the small of my back, holding me steady as his other hand slides up the backs of my thighs and between them.

He doesn't ask permission. Just hooks a finger under the lace and rips my panties down to my knees, cold air kissing the heat of my exposed cunt. I whimper, more from bashfulness than pain, and grip the sheet with my cuffed hands.

Two fingers between my legs now, blunt and thick, finding me soaked. He spreads me open and touches with deliberate slowness, just enough friction to make me buck against his hand.

"I could make you come like this," Blue says, lazy and cruel. "But I think you'd rather beg."

"I won't," I manage, but it's pure bravado, and he knows it.

He slides his fingers out, leaving me aching and empty. Then he smacks my ass, a pop that makes my whole body jolt forward on the bedspread.

"Count," Blue says.

I don't hesitate. "One."

He spanks harder, the sting blossoming into molten want. "Two," I breathe, before he even asks.

He delivers five, each strike landing precisely where it'll burn the longest. My ass prickles with heat, and my head empties of everything but this: him, the pain, the electric connection.

Then he gently rubs his palm over the reddened skin, soothing and almost tender. "Good girl," he murmurs. "Now, turn over."

I obey, rolling onto my back. He props me up with pillows, arranges my arms above me so the chain bites prettily into my wrists. There's no way to cover myself, so I don't even try; my thighs are already spread. Just like what he did to my ass, he does to my pussy. Spanking my folds as I gasp with each sting. He smirks at the rivers on my cheeks—I didn't realize I'd been crying, the release so sudden and intense.

Blue stands at the edge of the bed, looking down at me. "You want to say something?"

I should want more. Mercy, maybe, or at least a few seconds to compose myself. But what I want is to see what he'll orchestrate next. So I shake my head.

He climbs onto the bed, and his hands are everywhere at once: locking around my thighs, spreading me until muscles ache, then—without warning—filling me with three thick fingers at once. My body convulses, tries to clamp down, but he just shushes me. "You can take it," he growls, and fuck—he's right—I can, more than I ever thought, and hot shame floods my belly at how easily I yield to him.

He works me open until I can't tell pain from pleasure. I'm clenching around nothing, desperate for him to fill me for real, but Blue seems to relish the torment. He keeps his hand buried inside me, his other palm roaming slow circles up my torso, sometimes catching on an aching nipple, sometimes gripping around my throat just tight enough to threaten, never quite closing. I want to beg, but pride keeps my lips sealed.

He tests me—pushes harder, curves his fingers and finds the place that makes me see stars, then stops. Again and again. My whole body is a live current, straining for whatever end he decides I deserve.

"Does it hurt?" he asks.

I nod, biting the pillow so I don't scream.

"You like hurting, don't you?"

This time I can't muster a denial. Blue leans down, brushes his lips over my eyelids, my cheekbones, the corner of my mouth. It's weirdly intimate, like he's trying to memorize me at my most helpless.

Then he's up again, rubbing his cock along the mess between my legs, not letting himself in, just torturing me with the possibility. When he finally thrusts, it's with a single, brutal push that steals the air from my lungs. I arch up, caught between the pain and the relief of finally having him inside me.

He starts fucking, slow and deep, then gradually losing control until his hips are slamming into me so hard that the headboard hammers the wall with every stroke. I'm mewling, babbling, making sounds I haven't heard from myself before.

Blue watches my face the whole time, eyes locked on mine. "Good girl," he says again, and the words twist something in my chest.

"You're mine now, Saylor. Understand?"

I nod because I really can't do anything else, and he makes it quite clear every time he has his cock buried inside me.

The handcuffs hurt, but I do like the pain. They anchor me in the moment, make everything sharper. I lose count of how many times he brings me to the edge and yanks me back, like he's tuning an instrument by feel.

When he finally lets me come, it's because he wants to watch me lose my mind, wants proof of what he's done. And I do—I shatter, the whole world narrowing to a white-out of sensation, all nerves blaring at once. I think I scream, and maybe I cry, but Blue just keeps going, eyes never leaving my face.

He finishes with a low growl, pulls out and comes all over my stomach and tits, painting me in salt and proof. Then he untangles the cuffs and gathers me up against his chest, soothing until I come back to myself.

We lie there in the aftermath, my body raw and humming, his heart pounding through my skull where it rests against his sternum. He strokes my hair, gentle again, like I'm a thing worth treasuring.

"I don't want you sneaking around anymore," Blue says, soft but firm. "If you want to know something, ask me."

I nod, dazed, but already curiosity is rekindling in my gut. "Will you tell me?"

He thinks it over, then answers, "Not tonight."

CHAPTER TWENTY-SIX
SAYLOR

Waking up alone in Blue's bed is like the morning after the best concert of your life. Everything's quiet, but your ears are still ringing. The pillow still smells like whatever expensive soap he uses, mixed with something that's just him. My body aches in interesting places, a roadmap of last night's activities. The faint red marks around my wrists have faded, but I can still remember the weight of those handcuffs.

A piece of paper rests on the pillow beside me, written in that precise handwriting that screams expensive education.

Had to handle something. Back soon. Don't get into any trouble while I'm gone. – B

The note should be reassuring. Instead, it makes me realize how enormous and empty this house is when it's just me rattling around in it. Every footstep echoes off the vaulted ceilings, turning my morning routine into a one-woman percussion section.

I slip back to my room wearing one of Blue's shirts—a white button-down that hangs to my thighs. The fabric is stupidly soft, which explains why rich people always look so pleased with themselves.

Getting dressed means choosing armor for a battle I haven't figured out how to fight yet. I pick a vintage-inspired dress in deep emerald because green makes me feel powerful. My hair goes up in a simple chignon today—something sleek and controlled—and my lipstick is dark red like the doors of Grimlock.

If I'm going to plan my first *successful* murder, I should look the part. Fake it until you make it, right?

Wren has breakfast waiting in the smaller dining room. And by smaller, I mean it seats only twelve people instead of twenty. Even Blue's idea of cozy could house a small government.

"Just coffee and toast," I tell her, settling into one of the antique chairs.

"You need more than that. Can't plot revenge on an empty stomach."

I nearly choke on my coffee. "Plot revenge?"

"Whatever you want to call what you and Blue are up to." Wren sets down toast that's golden and perfect. "Point is, you need fuel."

"Speaking of Blue, where is he exactly?" I ask, trying to sound casual while spreading what's clearly butter that comes from cows with trust funds. "His note was pretty vague about this 'something' he had to handle."

Wren's energy changes slightly, a careful neutral that means she knows more than she's saying. "Blue has a restless soul. Keeps himself busy." She refills my coffee cup. "He and Hans will be gone most of the day, I expect."

The finality in her tone makes it clear this topic is closed. I focus on my breakfast instead, but the toast—thick artisan bread that tastes magical—might as well be sawdust. I can barely manage half a slice. Eating alone in this dining room makes me understand why Blue insisted we always eat together. The silence isn't peaceful; it's oppressive. The house is holding its breath, waiting for something interesting to happen.

Which is exactly what's going to get me in trouble again.

My brain keeps drifting back to the third floor. Those locked doors with their fancy keyholes, all those skeleton keys hanging in the hallway. Blue's "punishment" last night was definitely a distraction, but it didn't exactly kill my curiosity about what he's hiding up there.

And that kind of thinking is how I will end up handcuffed to his bed again, except next time he might not be in such a generous mood.

But more than that, I keep thinking about him and Hans out there somewhere, doing whatever it is Blue does when his restless soul needs tending. The helplessness claws at my chest, making me want to go exploring for answers, for proof that the stories about seven wives are more than small-town gossip.

"Wren," I call, pushing away my barely touched breakfast. "I think I need to get out of this house before I do something stupid."

She appears in the doorway instantly. "Something stupid, how?"

"Either trying to pick locks I have no business picking, or figuring out how to hot-wire that fancy car in the garage and going after Blue myself."

"Ah." Wren nods sagely. "Neither of those options would end well for anyone involved."

"Exactly." I stand up, smoothing my skirt. "Any chance I could get a ride into town? I promise not to get kidnapped, murdered, or otherwise ruin Blue's day."

Wren considers this while wiping her hands on her apron. With Blue and Hans gone, her protective duties have shifted. "I suppose I could use some things from town. And someone should check on Elliott. That man forgets to eat when he's experimenting with new recipes."

"Perfect," I say, already standing. "Give me five minutes to grab my purse."

I rush upstairs, trading my house slippers for black Mary Janes and checking my reflection one more time. The emerald dress still hugs my curves perfectly, the color making my skin look luminous instead of tired. I add the one piece of jewelry that matters—Dad's vintage compass necklace, its brass face worn smooth from decades of his thumb tracing over it. He gave it to me for my eighteenth birthday, saying every Mitchell needed to know how to find their way home. The weight of it against my chest is both comforting and heartbreaking, a reminder that I'm still trying to figure out where home is. At least my red lipstick is still perfect, which feels appropriate for whatever I'm about to get myself into.

Wren is waiting by the front door when I return, keys already in hand and a small shopping list tucked into her coat pocket.

Soon I'm riding shotgun in Wren's old but perfect Buick, watching Grimlock's twisted streets unfold. The morning fog clings to every surface like secrets made visible, transforming familiar buildings into something from a half-remembered dream. Cobblestones disappear and reappear through the mist, shop windows glow like lanterns floating in gray silk, and the whole town breathes with the rhythm of something alive and bygone. It's a beauty that makes you understand why people write ghost stories.

"Wren," I say as we navigate an alley that definitely wasn't designed for cars, "hypothetically speaking, if someone wanted to kill people but couldn't handle blood, what would you suggest?"

Wren doesn't even blink. "Hypothetically?"

"Completely hypothetically."

"Well, that's a bit of a pickle, isn't it? Wanting to kill people but squeamish about blood." Wren navigates another impossible turn. "It's a bit like wanting to bake bread but being afraid of flour."

"I'm not squeamish. I just . . . throw up when things get stabby."

"That's called being squeamish." Wren's tone is matter-of-fact. "Most people in the killing business just power through the mess. But there are alternatives."

"Such as?"

"Poison, obviously. Much cleaner than axes. More elegant too." She takes a corner that shouldn't be physically possible. "Although it takes patience. Can't just stab and run."

"I think I could manage patience." I watch a woman tending a garden where every flower is purple and not the usual black I've seen before. "Where would someone hypothetically get poison? Asking for a friend."

"Your friend has interesting hobbies." Wren's mouth twitches. "Toil & Trouble. Duffy stocks everything you need, no questions asked. She and Blue have an understanding."

An understanding. Because apparently when you're in the murder business, there's a whole network of suppliers.

"Could you drop me there?"

"Of course. Just promise me you'll be smart about whatever you're planning."

"Define smart."

"Don't get caught. Don't make messes for other people to clean up. And for god's sake, don't poison anyone at Blue's dinner parties. The man has enough social problems."

I'm really starting to love Wren.

Wren drops me off at Toil & Trouble with a promise to pick me up in an hour. The wind chimes on the wraparound porch create their unique melodic chaos as I approach the crimson door.

The familiar scent of lavender mixed with something that smells like a forest floor hits me the moment I step inside. Duffy's behind the bar, reorganizing her collection of spirit bottles, and when she spots me, her face breaks into a grin.

"Well, well. Look who's back." She sets down a bottle she's holding and reaches for the gin. "Let me guess—lavender gin fizz to start the day right?"

"Please. And make it a double."

"Starting early today, are we?" Duffy grins as she begins mixing. "Not that I'm judging. I heard about your performance at Blue's party from half the town. Sorry I missed it—my sisters and I tend to keep to ourselves during social gatherings."

"Introverts who own a bar?" I raise an eyebrow. "That seems counterintuitive."

"We serve drinks, we don't make small talk," Duffy says with a laugh. "There's a difference. Besides, most of our regulars prefer it that way." She pauses, searching for words while muddling lavender. "But from what everyone's saying, your singing was something else. Where'd you learn to sing like that?"

"My dad, mostly. He had this huge collection of old jazz records—Billie Holiday, Ella Fitzgerald, Nina Simone. I grew up listening to them." I settle onto a barstool, watching her work. The morning light streaming through the stained-glass windows turns everything amber and gold. "Started singing along when I was maybe five, and Dad said I had it. The ear, you know?"

"Natural talent." Duffy slides the finished drink across the bar. "That's rare."

I take a sip and close my eyes for a moment. The gin tastes perfect—floral and complex with just enough edge. "This is incredible. You really know what you're doing."

"Just a bartender who pays attention." Duffy leans against the counter, studying my face. "So what's your story, Saylor Mitchell? Before Grimlock, before Blue, before everything went sideways?"

"I came to New York when I was eighteen with nothing but a fake ID and a suitcase. Been singing in jazz clubs ever since, trying to make it." I laugh, but there's no bitterness in it. "I was convinced I was one good break away from making it. One record deal, one famous musician hearing me sing, one magical moment that would change everything."

"And instead?"

"Instead I learned that sometimes the universe has different plans." I touch the compass necklace through my dress. "Dad used to say that life isn't about getting what you want, it's about figuring out what you actually need."

Duffy softens. "What do you think you need now?"

Before I can answer, she reaches across the bar and touches my hand gently. Her fingers are warm, calloused from years of handling bottles and cleaning glasses.

"You know," she says thoughtfully, "most people who end up in Grimlock are looking for a place where they can stop pretending to be something they're not. A place where their darker impulses are understood, not judged." She studies my face. "You have that look—like you're tired of hiding who you really are."

I pull my hand back, surprised by how accurately she's read me. "Is it that obvious?"

"Only to someone who's been there." Duffy's smile turns knowing. "I like that about you. This town needs more people who are ready to embrace their true nature."

The compliment settles warm in my chest, but then reality kicks in. Duffy's being so understanding about all this—about Blue, about people embracing their "true nature." She makes it sound normal, even healthy.

And that should probably worry me more than it does.

"Duffy," I say, taking another sip for courage, "what do you actually know about Blue? I mean, besides those wife rumors you mentioned."

Duffy pauses, her hand stilling on the glass she's been wiping. "What do you want to know?"

"Anything real. He's so contradictory—in some ways he's completely open, tells me exactly what he's thinking. But then there are these walls, these things he won't talk about. What did he do before he came to Grimlock?"

Duffy sets down the glass and looks uncomfortable. "I don't know . . . it's his story to tell, you know?"

"Come on," I press. "I'm not asking for state secrets. I just want to understand how a man ends up living alone in a freaking castle. That's not normal, even by Grimlock standards."

She laughs despite herself. "Fair point. You want to know how Blue afforded that mansion?" Duffy glances around the empty bar, then leans closer. "Word is he inherited a fortune from some European arms dealer who died under mysterious circumstances. Blue was working for him when it happened." Duffy wipes down the same spot on the bar twice. "But here's the thing about Blue . . . He never keeps the money for himself. Half the businesses in Grimlock exist because Blue quietly funded them. The bakery, this place. He bought the building and lets me and my sisters run it rent-free."

That's not what I expected to hear. "Why would he do that?"

"Because Grimlock is his project. His attempt at . . . redemption, maybe? Building a community where people like him can exist without pretending to be something they're not. The man's trying to buy his way into heaven, one small business at a time."

Something about the way she talks about Blue—with understanding rather than judgment—makes me feel like I can trust her. And maybe it's the gin, or maybe it's the way she's been so matter-of-fact about everything, but I find myself wanting to tell her the truth.

"Can I tell you something?" I ask, glancing around to make sure we're still alone.

"I'm a bartender. Secrets are part of the job description."

I take a breath. "There are people who need to die. People who killed my father five years ago and got away with it." The words come out harder than I intended. "They're called the Crow, and they're the reason I've been running, hiding, pretending to be someone I'm not."

Duffy's expression shifts immediately. "The Crow." She says it like she's tasting something bitter. "Our charming neighbors across the Witchwood. Yeah, I know exactly who they are."

"I want them dead. I've wanted them dead for years. I have dreams about it, fantasies about making them pay." I take a shaky breath. "But here's the problem—I see blood and I completely lose it. Throw up, pass out, the whole pathetic show. So wanting revenge and actually getting it are two very different things."

"Ah." Duffy nods knowingly. "You need a method that keeps your hands clean."

"Wren mentioned you might be able to help with that."

Duffy's demeanor shifts, becoming more guarded. She crosses her arms and studies me carefully. "Did she now? And what exactly makes you think I'd help some newcomer settle a blood feud with our neighbors?"

"I'm not some newcomer," I say, heat rising in my voice. "I'm staying with Blue. And the Crow killed my father."

"Lot of people have grudges against the Crow. Doesn't mean I hand out party favors to anyone who asks." Duffy's eyes narrow. "What's your connection to Blue, really? Because if you're just some girl he's keeping around for entertainment, this conversation ends now."

The dismissive tone makes my jaw clench. "Blue knew my father. They were . . . friends. Close friends. My father asked Blue to protect me before he died."

Something in Duffy's expression softens slightly, but she's still wary. "Peter Mitchell."

I blink, surprised. "You knew him?"

"Knew of him. Blue doesn't talk much about his past, but Peter's name comes up occasionally. Usually when Blue's had too much to drink." She uncrosses her arms but doesn't move toward the apothecary shelves yet. "So the Crow killed Peter Mitchell . . . and now the daughter wants revenge."

"Now the daughter wants justice," I correct.

Duffy tilts her head, studying me like I'm a puzzle she's trying to solve. "Justice. Right." She's quiet for a long moment. "You sure you can handle this? Killing someone isn't like singing on stage. There's no applause at the end."

"I know," I say quietly. "I've already . . . it's not theoretical anymore."

Duffy's eyebrows raise and she looks at me with new interest. "Well then. That changes things." She finally moves toward the apothecary section with more purpose. "Looking for something cleaner than a blade, I take it?" She runs her fingers along various bottles. "You're definitely not the first. Half my customers are too squeamish for proper stabbing. Good thing I stock alternatives."

I watch her select a small bottle filled with tiny blue spheres that look like miniature boba pearls. "What are those?"

"These are rather special," Duffy says, holding up the bottle to catch the light. "Dissolves completely in any liquid, no taste, and gives about ten minutes of consciousness while everything shuts down. Enough time for a meaningful farewell speech but not enough for rescue."

I stare at the bottle, equal parts fascinated and horrified. "What are they exactly?"

"Trade secret, sorry. But they won't show up on any toxicology screen. My discerning customers love them." She pulls out a small velvet bag and drops the bottle inside. "And they're blue. I thought you might appreciate the aesthetic touch."

"Perfect," I say, taking the bag. "Thank you."

"On the house for a promising new artist." Duffy's smile is warm but knowing. "Just remember—poison is an art form. Start small, test your dosages, and never use the same method twice. Keeps things interesting."

The velvet bag feels heavier than it should in my purse, like it contains more than just tiny blue spheres—like it holds the weight of a decision I can't take back. But instead of fear, I feel something like relief. Finally, a path forward that doesn't involve me fainting at the first sign of blood.

I finish my gin fizz in one long pull, the lavender burning slightly on the way down. "Thank you," I tell Duffy. "For understanding. For helping."

"Don't thank me yet," she says, wiping down the bar where my glass was. "Wait until you see how this all plays out."

I settle back onto my barstool, checking the time. Still have twenty minutes before Wren comes back. The poison feels like a secret burning in my purse, and I can't stop touching the velvet bag through the leather.

"Saylor," Duffy says, her voice dropping lower. "The Crow aren't just killers. They're survivors who've done unspeakable things to innocent people. Men who deserve everything that's coming to them." She leans closer across the bar. "Little secret—my sisters and I also believe in 'justice.' But be smart about this. Don't underestimate them."

I look up at her, and for the first time in five years, I smile with real anticipation. "They underestimated my father once. That was their mistake."

Duffy nods slowly. "Just remember what I said about dosages. Start small."

I touch the velvet bag through my purse one more time. Such tiny little spheres to carry so much hope.

CHAPTER TWENTY-SEVEN
BLUE

"So," Jay says before I'm even through the door, "I have to ask—was the corpse centerpiece a planned part of the evening's entertainment, or did you just wake up that morning and think, 'You know what this dinner party needs? Dead people decor'?"

I settle into my chair while he frantically searches through desk drawers like he's looking for something stronger than his usual coffee. "You seemed to enjoy yourself well enough. I saw you having quite the conversation with Dame Gothel."

"I have to admit," he continues, finally locating a hip flask buried under a stack of case studies, "I'm still processing the fact that you used Samuel Crow as a floral arrangement. Very artistic, by the way. The blue flowers were a nice touch."

"Thank you. I thought the color coordination was important." I cross my ankle over my knee, settling in for what's clearly going to be a longer session than usual. "And before you ask—don't worry, I didn't fall off the wagon. Hans did the killing. Although that's not why I'm here today."

"Oh god." Jay sets down the flask without opening it. "What happened after I left the party?"

Jay blinks. Once. Twice. Then he uncaps the flask and takes a long pull.

"It's ten-thirty in the morning, Jay."

"Your sessions have completely destroyed my relationship with normal business hours." He wipes his mouth with the back of his hand. "So let me get this straight. You're telling me that retirement lasted exactly . . . what, forty-eight hours?"

"Retirement is overrated."

"Blue, we spent three years building your exit strategy. Three years of anger management, meditation techniques, finding healthy outlets for violent urges." Jay gestures wildly with the flask. "And you threw it all away for gift giving?"

"I prefer to think of it as targeted problem solving."

"With axes."

"Hans's axes," I correct. "There's a difference."

"Oh, there's a difference?" Jay's eyebrow arches dangerously. "You can't just have your staff handle all the killing and think that makes you murder sober, Blue. There are loopholes, and then there's . . . whatever the hell this is."

"It's called delegation."

"Delegation." Jay takes another swig from his flask. "Right. Because being murder sober doesn't mean you stop orchestrating deaths, it just means you outsource the actual stabbing."

"Hans's axe is just a tool, Jay. Like your pen, or your little stress ball that you keep hurling at the wall."

Jay retrieves said stress ball from behind the filing cabinet where it's apparently taken up permanent residence. "My stress ball doesn't decapitate people."

"Your stress ball is also significantly less effective at eliminating threats to the people I care about."

"And there it is." Jay stops mid-squeeze, his attention sharpening. "The people you care about. Singular person, really."

"Peter was my friend—"

"We're not talking about Peter anymore, and you know it." Jay leans forward in his chair. "We're talking about the fact that you came out of retirement not because someone killed your friend, but because someone threatened his daughter."

The distinction shouldn't matter, but somehow it does. Peter's death was a tragedy, a failure on my part to protect someone I cared about. But the thought of anyone hurting Saylor? That's something else.

"Fine. Yes. Saylor matters to me."

"How much?"

"Enough that I'd rather not see her tortured to death by criminals."

"Blue." Jay's voice takes on that patient tone that means he's about to make me say something I don't want to say. "How much does she matter to you?"

I stare at the chaos of his office, buying time while my brain tries to formulate an answer that doesn't sound completely insane.

Books scattered across every surface, coffee rings on important documents, that motivational poster about change that's hanging crooked behind his desk.

"She's different," I say finally.

"Different how?"

"She's not afraid of what I am. She should be, but she's not." I think about the way she looked at the Crow's corpse, the hunger in her eyes when she asked me to teach her violence. "She sees the monster and asks for more instead of running."

"That's concerning from a mental health perspective, but continue."

"Most people either want to fix me or use me. Saylor just wants to understand me." I pause as I realize the strength of my words. "She doesn't try to make me into something I'm not."

Jay makes a note in his pad. "And how does that make you feel?"

"Like I might actually deserve to be understood."

The admission hangs between us, and I immediately regret saying it. This is what happens when Jay gets me talking. Somehow he always manages to excavate thoughts I didn't even know I was having.

Jay clears his throat. "So how are those murder lessons going? Last session you mentioned she wanted to learn how to kill her father's murderers herself."

"She's really bad at it," I say finally.

"Bad at what, exactly?"

"The killing. She's an awful student, to be honest. Can't see blood without throwing up."

Jay blinks slowly. "And you're . . . persisting with this approach because?"

"Because she asked me to."

Jay sets down his pen very carefully. "So you're continuing to traumatize your girlfriend who clearly isn't cut out for violence because she asked nicely?"

"She's not my *girlfriend*."

"What is she, then?"

I don't have an answer ready for that. What is Saylor? My houseguest? My responsibility? My obsession?

"She's mine," I say finally. "I don't know what that makes her, but she's mine."

Jay reaches for his flask again. "Okay, we're definitely going to need to unpack that statement, but first—give me specifics. How bad are we talking?"

I think about Saylor in the basement with Julian, how she accidentally killed him and then threw up. Then later at dinner, the way her hand shook before she drove the knife through Leroy's palm. How she fainted when she saw the blood.

"She wants to kill people but can't handle the mess."

"She can't actually go through with it."

"She's getting better. Last night at dinner she managed to stab Leroy Crow through the hand before the nausea kicked in."

Jay stares at me. "You brought dinner guests home just so she could practice stabbing them?"

"I thought it would be a good learning opportunity."

"Jesus Christ, Blue." Jay downs the rest of his flask. "A formal dinner party? With place settings and everything?"

"Wren made braised short ribs. It would have been a waste not to use the good china."

"I'm not questioning the menu, I'm questioning the fact that you're treating murder like a dinner theater production." But there's almost amusement in his voice. "Don't get me wrong—I'm still on board with giving her agency back. Teaching her to defend herself is the right call. But did it have to be so . . . theatrical?"

"The Crow aren't going to attack her in a convenient location. She needs to be comfortable with violence in any setting."

"Fair point." Jay refills his flask. "And she actually went through with it? Stabbed him at the table?"

"Through the hand. Then vomited and passed out, but yes."

"But she did it." Jay considers this. "That's progress, right? First time she couldn't even hold the knife steady. Now she's actually drawing blood, even if her stomach protests."

"Exactly. She's learning."

"Learning." Jay shakes his head with a slight smile. "Only you would consider 'stabbed someone before fainting' as educational progress. But I have to ask—is this approach really working? Because it sounds like she's forcing herself through something she's not ready for."

"She asked for this."

"I know. And I think she should have the choice. That's why I supported this whole murder mentorship thing in the first place." Jay leans forward. "But maybe there's a middle ground between helpless victim and dinner party assassin? Something that doesn't involve traumatic vomiting?"

"You might be right." The admission surprises both of us. "The dinner party was probably overkill."

"Literally." Jay's lip twitches. "But hey, at least Wren got to show off her culinary skills."

"She does make excellent braised short ribs."

"See? Silver lining." Jay caps his flask. "Just maybe dial back the production value next time. Save the formal dinners for people who aren't on the menu. And be careful . . . she isn't like you."

"I know she's not like me," I say quietly. "She won't become what I became."

"How can you be so sure?"

"Because she still throws up when she sees blood. Because she asks questions about whether killing is right instead of just doing it. Because she—" I stop, realizing what I'm about to say.

"Because she what?"

"Because she makes me want to be better than I am."

The admission comes out before I can stop it, and Jay's entire demeanor shifts. He sets down his flask and actually focuses on me with attention that makes me want to leave.

"Now we're getting somewhere," he says softly. "Tell me about that."

"There's nothing to tell."

"Blue, you just admitted that someone makes you want to change. In three years of therapy, you've never said anything like that."

"I've changed plenty. I retired, didn't I?"

"You retired because you were tired of killing. That's different from wanting to be better for someone specific." Jay picks up his pen again. "What is it about Saylor that makes you feel this way?"

I stare at the motivational poster, wishing I were anywhere else. "I don't know."

"Try."

"She trusts me." The words come out reluctantly. "Not because she's naive or stupid, but because she chooses to. Even after seeing what I'm capable of."

"And that's important to you."

"No one has ever just accepted me before. Not the sanitized version or the useful version. But Saylor sees all of it and stays anyway."

"How does that make you feel?"

I consider giving him some therapeutic non-answer, but something about the way Saylor looked at me last night makes me want to try honesty for once.

"Like maybe I'm not completely irredeemable," I say finally.

"And now?"

"Now I think maybe I want to find out."

Jay makes another note. "This is progress, Blue. Real progress."

"It doesn't feel like progress. It feels like weakness."

"Caring about someone isn't weakness."

"It is when caring about them makes you vulnerable. When it makes you hesitate or second-guess or—" I stop, running my hands through my hair. "I've never cared about anyone the way I care about her. It's terrifying."

"Why terrifying?"

"Because I don't know how to do this. I don't know how to care about someone without destroying them."

Jay sets down his pen and looks at me directly. "Tell me about your parents."

The subject change is whiplash. "What does that have to do with anything?"

"Humor me. What were they like?"

"Dead. They've been dead for twenty-five years."

"Before they died. What kind of parents were they?"

"My father was a drunk who thought discipline meant breaking whatever was closest when he got angry. My mother was so afraid of him that she never spoke above a whisper." I don't know why I'm telling him this. "They died in a car accident when I was fourteen, and I felt nothing but relief."

"That's a lot of trauma to carry."

"Everyone has trauma, Jay. Not everyone becomes what I became."

"No, but it explains why you don't trust love. Why you think caring about someone means hurting them."

"Because it does. Look at what I've done to Saylor already—kidnapped her, put her in danger, turned her into someone who stabs people at dinner parties."

"Did you force her to stab Leroy?"

"No, but—"

"Did you make her ask you to teach her violence?"

"She asked for that, but I could have said no."

"Could you have?" Jay leans back in his chair. "If Saylor had asked you for something she needed, could you actually have denied her?"

The answer is immediate and certain. "No."

"Then you understand the difference between what your father did and what you're doing."

"Enlighten me."

"Your father hurt people because he wanted to. You're trying to protect someone because you love her."

The word *love* makes me want to leave the room. "I never said anything about love."

"You didn't have to. It's written all over your face every time you say her name."

"I don't fall in love, Jay. I help people. I protect them when necessary. But I don't fall in love."

"Why not?"

"Because love makes you weak. It makes you careless. It makes you—"

"Human?"

The question stops me cold. Human. Like that's something desirable instead of something to be avoided.

"I've spent my entire adult life learning not to be human," I say quietly. "Being human gets people killed."

"Being inhuman gets people killed too. Just different people."

"At least when I'm inhuman, the people who die deserve it."

Jay is quiet for a long moment, studying my face. "Blue, can I ask you something?"

"You're going to whether I say yes or not."

"When you think about Saylor, what scares you more—that she might get hurt, or that she might leave?"

The question cuts straight through every defense I've built. Because the truth is, I can handle the thought of fighting off the Crow, of protecting her from external threats. But the idea of waking up one morning to find her gone, having decided that I'm not worth the complications I bring to her life?

That terrifies me in ways I don't have words for.

"Both," I admit. "But if I'm honest . . . losing her scares me more than anything else."

"And there it is." Jay's smile is gentle, almost proud. "You love her, Blue. For the first time in your life, you're in love."

"That's not—"

"It is. And the sooner you accept it, the sooner we can figure out how to help you not screw it up."

I stare at the chaos of his office, at the certificates on his wall, at anything that isn't his knowing look. Love. Such a small word for something that's rewiring my entire nervous system.

"Assuming you're right," I say carefully, "what exactly am I supposed to do with that information?"

"You need to stop pretending this is just about teaching her self-defense."

"What's that supposed to mean?"

"It means you're in love with her, and you're acting like her personal violence tutor instead of telling her how you feel." Jay leans forward. "Blue, she stabbed someone at your dinner party. That's not normal girlfriend behavior."

"She's not my girlfriend."

"Exactly my point. What is she? Your student? Your protégé? Your revenge partner?" Jay takes on that patient tone again. "Or is she the woman you're in love with who happens to want to learn how to kill people?"

I don't have an answer for that, which apparently is answer enough.

"So what do I do?"

"Tell her you love her. Stop hiding behind murder lessons and start having actual conversations about what you both want." Jay picks up his stress ball, squeezing it thoughtfully. "And maybe stop acting like a serial killer with a teaching certificate."

"Serial killer with a teaching certificate," I repeat. "That's going on my business cards."

"I'm being serious, Blue."

"So am I. It has a nice ring to it."

Jay hurls his stress ball at the wall with more force than usual. "You're impossible."

"But I'm your favorite impossible patient."

"You're my only patient who brings dinner guests in body bags, so the bar is pretty low."

My phone buzzes with a text before I can respond. Wren's name appears on the screen, and I swipe to read her message.

Had to come to town for supplies. Need to head back. Can you give Saylor a ride home? She's at Toil & Trouble.

The woman has a restless soul and can't stay put, I think, already standing.

"Problem?" Jay asks.

"Wren needs me to pick up Saylor." I pocket my phone. "She's at Toil & Trouble."

"Blue?" Jay calls as I reach the door. "When you see her, try using words as your love language instead of murder."

"Right," I say, already heading for the door.

CHAPTER TWENTY-EIGHT
BLUE

The sound hits me before I even open the door—genuine laughter, bright and unguarded. I pause with my hand on the handle of Toil & Trouble, caught off guard by how foreign the sound seems in Duffy's usually quiet establishment.

When I push through the door, I find Saylor doubled over at the bar, tears streaming down her face from laughing so hard. Duffy's leaning against the back counter, grinning with the kind of satisfaction that comes from landing a particularly good story. They look like old friends sharing secrets, comfortable in a way that makes something warm settle in my chest.

I can't remember the last time I saw Duffy truly relaxed with another person. She's friendly enough with customers, professional with business associates, but this? This is different. Saylor's got her feet tucked up on the barstool rungs, completely at ease, and Duffy's actually remaining still instead of working—something I've seen maybe twice in all the years I've known her.

"Blue!" Saylor looks up, still catching her breath, and the sight of her face flushed with happiness does something dangerous to my composure. Her hair's escaping from whatever she'd tried to do with it this morning, and there's a lightness to her expression that I've never seen before. "Duffy was just telling me about Dame Gothel's love letters."

"She's been leaving them for the mailman," Duffy explains, barely containing her own laughter. "Romantic poetry about his 'strong hands' and 'noble dedication to correspondence.' Problem is, her handwriting looks like a serial killer's manifesto and he can't read a single word. The poor man is convinced she's sending him death threats."

This sets Saylor off again, and I can't help but smile at the sound.

I settle onto a stool, watching them with fascination. Grimlock doesn't welcome outsiders easily. We're a town full of people who've learned to be suspicious, who've all got reasons to prefer our privacy. Most newcomers sense the undercurrent of wariness and either leave quickly or spend months trying to prove they belong.

But Saylor's different. Maybe it's because she stabbed a man at my dinner party. Maybe it's because she looks at our darker edges and sees them as features rather than flaws. Or maybe it's simply that she understands what it means to carry secrets—and more importantly, what it means to keep them.

Whatever the reason, she's already carved out a place here. I can see it in how Duffy's shoulders have dropped their usual defensive tension, in the way they're sitting together like conspirators planning something delightfully wicked.

I check my pocket watch. Nearly two o'clock. "Ready to head back?"

Saylor nods, sliding off her stool. "Thank you for the drinks, Duffy. And the conversation."

"Anytime." Duffy's smile is warm but careful now. "Both of you are always welcome."

We leave money on the bar and step back into Grimlock's perpetual mist. The cobblestones are slick under our feet as we walk toward where Hans waits with the car, but something makes me pause at the entrance to the town square.

The clock tower rises from Grimlock's center like a Gothic prayer made stone. Its spire disappears into low clouds, and the massive clock face showing eternal midnight catches what little light filters through the fog.

"Have you been up there yet?" I ask, nodding toward the tower.

Saylor follows my gaze, tilting her head back to take in the impossible height. "I didn't know you could go up there."

"Most people can't. But I have certain privileges in this town."

Without waiting for her answer, I guide her across the square toward the heavy oak door set into the tower's base. I run my hand along the weathered stone frame until I find what I'm looking for—a loose brick that shifts when pressed. The iron key hidden behind it is blackened with age, left there by whoever decided Grimlock's clock should stay frozen at midnight.

"Blue, what are you doing?"

"Showing you something pretty amazing."

The door opens with a groan that echoes up the narrow spiral staircase. Stone steps worn smooth by centuries of feet wind upward into shadow, lit only by narrow windows cut into the tower walls. Each step demands effort, and we're both breathing hard by the time we reach the first landing.

"How many stairs?" Saylor asks, pressing her hand against cool stone.

"Too many to count. But the view makes it worth it. Promise."

We continue climbing, the staircase growing narrower as we ascend. The windows become more frequent, offering glimpses of Grimlock spread below us in miniature. Houses and shops shrink to dollhouse proportions, connected by streets that wind through mist in patterns that make perfect sense from this height.

The mechanism chamber houses the clock's guts. Massive gears and pendulums that haven't moved in decades fill the space. Brass and iron components the size of carriage wheels stand frozen, their surfaces green with age but still magnificent in their complexity. The air here smells of metal and time, of machinery that once kept perfect rhythm for an entire community.

"It's beautiful," Saylor breathes, running her fingers along a gear wheel taller than she is. "Why doesn't it work anymore?"

"The town decided they preferred time standing still."

She gives me a look that says she knows I'm being deliberately cryptic, but doesn't press. We climb the final stairs to the observation deck, and when we emerge onto the platform, Saylor's intake of breath makes the entire climb worthwhile.

Grimlock spreads below us in all directions, a perfect circle of civilization carved from wilderness. To the west, the Pacific stretches endless and gray, punctuated by jagged rocks where waves crash in silent explosions of white. The harbor curves around the town's edge, its piers reaching into water that disappears into mist.

To the east, the Witchwood Forest begins where Grimlock's last houses end. Ancient trees stretch unbroken toward the horizon, their canopy so dense it looks solid from this height. Somewhere beyond those trees, past miles of wilderness that would swallow a man whole, the Crow have carved out their territory. They're out there right now, in clearings we can't see from here, planning their next move and counting their dead.

"It's perfect," Saylor says, gripping the iron railing as wind whips her hair around her face. "You can see everything from here."

"That's the point. This building was built as a watchtower, to spot trouble before it reached town."

"And now?"

"Now it's just a good place to think."

She turns to face me, eyes bright with exhilaration from the climb and the view. Wind has brought color to her cheeks, and the way the afternoon light catches in her hair makes something tighten in my chest.

"Thank you for bringing me up here." She grips the railing tighter, taking in the view again. "I'm falling in love with this place, you know. Grimlock. I can see why my father kept coming back here."

"He really never mentioned it to you?"

"Never. Not once. But being here now, I can feel what drew him to this place." She pauses, watching the mist roll in from the ocean. "I'm surprised I never even heard of Grimlock before. A place this beautiful should be famous."

"That's how the residents prefer it. We're not exactly eager for tourist buses and vacation rentals." I lean against the railing beside her. "Small town living works best when it stays small."

"There's so much I want to explore. The shops, the neighborhoods, those walking trails I saw marked on signs." Her eyes drift toward the forest. "I'd love to go hiking in those woods. They look untouched."

"No hiking in the Witchwood," I say immediately. "But there is something happening tomorrow night in the forest. Something you might find interesting."

"Oh really?"

"The Dryad's Dance. It happens three times a year when conditions are right." I point toward a section of forest closer to town, where the trees thin slightly. "There's a grove where bioluminescent mushrooms grow. Tomorrow they'll be at peak brightness, and the whole town turns out to celebrate."

"Glowing mushrooms?" Her face lights up with genuine excitement. "That sounds incredible."

"It's quite a sight. Music, dancing, food you won't find anywhere else." I watch her carefully. "The folklore says the glowing mushrooms only light up when the barrier between our world and the fae realm grows thin. The paths they create through the forest are supposed to be doorways. Places where you can step from our realm into theirs." I lean against the railing. "Most people just go for the party, but some swear they've seen things. Heard voices that don't belong to anyone human."

"You mean like actual fairies?"

"Dryads, mostly. Tree spirits. That's why it's called the Dryad's Dance. Legend says they come out on these nights to dance with mortals." I shrug. "Could be the spores from mushrooms causing hallucinations, could be something else. Either way, it makes for an interesting evening."

"And everyone really goes?"

"Everyone. It starts after midnight, goes until dawn. Think you can handle a night in the Witchwood?"

"Are you kidding? I wouldn't miss it." She turns back to the view, but I can see her mind working. She nods, still staring out at the forest with new interest. "A midnight celebration in a glowing mushroom grove. My life has gotten very strange."

"Good strange or bad strange?"

"Definitely good strange." She smiles at me. "I'm never going back to boring after this."

"Boring's not your style anyway."

She laughs, and the sound gets caught by the wind and carried out over the water. For a moment we just stand there, taking in the view and the weight of everything that's brought us to this point.

Instead of saying anything else, I step closer and cup her face in my hands. When our mouths connect, she tastes of gin and lavender.

Her hands find my jacket lapels, pulling me closer as the kiss deepens into something that makes my head spin. When she bites gently at my lower lip, I groan against her mouth and back her toward the solid stone of the tower's central column.

"Here?" she whispers against my throat, breathless.

"Here."

The massive clock face dominates one side of the observation platform, its glass surface rising above us like a wall. The thick stone ledge at its base, where enormous Roman numerals are carved deep into the weathered stone, provides the perfect height. When I lift her onto this ledge, the clock's bulk shields us from the wind while she wraps her legs around my waist and pulls me between her thighs.

Her dress bunches around her hips as my hands find bare skin, and when she arches against me, I can feel her heat through thin fabric. The sound she makes when I trace my fingers along her inner thigh gets lost in the wind, but I feel it vibrate through her chest pressed against mine.

"Someone could see us," she says, but she's already working at my shirt buttons.

"Let them."

She shoves my shirt open and buttons ping off across the stone. My hands push up her dress, thumbs sliding the humid crease of her thigh high to her panties, which are nothing more than a black scrap—already damp, already begging. I pull them aside with two fingers, taking a moment to slide my thumb against her, slow and deliberate, smearing slickness over her clit. Her hips roll, needy, clamping tighter around my waist.

She fumbles my belt and undoes it. Instead of pushing my pants down, she peels the belt free and gives it a tug, grinning at me like a dare. I snatch it from her, wrap it twice around my fist, and double it back, then slide the loop over her neck. She shudders, lips parted, and tips her head into my hand. The wind whips her hair around her face, tangling it in the leather.

She's still got my cock pressed to her through my pants, grinding and frantic, but I won't let her have it yet. I tighten the belt, just enough, and use it to tilt her head up so I can bite along her jaw, her shoulder, the pale wing of her collarbone. She gasps, and I feel the sound travel up the column of her throat, the pulse against my palm.

"Blue—" she starts, breathless, but I cut her off with my mouth, pressing my tongue between her teeth until she yields and opens, hands raking through my hair and pulling me so close I can barely breathe.

I tighten the belt just a little more, and she whimpers, the sound barely escaping. Her attention goes glassy, pupils blown wide as the expansive sea, and her hands switch from grasping to clawing, catching on the nape of my neck, the cords of muscle at my shoulder.

She chokes down her own noises, biting the inside of her cheek hard enough to bleed. I can feel it, the way her breathing staggers, shallow and desperate. She lets go completely, trusting the pressure of my hand and the tension of the belt to keep her upright. I'll hold her for as long as she'll let me.

"Please," she says, one syllable, shaky, and I let go, not of her, but of the discipline holding me back. I unzip, freeing myself, and she grabs me, guiding my cock against herself without hesitation. Somehow I find a moment of clarity to reach for a condom in my wallet, but how I composed myself long enough to slip it on my dick, I don't know.

She yanks me in with her thighs as I line up and drive in, slow at first, then deeper. She's so ready for it she's shaking, hands still fighting for leverage, for a way to hold on to me or the world as I fill her up, every inch earning a new sound from the back of her throat. I brace one forearm against the clock face, palm flat on chilled glass just above her head, and thrust forward in short, eager strokes. Her dress is rucked high around her waist, dark fabric pooling beneath her, and I swear she looks like something painted, something baroque and religious, framed in stone and light.

She keeps her eyes on me, unblinking, drinking in every flicker of pleasure I let show. Her smile goes sloppy and fades, lips raw from my teeth, but she never stops moving, hips canting hard as I piston into her. I want to savor it, stretch it out, but she tastes like wind and ocean, and it's all I can do to keep from flying apart on the spot.

I take hold of the belt again and twist, the leather digging into my fist, and she arches, throat gleaming with sweat or fog or both. Her breathing becomes shallow, strained, and I watch her pupils dilate as the pressure builds. One twist too much and I could crush her windpipe. One second too long and she goes from gasping to unconscious.

She knows this. I can see it in her eyes—the exact moment she realizes I'm holding her life in my hands along with the belt. And instead of fear, instead of panic, she lets her head fall back farther, giving me more access to her throat. Offering herself completely.

Her pulse batters against the leather, frantic and wild, and I feel every beat through the belt. Her lips part but no sound comes out now, just the desperate draw of air through her constricted throat. Her hands claw at my shoulders, not to push me away but to pull me closer, even as I can tell her vision starts to blur at the edges.

This is the line. Right here. One more twist and I cross from lover to killer.

Her gaze blacks out for a moment and she is all nerve endings, nothing left but the direct line between her cunt and the sound my hips make when I bottom out. There is no world below us—just our pressed bodies and the fine line between pleasure and death.

I loosen the belt just enough to let air rush back into her lungs, and she gasps, the sound raw and desperate. But her eyes never leave mine, never show anything but complete faith that I'll know exactly when to stop.

She trusts me. She fucking trusts me and that truth makes my cock harder than it's ever been before.

She comes without warning and with no inhibition, clamping around me so hard I have to grit my teeth and grunt into her hair to keep myself from spilling right then. She chokes out a sob, raw and unselfconscious.

I keep thrusting, greedy now, the pressure gone from the belt but my fist still knotted in her hair. I sink into her and she holds me there, ankles crossed behind my back, locked tight. I come— white-hot, atomic—bursting behind my ribs all the way to my teeth, and I must make some kind of sound because she laughs, breathless and spent, and echoes it back at me. We don't move. My hand releases the belt and instead holds the smooth arch of her neck, thumb resting on her rapid heartbeat.

When we finally separate, she stays sitting on the ledge while I deal with the condom and fix my clothes. My shirt is probably ruined—half the buttons are scattered across the clock tower platform—but I don't give a damn.

"That was . . ." she starts, then trails off, laughing softly.

"Yeah."

She slides down from the ledge, smoothing her dress back into place. Her hair is a mess, her lips swollen, and there's already a faint mark blooming on her throat where the belt pressed against her skin. She looks thoroughly debauched, and the sight makes me want to push her back up against that clock face and start all over again.

But more than that, she looks content. Satisfied in a way that has nothing to do with sex and everything to do with the fact that she let me put a belt around her throat and never once doubted I'd keep her safe.

No one has ever given themselves to me that completely before.

"We should probably head back," she says, putting my shirt back on for me since I can't manage it with the missing buttons.

I watch her fingers work, so careful and domestic, and something twists in my chest. Not long ago I was a retired killer living alone in a house full of ghosts. Now I'm standing in a clock tower while a woman I'm falling in love with fixes my clothes after the most intense sex of my life.

Jay was right. I am in love with her. Completely, irrevocably, dangerously in love.

The realization should terrify me. Instead, it just makes me want to kill anyone who even thinks about hurting her.

CHAPTER TWENTY-NINE
SAYLOR

We walk up the drive to Maison Rouge in comfortable silence. Blue's hand rests on the small of my back, and I'm trying to look normal while my purse contains mysterious blue pills from Grimlock's resident poison dealer. The velvet bag moves against my hip with each step, a gentle reminder that I'm officially in the murder business now.

"I have something for you," Blue says as we reach the front door.

My stomach does a little flip. "What kind of something?"

"Another chance." He opens the door, watching my face carefully. "You don't have to if you're not ready."

Oh man . . . here we go . . . Another chance to prove I'm not completely useless at this whole revenge thing. "I'm ready," I say, but less confident than I'd like. "Actually, I went to the apothecary today with a goal. Got myself a different tool for the job."

Blue's eyebrows rise with interest. "Did you now?"

I pat my purse. "Turns out knives aren't really my thing. All that blood and stabbing." I make a face. "Duffy had some suggestions for . . . cleaner methods."

"Poison." Blue's smile spreads slowly across his face. "Very respectable choice. Requires patience and planning. Much more civilized than hacking people apart."

"That's what I thought." I'm so glad he approves. "Less mess, less chance of me puking on everyone."

"Absolutely. Some of history's most effective killers preferred poison." He opens the door wider. "Let's see how your new approach works."

I follow him down the stone steps, my hand gripping the velvet bag through my purse strap. The basement smells like damp stone and old blood.

Hans stands guard beside a chair occupied by Leroy Crow. His expensive suit is now wrinkled and stained with dried blood, his left hand wrapped in crude bandages that haven't quite stopped bleeding from where I drove the carving knife through his palm last night. Even wounded and captive, he still manages to look smug.

"Well, well," Blue says pleasantly. "Look who's recovered enough to join us again."

Leroy looks me up and down with clinical detachment. "Still playing at being a killer, I see. Tell me, did you enjoy watching me bleed all over your precious dinner table?"

"More than I probably should have." I set my purse down on Blue's knife table, fingers working to retrieve my purchase from Duffy. "How's the hand feeling, by the way? Still tender?"

"You'll find out soon enough when I return the favor." His smile is pure cruelty despite his obvious pain. "I have to say, you showed more spine than I expected. Most people hesitate before stabbing someone."

The smug satisfaction in his voice, even while wounded and tied up, makes something cold settle in my chest. Good. I need that ice-cold rage to get through what I'm about to do.

I pull out Duffy's bottle of blue pills, holding it up to catch the basement lights. "Well, Leroy, today's your lucky day. I brought medicine."

Leroy squints at the bottle. "What are those?"

"Health supplements." I shake the bottle, listening to the pills rattle. "Very good for you. Open wide."

"I don't want medicine."

"That's unfortunate, because you're going to take it anyway." I unscrew the cap, tapping one of the blue spheres into my palm. "Come on, just one little pill."

Leroy stares at me like I've lost my mind. "You want me to swallow random pills? Absolutely not."

"Oh, come on. It's just one tiny little pill." I hold the blue sphere between my thumb and forefinger, giving it a small shake. "Look how pretty it is. Matches Blue's beard."

"I'm not swallowing anything you give me, you deranged bitch."

"Rude." I step closer to his chair. "Hans, could you hold his head still?"

Hans moves behind Leroy's chair, placing his massive hands on either side of the man's skull. "Is very small pill, yes? Should not be difficult to swallow."

"This is ridiculous," Leroy snarls. "Blue, call off your psychotic girlfriend and let me die with some dignity. Use the axe like a professional."

Blue leans against the wall, arms crossed, clearly enjoying the show. "I'm just here for moral support."

I try to pry Leroy's mouth open with my free hand. "Come on, just open up. One tiny pill."

Leroy clamps his lips shut tighter, shaking his head as much as Hans's grip allows. I try pushing against his jaw, but he's got those muscles locked down tight.

"Hans, pinch his nose."

"Ah, is good idea." Hans releases one hand from Leroy's skull to clamp over his nose. "Now he must breathe through mouth, yes?"

Leroy holds his breath for an impressively long time, his face turning red, then purple. Just when I think he might pass out, his mouth opens in a desperate gasp for air.

I shove the pill toward his mouth, but he jerks his head sideways and spits.

"Missed," he gasps triumphantly.

"Damn it." I pick up another pill from the bottle. "Hans, hold him steadier this time."

"Is like trying to give medicine to very large, very angry child," Hans observes, repositioning his grip. "Perhaps we need different approach."

"I have an idea." I grab a glass of water from the side table. "Leroy, you seem thirsty after all that struggling."

"I'm not drinking anything either."

"Hans, tip his head back slightly."

We go through the same routine—nose pinching, waiting for him to gasp, then I try to pour water in his mouth. Most of it runs down his chin, but I manage to get enough in that he has to swallow or choke.

"There! See? You can swallow things." I hold up another pill. "One more time."

"This is insane," Leroy sputters. "Blue, this is torture. Actual torture."

"You would know," Blue says mildly. "Saylor's methods are significantly more humane than yours."

The third attempt goes better. I get the pill positioned right as Leroy opens his mouth to curse at us, and Hans gives his jaw a helpful little push upward. Leroy's eyes go wide as he realizes the pill is now in his mouth.

"Swallow," I command, pinching his nose again.

He tries to spit it out, but Hans's hand is covering his mouth now. Leroy makes muffled sounds of outrage, his eyes watering as he fights not to swallow.

But biology wins. After about thirty seconds of struggling, his throat bobs as the pill goes down.

"Success!" I step back, dusting off my hands. "See? That wasn't so bad."

Leroy glares at me with pure hatred. "What did you just make me swallow?"

"Something very good for you." I check my watch. "Duffy said it takes about ten minutes to work. Maybe fifteen."

"To work for what?"

"You'll see." I settle into the chair across from him, crossing my legs. I stare for several minutes. "So, while we wait, let's chat. Was it worth it? Killing my father for money?"

"Your father was a fool who thought he could outsmart us."

"Well, this fool's daughter is about to outsmart you." I check my watch again. "Eight more minutes, maybe."

Leroy tests his restraints, pulling against the ropes Hans tied around his wrists. "What did you give me? Poison?"

"Something like that."

Blue pushes off from the wall, moving closer. "How are you feeling, Leroy? Any symptoms yet?"

"I feel fine, you psychotic bastard. When I get out of here—"

"You're not getting out of here," I interrupt. "But please, continue your threats. They're entertaining."

Leroy keeps ranting about what he's going to do to all of us when he escapes, but after a few minutes he starts sounding slightly slurred around the edges.

"Is too quiet in here," Hans observes, glancing around the basement. "Maybe we need some music, Boss? Like the good old days when you always set your scenes to music. Has been long time."

Blue's face lights up. "Excellent idea, Hans. You're absolutely right." He moves to an ornate phonograph I hadn't noticed before, sitting on a carved wooden table between the wine bottles. The machine is gorgeous—brass fittings gleaming despite their age, a massive horn speaker that flares out like a morning glory, and intricate scrollwork decorating the mahogany cabinet. "Let's set the proper mood."

He selects a record from a collection stored beneath the phonograph, places it carefully on the turntable, and winds the mechanism with ease. The needle drops onto vinyl, and suddenly the basement fills with the smooth, dark tones of a jazz standard about love and death intertwining. Perfect murder music.

"Oh, I love this song," I say, starting to sway slightly in my chair. The music makes everything feel less like torture and more like . . . dinner theater. "Perfect choice."

"Leroy," Blue says pleasantly, "you're very lucky. Not everyone gets live entertainment during their final moments."

Hans starts nodding along to the bass line, his massive frame moving surprisingly gracefully. "Is very good song. Very . . . how you say . . . fitting."

I can't help myself—I start humming along, then quietly singing the chorus about dancing until dawn breaks. My voice echoes off the stone walls, turning the basement into an intimate concert venue.

"Feeling dizzy yet?" I ask Leroy sweetly between verses.

"I feel perfectly—" Leroy stops mid-sentence, blinking hard. "Actually, my mouth feels weird."

"Weird how?"

"Tingly. Like when you eat too much pineapple." He works his jaw experimentally. "What the hell did you give me?"

"Just wait for it."

Two more minutes, and Leroy's words come out thick and clumsy, like his tongue isn't working right.

"My vision's getting blurry," he says, sounding concerned for the first time since I've been down here.

"Mm-hmm." I check my watch again. "Right on schedule."

"Blue, seriously. What did she give me?" Leroy's question carries a note of panic now. "I can't feel my fingertips."

Blue examines his fingernails with casual interest. "I have no idea. This is Saylor's show."

"My heart's beating really fast." Leroy tries to lean forward, but his coordination is clearly off. "And I'm having trouble focusing on . . . on . . ."

"On what?"

"I can't remember what I was going to say." Leroy blinks slowly, like thinking requires enormous effort. "What's happening to me?"

"Well," I say cheerfully, "the good news is you're about to find out what all those people you tortured felt like. The bad news is you're about to die."

Leroy tries to surge forward in his chair, but his muscles aren't cooperating. "How long do I have?"

"Not long now."

Leroy turns back to me, his pupils now huge and unfocused. "Please. I'm begging you. Just . . . just use a knife. Something quick. This isn't . . . this isn't right."

"Neither was killing my father, but that didn't stop you."

Leroy's breathing becomes labored, each inhale sounding like work. His head lolls slightly to one side, and when he tries to speak again, only garbled sounds come out. Then his eyes roll back, and foam starts bubbling from his mouth.

White foam mixed with something that looks suspiciously like blood. It runs down his chin in pink rivulets, and the smell— metallic and wrong and definitely not something I was prepared for.

My stomach lurches violently.

"Oh god," I gasp, pressing my hand to my mouth. "Is that supposed to happen?"

"Poison affects different people different ways," Blue says calmly, like we're discussing the weather. "Some foam at the mouth, some just stop breathing. Leroy seems to be the foaming type."

More pink foam bubbles up, and Leroy's body starts convulsing against his restraints. Not violent seizures, but these awful, jerky movements that make the chair creak loudly.

My stomach rebels completely. I double over, dry heaving, but somehow manage to keep my breakfast where it belongs. Barely.

"You doing okay?" Blue asks, and I can hear the amusement.

"Peachy," I manage between waves of nausea. "Just . . . didn't expect the foam situation."

Leroy gives one final, shuddering breath, and then goes completely still. The only sounds are the jazz music still playing from the phonograph, my ragged breathing, and my heartbeat pounding in my ears.

I straighten slowly, wiping my mouth with the back of my hand. Leroy slumps in his chair, definitely dead, pink foam still staining his expensive suit.

"Is it over?" I ask.

Hans checks for life, then nods. "Very dead, Miss."

I stare at the body, waiting for guilt or horror or some emotional reaction beyond nausea. But all I feel is . . . satisfied. One down. However many Crow left to go.

"I did it," I say, more to myself than to anyone else. "I actually killed someone on purpose."

"You did," Blue agrees, moving to stand beside me. "How does it feel?"

"Messy. But good." I look up at him. "Really good."

Tightness in my chest wants to break open. Not from guilt or horror, but from relief. For the first time since Dad died, I feel like I actually did something for him instead of just surviving what happened to me. I'm not the helpless daughter who watched her father get stabbed. I'm not the victim who needed rescuing. I'm the woman who killed one of his murderers with her own hands.

I did this. I forced that pill down the Crow's throat and watched him die, and I didn't run or faint or throw up until it was over.

Would Dad be proud? I honestly don't know, but he's not here anymore and all I can do is seek justice for him.

Blue reaches out and gently brushes a strand of hair away from my face, his fingers lingering against my cheek. "Ready for the next one?"

I think about Dad, about his last moments, about all the pain the Crow caused. "Bring them on."

Blue chuckles softly, his fingers still tracing my cheek. "Maybe one is enough for one night. The other two can remain on ice." His smile is fond but practical. "No need to rush this or have an assembly line of carnage."

Blue's smile is proud but menacing as he pulls me closer, one hand sliding to the back of my neck. When he kisses me, it's soft but possessive—making out in front of a corpse should probably bother me more than it does.

Suddenly Leroy's body jerks violently in the chair, making me jump and break away from Blue's mouth with a small shriek.

"I thought he was dead!" I gasp, pressing my hand to my chest.

"He is," Blue says calmly, not even glancing at the body. "Just muscle spasms. Happens sometimes after death."

"Well that's horrifying," I mutter. "Does that happen often?"

"Often enough," Blue says. "Most people run screaming when they see it."

"Good thing I'm not most people." I step back toward him.

"No," he says, pulling me close again. "You're definitely not."

Hans starts untying Leroy's body from the chair. "Boss, should I dispose of this now?"

"Later. Right now, we all need to get ready for dinner. Time for your next lesson." Blue offers me his arm. "You did well."

As we head toward the basement stairs, leaving Hans and Leroy behind, I look back one more time at the still form slumped in the chair. I actually did it. No throwing up, no fainting, no humiliating myself in front of Blue.

I'm getting better at this.

CHAPTER THIRTY
SAYLOR

The relief flowing through me is intoxicating as we reach the main floor. For the first time since Dad died, I feel like I accomplished something meaningful. Like I'm actually becoming the person who can make them all pay.

Blue stops walking and turns to face me fully, his hands settling on my shoulders as he searches my face. "How are you feeling? Any nausea? Dizziness? Sometimes the adrenaline crash hits harder than expected."

"I'm starving, actually. Is that weird?"

"Perfectly normal. Murder works up an appetite." Blue offers me his arm with that pleased look that means he's proud of my progress.

His approval makes something warm unfurl in my chest. I find myself wanting more—wanting him to tell me I did well, that I'm learning. The hunger for his praise feels almost as sharp as my appetite for food.

"Get changed—wear something nice. There's an aspect of killing we haven't covered yet, and I want you to meet someone who can teach it better than I can."

I slide my hand through his arm, still buzzing from the adrenaline. The practical reality of what he's saying starts to sink in as we walk toward the main staircase.

"Disposal," he continues. "You can't just kill someone and not think about what happens next. The body is evidence. The scene tells a story. Every choice you make after the moment of death determines whether you walk away clean or spend the rest of your life looking over your shoulder."

This is why I trust him. Blue doesn't romanticize death or pretend it's cleaner than it is. He understands that wanting someone dead and actually making them dead are two completely different skill sets.

"An old friend of mine runs a restaurant built into the sea cliffs. Former colleague, you might say. He's traded his previous career for a Michelin star, but the skill set translates beautifully." Blue glances at me, gauging my reaction. "The view is incredible, and the food will be the best you've ever had."

When we reach my door, he stops and turns to face me. His hand comes up to cup my cheek gently before he leans down and presses a soft kiss to my forehead.

"I'm proud of you," he says quietly, his lips still close to my skin.

The warmth of his praise makes me bold. "What kind of grade would you give me? Was I an A student today?"

Blue pulls back just enough to meet my eyes, and that dangerous smile spreads across his face. "You were a very good girl."

Those two simple words. My knees actually wobble, and I have to grip the doorframe to keep from melting into a complete puddle of goo right here in the hallway. Jesus Christ, the man could probably make me combust just by reading a grocery list in that voice.

Blue gives me a playful swat on the ass. "Go get ready. Meet me downstairs in an hour."

I slip inside my room and close the door behind me, leaning against it for a moment to collect myself. This man . . . what is it about this man?

An hour later, I'm standing in my room trying to decide what constitutes appropriate dinner attire for learning about corpse disposal. I choose the black dress that skims my knees and makes my legs look longer than they are. Simple, elegant, but with enough edge that it doesn't scream *naive girl*. The shoes are lower heels than I'd normally choose for a dinner out, but something tells me tonight might involve more than just sitting at a table.

Blue's waiting in the main hall when I come down, and the way his dark eyes travel from my ankles to my face makes heat bloom under my skin. He's been careful to give me space since I killed Leroy in the basement. Polite distance, gentleman behavior, treating me like I need time to process what I've become instead of the woman who craves his touch and approval.

But the way he's looking at me now suggests that careful distance is getting harder for him to maintain.

"You look beautiful," he says, offering me his arm with old-fashioned courtesy.

He's wearing a dark suit that fits him perfectly, no tie tonight, the top button of his shirt undone.

Jesus, I'm turning into one of those women who gets hot and bothered by a man's collar bones.

I've never been the type to go for older men. My friends always dated guys our age—immature, loud, obsessed with gaming and craft beer. But there's something about Blue that makes my stomach flip in the best way. Maybe it's the way he moves through the world like he owns it, or how he can discuss murder over dinner without missing a beat. Whatever it is, this man has ruined me for anyone my own age.

"Thank you." I slide my hand through his arm, feeling the solid warmth of him through the expensive fabric. "So where exactly are we going for this disposal lesson?"

"The Cavern," Blue says, guiding me toward the front door where Hans is waiting beside Blue's sleek black Aston Martin, keys in hand. "About twenty minutes south along the coast. It's got the best views on the Oregon shore, and Axton Marrow takes his time with every dish." He takes the keys from Hans with a nod. "I'll drive tonight—the coast road requires someone who knows it well."

Hans's brow furrows, clearly uncomfortable. He leans closer to Blue, lowering his voice. "Boss, Brutus is back in town from the islands. He's—"

"I know," Blue cuts him off quietly. "We'll be fine."

Hans straightens, still looking worried. "You want me to follow close behind? Just in case?"

"We'll be fine tonight, Hans," Blue assures him. "It's just dinner."

Hans doesn't look convinced, but he nods reluctantly. "Have good time then. Drive careful on those cliffs." He glances at me with a slight smile. "Miss Saylor, you look very beautiful tonight. You are lucky man, Boss."

Blue's expression softens. "Yes, I am."

Blue opens the passenger door for me with his usual courtesy, offering his hand to help me in. "You'll understand why the location works so well once you see it," he says as I settle into the leather seat.

The drive south takes us along the coast road that winds between the forest and the ocean. The afternoon light is that particular Pacific Northwest golden that makes everything look like a postcard, dramatic cliffs and crashing waves and trees that seem determined to grow directly out of solid rock. I keep the window cracked just enough to smell the salt air and feel the cool breeze.

"Tell me about this friend of yours," I say as we navigate another hairpin turn that puts us closer to the edge than seems strictly safe.

"Professional cleaner for eight years. Bodies, scenes, evidence. If someone needed a situation to never have happened, Axton Marrow was the man you called." Blue downshifts as we climb higher up the cliff road. "He had an artist's eye for detail and the stomach for work that would send most people into therapy for life."

"What made him switch careers?"

"Same thing that drives most career changes. He got tired of the hours, the travel, the stress of working for people who might decide to clean up their own loose ends by having him disappear." Blue glances at me as we round another curve. "Plus, it turns out the same attention to detail that made him excellent at disposal also makes him exceptional at plating a perfect risotto."

The restaurant appears around the next bend like something out of a fairy tale. Carved directly into the cliff face, the Cavern looks like it grew from the rock itself. Floor-to-ceiling windows curve along the ocean side, offering views that probably make diners forget whatever they came here to eat. The building seems to hang suspended between the forest above and the waves below, like whoever built it had a death wish and excellent architectural taste.

Blue parks in a small lot hidden among the trees, and as we get out I can hear an unexpected sound echoing from below.

Sea lions. Hundreds of them, from the sound of it, barking and bellowing somewhere below.

"The sea lion colony," Blue explains as we walk toward the restaurant's entrance. "They've been using the caves under the restaurant as a rookery for decades. They're loud, but you get used to it."

"Sounds like quite the dinner soundtrack," I say.

The entrance is more like stepping into a natural cave than walking into a restaurant. The walls are raw stone, carved and polished to show off the natural grain and color. Warm light comes from fixtures that seem to emerge naturally from the stone, and the sound of waves echoes up from somewhere far below.

A hostess with intricate tattoos covering her arms greets us with professional warmth. "Blue. It's been too long." She hugs him like they're old friends, then turns to study me with intelligent eyes. "And this must be Saylor. Axton's been looking forward to meeting you."

"He has?" I ask, surprised.

"News travels fast in our community," the hostess explains, leading us deeper into the restaurant. "A protégé for Blue is big news. Especially one with your particular motivations."

The dining room is stunning. The ocean-side wall is entirely glass, offering an unobstructed view of the Pacific stretching to the horizon. Below, I can see the rocky outcroppings where the sea lions have claimed their territory, sleek brown bodies basking in the waning sunlight. The interior walls are the same polished stone as the entrance, and tables are positioned to take advantage of both the view and the acoustics that carry the sound of waves and sea lions throughout the space.

But what really catches my attention is how empty the restaurant is. Maybe ten tables total, all occupied by people who look like they've never filled out a job application in their lives. Well-dressed, careful about their conversations, dangerous in ways I'm only beginning to understand.

"Invite only," Blue murmurs as the hostess seats us at a corner table. "Axton only serves people he knows personally or who come recommended by people he trusts completely."

"Like you."

"Like me."

The hostess brings us wine without being asked—something that tastes like dark fruit and spice, smooth and complex in a way that screams expensive. I'm taking my second sip when a man emerges from what must be the kitchen.

Axton Marrow looks exactly like what you'd get if you crossed a chef with a mortician. He's tall and lean, with graying hair pulled back in a neat ponytail and hands that move with the careful attention of someone who's spent years working with very sharp instruments. His chef's coat is pristine white, but there's something about the man that suggests he's seen enough blood to last several lifetimes.

"Blue," he says, clasping Blue's hand with genuine warmth. "And the famous Saylor Mitchell. I've heard quite a bit about you."

"All good, I hope." I stand to shake his hand, noting the way he assesses me with the same attention most chefs probably reserve for evaluating a perfect piece of fish.

"All promising," he says with a smile that doesn't quite reach his eyes. "Welcome to the Cavern. I trust you'll enjoy the evening."

"The food smells incredible," I tell him.

"Wait until you taste it." He glances at Blue. "The usual?"

"Surprise us," Blue says. "But make sure the lady gets the full experience."

Axton nods. "Consider it done. I'll leave you to your conversation." He gives a slight bow. "Enjoy your meal."

As he disappears back into the kitchen, I turn to Blue. "He seems . . . intense."

Blue gestures toward the windows where I can see the sea lion colony lounging on the rocks below. "You hear that sound?"

I listen to the barking and bellowing echoing up from below. "The sea lions?"

"They're loud, messy, and they eat absolutely everything." Blue takes a sip of wine. "Best neighbors Axton's ever had."

"I'm guessing there's more to that story."

"Three things matter when you need to make a problem disappear," Blue says. "Where you do it, how you get rid of it, and when you need it gone."

The waitress brings our first course without interrupting. I cut into whatever Axton has prepared—some kind of seared fish with a sauce that tastes like it has actual magic in it.

"Oh my god," I moan, taking another bite. "This is incredible. What is this sauce?"

"Axton's secret," Blue says, watching me with amusement. "He's got a way with flavors most people can't replicate."

I take another bite, practically melting in my chair. "I could eat this every day."

"Just don't order the meat pies," Blue adds casually.

I pause with my fork halfway to my mouth. "Meat pies?"

"House specialty. The sea lions can't get enough of them."

"Like . . . shepherd's pie?"

Blue meets my eyes across the table. "Uh . . . sure. Although I haven't seen any *shepherds* around Grimlock lately."

The implication hits me like a cold wave. Oh.

"He's feeding them . . ." I can't quite finish the sentence.

Blue just raises an eyebrow and takes another bite of his dinner.

I sit back in my chair, staring at him. The casual way he just told me. The fact that I'm sitting here eating Axton's incredible food while he's apparently been turning people into sea lion snacks.

"That's actually brilliant," I say finally.

Blue's smile spreads slowly across his face. "I knew you'd get it. Plus, nobody suspects the guy winning James Beard Awards."

I grin. "Food critics are scrutinizing but not *that* scrutinizing."

"Exactly. And his friends know they can count on him." Blue raises his glass. "Loyalty's the most important ingredient."

The sun's setting as we finish eating, golden light hitting the water and the sea lions below. A few slip into the waves as we watch.

"Beautiful, aren't they?" Blue says, following my gaze. "Perfectly adapted. We should all be so efficient."

"How many people in your circle of friends have these kinds of . . . alternative career backgrounds?"

Blue considers this for a moment. "Most of them. Grimlock tends to attract people who've made their living in professions that don't have much in the way of retirement benefits or alumni networks."

"Do you trust all of them?"

Blue's expression grows more serious. "I trust exactly two people in this world now that Peter's gone. Hans and Wren.

"Hans has been with me for seven years. Found him in Prague, half-dead in an alley after a job went sideways. Someone had tortured him for information he didn't have." Blue's voice softens slightly. "He could have walked away once he healed up. Instead, he asked to stay. Said he'd never had anyone patch him up without expecting something in return.

"And Wren raised me. Not officially—she was the housekeeper

for the family that took me in after my parents died. But she's the one who made sure I ate, did my homework, didn't get myself killed being stupid." Blue glances at me. "When I bought Maison Rouge, the first call I made was to her."

"She said yes."

"She said it was about time I stopped being an idiot and settled down somewhere proper." There's genuine affection present. "Hans would take a bullet for me without thinking twice. Wren would take a bullet for me and then lecture me about why I put myself in that position in the first place."

I can hear the deep love and loyalty when he talks about them. "They're like family to you."

This is the first time Blue has truly opened up to me. Not just hinting at his past or giving me cryptic half-truths, but actually letting me see who he is underneath all that careful control. The man who found a broken stranger in Prague and gave him a home. The man who called his surrogate mother and asked her to come take care of him again. There's something vulnerable in the way he talks about Hans and Wren, something that makes my chest tighten.

"The only family I have left."

"There's so much about you that I don't know," I say quietly, studying his face in the candlelight. The admission slips out before I can stop it, but I don't regret it. Not when he's been this open with me.

Blue's dark eyes meet mine, and something morphs in his face. "What would you like to know?"

He's offering something here—a crack in that careful armor he always wears. Since he's being so open, maybe it's time I ask about something that's been nagging at me.

"The portraits in your house," I begin, then pause, a teasing smile tugging at my lips. "Should I be jealous that there are other women hanging in your hallway?"

Blue's entire body goes still. The warmth that had been in his eyes when talking about Hans and Wren disappears, replaced by something guarded and unreadable. His jaw tightens.

I can tell he doesn't want to answer, that I've stumbled on to something he'd rather avoid talking about. But after a long moment, he speaks.

"They are reminders of the good I've done." His voice is carefully controlled. "There is so much darkness in my mind, my soul . . . that in order to focus on changing that man that I was, I need a daily reminder of the good. Those women represent lives I saved, people I helped when they needed it most."

The raw honesty in his confession catches me off guard. This isn't what I expected—not wives or conquests, but some kind of penance.

"So not your wives?" I ask, unable to keep the relief out of my voice.

Blue actually laughs then, a genuine sound that breaks the tension. "No, not my wives. I've never been married."

He signals to the waitress, effectively ending the conversation about the portraits. But something has shifted between us— another wall down, another piece of the puzzle that is Blue revealed in the candlelight of the Cavern.

"Dessert?" he asks me.

"God, no. I'm so full I can barely breathe." I lean back in my chair. "There's no way I could eat another bite."

Blue's mouth curves into that smile that usually means he's got something planned. "Good. Because the lesson isn't over yet. There's one more place I want to show you."

CHAPTER THIRTY-ONE
SAYLOR

The drive from the Cavern takes us inland, winding through dense forest where the trees grow so thick our headlights barely penetrate the darkness between their trunks. I watch Blue navigate the narrow road like he could drive it blindfolded.

"So where exactly are we going?" I ask, still tasting Axton's incredible food in my mind.

"To see an old friend. Someone who knows her way around a body." Blue takes a sharp turn onto an even narrower road. "Like Axton, Vespera Nightshade also runs a . . . thorough disposal operation. Plus, she's got skills you might find useful."

The road ends at a sprawling Victorian house that someone clearly built during a serious obsession with turrets and gingerbread trim. Deep burgundy siding contrasts with bone-white shutters, and every window sports elaborate carved frames that probably took months to complete. A wraparound porch drips with so much decorative woodwork it looks like architectural lace. But it's the sign hanging beside the front door that makes me laugh.

Eternal Rest Funeral Home & Cosmetic Services:
Making Your Final Impression Count

"A mortician? Really?"

"Mortician with a side business," Blue corrects, parking beside a hearse that's been converted into what appears to be a mobile makeup studio. "Vespera discovered that the same skills that make someone excellent at preparing bodies for viewings also make them phenomenal at disguise work. Now she does both."

As we approach the front door, it swings open before Blue can knock. The woman who emerges looks exactly like what you'd get if Tim Burton designed a funeral director and then gave her a sense of humor. Deep brown skin with dramatic dark eye makeup, raven-black hair twisted into an elaborate updo secured with what appear to be tiny silver skulls, wearing a fitted black dress that manages to be both funeral-appropriate and fashion-forward. But it's her smile that catches my attention—wide, genuine, and absolutely wicked.

"Blue, you magnificent bastard," Vespera says in a voice like silk wrapped around steel, pulling Blue into an embrace that would be inappropriate at an actual funeral. "And this must be the infamous Miss Mitchell. The woman who's got our boy here breaking all his retirement rules."

"Guilty as charged," I say, shaking her surprisingly warm hand. "Technically, I think he's the one corrupting me."

Vespera throws back her head and laughs—a sound like champagne bubbles bursting. "Oh, I like her already. Come in, come in. I was just finishing up with a client."

The interior of the house is even more dramatically gothic than the exterior. Deep red wallpaper, antique furniture that looks like it belongs in a vampire's parlor, and enough candles to stock a cathedral. But what really catches my attention are the photographs lining the hallway—before and after shots of Vespera's work. The befores show people in various states of . . . well, death. The afters show the same people looking like they're simply sleeping peacefully.

"Impressive work," I observe, pausing beside a particularly striking transformation.

"Twenty-three years in the business," Vespera says proudly. "Working on the living is far more rewarding, I must say. Dead people never appreciate good contouring."

Vespera gestures toward a door marked Private in elegant script, then unlocks it with a key hanging from a chain around her neck. The room beyond is like stepping into a completely different world.

It's part laboratory, part workshop, and absolutely magnificent. Stainless-steel tables line one wall, equipped with drainage systems and ventilation that clearly handle messy work. Along the opposite wall, a massive industrial incinerator hums quietly, its door sealed with locks that look like they could stop a tank.

"Welcome to my sanctuary," Vespera says, spreading her arms wide. "Where problems disappear and secrets go to die."

Blue leans against one of the tables, completely at ease in this chamber of horrors. "Vespera handled Julian Crow for us last night. Had him processed and gone before dawn."

"Julian Crow?" Vespera perks up with professional interest. "Oh, that was delightful work. Young man, good bone structure. Shame about the personality, but they can't all be winners." She glances at me with something that might be pride. "I heard you were the one who did the actual honors. How was your first kill?"

The casual way she asks the question should probably disturb me more than it does. "Honestly? Terrible," I say, feeling heat creep up my neck. "I mean, he died, so mission accomplished, but I have no idea what I'm doing. I'm basically winging it and hoping nobody notices I'm a complete amateur."

"Ah, honesty! How refreshing." Vespera claps her hands together with genuine delight. "Blue, darling, you've brought me a protégé who actually admits she's a work in progress. How absolutely wonderful.

"The Crow are an awful bunch," Vespera continues, her tone shifting to something darker. "They deserve whatever's coming to them. Thank goodness Blue finally got some sense into that thick skull of his and left them behind."

I stop breathing. "Wait. What?"

The room goes quiet except for the hum of the incinerator. I look between Blue and Vespera, suddenly understanding that I've just learned something huge.

"You were one of them?" I ask Blue, my voice barely above a whisper. "You were a Crow?"

Blue runs a hand through his hair, messing up that perfect styling.

"Shit," Vespera says, covering her mouth too late.

"What do you want to know?" Blue asks, already knowing what I'm going to demand.

"Everything," I say without hesitation. "I need to know everything."

Blue is quiet for a long moment, studying my face like he's looking for something. Finally, he nods. "Blue Crow."

Vespera busies herself organizing tools on one of the tables, but I can tell she's listening to every word.

"I was in my early twenties when Brutus recruited me," Blue continues. "Fresh out of the military, looking for purpose, to apply the skills I'd picked up. Brutus saw potential in me that I didn't even know I had. He convinced me I was wasting my talents in civilian life, that I could be part of something bigger." Blue's hands clench into fists at his sides. "He made it sound like an honor. Like joining the Crow was the most important thing I could ever do."

"He was your mentor."

"He was my father figure, my teacher, my god." The admission comes out bitter. "For eight years, I was Blue Crow. I killed whoever Brutus pointed me at, however he wanted it done. I thought I was part of something legendary."

"What changed?"

Blue meets my eyes across the room. "Your father."

Vespera has gone completely still, her usual theatrical energy replaced by focused attention.

"He said he knew there were people who needed help escaping. Said if I helped him save the innocent ones, he'd help me find targets who actually deserved to die."

My heart is pounding so hard I can hear it in my ears. "And you said yes."

Blue looks at Vespera, who nods encouragingly. "Peter and I spent years working together. He'd identify people who needed help disappearing, and I'd handle their 'deaths' while he got them new identities, new lives."

"That's . . . actually beautiful," Vespera says softly.

"It was perfect," Blue agrees. "Until Brutus figured out the pattern. Too many of our targets were surviving their 'murders,' disappearing without a trace." His expression darkens. "When he confronted me, I had to choose. Peter or the Crow."

"You chose Peter."

"I chose myself," Blue corrects. "I chose to stop being Blue Crow and just be Blue. But that meant war with Brutus, and Peter . . ." He trails off, pain flickering across his face.

"Peter paid the price," I finish quietly.

I'm quiet for a long moment, processing everything he's told me. "Blue Crow . . ." I finally say. "Doesn't sound right."

"It wasn't right," Vespera says.

Blue clears his throat, breaking the heavy weight in the room.

"Enough about the Crow. *This* is why I wanted to bring you here," he says, gesturing around the room. "To meet Vespera and see the incinerator. So you'd know where to come if things go sideways."

"Consider me your backup plan," Vespera adds with that wicked smile returning. "If you ever need help making problems disappear, I'm your girl. And if you ever need a glam squad for an undercover job, well, I do that too."

Blue pushes off from the table. "We should go. We've got dessert waiting at home." His grin turns predatory. "Two Crow sitting on ice, and I'd hate for them to spoil."

CHAPTER THIRTY-TWO
BLUE

The basement air carries the scent of champagne and anticipation—two of my favorite combinations. Hans has outdone himself with tonight's presentation. The stone walls are softened by warm lighting, and he's arranged a proper dessert service on the antique sideboard: crystal flutes, vintage champagne chilling in silver buckets, and delicate petit fours that Wren must have prepared before she turned in for the evening.

Our two remaining dinner guests complete the tableau.

Jack "The Knife" Crow sits in the chair closest to the champagne setup, his wrists secured with Hans's trademark efficiency. No gags this time—I want to hear what they have to say. Victor "The Veteran" Crow occupies the chair beside him, his confiscated cane sword leaning against the wall like a decorative accent.

Both men eye the champagne setup with obvious wariness. Smart. They should be wary.

"Gentlemen," I say, guiding Saylor down the final steps with my hand at the small of her back. "I hope you weren't waiting long."

"Not at all," Victor replies, but he carries less of the confidence he showed at dinner. "Though I have to say, your hospitality has taken quite the turn since the soup course."

Jack snorts. "Hospitality? Your psychotic girlfriend stabbed Leroy through the fucking hand. Where is he, anyway?"

I can feel Saylor's posture straighten beside me, but when I glance at her profile, there's no trace of the earlier nausea. If anything, she looks . . . eager.

"Leroy's indisposed at the moment," I say pleasantly. "But don't worry—you'll be joining him soon enough."

"Hans," I call, and the big German emerges from the shadows near the wine storage. "Would you mind opening the champagne? I think tonight calls for a celebration."

"What exactly are we celebrating?" Jack asks, testing his restraints with casual interest. "Your girlfriend's impressive stabbing technique? Because I have to say, the follow-through was shit."

Saylor moves toward the champagne setup with fluid grace, pulling a small velvet bag from her purse. "We're celebrating progress," she says, her voice carrying a confidence that wasn't there when we first met at dinner. "Personal growth. Learning new skills."

Hans pops the first cork like he's done it a thousand times before, the sound echoing off the stone walls like a small gunshot. Victor flinches despite himself, while Jack just watches Saylor with growing unease.

"You know what your problem is, sweetheart?" Jack says with less swagger now. "You think one lucky stab makes you dangerous."

Saylor extracts a bottle filled with tiny blue spheres from the velvet bag. "Actually, Jack, I think my problem was trying to be something I'm not." She unscrews the cap with steady hands. "All that dramatic knife work. Very messy. Not really my style."

My pulse quickens as I watch her tap not one, but two blue orbs into her palm. Christ, she's learning fast.

"What are those?" Victor asks, his earlier composure finally cracking.

"Medicine," Saylor says sweetly, studying the blue spheres in her palm. "For your nerves. You both seem so tense."

"Two?" I can't keep the admiration out of my voice. "Feeling efficient tonight?"

She glances at me, and the heat in her gaze makes my blood sing. "It's been a long day. I don't feel like waiting around." She drops both orbs into the first champagne flute, watching them dissolve with scientific interest. "Plus, Duffy said I should experiment with dosages. Test different approaches."

Hans pours the second glass, the bubbles rising in perfect streams. Saylor drops two more blue spheres into this flute as well, her movements becoming more confident with each repetition.

"Duffy?" Victor's voice cracks slightly. "You got poison from that witch?"

"Witch? I thought you men burned all the witches at the stake years ago," Saylor says, accepting both glasses from Hans. She holds them up to the light, watching the last traces of blue fade completely. "But call her whatever you want."

Jack laughs, but there's no humor in it—just the desperate bravado of a man who knows he's fucked. "You really think we're just going to drink whatever you hand us?"

"Oh, you absolutely are." Saylor moves to stand directly in front of his chair, champagne flute extended like an offering. "Hans is going to help you remember your manners if needed."

Hans flexes his fingers like a pianist preparing for a concert.

"This is fucking ridiculous," Victor says, yanking at his bonds. "Blue, what happened to professional courtesy? Just put a bullet in our heads and be done with it."

"Now where's the fun in that?" I lean back in my chair, thoroughly entertained. "Saylor's been practicing. I'd hate to deny her the opportunity to show off her new skills."

Saylor kneels gracefully beside Jack's chair, holding the champagne flute like a communion chalice. "Come on, Jack. One little sip. It's excellent champagne—Wren doesn't stock anything cheap."

"Go fuck yourself."

"Hans, could you help Jack open his mouth? I think he's forgotten how to be polite."

Hans moves behind Jack's chair with predatory grace, placing one massive hand on the man's forehead while using the other to grip his jaw. Jack tries to keep his mouth clamped shut, but Hans knows exactly how much pressure to apply until his lips part.

Saylor tilts the glass, pouring a small amount between his teeth. "Just swallow, Jack. Fighting it only makes things take longer."

Jack spits, spraying champagne across the stone floor with defiant fury. Hans immediately pinches his nose while keeping his jaw forced open, cutting off his air supply.

"There we go," Saylor says pleasantly, pouring another measure when Jack's mouth opens in a desperate gasp for air. "Much better cooperation."

This time, Jack has no choice but to swallow or drown. The fight goes out of him as soon as the champagne hits his system—he knows it's over.

Victor is easier. The old gangster doesn't fight when Hans grips his jaw, just opens his mouth and lets Saylor pour the champagne down his throat. He swallows it all with the resignation of someone who's lived too long in this business to expect mercy.

Saylor settles back to watch like she's got front row seats to her favorite show.

Hans sets the empty glass aside.

Victor's voice is already getting weaker as he speaks. "You know this won't end with us. The Crow have been around for years, Blue. Kill us, and ten more will take our place."

"I'm counting on it," Saylor says, echoing my words from dinner with a confidence that makes something hot and primal uncoil in my chest. "More practice."

The casual way she discusses multiple murders, the complete confidence in her voice—watching her discover this side of herself is better than any drug I've ever tried.

The basement falls quiet except for the increasingly labored breathing of our guests. Jack's face has gone pale, sweat beading on his forehead despite the cool air. Victor tries to speak but can only manage a whisper.

"This . . . this isn't justice," Victor manages. "This is revenge."

Saylor tilts her head, considering his words with genuine curiosity. "Is there a difference?"

Victor's head drops forward, his breathing becoming shallow and irregular. Jack follows a moment later, the last traces of defiance finally leaving his body.

I watch Saylor as she studies their faces, taking in every detail like she's memorizing it. Her breathing is steady, her color normal, her stomach apparently settled. No nausea, no fainting—just watching them die by her own hand.

"Well?" I ask quietly.

She turns to look at me, and the satisfaction blazing in her expression makes my pulse pound. "I could get used to this."

The way she says it—the quiet conviction, the complete absence of guilt or regret, the flush in her cheeks that has nothing to do with exertion—makes something primitive and hungry rise in my chest. Watching her kill, seeing her embrace this part of herself without apology, is the most erotic thing I've ever witnessed.

I stand slowly, moving toward her with deliberate intent. She meets my gaze without flinching, and when I cup her face in my hands, her lips part in anticipation.

"You're incredible," I murmur against her mouth before kissing her with all the heat and admiration I've been holding back.

She responds immediately, her hands fisting in my shirt as she pulls me closer with desperate hunger. The kiss tastes like victory, and when she breaks away to look at me, her eyes are dark with the same arousal that's coursing through my veins.

"Bedroom," she whispers, her voice breathless with want. "Now."

I don't need to be asked twice.

CHAPTER THIRTY-THREE
SAYLOR

A knock on my door at 9 p.m. reveals a garment bag hanging on the handle with a note attached.

For tonight. The fae prefer their mortals dressed appropriately. – B

I unzip the bag and stare at what's inside.

"Holy shit," I whisper to my empty room.

The centerpiece is a black corset dress crafted by someone who not only understands but worships the female form. The bodice is made of black silk with intricate silver embroidery that catches light when I move. The corset laces up the front with silver ribbon, pulling everything into a perfect hourglass silhouette. The skirt is layers of black tulle and silk that flow to just above my knees, short enough to show off the thigh-high stockings with delicate lace tops.

The boots are black leather and lace up to mid-thigh, with silver buckles and a higher heel than I usually wear. They're clearly expensive, custom-made to fit perfectly, and designed to look both elegant and slightly dangerous.

But it's the wings that make this costume look like it came from one of my dreams.

They're massive black feathered wings that span at least six feet when fully extended. Each feather looks real, ranging from deep black to hints of iridescent purple and blue that only show when light hits them just right. The wings attach to a harness hidden beneath the corset, positioned so they look like they grow naturally from my shoulder blades. When I move, they respond slightly, creating the illusion that they're actually part of me.

The accessories complete the transformation. A delicate silver circlet that looks like twisted thorns, dark eye makeup that makes my eyes look huge and mysterious, and silver jewelry that catches the light. My hair falls in loose waves over my shoulders, contrasting perfectly with the black feathers.

I slip everything on, and when I look in the mirror, I see a dark angel, something powerful and hauntingly nightmarish. Something that might grant your prayers or might drag you into beautiful darkness, depending on her mood.

Twenty minutes later, I'm making my way downstairs, the wings creating a dramatic silhouette against the walls.

Blue stands at the bottom of the staircase, and the sight of him stops me completely.

The plague doctor costume is flawless and absolutely terrifying. The long black leather coat reaches almost to his ankles, fitted to emphasize his broad shoulders and lean build. The leather is aged and weathered, making it look authentic rather than theatrical. Black leather gloves extend past his wrists, and his pants are tucked into tall black boots that look like they could kick down doors without showing a scuff.

But it's the mask that makes my breath catch. The plague doctor's beak is longer than I expected, crafted from dark leather that's been treated to look centuries old. Dark glass lenses hide his eyes completely, giving him an inhuman appearance that makes my skin crawl in the best possible way. The beak extends far enough that it completely changes the shape of his face, making him look like some hybrid between man and bird of prey.

A black leather hat sits low on his head, and when he turns slightly, I catch the outline of his axe handle beneath the back of his coat. The weapon is positioned along his spine, completely hidden by the flowing leather but obviously accessible if needed.

He looks like Death's personal surgeon. Like something that would haunt plague-ravaged cities and collect souls for processing.

"You look . . ." He stops, tilting his head to study me. "Terrifying."

I laugh. "You look like you stepped out of a medieval nightmare."

"And you look like a death angel." There's something satisfied in his observation, like he's pleased with how we turned out. "We match." He offers me his arm, then pauses. "I should have mentioned— everyone dresses up for the Dryad's Dance."

"I figured that out from the costume." I gesture at my wings. "But why? Is it just tradition?"

"Folklore. The story goes that during the Dryad's Dance, when the barrier between realms grows thin, the fae use the opening to lure humans back to their world." Blue's voice takes on the tone of someone reciting an old tale. "But if there are no humans to be found—only other creatures, other magical beings—then there's no one for them to trick."

"So everyone pretends to be something else to avoid being kidnapped by fairies."

"Exactly. Hide in plain sight."

"Smart. I can work with that."

He offers me his arm. "Ready?"

Outside, a black carriage waits in the circular drive, complete with two midnight-colored stallions that stepped out of a fairy tale written in shadow and starlight. These aren't ordinary horses—they're magnificent creatures with coats so dark they absorb light, their manes flowing like liquid silk in the evening breeze. Steam rises from their nostrils in the cool air, and when they shift their weight, muscles ripple beneath their glossy coats like coiled steel ready to spring. Their eyes are intelligent, almost knowing, and when one turns to study me, I swear I see recognition pass through those dark depths—like it knows exactly what I am.

The driver perched on his seat wears a tall black hat and cape that billows dramatically in the wind, his face hidden in shadow. The whole thing is so dramatically over the top that I stop walking.

"Seriously?" I stare at the carriage with its ornate silver details and lacquered black finish that reflects the estate's lights like a dark mirror. "We're taking a carriage to a forest party?"

"Right for the occasion."

"How far is this thing anyway?"

"Not far. But you're wearing wings." He helps me up into the carriage, careful not to crush the feathers. "And I thought you might enjoy the entrance."

I settle into the velvet seats, my wings spreading behind me. The interior is sumptuous—black velvet cushions so soft they embrace me, silver trim that catches the moonlight filtering through the small windows, and enough space that my costume doesn't feel cramped. "You really don't do anything halfway, do you?"

"Where's the fun in that?"

The driver clicks his tongue and the stallions begin moving, their hooves creating a steady rhythm on the gravel drive that sounds like distant thunder. The carriage rocks gently as we make our way down the winding path toward the forest, and I have to admit there's something magical about arriving this way.

As we settle into the rhythm of the journey, Blue reaches across the space between us and takes my hand. The gesture is simple, normal—something boyfriends do with their girlfriends on the way to parties. His fingers intertwine with mine, thumb tracing gentle circles across my knuckles, and for a moment we're just two people holding hands in a carriage.

It's the first genuinely normal thing that's happened between us.

Everything else has been wrapped in shadows and danger— kidnapping and murder, handcuffs and belt around my throat near suffocation, passion that burns so hot it leaves marks. Even our tender moments carry an edge of darkness, a reminder that Blue is something beautiful and terrible that I should probably run from but can't bring myself to leave.

But this? This is what regular couples do. Exist in moments that don't require wondering if someone's going to end up dead by morning.

The strange thing is, I'm not sure I want normal. The darkness that surrounds Blue isn't what I'm enduring—it's what I'm falling into willingly. There's an intoxication in loving a man who can kill without hesitation but touches me like I'm made of glass. Who can teach me murder as casually as teaching someone to ride a bike. In being claimed by someone whose idea of romance involves corpses and midnight flowers.

I study his profile in the carriage's dim light—the perfect line of his bearded jaw beneath that plague doctor mask, the way his free hand rests casually on his thigh, the controlled grace in everything he does. Even dressed as Death's personal surgeon, he's the most attractive man I've ever seen.

Maybe especially because he's dressed as Death's personal surgeon.

"So this is how you normally travel to parties?" I ask, watching the trees pass by through the carriage window, his hand still warm in mine.

"Only the important ones."

"And what makes this one important?" I adjust my wings so they don't get destroyed against the seat back.

"You're going."

Jesus . . . this man may be perfect.

The Witchwood forest beyond Grimlock's borders has been transformed into something that exists in the space between dreams and reality.

Bioluminescent mushrooms line every path through the trees, their caps glowing with ethereal blue light that pulses gently, creating the effect of a living constellation spread across the forest floor. The paths themselves seem to shift and change as we walk, the mushroom lights leading us deeper into woods that feel primordial and wild.

String lights hang from every branch—tiny bulbs that twinkle and flicker in patterns that seem almost choreographed. They're strung at different heights, creating layers of light that weave between the trees. Some hang low enough to walk under, others stretch high overhead, and the overall effect makes the forest feel like it's been wrapped in captured starlight.

But it's the death moths that make the scene truly otherworldly. Hundreds of them flutter through the air, their dark wings marked with pale skull patterns that glow faintly in the mushroom light. They move in spirals around the string lights, creating shifting shadows that dance across the forest floor. Some settle on tree branches, their wings spread to display the intricate bone-white markings, while others drift between costumed guests like living omens that somehow make the celebration feel more magical rather than sinister.

Everyone is here, just as Blue promised, but dressed so dramatically I have to look twice to recognize faces. Dame Gothel has come as some kind of nature goddess, her hair woven with living vines and her dress formed of leaves that seem to grow and morph as she moves. Dr. Finch is a mad scientist, complete with goggles and a coat covered in mysterious stains. Duffy has dressed as a forest sprite, which suits her auburn hair and mischievous grin perfectly.

Musicians play from platforms built into the trees themselves, their instruments creating melodies that sound like wind through leaves and water over stones. The music has no clear rhythm, but somehow everyone knows how to move to it, swaying and spinning in patterns that seem to come naturally.

"This is incredible," I whisper to Blue as we make our way deeper into the celebration.

"Wait until you see the heart of it."

We follow a path marked by mushrooms that glow brighter than the others, their light shifting from blue to purple to silver as we pass. Other costumed figures drift around us—a woman dressed as a raven, a man who appears to be made of bark and moss, someone in flowing robes that shimmer like water in the mushroom light.

The path opens into a clearing where the real magic happens.

The trees here form a perfect circle, their branches intertwining overhead to create a natural cathedral. In the center, a ring of massive mushrooms pulses with light so bright it's almost blinding. The glow changes color, casting everyone in the clearing in shades of blue, purple, and silver that make them look like beings from another world.

People dance within the mushroom circle, their movements hypnotic and strange. Some dance alone, lost in the music and the lights. Others move in pairs or groups, their costumes blending together until it's impossible to tell where one person ends and another begins.

"The Dryad's Dance," Blue says. "This is where the barrier between worlds is thinnest."

As if to prove his point, the lights from the mushrooms suddenly flare brighter, and for just a moment, I swear I can see figures moving between the trees that aren't wearing costumes at all. Tall, graceful shapes that seem to be made of moonlight and shadow, watching the human celebration with knowing eyes.

I blink, and they're gone.

A figure approaches us, and it takes me a moment to recognize

Elliott beneath his butterfly costume. His wings are enormous, iridescent things that seem to catch every color of light and throw it back transformed. His face is painted with intricate patterns that make his green eyes look otherworldly.

"Saylor! You look absolutely divine, my dear." His compliment has that dreamy quality it always carries, but tonight it seems more appropriate somehow. "And Blue, perfect costume for you."

"Elliott," Blue nods. "How's the party treating you?"

"Oh, it's wonderful. Simply wonderful. The lights are speaking tonight, did you know? They're telling stories about the time before time, when the trees were young and the world was wild." Elliott's painted face breaks into a smile. "Would you like to dance, Saylor? The mushrooms are calling for new partners."

I glance at Blue, who gives me an almost imperceptible nod.

"I'd love to."

Elliott takes my hand and leads me toward the ring of glowing mushrooms. The moment I step inside the circle, the world changes.

The music becomes something I can feel in my bones, a rhythm that matches the pulsing of the lights and the beating of my heart. Elliott moves with surprising grace for someone his age, spinning me through patterns that seem to write themselves in the air. Other dancers swirl around us—the raven woman, the bark man, figures in costumes so detailed I can't tell what they're supposed to represent.

The lights grow brighter, the music more intense, and there's something shifting in the air around us. The boundary between performance and reality begins to blur, and for a few moments, I almost believe we really are dancing with creatures from another world.

Then Elliott spins me one final time and releases my hand, bowing low as the music shifts to something softer.

"Thank you for the dance, dear one," he says, his painted face glowing in the mushroom light. "The Witchwood approves of you."

As I make my way back to Blue, weaving between dancers and glowing fungi, I catch sight of something that makes me stop cold.

Ash Cupp stands at the edge of the clearing, and he's not in costume. He's wearing his usual cream linen shirt and dark pants, completely out of place among the theatrical disguises surrounding him. But it's the look on his face that worries me—tense, alert, scanning the crowd with the focus of someone expecting trouble.

When he spots me looking, he makes his way over, moving through the costumed dancers with ease.

"Saylor," he says when he reaches me. "I need you to find Blue. Now."

"What's wrong?"

"They're coming. The Crow. At least six of them, maybe more." His gray eyes are hard, calculating. "My sources say they'll hit during the celebration when everyone's distracted. They know Blue will be here."

My blood turns cold. "Are you sure?"

"I'm sure." Ash glances around the celebration, and I see him catalog potential like someone who's done this before. "I need to find him."

I scan the crowd, looking for the distinctive plague doctor mask. The clearing is packed with costumed dancers, all moving and swaying to the hypnotic music. For a moment, I can't find him anywhere.

Then I see the black leather coat near the far edge of the circle, and my stomach drops instead.

"There," I point. "By the musicians' platform."

Blue stands near the edge of the clearing, but his plague doctor mask hangs loose in his hand instead of covering his face. He's deep in conversation with a woman whose gown seems to flicker between blue and silver in the mushroom light. She's standing too close to him, one hand pressed to his chest, speaking urgently with obvious distress.

When she turns slightly, I get a clear view of her face and my stomach drops. I can see tears streaming down her cheeks, but more importantly, I know that face. I've seen it every day since I've been living at Maison Rouge.

She's one of the women from the portraits in the main hall.

"What the hell?" I breathe.

Ash follows my gaze and his entire face hardens. "That's impossible."

"Who is she?"

"That's Cordelia Lynd." Ash's voice is tight with something between confusion and alarm. "She's supposed to be dead."

The woman—Cordelia—grips Blue's coat with both hands now, speaking urgently. Blue's posture is tense, his free hand raised as if trying to calm her down, but I can see the way his body angles away from her. Whatever she's saying has him upset.

I can't stop staring at the woman. At Cordelia. At whatever the hell she's supposed to be.

"Come on," Ash says, starting toward them. "We need to warn him about the Crow."

We push through the costumed dancers, weaving between a woman in a dress made of peacock feathers and a man wearing an intricate clockwork mask with moving gears. The music continues its hypnotic rhythm, but all I can focus on is the scene unfolding ahead of us.

When we finally reach Blue, he looks up at our approach but doesn't step away from the woman. He appears carefully calm, giving nothing away.

"Blue," Ash says without preamble. "We have a problem. The Crow are coming. Tonight. They'll hit during the celebration when everyone's distracted."

Blue's jaw tightens, but he just nods. "How long?"

"Soon. They know you'll be here."

Blue nods and looks at Cordelia. "So I hear."

"I told you! He's coming," Cordelia says. "And it's not just about tonight. Brutus is building an army to take over Grimlock next . . . just to get back at you."

Blue glances around the celebration, his mind clearly working through scenarios and exit strategies. The woman beside him wipes at her tears but says nothing, just watches me with curious eyes.

"Saylor needs to go back to the house," Blue says finally. "Now."

"What? No." I look between him and the crying woman who's supposed to be dead. "I'm not going anywhere until someone explains what the hell is going on."

Blue raises his hand, making some kind of signal toward the edge of the clearing. Within moments, Hans appears through the crowd, dressed as a medieval knight with chainmail and a sword at his hip. Behind him, I spot Wren dressed as a witch, complete with pointed hat and black robes that somehow make her look even more formidable than usual.

"Take her home," Blue tells Wren. "Call up security and have them man the doors. Stay with her until I get back." He turns to Hans. "You're with me."

"Blue, you can't just—" I start, but he cuts me off.

"Saylor—"

"I'm not a little girl that needs to be protected. You've been training me for this. It's my fight too."

"Your poison isn't going to help here," he snaps, and it's the first time I've seen him mad . . . losing control . . . and at me.

"I can help. I can fight—"

"This isn't up for discussion." There's a tone that makes it clear arguing would be pointless. "You're leaving. Now."

Wren steps forward. "Come along, dear. We'll get you safely back to the house."

I want to argue, want to demand answers about why this woman who hangs in a picture in his house can stay but I have to leave, about why Blue won't look me in the eye, about what the hell any of this means.

My mind spins as I keep my eyes locked on Cordelia.

What the fuck is going on?

"I'll be back soon," Blue says, finally meeting my eyes. But there's something in him I can't read, something that makes me want to demand answers and run away at the same time.

Wren takes my arm gently but firmly. "Come now, dear. Time to go."

As Wren guides me away from the clearing, away from the glowing mushrooms and death moths and whatever confrontation is about to happen, I keep looking back over my shoulder.

Blue is already deep in conversation with Ash and the woman who shouldn't exist, his plague doctor mask forgotten in his hand.

And I'm being escorted home like a child sent to bed while the adults handle the real problems.

CHAPTER THIRTY-FOUR
BLUE

The first crossbow bolt punches through the bark inches from my head, sending splinters into the night air like wooden shrapnel.

I shove Cordelia behind the nearest tree as chaos erupts across the celebration. Costumed dancers scatter in every direction, their screams cutting through the hypnotic music as black-clad figures emerge from the forest like Death itself stepping from shadow.

The Crow have come calling.

"How many?" Ash appears at my elbow, his casual linen shirt a stark contrast to the violence unfolding around us.

I count muzzle flashes between the trees, catalog the advancing shapes cutting through the bioluminescent maze like they've done this before. "Twenty. Maybe thirty."

"Fuck." Hans materializes on my other side, his medieval knight costume suddenly looking less theatrical and more practical. The chainmail across his chest could actually stop a blade, and the sword at his hip isn't a prop. "We are very outnumbered, Boss."

Another crossbow bolt shatters the glowing mushroom beside Cordelia's head, spraying phosphorescent spores across her silver dress. She doesn't scream or run like the other civilians. She just crouches lower, waiting for instructions.

"Go! Now!" I shout to her. I turn to Ash, "What about the residents?" I ask, already knowing the answer will complicate everything.

"Dame Gothel's getting people out through the old logging road," Ash reports, calm despite the gunfire now echoing through the trees. "But they'll need time."

Time we don't have. The Crow are advancing in a coordinated pattern, driving people away from the paths that lead back to town. They're herding us toward the heart of the clearing where the scattered trees provide cover but no escape routes.

I pull my axe from beneath my coat, the familiar weight settling into my palm like coming home. "How long can we hold them?"

"Long enough," Hans says, but it seems he's not fully convinced.

My plague doctor mask lies somewhere in the chaos behind me as I scan the tree line, forgotten the moment the first bolt flew. The Crow are positioned to cut off every escape route. Professional killers using a magical forest celebration as their hunting ground.

The irony isn't lost on me.

"There!" Ash points toward a figure stepping into the clearing's edge. "Brutus."

Brutus "The Beast" Crow steps into the clearing, and I remember why they call him the Beast. He's massive—six and a half feet of muscle and scar tissue wrapped in tactical gear. The man looks ready for war, which makes sense considering the circumstances.

The gunfire stops with the sudden finality of an orchestra conductor dropping his baton. Brutus raises his hand, and every Crow in the forest freezes in position. Discipline like that comes from years of working together, of trusting absolutely in your leader's judgment.

We're fucked.

"Blue!" Brutus booms across the clearing. "I hear you've been redecorating with my people. You need serious fucking help, my man. I thought I was sadistic but you . . ."

I step away from the tree, axe loose in my grip. "Brutus. Should have known you'd show up eventually."

"Couldn't let you have all the fun." His laugh is exactly as unpleasant as I remember. "But I've got a proposition for you."

"I'm listening."

Brutus gestures to his men positioned throughout the forest. "We've got you completely surrounded. No way out except through us, and there's a lot more of us than there are of you." He pauses, apparently enjoying his moment of tactical superiority. "But I'm feeling generous tonight."

"Generous how?"

"Fair fight. You, me, and whoever wants to dance. No guns." Brutus pulls a massive machete from his belt, the blade gleaming in the mushroom light. "Just steel and skill. Old school."

Hans steps up beside me. "Boss, this is obviously trap."

"Of course it's a trap." I don't take my eyes off Brutus. "But it's the only chance we've got."

Ash appears on my other side, and I notice he's somehow acquired a knife that clearly was designed for killing rather than cake decorating. "What are the terms?"

"Simple," Brutus calls back. "Last man standing wins. You kill us all, you walk away. We kill you . . ." He shrugs. "Well, we'll make it quick. Professional courtesy."

I consider our options, which is a short mental exercise since we don't have any. Twenty trained killers versus the three of us and a forest full of panicking locals. The math isn't encouraging.

Years of murder sobriety, gone in an instant. But if this buys Saylor and Wren time to get away, if this keeps her alive, then it's worth it. Peter asked me to protect his daughter. Hans is willing to die for that promise. The least I can do is break my sobriety.

"Deal," I call back.

Brutus grins, the act transforming his scarred face into something genuinely terrifying. He makes another hand signal, and suddenly every Crow in the forest steps into view. They're not carrying guns anymore—just blades. The message is clear: They're going to carve us apart piece by piece.

"Gentlemen," I say quietly to Hans and Ash, "it's been an honor."

"Likewise, Boss," Hans replies, testing the weight of his sword.

"Save the eulogies for after we're dead," Ash suggests, flipping his knife to a reverse grip. "We might surprise them."

The first Crow charges across the clearing, screaming like a banshee and swinging a machete in wild arcs that would be impressive if they weren't completely uncontrolled. I step inside his reach and bury my axe in his sternum. The metal punches through bone and gristle, and when I wrench it free, blood arcs across the glowing mushrooms like abstract art.

Then all hell breaks loose.

They come at us from every direction, a wave of black-clad killers with steel in their hands and murder in their eyes. Hans meets the first one with his sword, the clash of metal on metal ringing across the clearing. Ash moves like liquid shadow, his knife finding throats and hearts. He's done this dance many times before.

I lose myself in the rhythm of violence. Duck under a sword thrust, pivot, axe through a neck. Sidestep a machete swing, reverse grip, axe between ribs. Forward, back, spin, chop. Each movement flows into the next with muscle memory built over fifteen years of killing.

A Crow with intricate facial tattoos comes at me with paired knives, spinning them in complex patterns that look impressive but leave his center exposed. I take his head off with a horizontal swing that sends blood spraying across three nearby mushrooms.

Another one tries to flank me from the left, machete raised high for an overhead chop. I catch his wrist with my free hand, twist until something snaps, then drive my axe through his ribs. He goes down gurgling, clutching at the wound like he can hold his life inside.

The clearing has become a charnel house. Bodies in tactical gear sprawl between the glowing fungi, their blood mixing with phosphorescent spores to create patterns that would be beautiful if they weren't so horrifying. The air reeks of copper and shit and the ozone smell that comes from violence done efficiently.

Hans is holding his own near the musicians' platform, his sword work clean and economical. Every strike finds its target, every movement serves a purpose. He's cut down four Crows already, and his chainmail has turned aside two blade strikes that should have opened him to the spine.

Ash fights like he was born to do it, which maybe he was. The knife in his hand moves like an extension of his will, opening arteries and puncturing lungs. He's taken down three Crows without taking a scratch, dancing between their attacks like death wearing linen.

For a moment, I actually think we might survive this.

We're outnumbered six to one, but we're not going down easy. Ash moves like he never left this life behind. Bodies drop around me, blood feeding the glowing mushrooms until the clearing looks like an abattoir lit by fairy lights.

But they keep coming.

For every Crow we drop, another takes his place. They're coordinated, patient, willing to take losses to wear us down. Professional killers who understand that numbers always win in the end.

Ash appears beside me, breathing hard. "We're making a dent."

"Not big enough," I reply.

He's right though. The clearing is littered with Crow bodies. We've cut their numbers in half, but there are still too many. And we're getting tired.

Time to end this.

I start moving toward Brutus, cutting through the chaos with single-minded purpose. A Crow tries to block my path with twin blades. I take his arm off at the elbow with one swing, then split his skull with the return stroke.

Another one comes at me from the side, machete raised for a killing blow. I pivot, catch his wrist, and drive my knee into his elbow. The joint bends backward with a wet snap, and he drops his weapon. My axe opens his throat before he can scream.

Brutus sees me coming and grins, raising his machete in salute. "Blue! Ready for the main event?"

But I can see the fear behind his bravado, the way his eyes dart to the bodies scattered around me. And fucking good. He should be afraid.

"Let's dance."

We circle each other through the carnage, stepping over bodies and around the glowing mushrooms that continue their eternal pulse of ethereal light. Blood steams in the cool night air, and somewhere in the distance I can hear the clash of steel on steel as the battle rages on.

Brutus moves faster than his size should allow, the machete whistling through the air in patterns designed to take limbs rather than just wound. I give ground, letting him commit to his attacks while I read his rhythm.

He's good. Better than I remember. But he's also angry, and anger makes people stupid.

His next swing comes in too high, leaving his ribs exposed. I step inside his reach and drive my axe toward his heart, but he's already moving, catching my wrist with his free hand. For a moment we're locked together, struggling for control of our weapons.

He's stronger than me, but I'm faster. I hook my foot behind his ankle and drive my shoulder into his chest, sending us both tumbling to the ground. We roll across the mushroom-lit earth, each trying to pin the other long enough for a killing blow.

I come up on top, axe raised, but he gets his knees between us and kicks. The impact launches me backward into a cluster of glowing fungi that crush under my weight, their light dimming as I roll away.

Brutus rolls to his feet, machete gleaming in his fist. "You always were trickier than you looked."

"And you always talked too much."

We close again, weapons clashing in a shower of sparks. His blade catches my axe handle, scoring the wood but not biting deep enough to matter. I twist the handle, using the hook of my axe to catch his machete and wrench it aside, then bring my knee up toward his groin.

He blocks with his thigh, counters with an elbow that catches me in the temple hard enough to make my vision blur. I stumble backward, black spots dancing across my sight.

He presses his advantage, machete cutting through the air where my head was a second earlier. I duck, roll, come up swinging. My axe catches him across the back of the thigh, opening a gash that sprays blood across the nearest mushrooms.

He roars, more rage than pain, and lunges forward with his machete extended like a spear. I sidestep, let the metal whistle past, then bring my axe around in a horizontal arc aimed at his neck.

He drops under the swing, sweeps my legs out from under me. I hit the ground hard, axe spinning away into the darkness. Brutus looms over me, machete raised for the killing blow.

"Should have stayed retired," he snarls.

That's when I hear Hans scream.

The sound cuts through the battle noise like a blade through silk—raw, agonized, ending too abruptly. I turn my head and see him twenty feet away, a Crow's machete buried in his spine between his shoulder blades. The chainmail that protected him from slashing attacks can't stop a thrust from behind.

Hans drops to his knees, sword falling from nerveless fingers. The Crow behind him—one I don't recognize, probably backup they called in—grins as he wrenches the machete free. Blood gushes from the wound, and Hans pitches forward onto his face.

The moment of distraction costs me everything. Brutus's machete descends toward my throat, and I can see death approaching with crystalline clarity.

Then Ash appears like a ghost, driving his shoulder into Brutus and sending us all tumbling across the bloody ground. We roll apart, and when I look up, Brutus is already on his feet, backing toward the tree line.

"This isn't over," he snarls, pressing one hand to a gash Ash opened on his arm and the other to his thigh.

"Coward," I spit, getting to my feet. "Running from a fair fight."

Brutus's face twists with rage, but he's smart enough to know when he's beaten. He whistles, and the remaining Crow begin melting back into the forest. Three, maybe four of them left alive.

"Next time I won't be so generous," Brutus calls over his shoulder before disappearing into the darkness.

The clearing falls silent except for our ragged breathing.

Victory, but I can already see it's come at a horrible cost.

I spin around, looking for Hans, and my blood turns to ice. He's on the ground twenty feet away, alive but barely, raising his arms weakly to block the Crow standing over him. The bastard with the bloodied machete swats Hans's feeble defense aside and raises the weapon high, preparing to split his skull.

I'm too far away. I'll never make it in time.

"No!" The word tears from my throat as I sprint across the corpse-littered ground.

The Crow brings his machete down in a vicious arc, and I watch helplessly as the blade bites deep into Hans's skull with a wet crack that echoes across the clearing. Blood and brain matter spray across what's left of the mushrooms that haven't been trampled.

I reach the Crow three seconds too late, my axe taking his head clean off. Blood sprays across the clearing, but the damage is done.

Hans is dead.

Hans is on his back, face turned toward me, eyes open but vacant. Blood pools beneath him, soaking into the earth. The chainmail across his chest has been shredded by the machete thrust, and I can see white bone gleaming through the wound.

I kneel beside him, cradling his head in my lap. His face is peaceful, younger somehow in death than he ever looked in life. Seven years he worked for me. Seven years of perfect loyalty, of following orders without question, of protecting the people I cared about.

And now he's gone.

"Hans," I whisper, smoothing his blood-matted hair away from his forehead. "Mein treuer Freund."

The grief crashes over me, doubling me over his still form. Hans, who died protecting people he barely knew because I asked him to.

Gone.

I look up at the night sky, at stars barely visible through the forest canopy, and let the words come. Words that I've heard Hans give over other fallen men in our past. It was always his ritual. His way to pay respect. Words I know he'd want said over his body:

"Hear me, spirits of the night. Take this warrior from my sight. Hans the faithful, Hans the brave. Deserves far more than earthly grave.

"Seven years he stood with me. Now his soul flies wild and free. Blood and iron, steel and bone. He shall never fight alone.

"In the mist between the worlds. Where the ancient banner unfurls. Wait for me, you stubborn friend—this is not our story's end."

My voice cracks on the final words, and something hot spills down my cheeks. When was the last time I cried? I can't remember. But Hans deserves tears, deserves grief, deserves better than dying in a forest while protecting people he chose to call family.

I smooth his blood-matted hair one last time, then gently close his eyes.

"Wait for me on the other side, mein Freund," I whisper. "See you soon."

CHAPTER THIRTY-FIVE
SAYLOR

I slam through the front door of Maison Rouge like a hurricane with black feathers in a rage. Wren looks up from where she's checking window locks, her witch costume making her look like she could hex someone just by glaring at them. "Saylor, dear—"

"Don't." I rip off the thorny circlet and throw it onto the marble floor where it clatters like broken promises. "Just don't."

My wings catch on the doorframe as I storm toward the staircase, and I have to wrestle with the harness to keep from tearing the damn things off completely. Everything about this costume that felt magical an hour ago now feels like theatrical dress-up for Blue's entertainment.

"The security team is on their way," Wren calls after me. "Blue wants—"

"I don't give a shit what Blue wants right now." My defiance echoes off the vaulted ceilings as I hit the stairs. "Blue can kiss my ass."

Wren's shocked silence follows me up to the second-floor landing, where I stop in front of the portrait gallery like I'm preparing for war.

Cordelia beams down at me from her gilded frame, all platinum curls and radiant confidence. The same face I just saw at the Dryad's Dance. The same woman who was sobbing into Blue's arms like her world was ending.

"What the actual fuck?" I whisper to her portrait.

Margaret's portrait hangs next to her, then Eleanor, Vivian, Catherine, Penelope, Sophia. Seven secrets watching me from gilded frames. Seven reminders of just how much I don't know about Blue. Seven women who all look content in a way that's hard to define, all holding his signature blue roses. Seven mysteries I should have pushed harder about when I had the chance at the Cavern.

I know what I saw. That was Cordelia—the same face, the same bone structure, the same platinum blonde hair styled in those perfect finger waves. I'd stake my life on it.

Which means Blue has deep, personal relationships I know nothing about.

"Who the fuck are you?" I whisper to her portrait.

But Cordelia's painted expression offers no answers, no explanations for how someone can be both in a portrait here and crying in a forest at the same time.

So many fucking secrets . . . like the third floor . . .

"No more guessing," I say out loud. "No more wondering. No more being the clueless girlfriend who gets all her information secondhand."

I've never been the dumb girl in any story, and I'm sure as hell not starting tonight.

The third floor beckons from above like a challenge wrapped in Blue's explicit instructions to stay away. Well, fuck his instructions. I'm tired of locked doors and careful explanations and being dismissed whenever things get complicated.

The hallway of skeleton keys stretches before me, a curtain of metal that clinks softly as I push through. Keys of every size and era hang at eye level, forcing me to duck and weave between them. Tonight they're not mysterious or romantic. Tonight they're just obstacles standing between me and whatever fresh hell Blue's been hiding up here.

I start grabbing keys at random, working my way down the hallway with systematic fury. The first key I try is too big for any of the keyholes. The second is too small. The third fits the lock on the burgundy door but won't turn no matter how hard I twist.

"Come on," I mutter, moving to the next key, my wings bumping against the hanging metal with each movement. "One of you bastards has to work."

The blue door. The silver one with carved roses. The door that is covered in black velvet. I try key after key, lock after lock, growing more frustrated with each failure.

Some keys go in but won't turn. Others are obviously the wrong size. A few seem promising until they stick halfway, refusing to budge in either direction. My hands start cramping from gripping the ornate metal, and my wings keep getting tangled in the swaying keys like some gothic obstacle course designed by a sadist.

Fifteen minutes in, I'm seriously considering finding something heavy and just smashing whatever door catches my eye first. Twenty minutes, and I'm muttering curses that would make a sailor proud.

Then I reach for a key near the end of the hallway—an ornate thing made of tarnished silver with a head shaped like a raven in flight. It's heavier than the others, older, with a weight that suggests it was made to lock something important.

Something secret.

The door I try it on is painted the color of dried blood, with a key-hole surrounded by carved skulls so small they're almost hidden in the decorative woodwork. When I slide the key in, it fits like it was waiting for me.

When I turn it, the lock clicks open with a sound like breaking bones.

"Finally," I breathe, pushing the door open.

And immediately wish I hadn't.

The smell hits me first—dust and old stone, something stale and unused that makes my nose wrinkle. The musty odor of things that have been locked away from air and light for far too long.

The room beyond is larger than I expected, with stone walls that look older than the rest of the house. I fumble along the wall until I find a light switch, and when the overhead lights flicker on, what I see makes my stomach drop.

But I can't look away.

Seven tables line the room like some macabre exhibition. Each one holds a single human skull, positioned with the same careful attention Blue brings to everything else in his life.

The skull on the first table, according to a small placard written in Blue's careful handwriting, belongs to Margaret.

Eleanor's skull sits on the next table, arranged with deliberate care.

Vivian's skull occupies the third table. When I look at it, my stomach churns thinking this was once the smiling woman from the portrait downstairs.

Catherine's skull is centered perfectly on the fourth table, the bone gleaming under the electric lights.

Sophia's skull sits on the fifth table, placed with the same methodical attention.

The sixth table holds another skull with the name Penelope, set with reverence equal to all the others.

And then I see the seventh table.

A complete skull sits there like someone took their time polishing every surface. The bone gleaming white and perfectly positioned, the empty sockets seeming to track my movement. A small placard at the foot of the table reads "Cordelia" in Blue's neat handwriting.

"What. The. Fuck."

But Cordelia was just at the Dryad's Dance. I saw her. She was alive, breathing, sobbing into Blue's chest like her world was ending.

"Seven," I whisper, backing toward the door. "One, two, three, four, five, six, seven."

Seven skulls. Seven women whose names match the portraits downstairs.

But if they're all here, displayed in Blue's private museum of horrors, then who the hell was crying all over him at the Dryad's Dance?

I count again, needing to be absolutely sure. Seven tables. Seven skulls positioned like trophies. Seven names on small placards marking each display.

My stomach heaves, and I taste bile at the back of my throat. The air feels thick and wrong, clinging to my skin like I'm breathing in secrets and death.

I should run. I should get out of this room, out of this house, out of Grimlock before Blue comes home and finds me standing in his chamber of secrets. I should call the police, the FBI, whoever handles cases like this.

But my feet won't move. I'm frozen in the doorway, staring at seven skulls whose owners I just saw smiling in portraits downstairs.

What the hell is Blue hiding? And how many more secrets does he have?

These are his trophies, displayed in his private museum where he can visit them whenever he wants. Where he can remember whatever twisted connection he had with each of them.

From somewhere far below, a sound rips through the silence that makes my blood freeze. Wren's voice, but not like I've ever heard it—raw, broken, animalistic. A howl of pure agony that echoes up through the floors and seems to shake the very walls of Maison Rouge.

"No, no, no, no!" The words tear from her throat like pieces of her soul being ripped away. Not the controlled, capable Wren who manages Blue's household like a general. This is the sound of a woman's world ending in real time.

The sobbing that follows is worse than the screaming. Deep, wracking sobs that speak of loss so profound it has no words. The kind of grief that hollows you out and leaves nothing but an empty shell breathing.

I scramble to my feet, adrenaline cutting through my shock. Whatever's happening downstairs is bad. Catastrophically bad.

But before I can even reach the top of the stairs, a shadow fills the doorway at the end of the hall.

Blue stands there, still wearing his plague doctor costume, but the leather coat is soaked with blood. Fresh blood, dark and wet, covering his chest and arms like he's been bathing in it. His face is a mask of something I've never seen before—exhaustion, grief, rage all twisted together.

Terror floods my system so fast I can barely breathe. "What's going on?" The question comes out high and thin. "What's wrong with Wren? Whose blood is that?"

His dark eyes find mine across the hallway, and for a moment he just stares at me like he's seeing a ghost. Like he's surprised I'm real.

"Who are these skulls?" I demand, my voice getting stronger even as my hands shake. "I saw them, Blue. I saw all of them. Seven skulls with the same names as the women in your portraits like some sick exhibit. Margaret, Eleanor, Vivian, Catherine, Sophia—all of them!" My pitch climbs higher with each name. "What the fuck is happening? Where is Cordelia? What the hell is happening?" I take a shaky breath, trying to make sense of the impossible. "I saw her at the Dryad's Dance tonight—alive, breathing, crying all over you. But her skull is upstairs with a nameplate that says she's dead. How can she be both places?"

Blue steps into the hallway, and I can see the weight of whatever happened at the Dryad's Dance crushing down on his shoulders. When he speaks, he's hoarse, broken.

"Hans is dead."

"Hans?" The name comes out like a question, like maybe I misheard him. "What? *WHAT?*" I shake my head. "How?"

Blue looks at me with hollow eyes, then looks down at his gore-soaked coat like he's just now noticing it. "There were too many of them. I tried to . . . I couldn't save him."

Blue takes a step toward me, then another, but halfway down the hall his legs give out. He stumbles against the wall, sliding down until he's sitting on the floor, his back pressed against the stone. His head falls forward into his hands, and I can see his shoulders shaking.

I've never seen Blue show weakness. Not once. He's always been controlled, composed, dangerous in that careful way that makes people step aside when he walks into a room. But this isn't weakness. This is something much more powerful—grief so raw and devastating that it's stripped away every defense he's ever built.

CHAPTER THIRTY-SIX
SAYLOR

The church bells aren't ringing—they're pounding out a funeral march that vibrates through the stone floor and into my bones.

I sit in the third pew, watching Blue move through clusters of mourners, shaking hands and accepting condolences while his mind is clearly somewhere else. Dame Gothel touches his arm and speaks words I can't hear. Dr. Finch grips his shoulder. Elliott offers a flask disguised as a prayer book.

Everyone wants to comfort the grieving, broken man. Except Blue isn't that man. Blue is the man who keeps seven skulls on the third floor of his mansion and attends funerals for friends who died protecting his demons.

Two days of silence between us. Two days of him appearing at meals, eating without tasting, disappearing into parts of the house I don't dare follow. Wren moves through her duties, but every task seems to require twice the effort it used to. The whole estate feels deflated, a balloon slowly leaking air.

And I've been hiding in storage units, sitting among boxes of my old life, trying to figure out what the hell comes next. Because I can't stay here. Not knowing what I know. I could handle Blue being a killer—hell, that turned me on if I'm being honest. But killing women and preserving them upstairs? That crosses a line.

Doesn't it?

The rational part of my brain keeps circling back to the same arguments. I've murdered now too. I poisoned men and felt nothing but satisfaction watching them foam at the mouth. I stabbed Leroy and the only thing that bothered me was the mess. I even slit a man's throat—accidentally, yes—but still a kill. Who am I to judge anyone for their relationship with death?

But this feels different. Sick. Twisted. Demented even. He mentioned that those portraits remind him of the good. How can that be? How can skulls of these women be good? And if Blue could kill them, display them, visit them whenever nostalgia struck . . .

Would he kill me?

Of course not. Blue protects me, cherishes me, looks at me like I'm the answer to questions he's been asking his whole life.

But maybe Margaret thought that too. And Eleanor. And all the others whose skulls are organized so carefully upstairs.

Then there's the Cordelia problem. I saw her at the Dryad's Dance—alive, breathing, sobbing into Blue's chest. But her skull sits upstairs with a nameplate marking her as dead. What kind of game is Blue playing?

I feel like I'm losing my mind, and mourning Hans on top of everything isn't helping. I don't know what to do. I don't know what to say. I'm swirling in an abyss of death and secrets.

I need answers. But Hans died protecting me, and Blue's grief is this raw thing that makes him untouchable. Every time I've considered asking about the women, about Cordelia, about what any of this means, I look at him and see someone barely holding himself together.

Besides, there are practical considerations. The Crow are still out there. Brutus and whoever else escaped the forest are probably planning their next move. And I'm not done with my own killing spree. I still have names on my list, men who need to pay for what they did to Dad.

But what if they get to me before I get to them?

So when do I leave? How? Do I sneak out in the middle of the night and hope I can survive whatever's waiting beyond Grimlock's borders? Do I confront Blue first and risk . . . what exactly?

The questions chase each other in circles while Blue continues accepting condolences from people who sort of know what he really is. But does anyone really know who Blue is? I sure as hell don't.

But . . . but, and this is a very big but . . . I don't want to leave. I should. I fucking should. But I . . . Jesus, I love the man. Skulls, unanswered questions, and all. And the man I love . . . the man I want to hold as he grieves, has been pushing me away. He doesn't want me. He doesn't need me.

The pain of that is worse than anything else.

The church fills around me. Grimlock's entire population, it seems, dressed in their funeral finest. Black wool and silk, expensive shoes on weathered stone. Everyone knew Hans. Everyone now mourns him. The man who called me Miss and smiled through every awkward situation.

Hans, who died because the Crow came hunting for me. Because of my kills.

Blue finally takes his seat beside me without acknowledgment. He smells of expensive soap and grief. His hands rest on his knees, perfectly still, but I can see the tension in his shoulders.

Reverend Bridger approaches the pulpit, and the murmuring congregation falls silent. He's elderly—maybe eighty, maybe a hundred—with wild white hair and eyes so pale they're almost colorless. His voice, when he begins, carries an accent I can't place.

"We are gathered in the shadow of loss," he intones, raising his arms, "but death is not the end. It is transformation."

A brass band emerges from somewhere behind the altar. Not church musicians—these are professionals, instruments gleaming, faces serious. They position themselves around Hans's coffin in formation.

"Hans Müller lived with honor. He died with honor. And he shall be honored in the ancient way."

The reverend strikes a ceremonial gong that hangs beside the pulpit. The sound rolls through the church, deep and resonant. Every person in the congregation stands as one, moving like they've done this before.

"Form the procession," Reverend Bridger commands. "We march as one family, united in grief, united in love."

The brass band begins a slow, hypnotic rhythm. Not quite military, not quite funeral dirge—something older, more primal. The bass drum sets a heartbeat pace that seems to sync with my body.

Blue stands, offers me his arm. Around us, the entire congregation files into formation behind Hans's casket. Dame Gothel and Dr. Finch move to the front, followed by Elliott and Ash. Duffy falls in behind us, along with Luna and Arthur and faces I recognize from the party, from my walks through town.

We step in perfect unison.

Left foot. Right foot. Left foot. Right foot.

The rhythm is infectious, impossible to resist. My body finds the beat without conscious thought, matching the pace of everyone around me. We move as a single organism, a human river flowing behind Hans's casket through the church doors and into the gray afternoon.

The brass band leads us down Grimlock's winding streets, their music bouncing off the buildings and back in complex layers. Drums and trumpets and a deep tuba, all working together to create a symphony of grief that transforms the entire town into a concert hall.

Residents who aren't part of the procession stand in doorways and windows, heads bowed as we pass. Some hold candles despite the daylight. Others scatter flower petals in our path. An old woman steps out from her house with fresh bread, breaking it and offering pieces to the marchers.

We accept the bread without breaking stride, chewing in rhythm with our steps.

Left foot. Right foot. Left foot. Right foot.

The music builds, becomes more complex. Individual instruments break away from the main melody to create counterpoints that weave through the procession. A trumpet here, a clarinet there, each one picked up and amplified by the acoustics of the narrow streets.

I start humming along even though I don't know the melody. Everyone is humming or singing words in languages I don't recognize. German, maybe others. The sound rises around us, human voices joining with brass and percussion to create something powerful and ceremonial.

The cemetery gates stand open, wrought iron painted black and decorated with ravens that seem to watch our approach. Jasper Crane, the gravedigger, waits inside, dressed in formal black instead of his usual dirt-stained work clothes. He falls into step beside the procession, adding to the growing chorus.

The cemetery itself has been transformed. Every headstone bears a candle. Paths between graves are lined with flowers—not the cheerful bouquets you see at spring funerals, but something darker. Dark roses and deep purple blooms that look almost black in the dim light.

We wind between the graves in serpentine patterns, the brass band never missing a beat. The music grows louder, more triumphant. What started as a funeral march has become a celebration, a declaration that death cannot diminish the impact of a life well lived.

Hans's burial plot sits beneath an enormous oak tree, its branches spread wide enough to shelter the entire gathering.

The brass band forms a circle around the grave, still playing, still maintaining that hypnotic rhythm. The rest of us fill in behind them, creating concentric rings of mourners that pulse with the music.

The rhythm changes, becomes triumphant. Around me, people begin to dance—not the wild abandon of the Dryad's Dance, but something structured, ritualistic.

They move in patterns around Hans's grave, weaving between headstones, hands joined and faces turned skyward. The brass band follows, instruments gleaming in the gray light, creating music that makes the air itself seem to glimmer.

I find myself swept up in the movement, following steps I don't know but somehow understand. Blue's hand finds mine, steady and warm, guiding me through turns and spirals.

The dance builds to a crescendo that seems to shake the earth. Every instrument playing at full volume, every voice raised in harmony, every body moving in perfect synchronization. For a moment, the boundary between life and death feels thin enough to step through.

Then, suddenly, silence.

Complete, absolute silence that rings in my ears after the overwhelming symphony. We stand frozen in our dance positions, breathing hard, connected by invisible threads of shared experience.

Reverend Bridger approaches Hans's casket, places his hands on the polished wood.

"Go well, faithful friend," he says simply. "The doors between worlds are open today. Choose your path."

The casket begins its descent into the earth, lowered by ropes that move in perfect rhythm. No mechanical winches, no modern funeral home efficiency. Just human hands working together to send Hans to his final rest.

As dirt falls onto the casket, each person in the congregation drops something into the grave. Flowers, yes, but also personal items. Dr. Finch drops a small notebook. Dame Gothel contributes a silver bracelet. Elliott places a perfectly formed pastry beside the flowers.

When it's my turn, I drop in the compass necklace Dad gave me. The one that's supposed to help me find my way home.

Hans deserves something that mattered to me. Something that meant direction when everything else felt lost.

Blue steps forward and drops in his pocket watch—the one he checks constantly, the one that's clearly precious to him. Then he steps back beside me.

"It's finished," Reverend Bridger announces. "Hans Müller has joined the honored dead. Let us return to the business of living."

The brass band strikes up a different tune—lighter, more hopeful. The procession reforms, but the energy has changed. People talk and laugh as we make our way back toward town, sharing stories about Hans, about life, about the peculiar magic of Grimlock funerals.

"That was beautiful," I tell Blue as we walk.

He nods but doesn't respond. The wall between us remains intact.

By the time we reach Maison Rouge, the sun is setting. The house looms against the darkening sky, all towers and Gothic windows that catch the last light.

Blue stops at the front door, finally turning to face me directly. But he doesn't say anything.

I wait.

I wait.

Finally, I break the awkward silence. "We need to talk."

CHAPTER THIRTY-SEVEN
BLUE

"Have a nice evening," I tell Saylor at the front door, each word clipped and cold.

She stops on the threshold, one hand on the doorframe, and I can see her building up to another attempt at conversation. Another push against the walls I've built between us since Hans died. But I don't have the energy for whatever she wants to discuss, and I sure as hell don't have the strength to pretend everything is normal when Hans's body is cooling in the ground because of choices I made.

"Blue—"

"I have some business to handle," I say, already turning away. "Wren will see to whatever you need."

"No." The word stops me mid-step. When I turn back, Saylor has moved fully inside, closing the door behind her with deliberate force. "I said we need to talk, and I meant it."

"There's nothing to discuss."

"Bullshit." Her voice cuts through the entrance hall. "You've been avoiding me for two days. Two days of showing up to meals and eating in silence while I sit there wondering what the hell happened between us."

I try to remain neutral, but something in her tone makes me want to end this conversation before it starts. "Hans died. That's what happened."

"I know you cared about Hans, and his death is devastating." She steps closer, and I can see the exhaustion in her eyes. "But that doesn't explain why you've shut me out completely. Why you won't even look at me anymore."

"I'm looking at you now."

"No, you're looking through me. There's a difference." Saylor crosses her arms. "Talk to me, Blue. Tell me what's going on in your head."

"What's going on in my head is that good people die when they get too close to me. Hans is proof of that."

"So what, you're going to punish me for Hans's death? Make me feel like I don't belong here because someone else made a choice to help us?"

The accusation stings because it's partially true. "This isn't about punishment."

"Then what is it about?" She moves closer, close enough that I can smell her perfume. "Because from where I'm standing, it seems like you're using Hans's death as an excuse to push me away."

"Maybe you should be pushed away." The words are out before I can stop them, and I watch her face crumple. "Maybe the smart thing would be to get as far from me as possible before you end up like everyone else who gets too close."

Part of me knows I should be angry about the third floor—about her finding the skulls, violating the one boundary I set. But after watching Hans die, after feeling his blood soak into the earth, her snooping through my most private space seems insignificant. She broke my trust. She saw what I keep locked away. A week ago, that betrayal would have consumed me. Now? Now all I can think about is that she's at least alive to betray me, and I need to keep it that way—even if it means pushing her away.

"Fine." She straightens, composing herself. "I have some business to handle too, then."

"What business?"

"I think I'll have the driver take me to town. Get a drink at Toil & Trouble." She watches my face carefully as she says it. "Talk to Duffy. Talk to *someone*."

"Good idea," I manage, although my jaw is clenched tight enough to crack teeth at the thought of her going anywhere without me. But I can't lock her in this house, even though part of me wants to. "I have a . . . driver out front with the car you can use."

"Fine."

The door closes behind her with deliberate force, and I wait until I hear the car pull away before heading toward my study. What I need is a drink and silence and maybe a few hours to figure out how to keep the rest of the people I care about from ending up dead.

I push open the study door and freeze.

The room that used to be my sanctuary now feels haunted. Dark wood paneling climbs the walls, broken by floor-to-ceiling bookshelves filled with first editions and rare manuscripts. The massive fireplace dominates one wall, its mantelpiece carved with hunting scenes that seem too violent now. Persian rugs in deep burgundy cover the hardwood floors, and brass reading lamps cast pools of warm light over leather furniture chosen for comfort rather than display.

But all I can see is Hans three weeks ago, standing by the window with a cup of coffee, watching the sunrise while he waited for me to finish reviewing security reports. He'd been humming something—some German folk song from his childhood—completely off-key but utterly content. When I'd looked up from my papers, he'd grinned and said, "Beautiful morning, Boss. Good day to be alive, ja?"

Now Hans will never see another sunrise, and this room feels like a tomb.

Dr. Jay Finch sits in my leather chair behind my desk, feet propped up on the mahogany surface, reading my personal correspondence with the casual attention of someone who belongs there.

"Evening, Blue," he says without looking up from the letter in his hands. "Quite the send-off for Hans. The whole town marching in perfect time? That was something else."

"What are you doing in my house, Jay?" I close the door and move toward the liquor cabinet, because if I'm going to deal with an uninvited therapist, I'm going to need whiskey. "And in my chair."

"You haven't been returning my calls." Jay finally looks up, and I can see the professional concern masquerading as casual interest. "Thought I'd make a house call. Check on my favorite homicidal patient after he lost someone who mattered."

"I'm fine."

"Clearly." Jay gestures at the stack of unopened mail, the empty glasses scattered across my desk, the general air of a man avoiding his own life. "That's why you've been holed up in this mausoleum for two days, speaking to no one and avoiding the world."

I pour three fingers of whiskey and down half of it before responding. "Grief has its own timeline."

"Grief, yes. Self-destruction masquerading as grief, no." Jay swings his feet down and leans forward. "Blue, you've shut down completely. You're not processing what happened, you're just . . . existing in a state of suspended animation."

"Hans is dead because of me." The words come out flat, factual. "He died protecting someone I brought into his world. How exactly am I supposed to process that?"

"By talking about it instead of drinking yourself into a coma and shutting out everyone who cares about you."

I set down my glass harder than necessary. "I'm not in the mood for therapy, Jay. Save the analysis for someone who gives a damn. Plus, after the other night, I'm no longer murder sober so . . ."

"That was self defense."

"Well what comes next for the Crow won't be."

Jay sighs. "We can address your sobriety at another time, but today I'm here because of your grief over Hans."

"Jay . . ."

"Right. Because you've never lost anyone before in your line of work." Jay's tone becomes more clinical. "Blue, you've seen more death than most people see in ten lifetimes. You've lost contacts, allies, people you worked with. Hell, you lost Peter—your best friend—and you handled that by going on a murder rampage. This is part of what you do. Part of what Hans signed up for when he chose to work with you."

"This is different."

"How? How is this different from Peter's death? How is this different from all the other times?" Jay sits back in my chair. "Hans knew the risks. You knew the risks. So explain to me why this particular death has you hiding away instead of moving forward."

The question sits in the air between us, and for a moment I consider throwing him out. But the whiskey has loosened something in my chest, and maybe I need to say this out loud.

"Because losing Hans is like losing Peter all over again." The words scrape out of me. "Peter saw something in me worth saving when I was just another killer with blood on his hands. He believed I could be more than the monster everyone expected. And

Hans . . . Hans was the same. He chose me. Not my money, not my connections, not what I could do for him. He saw the good in me even when I was doing terrible things." I stare into my glass. "Peter showed me I was worth saving. Hans showed me I was worth staying saved. And now they're both gone because I couldn't protect them." I pause, searching for the right words. "Hans was good. Really good, even when he was helping me do terrible things. He showed me that sometimes you have to do bad to do good, but he also made me realize I was fucking exhausted. Tired of the killing, tired of the violence, tired of being the monster everyone expected me to be. And Hans . . . Hans made me realize it was okay to feel that way. That maybe it was time to stop."

"And now he's dead because of that choice."

"Now he's dead because I brought violence back into our lives." I drain the rest of my whiskey. "He died protecting me from a choice I made to come out of retirement."

Jay is quiet for a long moment, studying my face with that calculating look that means he's processing everything I just said.

"Hans wouldn't want you to carry this guilt," he says finally.

"Well, Hans isn't here to have an opinion about it."

"No, but I am. And my professional opinion is that you're using grief as an excuse to avoid dealing with the real problem."

"Which is?"

"You're terrified that what happened to Hans will happen to Saylor." Jay leans back in my chair. "Based on what I saw at the funeral, you're shutting her out because you think distance will keep her safe. But all you're doing is pushing away the one person who might actually understand what you're going through."

"Saylor doesn't understand anything about what I'm going through."

"Doesn't she? She watched her father get murdered. She's living in a world of violence she never asked for." Jay cocks his head to the side. "Sound familiar?"

The comparison stings. Saylor and I, both dragged into darkness by circumstances beyond our control. Both trying to figure out how to live with blood on our hands.

"That's different."

"Is it?" Jay studies my face. "You know what I think? I think you're using Hans's death as an excuse to avoid something that scares you more than any Crow ever could."

"And what's that?"

"Actually caring about someone enough to let them in."

I finish my whiskey and pour another. "Your point?"

CHAPTER THIRTY-EIGHT
SAYLOR

The driver won't stop checking the rearview mirror, his eyes darting between the road and my face every few seconds. I'll never get used to this—having drivers, housekeepers, people whose job it is to watch me and worry about my moods.

"Drop me at the town square," I tell him. "I need to walk."

He nods without argument—probably relieved to get the angry woman out of his car before she starts throwing things. The moment we stop, I'm out and moving, my feet finding pavement with the steady rhythm of someone working off fury one step at a time.

Blue thinks he can dismiss me? Shut me out like I'm some fragile thing that can't handle whatever darkness he's drowning in? Well, fuck that. And fuck him for making me feel small in my own life.

The evening air bites at my skin, carrying the salt tang of ocean and damp earth from gardens settling into twilight. Grimlock in the fading light becomes a different creature. Windows begin to glow against stone walls, and the narrow streets transform into arteries of shadow and golden light that vibrates with secrets.

I walk without direction, letting my anger guide me through alleys I haven't explored before. Past a clockmaker's shop where gears tick behind dark glass, around a corner where ivy climbs so thick it swallows the building's original lines. My feet find their own path while my brain churns through everything Blue said, everything he didn't say, everything that sits between us like broken glass.

That's when I see it.

A burst of color against gray stone, so vivid it stops me mid-step. Someone has been painting a mural on the side wall of a narrow building. Paint covers the stone in sweeping arcs of crimson and gold, deep purple and forest green, all blending together in patterns that flow and spiral across the surface.

The artist is still there, a woman who looks maybe a few years older than me with wild black curls that escape from a messy bun secured with what appears to be a paintbrush. Her clothes tell the story of someone who lives in color—a paint-splattered canvas apron over jeans that have been tie-dyed in shades of teal and amber, work boots so covered in dried paint they've become art themselves. She's reaching high above her head, pressing her palm against the wall to leave a handprint in brilliant blue, and that's when I realize there are no brushes other than in her hair anywhere. Just buckets of paint and hands as tools.

"Don't stop," she calls over her shoulder without turning around. "I can feel you watching, but don't let that stop you from joining in."

"I'm sorry?"

She turns then, and I see colors smeared across her cheek like war paint. "The wall. It's been waiting for someone new." She gestures to buckets of paint arranged on the ground, colors so rich they seem to glow. "Maya Delacroix. Town muralist, unofficial therapy provider, and firm believer that sometimes you need to get your hands dirty to clean your soul. Saylor, right? I met you at the party."

I approach slowly, studying the patterns spreading across the stone. They're not pictures of anything I can name. Just raw emotion turned into swirls and spirals and bold slashes that make me want to grab some paint myself.

"I don't know how to paint."

"Everyone knows how to make marks. The wall doesn't judge technique—it just wants honesty." Maya dips her hands in a bucket of deep orange paint. "What color feels right for whatever you're carrying?"

Without thinking, I point to a bucket of dark red that seems to glow with its own inner fire. Maya nods approvingly.

"Anger red. Perfect. That color knows what it wants."

I roll up my sleeves and plunge my hands into the paint. It's warmer than I expected, thick and smooth between my fingers. Maya guides me to a blank section of wall, then steps back and lets me find my own way.

I start with just my palm against the stone, leaving a crimson handprint. Then my fingers are dragging across the surface in long lines that feel like screaming without making any noise.

I paint my frustration with Blue's behavior, my confusion about the skulls upstairs, my grief for Hans, my fury at being treated like something fragile. Each stroke releases something I've been holding too tightly, and soon my hands are flying across the stone with surprising confidence.

Maya works beside me, adding touches of gold that flow into my angry red. Other people drift into the courtyard—an elderly man who adds careful dots of white, a teenager who splashes purple with joyful abandon.

No one speaks. We just paint, our separate emotions blending into something larger. The wall grows and changes as more hands join the work, my red spreading into Maya's gold, flowing into the man's precise details, dancing with the teenager's wild purple.

When my arms finally grow tired, I step back to see what we've created. The wall pulses with life—not a mural in any traditional sense, but a record of this moment, this evening, this group of people who found each other through color and stone.

"How do you feel?" Maya asks, wiping her hands on a paint-stained rag.

I look at my paint-covered hands and feel something ease in my chest. "Lighter."

"That's what the wall does. Takes the heavy stuff and turns it into something everyone can see, something that becomes part of the town." Maya steps back to admire our combined work. "Your anger isn't gone—it's just not only yours anymore."

The paint is starting to dry on my skin, but I don't want to wash it off yet. There's something satisfying about carrying this evidence of creation, proof that I can make something beautiful even when I'm furious.

Maya starts gathering empty paint buckets. "Whatever's eating at you, don't let it shrink you down. Anger like that"—she gestures to my bold red strokes spreading across the stone—"that's meant to take up space."

I study the wall where my anger has become something others can see and touch. "Thank you. For the paint, for the wall, for . . ." I trail off, not sure how to explain what just happened.

"For letting you be mad without judgment?" Maya grins. "That's what walls are for. Come back anytime you need to get loud."

I nod, already stepping back toward the street. The fury that brought me here has burned off, leaving something steadier behind.

Toil & Trouble sits three blocks away, its windows glowing with warm light and the promise of strong drinks and sympathetic company. I walk toward it with purpose now, my steps finding a different rhythm on the cobblestones—not the angry march I started with, but the confident stride of a woman who knows exactly what she wants.

The wind chimes on Duffy's porch sing their metallic song as I approach, and when I push open the door, the whole bar turns to look at me.

"Paint," I announce, holding up my red-stained hands before anyone can panic.

Duffy looks up from wiping down the bar, her eyes taking in my paint-covered palms and the wild look in my eyes. A slow grin spreads across her face. "For a second there, I thought you'd killed another one of those Crow bastards."

"The night is young," I mutter, settling onto my usual barstool.

"Lavender gin fizz?" she asks, already reaching for the bottle.

"Make it a double. Actually, make it whatever's strongest."

Duffy's eyebrows climb toward her hairline, but she doesn't argue. She pours whiskey instead—the good stuff, judging by the amber color and the way it catches the light. "Rough evening?"

I down half the glass in one gulp, feeling the burn all the way to my stomach. "You could say that."

"Paint therapy, huh? Maya's been getting a lot of customers lately. Good for the soul, apparently." Duffy leans against the bar. "What a funeral today. Hans was a treasure—one of the truly decent ones. Can't imagine what Blue's going through right now."

I stare into my whiskey, thinking about Hans's grin, his off-key humming, how he always made sure I had everything I needed before I even asked. "Hard to believe he's gone."

"Hans always looked out for people. Even customers he barely knew." Duffy wipes down the same spot on the bar twice. "Seven years he worked for Blue. That kind of loyalty . . . you don't see it much anymore."

We sit quiet for a moment, both lost in our own thoughts about Hans.

"Tell Blue if he wants, I can do a bone reading for Hans," Duffy says quietly, wiping down the same glass twice. "Sometimes it helps with the grief. Gives people closure."

"A bone reading?"

"It's something my sisters and I do. We can read the last memories of the deceased through their bones, or sometimes through flowers left at gravesites." Duffy's voice takes on a reverent quality. "See their final moments, understand what they experienced before passing."

I stare at her, not sure if I'm more fascinated or disturbed. "You can actually see what happened to them?"

"Every detail. Their last thoughts, their final emotions, what they saw." She sets the glass down carefully. "It's not always pleasant, but families find comfort in knowing their loved ones weren't alone, or that they died peacefully."

"But what if the last thoughts aren't good? Aren't peaceful?" I lean forward, genuinely curious. "What if someone died violently, or in fear?"

Duffy's eyes take on a darker gleam. "Well, that's when things get interesting. Justice. Revenge." She meets my gaze directly. "You know all about that."

I nod slowly, and she gives me a knowing smile.

After a pause, Duffy's expression shifts. "Grieving Hans must make all the planning really tough right now."

"Planning?"

She studies my face carefully, looking confused. "All the planning it takes to move?"

"Move?"

Duffy's face goes pale. "Oh. Oh shit. You have no idea?" She sets down the bottle carefully. "Saylor, please tell me you're joking."

"Duffy, what the hell are you talking about?"

"The rumor mill is that you're leaving town. Moving away. At least that's what was told at the funeral."

"What the absolute fuck?" The words tear out of my throat loud enough that several people at nearby tables look over.

Duffy winces sympathetically. "I take it you weren't consulted about the move?"

"This is insane. This is completely fucking insane. He's kicking me out," I whisper, more to myself than to Duffy.

I stand up so fast my barstool tips backward, clattering against the floor. "I have to go."

"Saylor, wait—"

But I'm already moving and heading for the door. The fury that had burned off during the painting session roars back to life, twice as hot as before.

Kicked to the curb with no notice.

Without my knowledge, without my consent, without even the courtesy of a conversation.

The wind chimes crash together violently as I storm off the porch, their metallic song turning discordant and angry, matching the rhythm of my heart as I head back into Grimlock's twisted streets.

CHAPTER THIRTY-NINE
BLUE

The front door slams so hard it rattles the chandelier. I'm halfway through explaining to Jay why having Saylor be sent away is the only logical solution when the sound of her fury echoes through every floor of Maison Rouge. Her footsteps pound up the grand staircase, each one a declaration of war.

"Blue!" A momentary pause. "Where the hell are you?"

Jay raises his eyebrows. "I'm guessing she found out about your plans."

"Seems likely." I down the rest of my whiskey and head for the door. "This conversation isn't over."

"Oh, it's definitely over," Jay calls after me. "Good luck surviving the next ten minutes."

I find Saylor in the main hall with red-stained hands clenched into fists. Her dark hair is wild from the evening wind, her cheeks flushed with anger.

She's never been more beautiful.

"What. The. Fuck. Is. Going. On?" Each word comes out like a bullet.

"Saylor—"

"No! I'm talking now." She starts pacing across the polished floor, her fury filling the space like wildfire. "What person kicks someone out without even telling them? What psychopath tells other people and not the person actually moving? If you wanted me out, you should have said something! Why did I have to hear about this from Duffy? What kind of person are you?"

"Someone who's trying to keep you alive."

She stops pacing to stare at me. "By kicking me out with no notice and no place to go? How does that work exactly?"

"I have a place for you to go. A plan."

"A plan? Oh my God, you're serious." She laughs, but there's no humor in it. "You actually have been planning this? For how long? And is there some reason you didn't let me in on this?"

"I have my reasons."

She resumes pacing, her anger building steam again. "And if I say no to *your plan*? What's next? Maybe I'll just end up like the other seven women—a pretty picture on the wall and then a skull upstairs!"

The words explode out of her, and I can see the real fear behind her fury.

"If I don't obey the mighty Blue, you'll add me to your collection upstairs?"

"Do you really believe that?" I step closer, studying her face. "Do you honestly think I want to hurt you?"

Her certainty wavers for just a moment. "I don't know what to believe anymore."

"Then ask me what you really want to know."

"The skulls!" The words burst from her like a dam breaking. "I've been trying not to bring it up because of Hans, but Jesus Christ, Blue. There are seven skulls in your house!"

"I know."

"You know? That's all you have to say? You know?" She gestures wildly at the portraits above us. "Margaret, Eleanor, Vivian, Catherine, Sophia—they're all up there as skulls while their portraits smile down at us like some twisted fairy tale."

"Yes."

"And I saw Cordelia at the Dryad's Dance. Alive. Breathing. Crying. But her skull is upstairs with a nameplate. How is that possible?"

I wait for her to finish, letting her fury burn itself out. She needs to say all of this, and I need to hear it.

"Look, I know you kill people," she continues. "I've never judged you for that. Hell, I've joined you. But keeping their bones upstairs with name tags? What kind of person does that? What did they do to deserve death? Were they threats? Were they criminals? Or did they just ask too many questions?"

"Are you finished?"

"No! I'm not finished! Because this isn't just about murder, Blue.

This is about trust. This is about all your damn secrets, about what you're planning for me, about—"

"Follow me."

I head for the stairs, not waiting to see if she follows. Her footsteps echo behind me, laced with anger but curious enough to keep pace.

We climb to the third floor, walk through the hallway of skeleton keys that sway gently as we pass. At the blood-red door, I pull out the raven key and unlock it.

"After you."

Saylor steps into the room, and I watch her face as she processes what she's seeing. She's been here before, but now she's looking with different eyes, searching for answers instead of just recoiling from the horror.

"There," I say, pointing to an empty eighth table. "That's where your hunter would go."

"My hunter?"

"Brutus Crow," I say conversationally. "His intent is to kill you. When I finally get him, his skull will be sitting on that table with your name on the placard. In due time.

"The skulls aren't of the women—they're of the women's hunters. Each skull represents a man who was hired to kill the woman whose name is on the placard." I move to stand beside her. "I know it may seem twisted that I keep their skulls, but I like to keep reminders. Just like my cemetery in the garden for all the souls I couldn't save, or the portraits of the ones I did to remind me of the good, I wanted to keep these to remind me of the bad, the darkness, the reason I'm trying to not be like them. These are my reminders."

"So all the women on your wall . . ."

"Are alive and well, living under new identities far from whatever danger brought them to me in the first place.

"Margaret was running from an abusive ex-husband who had connections in law enforcement. Eleanor needed to disappear from a stalker who'd killed her sister. Vivian got on the wrong side of a human trafficking ring." I point to each table in turn. "Catherine had evidence against a cartel. Sophia witnessed a political assassination.

The sixth woman—Penelope—was a federal prosecutor whose family was threatened."

"And Cordelia?"

"Cordelia was the first. Ten years ago. She was Brutus Crow's girlfriend, but she got smart and tried to leave him." I run my hand along the edge of her table. "She came to me because she'd heard rumors about what I do. Begged me to help her disappear because Brutus doesn't let anyone walk away alive."

Saylor is quiet, processing. "So you faked their deaths."

"Your father and I gave them new identities."

"So all these skulls are actually bastards?"

"Every single one. Men who threatened, stalked, or tried to kill the women I was protecting." I point to the table labeled Margaret. "That's her ex-husband. Tracked her down three times before I convinced him to stop permanently."

Saylor moves from table to table, reading the nameplates with new understanding. "Eleanor's stalker. Vivian's trafficker. Catherine's cartel contact."

"Justice served with a little reminder of the darkness I'm fighting against."

She stops in front of the table labeled Cordelia. "And this is?"

"One of Brutus's lieutenants. I wanted Brutus himself, but he was too well-protected. This bastard had to do." I shrug. "Took me two years to track him down, but I'm very patient when it comes to revenge."

"I saw Cordelia at the Dryad's Dance. She was out of hiding."

"Was teaching elementary school in Portland under the name Lisa Davies. Married to a nice accountant who thinks her first boyfriend died in a motorcycle accident. She was at the Dryad's Dance because Brutus found her. Somehow tracked her down despite everything we did to hide her. She got away, but not before she heard them plotting. She came to warn me that they were planning the attack, even though showing her face put her right back in danger."

Saylor sinks into the chair I keep in the corner—the same one I sit in sometimes when I need to remember why I do this work.

"I would never kill an innocent on purpose. I am a serial killer. I just happen to be very selective about my victims."

"All the women are alive and free."

She stares at the empty table where Brutus's skull will eventually sit.

Saylor is quiet for a long time, processing everything I've told her. When she finally speaks, her voice is soft.

She stands up, moving toward me with heat in her eyes.

"You aren't the villain in this story, Blue. You're the hero." Her smile turns fierce as her fingers find my shirt buttons.

"Saylor—"

"Shut up." She yanks my shirt open, buttons scattering across the stone floor. "I'm done pretending I don't love every twisted, beautiful thing about you."

She shoves me back against the wall, her mouth finding mine with desperate hunger. When she bites my lower lip hard enough to draw blood, I groan and flip us around, pressing her against the cold stone while the skulls of criminals watch from their tables.

"Here?" I ask against her throat. "You want to do this here?"

"Especially here." Her hands are already working at my belt. "With all your trophies watching. With the proof of what you really are spread out around us."

I slide my hands under her thighs, lifting her until her legs wrap around my waist. The stone wall is cold against my palms as I brace us, but Saylor is fire in my arms, her body arching against mine like she can't get close enough.

Saylor makes a noise like she's been set on fire, and it lights up every molecule inside me. Her body wraps around mine, pulling my hips to her as if she's afraid any sliver of space will let the world slip in and ruin this. She tears at my shirt, popping another button and scraping her nails over my skin hard enough to remind me what pain is meant to do: keep you awake, keep you honest, keep you here. The taste of blood is on my tongue—hers, mine, I couldn't care less—as the world narrows to the pair of us pressed against a wall in a sanctuary of death.

Her legs tighten around me and I'm already bone-hard, the animal in me roaring at the rawness of it, the mess, the stench of acid and rot. I push her panties to the side and she's already soaked, primed from her earlier rage. My cock is so fucking hard that I can't wait another second. I thrust into her, one hard stroke and then another, no hesitation, no foreplay—her dripping wet cunt tells me she doesn't need it and neither do I. Sliding into her tight pussy with one brutal movement, her breath catches on a gasp that's half pain and half laughter as I moan out her name.

She clings to me, clawing at my back, her teeth finding my shoulder and biting down just enough to make me see white at the edge of my vision. I fuck her hard against the wall, the edge of the stone catching her hips and marking her, her glorious mess of hair tangling in my hands. The ghosts in the room see everything: my hunger, my need, the way I can't distinguish lust from grief from relief.

Wet heat pulses around my cock, every thrust met with a sound from her that gets louder, more ragged.

"Fucking love you," she hisses in my ear, and it tears something open. I rut in deeper, driving her into the stone hard enough that her spine will remember it. My hands find her wrists, pin them above her head—a little leverage, a little violence, the old language we speak best. She fights me, because she wants to, because she can, and that resistance is pure fire. Her thighs squeeze so tight around my waist it hurts.

She cocks her head back and grinds into me, meeting every thrust with more. The wall thuds, and I realize, distantly, that the friction of her ass against the stone might be scraping her raw. I don't stop. She doesn't want me to stop. There's nothing gentle to this, nothing that could be called loving by any sane definition, but we were never built for sane.

I want to devour her, and I almost do, kissing her hard enough to bruise, biting at her jaw as I piston deeper. She meets me, thrust for wild thrust, grinding down to chase the pressure just right. Her hands fight my grip and I let go, just so she can slap me, once, across the face. It's not even a slap, more like a wake-up call, and I want to say thank you, but I'm too busy breathing in all of her.

She comes first, sudden and violent, the muscles inside her clamping down on my cock like a vise. Her whole body seizes and she screams, actually screams, so loud I hear it bounce off the stone and down the hallway, a call to every ghost in the building. I lose my grip for a second and she bites my jaw, hard, leaving a wet patch of blood. The pain brings me over, and I bury myself in her and fill her up, shaking with it, every ounce of control gone.

She milks me with her aftershocks, writhing and cursing with every jolt, squeezing me dry before I let go of her wrists and drag her mouth back to mine. The first time I come it's half rage, half relief, and all of it inside her. I want every one of these corpses to watch, want the past to see what it can't have. I fuck her through the end of it, cock softening just enough to keep going, the salt-bitter mess of her and my blood slicking our bodies together like paint.

When I finally pull out, she drops her feet to the floor and goes slack against me, panting like she just ran ten flights of old stairs. For a minute we just cling together, silent except for the sound of skin and heartbeat and Saylor's breathing.

"Jesus Christ," she finally says, pushing her hair out of her face.

She looks around the room, taking in the tables with their grisly displays, then back at me with something between amazement and horror. "This is officially the most unhinged thing I've ever done. And I poisoned a man, so that's really saying something."

"The poison thing was fairly tame compared to this."

"Right?" She laughs, but it's slightly hysterical. "Most people have sex in beds. Normal people. But no, I decide to jump you in your creepy death museum because apparently that's who I am now."

I start buttoning what's left of my shirt while she smooths down her dress.

"But I'm still fucking pissed at you."

"About?"

"The move, Blue. Trying to get me to leave without asking me." Her anger is returning, sharpening. "How the hell do we let all of Grimlock know this is false info? Everyone is just getting to know me, and now I'm going to look like a flake, or there's going to be rumors of trouble in paradise or . . ." she pauses. "I know you don't care about reputation . . . clearly. But—"

"You're *still* leaving."

She stares at me. "What?"

"You heard me. You still aren't safe here. You're moving as planned. Just like these women before. You'll be safe far from here so I can go after Brutus."

"The fuck I am. We are going to come up with a plan on how to handle Brutus Crow together. You and me. I'm not one of those girls on the wall. I don't need to be protected. I'm staying by your side to take the man down."

"No," I say quietly. "You're not."

"Excuse me?"

"Hans is dead." The words come out flat, final. "I no longer have him by my side to help. I can't protect you from the Crow. Nothing has changed in my plan. The move is happening whether you like it or not."

CHAPTER FORTY
SAYLOR

Has Blue lost his mind?

I stand in the forbidden room surrounded by killer skulls, and Blue is giving me that stubborn look I'm starting to recognize.

"What part of 'I'm ready to fight' don't you understand?" I cross my arms, staring at him. "Your attempt at forcing me out is taking away my power. I'm not disappearing. I'm not hiding."

Blue's jaw tightens. "It's not that simple."

"It's exactly that simple." I gesture around the room at his macabre museum. "These women needed new identities because it was the only way they could save themselves. I can save myself another way. Problem solved."

"The Crow—"

"Will get exactly what they deserve," I interrupt. "And I'll be there to help give it to them."

Blue runs his hands through his hair, which I now realize he does often, making it stick up at odd angles. "Saylor, you don't understand—"

"I'm getting sick of standing here," I snap, "and it's not because of the bones."

Blue blinks at me like I've started speaking old world Greek.

I turn on my heel and storm toward the door. Behind me, Blue calls my name, but I'm done with this conversation. He can stand up there arguing with his bone collection for all I care.

I stomp down the stairs. The main hall stretches before me with gothic arches and expensive art.

Wren appears from the direction of the kitchen, looking harried in a way I've never seen before. Her usual unflappable composure has cracks around the edges, grief written in the lines around her eyes.

"Saylor, dear." She attempts a smile that doesn't quite reach her eyes. "I had luggage and boxes sent to your room. I'll come up and help—"

I stop dead in the middle of the hall. "No." The word comes out flat and final. "I'm not leaving."

Wren blinks rapidly. "I beg your pardon?"

"I'm staying here." I gesture vaguely around the mansion.

Wren's confusion deepens, but before she can respond, Blue appears behind me. I can feel his presence without turning around, that familiar electricity he brings to any room.

Wren's eyes dart between me and Blue, clearly looking for guidance on how to handle this situation. Blue gives her a look—one of those silent communications that speaks volumes.

"Stop talking with your eyes," I snap, spinning around to face him. "Both of you. If you have something to say, say it out loud."

Before Blue can respond, the doorbell echoes through the house. Wren bustles toward the front door, muttering about unexpected visitors and proper calling hours.

When she opens it, Ash steps inside, and for the first time in two days, something shifts in the oppressive atmosphere of Maison Rouge. He looks like he's been running, his casual clothes slightly disheveled, but his eyes are bright with purpose.

"Blue," he says immediately, spotting him behind me. "Got it done."

"What did you get done?" I interrupt before Blue can respond. That familiar prickle of being excluded from important conversations starts up my spine.

Ash glances between Blue and me, clearly sensing the tension. Blue opens his mouth, probably to suggest they adjourn to his study for a private conversation.

"Stop," I say, holding up my hand. "Just stop. If this has to do with the Crow, then I have a right to know too. We're not doing the whole 'let's go talk in private while Saylor waits in the hall like a good little girl' thing."

Blue closes his mouth, looking slightly put out.

"So what did you get done?" I ask Ash.

"I managed to bribe the Crow responsible for guarding the roads and perimeters around Brutus's hideout," he explains. "Had some past contacts with a few of them from when I was a Crow. Turns out some of them hate Brutus as much as I do."

"And?" I lean forward.

"We can move in tonight without being detected." Ash grins. "Time for revenge."

Finally. Finally, we're going to make them pay for Hans, for Dad, for everything they've stolen from us.

"I'm coming," I announce immediately.

"No," Blue says, his tone carrying that edge that usually makes people obey without question. "You're not."

"Yes, I am."

Blue's jaw tightens. "Saylor, this isn't—" He stops, runs a hand through his hair. "I can't lose you too. I can't watch another person I'm supposed to protect die because I wasn't careful enough."

The raw honesty in his voice catches me off guard. This isn't about my capabilities. This is about Hans. About Peter. About everyone he's lost.

"Hans died protecting me," I say, keeping my voice steady. "My father was murdered by these same bastards. How is this not my fight?"

"You can't even see blood without passing out," Blue points out, which stings because he's absolutely right. "You're not equipped for combat."

The honesty cuts deeper than I want to admit, but it doesn't change anything fundamental. "I'm still going."

"No."

"Yes."

We stare at each other across the foyer, and I can see him trying different arguments in his head, discarding each one as it occurs to him. Wren stands frozen by the door like she's watching a tennis match, and Ash appears to be trying not to laugh.

"These aren't the men from my basement," Blue says finally. "This is real combat. Real violence. People are going to die, and it's going to be messy and brutal and—"

"And I want to be there for it." I step closer to him, close enough to see the flecks of amber in his dark eyes. "It's not just Hans that needs revenge, Blue. My father's death hasn't been fully avenged either. These are the same people on my list. And even if they weren't on the list, they are still the Crow. The same organization that murdered the only family I had left."

I can see him processing this, weighing it against his need to protect me.

"I'm going," I say again, softer this time but no less determined. "This is my choice."

"No."

"Yes."

"No."

"Yes."

The standoff stretches until Ash throws his hands up in exasperation.

"Fuuuuuuck, she's going!" he declares. "Blue, you've been outmaneuvered. Accept defeat gracefully."

Blue turns his glare on Ash, who just grins back without an ounce of concern. But I can see something in Blue's posture shifting, the fight going out of him as he realizes he's lost this particular battle.

"Fine," Blue says finally, the word coming out like it tastes bitter. "But you follow orders. No heroics, no improvisation, no getting yourself killed because you want to prove a point."

"Deal," I say immediately, before he can change his mind.

"We move at midnight."

The finality in his voice should feel like victory, but something doesn't sit right. I watch Blue's face—the tight set of his jaw, the way his hands have already curled into fists like he's preparing for battle. He's going to walk into that hideout expecting to die. Expecting this to be some kind of redemption through violence.

That's not what I want.

"Wait," I say, the idea forming even as I speak. "What if there's another way? Another way where vengeance can . . . taste better."

Blue and Ash both turn to look at me, curiosity replacing the tension.

"I'm listening," Blue says carefully.

I take a breath, knowing what I'm about to suggest is insane. But it's also perfect.

"But the plan does require both of us to die," I add, watching his face for his reaction.

CHAPTER FORTY-ONE
SAYLOR

The mirror in Vespera's workshop reflects someone I barely recognize.

Gone is the girl who sang at White Note in sequined dresses and hoped nobody would notice she was falling apart. The woman staring back at me has sharp cheekbones courtesy of expert contouring, lips painted dark enough to look like dried blood, and eyes so dramatically lined they could cut glass. Vespera has given me a wig that transforms my dark hair to platinum blonde, sleek and straight in a way that completely changes the shape of my face.

"Stop fidgeting," Vespera says, making final adjustments to the wig that's giving me this new identity. "You look perfect. Dangerous and beautiful—exactly what we need."

The dress she's chosen makes me look like I belong at the kind of party where people disappear forever. Black silk that hugs every curve, with a neckline just suggestive enough to be distracting. The heels add four inches to my height and make me feel like I could step on someone's throat without breaking stride.

"How do I look?" I ask, though I already know the answer.

"Like death in designer clothing." Vespera grins with artistic pride. "Blue is going to swallow his tongue when he sees you."

Through the workshop windows, I can see Blue pacing in the clearing beyond Vespera's house. He's been out there for twenty minutes, checking his watch and running his hands through his hair. The sight makes my stomach flutter with something that isn't fear.

"Remind me of the story again so I don't fuck this up," I say, smoothing the silk over my hips and still getting used to how the dress moves.

"You're Scarlett Rose, the daughter of a recently deceased arms dealer from London. Word on the street is that you're looking to expand Daddy's old business relationships, and you've heard Brutus runs the most efficient operation on the West Coast." Vespera hands me a small evening bag that matches the dress perfectly. "Ash's contacts have been spreading rumors about you for weeks. Tonight's their monthly celebration—they think they're meeting a potential new business partner with deep pockets and flexible morals."

Inside the bag are my instruments of destruction: a dozen tiny blue spheres that look like decorative beads, each one capable of killing a grown man in ten minutes. Enough to wipe out every Crow in that lodge, with a few extra for good measure.

"They're celebrating what they think is Blue's death," Vespera continues, applying a final coat of lipstick to my mouth. "Word spread that some rival outfit took him out with a car bomb in Portland. Same explosion supposedly killed his girlfriend too—meaning you're officially dead as well." She pauses, her smile turning vicious. "Ash has been working overtime selling the story. All of Grimlock is in mourning, and the few locals who've spotted Blue around Maison Rouge swear they're seeing his ghost. The man's going to be absolutely legendary when he rises from the dead after this is all over."

I stare at my reflection one more time. The woman in the mirror looks capable of anything. She looks like someone who could walk into a room full of killers and walk out alone.

She looks like someone who could get justice for her father.

"I'm ready," I say, and for the first time in five years, I mean it.

Vespera opens the workshop door, and Blue nearly trips over his own feet when he sees me. His eyes travel from my face to my dress to my legs and back again, and the heat in his gaze makes my pulse race.

"Jesus Christ," he breathes. "Saylor?"

"Scarlett Rose, actually," I say, letting a posh British accent slip into my voice as I practice the sultry tone I'll need for tonight. "Pleased to meet you."

Blue approaches slowly, like he's afraid I might disappear if he moves too fast. "You look . . ." He stops, swallows hard. "You look like you could kill every man in that room without breaking a sweat."

"That's the idea."

He reaches out to touch my cheek, his thumb tracing the sharp line Vespera created with her contouring. "Are you sure about this?

You'll have to be Scarlett Rose completely. No hesitation, no second-guessing. I won't be there beside you."

"You're a good teacher," I say, leaning into his touch. "I've got this. It's what I've been waiting for." I smile and give him a wink. "I'm an A student after all."

His eyes darken with pride and something hungrier. "Good girl," he murmurs, then kisses me with enough heat to melt steel.

When we break apart, I'm breathless but steady. "Besides, you're retired, remember. Let's get you back on the wagon. But I also know you'll be watching from the woods. If anything goes wrong—"

"If anything goes wrong, murder sober or not, I'm coming in after you." His voice carries a promise that makes my chest tight. "Consequences be damned."

Vespera clears her throat delicately. "Much as I love watching you two have a moment, we're on a schedule. Scarlett needs time to make her entrance."

Blue nods reluctantly but doesn't step away from me. "Remember what we practiced. You're confident, you're mysterious, and you're absolutely lethal. Everything else is just acting."

"I'm not acting anymore," I say quietly. "This is who I am now."

The look he gives me could burn down cities—pride mixed with hunger and a darkness that matches my own. "Then go show them what Peter Mitchell's daughter is capable of."

I kiss him once, hard and desperate, then follow Vespera to the car that will take me to the Crow lodge. As we drive through the Witchwood toward my destiny, I practice being Scarlett Rose in my head.

Scarlett Rose doesn't throw up at the sight of blood.

Scarlett Rose doesn't hesitate when it's time to kill.

Scarlett Rose gets what she wants, and what she wants is every Crow in that lodge dead by midnight.

The headlights cut through the darkness ahead, and I can see yellow light spilling from the windows of the hunting lodge where my father's killers are gathering to celebrate another successful year of being monsters.

By the time the sun rises, they'll all be corpses.

And I'll finally be free.

The hunting lodge blazes with light and laughter when Ash's contact leads me through the front door. Inside, it's exactly what I expected from a group of killers celebrating what they think is their greatest victory: expensive whiskey, cigar smoke thick enough to choke on, and the kind of reckless joy that comes from believing you've finally eliminated your biggest threat.

"Gentlemen," one of Ash's contacts announces, his voice carrying across the main room. "I'd like you to meet Scarlett Rose. She's here to discuss potential business arrangements."

Every conversation stops. Every eye in the room turns to assess the blonde woman in the silk dress who just walked into their sanctuary. I count twelve men total—more than we expected, but not more than I prepared for.

At the head of the main table sits Brutus himself, exactly as Blue described him. Massive shoulders, scarred face, and eyes that have seen too much violence. He raises his whiskey glass in greeting, and the gesture is both welcoming and threatening.

"Ms. Rose," he says in a way that reminds me of gravel in a cement mixer. "We've been hearing interesting things about you. Something about expanding your father's business into our territory?"

I move deeper into the room, letting my hips sway just enough to hold their attention. "Daddy always said you Americans know how to spot opportunity," I say, my British accent making the words sound casual but sharp. "I'm after partners who don't fuck around."

"Quality work." Brutus grins, the expression transforming his face into something genuinely terrifying. "I like that. Sit. Let's discuss what quality means to people like us."

The chair they offer puts me directly across from Brutus, with six men on each side of the long table. Perfect positioning for what I have planned. As I settle into my seat, I notice the table is already set with crystal glasses and opened bottles of what looks like very expensive wine.

"We're celebrating tonight," Brutus explains, gesturing to the bottles. "Got word this morning that someone finally took care of a problem we've had for years. Car bomb in Portland took out an enemy of ours. Hell of a way to go."

The room erupts in laughter and congratulations. Men toast the unknown killers' success, bitching that they didn't get to do the honors themselves but celebrating the result. I smile and nod, playing the impressed potential partner while fury builds in my chest.

They think Blue is dead. They're celebrating his murder.

"To whoever blew that bastard to pieces," someone calls out, raising his glass. "And to one less problem to worry about."

"Cheers to that," I say with a smile, accepting a crystal glass filled with dark red wine. The liquid catches the lamplight, and I can see my reflection swimming in its surface. "But hang on—let me do this right."

I stand gracefully, glass raised, commanding attention with the simple act of movement. Every eye in the room follows me as I walk to the sideboard where the wine bottles wait like soldiers in formation.

"Back home, we always add a little something special to celebrate big wins," I continue, my British accent flowing naturally as I set down my glass and reach into my evening bag. "Trust me, it makes everything taste better."

The blue spheres roll across my palm like tiny pearls, each one containing enough poison to kill a grown man in ten minutes. I've practiced this so many times in Blue's basement that my movements are automatic now.

"What's that?" one of them asks, craning his neck to see.

"Something brilliant from back home," I say with a wicked grin, my accent making it sound exotic. "Think ecstasy meets cocaine, but your head stays clear while your cock thinks it's Christmas morning. The high lasts for hours."

The room erupts in interested murmurs and crude laughter. "Hell yes," someone shouts. "Count me in."

"My dealer calls it 'executive candy,'" I continue, dropping three spheres into the first bottle and swirling gently until they dissolve completely. "All the fun, none of the stupid decisions. Well, except maybe fucking like a god."

I move to the second bottle, then the third, adding poison to each one while the men watch with the fascination of children witnessing a magic trick. They have no idea they're watching their own execution.

"There," I announce, returning to the table with my enhanced wine collection. "Now we can truly celebrate properly."

I pour fresh glasses for everyone, making sure each man gets wine from one of my treated bottles. The poison is completely tasteless, just as Duffy promised, and it dissolves without leaving any trace of blue.

But I catch Brutus watching me carefully, his eyes tracking my movements as I pour. Smart bastard. He's not going to drink until I do.

I reach for my own glass—the one I poured from the single untreated bottle I kept separate, marked with a tiny scratch on the base that only I can see—and raise it high.

"A toast," Brutus declares, raising his glass high. "To new partnerships and the death of old enemies."

"To justice served," I reply in my refined accent, touching my glass to his with a crystalline chime that sounds like a funeral bell.

They drink deeply, savoring what they think is triumph. I take a small sip from my own untreated glass and watch them swallow their doom with smiles on their faces.

The conversations resume, business discussions mixed with graphic descriptions of how they imagine Blue died. They describe his supposed fear, his desperation, the satisfaction they felt watching him fall. Each word makes my hatred burn brighter, but I keep smiling, keep playing the interested businesswoman while death spreads through their systems.

Five minutes pass. Then eight. Then ten.

"You know what?" the man to my left says suddenly, setting down his glass with slightly shaking hands. "I don't feel so good."

"Same here," another one admits, loosening his collar. "Getting warm in here."

Brutus frowns, studying his own hands as they begin to tremble. "What the hell—"

That's when the first one collapses.

He pitches forward onto the table, wine glass shattering against the wood. His body convulses once, twice, then goes still. Blood trickles from the corner of his mouth, dark against his pale skin.

"What—" another one starts to say, but the words dissolve into choking sounds as he grabs his throat, eyes wide with terror.

Panic erupts around the table. Men try to stand, to run, to call for help, but their legs won't support them. The poison is working exactly as expected—consciousness remains while everything else shuts down.

"You," Brutus gasps, pointing a shaking finger at me. "You did this. You fucking poisoned us."

I lean back in my chair, completely calm while chaos unfolds around me. "Guilty as charged," I say, my British accent now carrying an edge of steel.

"Who are you?" he demands. "Really?"

I stand slowly, smoothing my silk dress while men die around me like dominoes falling in sequence. When I speak, my voice carries across the room with perfect clarity, the British accent now dropped completely.

"My name is Sara Mitchell. My father was Peter Mitchell. Five years ago, you murdered him in front of me, and I've been dreaming of this moment ever since."

Brutus's eyes widen with recognition and fear.

"You searched for a broken little girl," I add, walking slowly around the table while he struggles to stay upright in his chair. "But she grew up. She learned things. She made friends who taught her exactly how to get to you."

Three more bodies hit the floor. The sounds are wet and final.

"Blue Crow," Brutus rasps, understanding finally dawning. "He's not dead."

"Very much alive," I confirm pleasantly. "And probably wondering how I'm doing right about now."

I reach Brutus's chair and crouch beside him, studying his face as the poison works its way through his system. He's still conscious, still aware, just as Duffy promised. Still able to feel everything that's happening to him.

"I want you to know something before you die," I whisper, close enough that only he can hear. "My father was a good man. He saved people. He made the world better just by being in it. And you killed him because he refused to let you hurt someone innocent."

Brutus tries to speak but only manages bloody foam.

"He begged you to let me live," I continue. "Do you remember that? How he offered you everything—his life, his money, his complete surrender—if you would just let his daughter go?"

His eyes are starting to glaze, but I can see he remembers.

"Well, congratulations. You got exactly what you wanted. Peter Mitchell is dead." I lean closer, my lips almost touching his ear. "But his daughter is very much alive. And she just killed every single one of you."

Brutus tries to respond, but the poison has other plans. Blood starts pouring from his nose in thick streams, followed by his ears. His body convulses violently, and he vomits blood across the table with wet, choking sounds. His eyes roll back, showing only whites, while his fingers claw uselessly at his throat.

I watch every second of it with a smile. The girl who used to faint at the sight of blood is long gone. This is who I am now—someone who can watch a man die in agony and feel nothing but satisfaction.

A man that deserves it, of course.

I stand and walk to the window, looking out into the Witchwood where I know Blue is waiting. The silence behind me is complete now—twelve men who woke up this morning planning to celebrate Blue's death, now dead themselves.

The irony is so perfect it makes me smile.

I pull out my phone and send a simple text: "Come collect me. It's finished."

Then I sit down to wait, and take a long, luxurious drink of my wine surrounded by the corpses of my father's killers.

I know my father would be proud of me.

CHAPTER FORTY-THREE
SAYLOR

"We should get ready," I say, glancing toward the window where cars are already pulling up the drive. "The guests are starting to arrive."

Around me, Maison Rouge pulses with music and laughter and the particular energy that comes from celebrating something that shouldn't be possible. We're throwing a back-from-the-dead party—a very merry resurrection celebration—toasting our miraculous return to the land of the living while half of Grimlock drinks to our survival.

"Saylor!" Dame Gothel appears at my elbow with champagne and a grin that could power the entire town. "Congratulations on being gloriously alive, darling."

Duffy slides up beside her, cocktail in hand. "Miraculous, really. We thought we'd lost you both for good."

I look between them. "This is surreal. A week ago you thought we were dead."

"Well, it's not every day someone comes back from the dead," Dame Gothel says, taking a delicate sip. "Blue knows how to throw a party for any occasion."

"Death looked so final when we heard the news," Duffy says, raising her glass. "But here you are, defying the grave itself."

I bite back the urge to tell them exactly how close we actually came to not making it back—whatever happened while we were gone, however Blue managed our disappearance and return. Hell, I know the whole town believed we were truly gone, and now here we are, very much alive. The rumors will spread even further tonight, growing more elaborate with each telling, and our enemies will have to reckon with the fact that we're much harder to eliminate than they thought. Instead, I just nod solemnly. "Right. Very risky business, cheating death."

"Exactly!" Dame Gothel raises her glass. "To Saylor and Blue—the first people in Grimlock to successfully rise from the grave."

"Enjoy the party," I tell them, already scanning the room. "I need to find Blue."

The ballroom is set up much like the welcome party. Blue clearly knows exactly how I like things. Edison bulbs strung between iron candelabras cast everything in warm amber light, while black roses—actual black roses, because of course Blue went there—spill from silver urns placed strategically around the room. The tables groan under platters of food that could have been conjured by some very stylish witch: dark bread shaped like ravens, wine that's so deep purple it's almost black, and desserts with names like "Death by Chocolate" and "Broken Hearts Tart."

The crowd spreads throughout the ballroom, everyone moving with the relaxed enthusiasm of people who know they're in for a good time. Conversations resume as guests begin filling their plates, the atmosphere warm and convivial despite the elegant setting.

So many people from Grimlock are eager to congratulate us personally about our miraculous survival. The relief in their faces is genuine—pure joy at seeing us both still breathing. There's something beautiful about a town that celebrates life this enthusiastically.

Musicians have claimed the corner near the fireplace, their instruments weaving melodies of celebration and mourning wrapped together. The violin particularly seems to understand that we're toasting both victory and loss, joy and the particular satisfaction that comes from surviving when everyone expected us to die.

Blue appears beside me with two glasses of liquid midnight. "Having second thoughts about the no-marriage thing?"

He's traded his usual dark suits for something more formal tonight—a perfectly tailored tuxedo that makes his shoulders look impossibly broad and emphasizes the lean lines of his body. His dark hair is styled with just enough product to look effortless, and his beard is trimmed to perfection, the blue-black color catching the candlelight. The mustache that frames his mouth draws attention to lips that have no business being that perfectly shaped on a man who's already unfairly attractive.

It's honestly criminal how good he looks. Like he stepped out of some vintage Hollywood movie where all the leading men were devastatingly handsome and knew exactly how to use it.

"No second thoughts," I say, taking a sip of the drink. "Let's focus on the party. No more marriage talk." I glance around the ballroom, taking in the perfect details, the happy faces, the celebration of life itself. "This is actually incredible. Only you would throw the most beautiful party to celebrate us rising from the dead."

"Good," he says, and I can hear the genuine relief. "I wasn't sure how you'd feel about celebrating . . . this."

"You mean celebrating the fact that we're both still breathing and very much alive? I'm discovering I'm very much in favor of both of us surviving."

He looks at me for a long moment. "Jesus, Saylor. That blue dress . . . Wren has excellent taste. You look . . ." He stops, shakes his head. "I'm trying to think of something that isn't completely inappropriate to say at your back-from-the-dead party."

When Wren had brought the dress earlier, I'd been a little worried about the neckline—it's lower than anything I'd usually wear, showing off more cleavage than I'm comfortable with. But she'd insisted it was perfect, and now I'm starting to see why. The dress hugs my curves in all the right places, the blue silk flowing in a way that somehow manages to be both elegant and rebellious. She'd even gotten the vintage details right—the fitted bodice, the full skirt that hits just below my knees, the subtle piping along the seams.

I'd planned to wear my hair down, loose and casual, but Wren had other ideas. She'd swept it up into this intricate vintage style that shows off the diamond earrings she'd also mysteriously produced. The whole look is pure vintage glamour with an edge—like a 1940s pin-up girl who could probably kill you with her stiletto and look gorgeous doing it. Which, considering where I am and who I'm with, feels surprisingly appropriate.

A crash of laughter erupts from somewhere near the dessert table, where Elliott appears to be telling some story that involves a lot of dramatic arm waving and spinning. He narrowly misses a candelabra.

"Saylor, my dear!" He abandons his audience to flutter over, somehow managing to make even walking look theatrical. "This is absolutely divine. A celebration of resurrection, of defying death, of the beautiful chaos that comes from refusing to stay buried."

"Elliott, are you drunk?" I ask, trying not to giggle.

"Drunk on the miracle of survival!" He gestures broadly, nearly taking out a passing server. "Do you know how rare it is to see two people cheat death so spectacularly? You both have the most impressive track record of survival I've ever witnessed."

The party swirls around us, conversations flowing like water around stones. I catch fragments of dialogue that sound like they belong in a different century—mentions of ancestral families and old debts, of favors owed and mysteries solved. Someone near the piano is discussing the proper way to preserve certain types of flowers, while another group debates the merits of various wines for specific occasions that probably aren't dinner parties.

The whole scene feels beautifully strange and perfectly suited to this impossible town that's somehow become home.

Blue's hand finds the small of my back, warm through the silk of my dress. "Want to get out of here for a minute?" Blue's hand finds mine. "I have something to show you."

I glance around at the party, but there's something in the way he speaks that makes me curious.

"Yeah, okay."

He leads me through the crowd, past Dame Gothel, who raises her champagne with a knowing smile. Instead of heading outside, he guides me toward the main staircase, up to the second floor where the hallway stretches in both directions.

"Where are we going?"

"Somewhere I should have shown you before now."

We walk down the hallway past doors I've never opened, until we reach the end where a narrow staircase spirals upward. Blue pushes open a heavy wooden door, and suddenly we're climbing stone steps that wind up and up.

"Where are we going?" I ask, slightly out of breath from the climb.

"You'll see."

The stairs are steep and narrow, winding up through stone walls until finally we emerge into a circular room with windows all around. But Blue doesn't stop there—he pushes open another door, and we step outside onto a balcony that wraps around the entire tower.

The view takes my breath away. Grimlock spreads out below us like a living map painted in gold and shadow. The lights from windows and streetlamps create constellations across the town, while beyond them, the dark forests stretch toward the ocean like velvet. I can smell salt on the wind mixed with woodsmoke from chimneys, and underneath it all, the green scent of growing things that never quite goes away in the Pacific Northwest.

The stone railing is cool under my palms, worn smooth by years of weather. Party music drifts up from below—muffled laughter and the faint sound of someone playing piano—but up here the night air carries other sounds too. The distant crash of waves against cliffs, the rustle of leaves in towering evergreens, an owl calling somewhere in the darkness.

From this height, I can see the whole town laid out like a storybook illustration. The gothic mansions perched on their hills, the winding streets that connect them, the clock tower in the town square with its hands forever frozen at midnight. Lights glow warmly in cottage windows tucked between the larger estates, each one holding its own secrets.

"My god," I say, moving to the stone railing. "You can see everything. It's like the clock tower but different angles."

"Yeah." But when I look at him, he's not looking at the view. He's looking at me. "I know I planned for you to move . . ."

My chest tightens, but not in panic. "Blue . . ."

"But I want you to stay." He gestures to the view, to Grimlock spread out below us. "I want to make this place ours together."

I turn to face him fully, searching his eyes. "You really want that?"

"For so long, I thought I had to change to find redemption." He swallows hard. "I thought I had to become someone different, someone better. Pretend the violence wasn't part of me. Hide what I really am." He pauses, looking out over Grimlock before meeting my eyes again. "But when I look at myself through your eyes . . . I like what I see reflected there. For the first time in my life, I like who I am."

"I do too . . ."

"You don't see a monster who needs fixing. You see someone worth staying for." His hands find my face, thumbs brushing across my cheekbones. "You accept all of it—the darkness, the violence, the parts of me I thought made me irredeemable."

I think about all the times he could have asked me to forgive him for what he's done, what he is. But he never did. He never asked for forgiveness. Just a witness. And maybe that's all redemption is— bleeding out beneath the gallows with someone willing to look you in the eye.

"Because those parts aren't separate from the rest of you," I whisper. "They're not flaws to fix. They're just . . . you. And I love you."

His thumb traces my bottom lip, and I see the exact moment he can't fight whatever is holding him back. When he leans down, I rise up to meet him halfway.

The kiss is soft, tender in a way that surprises me. It's nothing like the desperate hunger from the greenhouse or the claiming fire from that first night in the jazz club. This is different, like he's trying to memorize the shape of my lips, the way I taste, the small sound I make when his hand caresses my lower back.

I can feel everything in this kiss—years of loneliness, the fear that he'd never be worth loving, the wonder of finding someone who sees his darkness and calls it beautiful. When we finally break apart, we're both breathing hard, foreheads pressed together in the tower's quiet.

I pull back slightly to look at him, something shifting in my chest. "Can I ask you something?"

"Always."

"What if I don't want to be murder sober like you? Now that Brutus is dead?" I search his eyes in the moonlight. "You said more Crows will come eventually. What if I want to be there waiting when they do?"

The smile that spreads across his face is absolutely wicked, predatory in a way that should probably frighten me but instead sends heat racing through my veins. He cups my face in his hands and kisses me deeply, possessively, like I've just given him the most perfect gift.

When we break apart, his eyes are dark with something that looks like pride and hunger and pure satisfaction.

"I was hoping you'd say that," he murmurs against my lips. "Because I like being the teacher."

"Good," I whisper back, rising up on my toes to meet his gaze. "Because I like being the student."

He turns me gently in his arms until my back is pressed against his chest, his hands settling at my waist as he pulls me close. The warmth of his body surrounds me completely, and when he leans down to press his lips to the curve of my neck, I can feel his smile against my skin.

"Look at it," he murmurs near my ear. "All of it. This is ours now."

I lean back into him, watching the lights of Grimlock spread out below us like fallen stars. His arms tighten around me, protective and possessive, and I can feel the steady rhythm of his heartbeat against my back.

We stand on the tower balcony. The party continues in the ballroom, but up here it's just us and the night sky and the promise of time.

Tomorrow there will be plans and decisions and the ordinary magic of building a life together. But tonight, there's this—two people who found home in each other's darkness, promising not forever, but today, and today, and today.

It's enough. More than enough.

It's everything.

Once upon a time, I believed in fairy tale endings. White dresses and church bells and happily ever after that looked like everyone else's version of perfect. But maybe the best stories are the ones where the monsters get to be happy too. Where the villain and the hero are the same person, just seen from different angles.

Maybe the real question was never who is the villain. Maybe the question was always this: What happens when the villain wins?

ACKNOWLEDGMENTS

I'd like to thank my family for cheering me on for the last fifteen years of my author journey. To my husband for keeping me watered, fed, and loved. To my daughters, who understand exactly what it takes for me to finish a book and for their patience through it. It's because of you that I keep my dream alive. You are my inspiration.

I'd also like to thank my bestie, Zoe Blake, for being there daily. Your support, your advice, and your encouragement get me through the days. I love knowing you are only a call away. We are now old ass friends. We ride at dawn, bitch!

I also need to thank all my fellow author friends out there, which are too many names to list. I have been so lucky to have made so many friends in this Romancelandia of ours. I found my people!

And I also want to thank the women who recently made my dream of seeing my books in bookstores come true. Katie, Laura, Michelle, Catherine, and all the staff at Avon . . . you have made me cry happy tears countless times. It's because of you that I even get to type these words.

Thank you!

ABOUT THE AUTHOR

ALTA HENSLEY is a *New York Times* and *USA Today* bestselling author of dark romance. Twisted, clever, and occasionally unhinged, her books deliver morally gray antiheroes, sharp-tongued heroines, and happily ever afters that taste even sweeter after a little ruin. With a signature blend of grit, wit, and heat, Alta's stories prove one thing: Villains deserve love too. Alta lives on the foggy coast of Oregon with her husband, two daughters, and a pair of dogs who think they're in charge. When she's not writing redemption for the irredeemable, she's walking the coastline or sipping craft beer in eccentric little bars that feel like they belong in her books.